Maria Lewis was born and raised in Hackney. She has always loved writing and dreamt one day of writing a book. One Girl & Three Guys is her dream come true. (Well, one dream at least.)

One Girl
&
Three Guys

Maria Lewis

IncorPlus

First Published in paperback in 2009 by IncorPlus Limited

British Library Cataloguing in Publication Data
A Catalogue Record for this book is available from the
British Library

ISBN: 978-0-9560842-0-0

Typeset in Plantin with Utopia Italic by BookType

Printed and Bound in Great Britain

IncorPlus Limited
91 Montague Road, London E11 3EW

www.incorplus.co.uk

For Me ☺

Acknowledgements

Ricardo Jordan, whose continuous encouragement helped turn a few pages on a computer into a book.

Nigel Davis, who gave me a deadline that inspired me to finally finish this LONG time coming project. I was a little overdue, but made it in the end Nigel – and I'm still waiting for that surprise party!

Deborah Alexander, who took the time to read all my drafts (of which there were many!) and give that essential 'reader's' opinion with a chockablock work schedule, planning a wedding and baby on the way!

Davina Victory for her no holds barred critique.

Amanda Laws (nee Stevens) for just about everything! I can truly say this book would not have been possible without you!

Craig Wilson for his endless patience with my hundred and one book cover changes and his superb cover design.

Lauren and Billy for just being…Lauren and Billy!

Everyone who over the years have kept me going – sometimes through embarrassment, mostly through determination – by simply asking 'What's happening with the book?!' Definitely might have been a longer time coming without ALL of you!

Lastly but not least, My Mother, Irene Lewis who I know deep down wasn't sure this book would happen – but kept asking about it anyway!

Thank you all!

Prologue

'Bobby, we're in the middle of a conversation! This is important, I need your input here. This affects both of us! Just for once, help me out here. Please!' Jess wanted to shout her frustration.

'Jess, I said I'd meet the guys; we can continue this later. Or, better still just do what you think is best. I trust your judgement totally.' Bobby stood up and began to shrug into his jacket.

'Bobby, I'm struggling here; this is serious. I don't want this to be based on just my judgement this time. You trusting my opinion is not the point. You giving yours is! And you walking out all the time is not helping.' Jess sat down heavily. 'This is starting to affect us Bobby, I don't know how much longer I can do this solo thing.'

Bobby turned to look at her. 'Jess, you worry too much. Everything will be fine. It always is in the end, isn't it?'

'But will *we* be fine, Bobby?' Jess looked unblinkingly up at him. He raised an eyebrow in surprise. 'What sort of question is that?' he asked, almost incredulously. 'Of course we'll be fine, Jess. We're as solid as a rock. Stop being so dramatic. This really isn't that big a deal.'

He gave her a quick kiss on the lips. 'We'll finish when I get back.' This time Jess raised her eyebrows.

'Honest, Jess, we'll pick up exactly where we left off. It's not going to be a late one so see you soon.' He winked at her, then turned and left the room without further ado. Seconds later Jess heard the front door slam.

She sat there with a faraway look in her eyes, gently rubbing her arms, suddenly feeling a chill. She sighed wearily and softly repeated to the empty room.

'But *will* we be fine, Bobby?'

1

Jessica

I wouldn't ever say I knew everything about relationships, I mean who can? But what I do know as, sure as Superman can fly, is that the love is so over in this one. I'm not kidding. It's dead.

I know that may sound a bit off the cuff and I don't mean to be, but seriously, when the love's gone, it's just gone, isn't it? I mean, what can you do? It's not like I didn't attempt to try to find the love again. You have to, don't you? After ten years with someone. It's the expected thing to do, isn't it? It's just really difficult to find these things when you don't even know where to start looking. And that's why this one has to end.

Now, don't think I'm being blasé and just carelessly wanting to toss all those years to the wind. It's not like that. It's about me finally realising what time it is on this relationship clock and setting the alarm to do something about it. Time to do the 'nasty', so to speak, but in as nice a way as possible. *If* that's possible, since the person you're giving the nasty news to doesn't have the slightest inkling that anything's wrong. I'm getting cold feet again just thinking about his reaction, but I'm not going to let that stop me like it has the last four times. Cold feet is now not an acceptable excuse for not getting the end finally off my chest.

Hmm … speaking of chests, it's either the mirror or this wonderbra really is doing wonders for mine. When a slip of material like this can make mountains out of these molehills, then you have to ask yourself, does anybody really need surgery? It's a shame that, if all goes to plan, I'll soon be the only one admiring these molehills.

My current-but-soon-to-be-ex-if-all-goes-to-plan boyfriend and I are going out for dinner tonight for me to break the news to him that I want to break it off. I've booked us somewhere really fancy called Galleon something de something or another, in the hope that all the grandeur will overwhelm him into silence when he hears what I've got to say. Normally I'd discuss this whole break-up thing with my best friend, Maddy, beforehand, but this is something I know I can't have a practice run on.

* * *

'Why do you want to go somewhere so upmarket?' Maddy asked as Jess put down the phone after confirming her dinner booking. 'What's the occasion? It's not your birthday, or Bobby's, not your anniversary, not ...'

Jess stopped her mid-sentence. That was something you had to do on a regular basis with Maddy if you wanted to get a word in edgewise. 'Was it not you that said every day should be Valentine's, not just the 14th of February? Well, today, April 19th is going to be our Valentine's.' Jess shrugged her shoulders in the hope that that would be enough explanation. She didn't like lying to Maddy, but she knew that if she told her the true nature of the dinner, then Maddy would try to discourage her, want her to think about it some more, extol the virtues of Bobby – all stuff that she didn't need to hear, just in case it worked. Like it had the last four times. Maddy could be very persuasive and she wasn't about to give her a fifth opportunity to test those skills now that she'd got this far. She'd let her know straight after the deed was done – promise. But Maddy's puzzled frown was already telling Jess that her Easter Valentine dinner story was not cutting it.

'But why TODAY?' she persisted.

'Why not today?' Jess nonchalantly started plumping the sofa cushions, hardly believing her luck when Maddy finally seemed to accept her rationalisation and started talking about a Valentine dinner where she'd puked on the guy's shoes.

★ ★ ★

Tonight is the night that I end things with Bobby. I think I'm finally ready to do it, and sending him on his way with a good meal inside him is the very least I can do. That sounded kind of flippant, didn't it? It's not that I don't appreciate the gravity of the situation; it's just my way of dealing with things. I mean, I'm about to end an era here; a relationship that has spanned more than a decade. That sounds quite epic, doesn't it? It feels epic too. I just feel that I have to treat it like it's not a deal, otherwise it could turn out to be a very big deal indeed. So big that I may not be able to go through with it and it's taken me so long to get here that backing out now is not an option.

So here I am, Jessica Montrose, standing in front of the mirror adding the last touches to my reflection before I go out to my last supper with Bobby, short for Robert. Bobby Phillips, Robert Phillips; one and the same, same being the operative word both for his name and our relationship; the same for ten years, three months and six days. Okay, to be fair, it hasn't been the same for the whole ten years, but a good amount of the last seven, including the extra months and days. We've somehow gone from party whoopy-ing all over town to party poopy-ing just in the house. And this just seems to have seeped its way into all the other areas of our life together. Our increasingly separate lives together.

* * *

'Bobby, you're not working today and the weather's really nice. How about we all go for a drive? I mentioned it to Martell and he's really excited.' Jess smiled.

'Oh babe, it's the final of Football Frenzy tonight. I can't miss that!'

'But we haven't done any family stuff for a while and he'll be so disappointed.' Jess now frowned.

'He's young, he'll bounce back. Kids do, you know. You guys go if you think it'll bother him that much.'

'Bobby, I've been cooking all week. Fancy going out for a meal tonight?'

'I could fancy a frozen pizza. That's not exactly cooking 'cos you can just shove it in the oven AND we can stay in.'

'Bobby, shall we watch a DVD tonight?'

'Sorry babe, I said I'd go out with the lads tonight.'

'Oh … but we haven't done anything together for ages.'

'Neither have me and the lads.'

'Erm … I believe you went out for a drink with them last week, and you went around Eric's for hours a couple of days ago.'

'So I see the guys once in a while. At least I see you every day, Sweetheart.'

* * *

And on the rare occasion that we do manage to do something together, it'll only happen if I organise it, which really takes the fun out of birthdays, anniversaries, Christmas card buying and just about every other occasion you can think of. I do hold my hand up and take some of the blame in things turning out this way, though. It definitely all started to go wrong when I started doing everything. Not that everything I did went wrong, but it made our relationship go wrong … stop going right … oh, you know what I mean. Anyway, I'm going to hold the same hand up again, except this time it's to stop all of this happening anymore. It shouldn't have taken me so long to come to this conclusion. It's not like I wasn't tipped off. Back when I was growing up in Philadelphia – where I'm originally from despite my cockney-tinged accent – I remember my Grandma warning me about stuff like this. It's just a pity I didn't remember her warning in time to stop me going prematurely grey; it would have saved me a fortune in hair dye. Grandma, God rest her soul, could always shine a light of common sense on any dark situation.

★ ★ ★

'Grandma, boys suck, they really do.' Jess hugged her knees as she sat at her Grandmother's feet.

'Why's that, Baby?' Grandma Pearl stroked Jess's hair.

'Well, for a surprise, I fixed the pedal on Toby's bike 'cos he didn't know how, but he got mad at me for doing it. I was only trying to help, Grandma! Boys are stupid.'

'Baby, if you pout any harder, your bottom lip will stay that way.' Grandma Pearl always told Jess that. It had never happened, but Jess didn't want to tempt fate, so quickly pulled her bottom lip in.

'Baby, know this. When you take away a man's right to be responsible, you take away his right to be a man.'

Jess nodded sagely at her grandma's words. At the tender age of nine, she wasn't entirely sure what they meant, but she knew it must be true. Her grandma knew everything.

★ ★ ★

I guess I've always had this idea that the man is supposed to be the strong one; the Captain of the Relation-ship so to speak, who'd be able to sail us through troubled waters. It's only taken ten years for Bobby to titanically sink the boat that idea came sailing on. Whenever there was a situation, I had to become the Baywatch Babe (obviously without the boobs hence the wonderbra) with Bobby being the stand-on-the-sand-waving-arms-and-pointing-towards-the-sea kind of bystander.

Somebody had to step up to get things done. It just gets a bit much after so many years of continually being the sole decision-maker, home-maker, relationship-maker, tea-maker (Bobby makes *really* bad tea) – in fact every-thing-maker.

Want to go see a movie? Jess'll find out what films, what cinemas, what showings. Want to go eat out? Jess'll find out what restaurants, what sittings, what menus. Need a sitter for Martell? Jess'll find out who, when, for how long. Want a gift for my birthday? Jess'll choose it and buy it too. After all, who knows what Jess likes better than Jess, right?

That's how it's been, not so much in the beginning, but certainly in the middle, and definitely now at the end. Want to end the relationship? Jess'll do it.

Do you want to know what really made me decide that

my relationship was on route to Nowheresville? There're a few things, but one that particularly springs to mind was when I was offered a new position where I work. It was in the designer section at Jarrod Jones – also known as Jarrod's, a department store in the West End of London that's considered to be the place to shop, mainly by B list celebrities. You know, the ones from your regular weekly soaps or reality TV save-me-from-the-jungle shows.

The new job was going to be one with a lot of new responsibilities, but most importantly of all, it was going to involve choosing new designer lines. If you can imagine someone on a diet simply dying for that piece of choco-late gateau then you have some idea how I felt about this opportunity. I. Love. Designer. Clothes. It's that simple. I mean, who doesn't? I knew the position was going to be a challenge, but like with any new thing you take on, even though you might feel like you're up for the task, you still have doubts as to whether you can actually do it. And then there's that comfort zone to break out of. You've been in charge of the Teen Wear section for yonks and can run the department with your eyes closed (and on the odd late night out drinking before work the next morning, literally had to). On top of that, my Teen Wear team thought I was the coolest boss ever – I don't know if it was because of the cream cakes I bought them every Friday lunchtime or the end of month team bonding at the local bar. Or maybe I simply was a cool boss. I mean, they did buy me a really nice DKNY purse for my birthday. If they'd had reserva-tions about my management style, a purse from Primark would have confirmed it. Saying that, Primark *did* have some nice purses in there the other day...

Anyway, I'm sure you can appreciate that leaving all

of that behind (*especially* DKNY birthday purses – did I mention it was a limited edition?) was a decision in itself and therefore one that I needed a little help with. Adoration and wonderful designer birthday purses or exclusive designer frocks with fifty percent discount? What choice should I make? Or in the great words of that song: should I stay or should I go? So I ran it past Bobby to see what he thought. A few times.

★ ★ ★

'*Bobby, do you think I should take the new job? I have to give them a decision in a week.*'

 '*Sweetheart, I'm kind of in the middle of a game here. Ask me again at half-time. Actually, maybe after that because there'll be analysis. Actually, maybe after that because there'll be highlights. Actually, maybe tomorrow.*'

'*Bobby, what do you think I should do about the new job? They need an answer from me in a few days*'

 '*Well, whatever you do, can you do it after you write that letter for me about the invisible parking ticket? They definitely didn't put it on the car, Jess!*'

'*Bobby, I have to tell them tomorrow and I still don't know what to do!*' *Jess was twisting her fingers so much that at one point they were nearly in a knot.*

 '*If you want to stay with your team, then do that, Jess.*'

 '*I know, but this move could futuristically expand my horizons!*' *Jess had a tendency to get a little dramatic when she was anxious.*

 '*Then follow your mind and go for the new job.*' *Bobby acknowledged.*

'I know, but we just won the team of the month award and the guys are really stoked to do it again. We'll get an all-paid-for day out if we do a double. No team's done a double before. And no team's bought me a DKNY purse before."

'Probably best to stay where you are then.' Bobby nodded.

'I know, but this new offer … it'll be a new challenge, new team, yada yada yada.'

'Probably best to go then.' Bobby reached for the remote and started flicking through the channels. His responses frustrated Jess. She restrained herself from wrapping her fingers around his throat only because he would then be even more unlikely to give her any constructive advice. Jess breathed a sigh of annoyance.

★ ★ ★

I eventually decided – on my own – to move on and potentially up with the new section. I do miss my guys from Teen Wear though, got my work cut out trying to get that admiration thing going again with the new team, a diet-mad crew so the cream cake thing is out. I'm thinking maybe deluxe crackers? Okay, so I got a little pleasure from being up on that pedestal. So I'm human. So sue me.

In case you're thinking is that what her dramatic relationship exit is all about – it isn't. It's not just with me that Bobby falters in his decision-making process. It's Martell too. Who is Martell, I hear you ask? None other than our adorable son, Martell Christopher Montrose-Phillips. Named after Bobby's favourite brandy.

Well, to be totally honest, we didn't just think: we like

brandy so let's name our baby after a bottle. The name came about more because Bobby did something or other to upset me. I can't even remember what it was now

* * *

'Oooooh! Robert Phillips … you … you …' Without thinking, Jess grabbed the glass of brandy from Bobby's hand and threw it in his face.

'What the …!' Bobby looked down at himself and then at Jess, speechless with shock.

'Let me tell you, mister, if you think … oh!' Jess suddenly felt a sharp pain, but was too angry to consider it as any more than an annoying interruption to her tirade.

'… if you think that … OH! Oh! Oooooh!' Okay, that hurt way more than before. Jess held onto her stomach.

'Oh my gosh, Jess, look …' Bobby still looked shocked, but a slightly different shocked.

'Don't try and change the subject! I … Aaah!' What the hell was wrong with the demon child within her?

'LOOK!' Bobby's shout stopped Jess's wordflow. 'Look Jess, you're dripping on the floor!'

Jess looked down and, true enough, she was standing in a puddle of broken waters.

* * *

Bobby didn't even get a chance to wipe the chucked brandy off his face before our baby came into the world. It dripped down his face along with his tears of joy when the doctor exclaimed, 'It's a boy!' The name Martell just seemed fitting. It didn't even occur to me about kids teasing him at school. I mean the only brandy they should know about at that age was a singer with braids.

Thankfully Martell – who by the way is nine years old – never did have that name-calling problem. He did, however, have the problem of whether to change schools.

Picture this. The headmistress of your child's school – Mrs Ragon (the children added a 'D' to her name and called her Mrs Dragon because she was quite hot-tempered and fierce looking). Now, I know that every child has a potential bright spark in them, but Martell's was starting to glow a little early, so I requested he be moved into the year above. It was already standard practice at his private school, so I really didn't think it would be an issue. I made an appointment with the school to speak to the head.

* * *

'Mrs Ragon, Martell, as you know, has been doing really well here and now seems to be finding the work a little less challenging. He's getting top marks in everything so I'd like to formally request that he be moved up a year. I know this is something that the school offers.' Jess smiled at the end of her little speech, quite proud of the way she had constructed all her nouns in the face of this beacon of intelligence. She started to rummage around in her bag for a pen to sign her authorisation for the move.

'I'm sorry Ms Montrose, but I'm afraid that I can't allow that.' Mrs Ragon politely smiled back.

Jess stopped rummaging and gave the head a can-you-say-that-again-because-I-don't-think-I-heard-you-right kind of look.

'It's not that I don't think he can handle the work in a higher class, I acknowledge your son is very advanced for his age ...' she continued.

Jess smiled proudly and started rummaging around for the pen again.

'… but in light of recent views on pre-teen esteem in children, it could create an inferiority complex amongst his class members to know that Martell was moved to a more advanced class, and they were not, even though they are the same age.'

She still had that polite smile on her face, which for some reason Jess suddenly had the urge to physically remove, even though she wasn't usually an advocate of violence. She took a deep breath.

'Just to clarify, you're not going to move Martell up a year, not because he's not bright enough?'

Mrs Ragon nodded agreeingly.

'… And not because it's against school policy.'

Mrs Ragon smiled acknowledgingly.

'But because it might, not definitely will mind you, but just possibly might, make another kid in his class feel like they will not be able to face the world?' Jess's voice rose in line with her incredulity.

'That's correct, Ms Montrose.'

'So, Martell's progress should be held back because Johnny who sits at the next desk may somehow be traumatically affected for life due to something that has absolutely nothing to do with him, and that, in actual fact, he probably doesn't give a toss about because he's just glad that it's not him that'll have to do extra homework. Is that what you're telling me, Mrs Ragon?' Jess was taking several deep breaths now.

'Well, Ms Montrose I wouldn't have put it quite like that, but in essence, yes.'

★ ★ ★

At that point, I was probably exhibiting more dragon-like qualities than Mrs Ragon. There might not have been fire coming out of my mouth, but there sure as hell was steam coming out of my ears. Since when was ensuring a pupil was being educationally challenged be regarded as anything other than ... well, than being educationally challenged? Political correctness gone potty!

The way Mrs Ragon looked at me I knew there wasn't any point in trying to appeal to her sense of better judgement. For her to think her decision had any sort of logic attached to it made me seriously question whether she had any sense – full stop. It also made me suddenly grudgeful that part of the two and a half thousand pounds per term I was paying for Martell's private education was ending up in this woman's wage packet. It seemed there were only two options available to me. Accept the 'dumbing down' offered by this school, or change schools. Okay, I know that my options sounded really drastic, but it was a drastic situation! Children are our future; you can't afford to play around with their education. Without a proper education, Martell could fall by the wayside, be less a pillar and more a pillock of the community. He could even end up with an ASBO against his name! Nope. No way. I couldn't let that happen. Bobby and I had to make a decision. He was Martell's father after all, and naturally would want a say in what was going to be the best thing for his son.

★ ★ ★

'So what do you think, Bobby? Do you agree we should change Martell's school?'
   'Not necessarily'

'So you think we should leave him there?' Jess asked.

'Maybe.'

'So we maybe need to change his school?' Jess was confused.

'Possibly.'

'So we possibly need to leave him there?'

'It's an option.'

'It's an option that we change his school?' Jess was even more confused.

'Jess, you're the one that's on top of all this kind of stuff. Whatever you decide is fine with me.' And for added effect, Bobby turned to a new page in the sports section of the newspaper that Jess wanted to grab and whack him with.

★ ★ ★

At least I was right in that he would want a say. He just didn't say anything which would constructively help the decision-making process, which was just what I already knew he would say. Fortunately, Mrs Ragon did eventually see sense and moved Martell up to the next class, but only after a lot of fussing and threats from me to form a Paying Parents Union that would march to Parliament Square on the injustice of her decision. It was either that or the fact that she'd been asked out by Mr Romaine, the physics teacher, a week after our meeting. I'm sure he would have asked her out anyway, and that me mentioning, when I saw him in the corridor after my meeting with Mrs Ragon, that she'd said some very flattering things about him had nothing to do with it.

Anyway, it's a culmination of situations like this that has brought me to this point. Believe me when I say, this incident is just one that has been plucked from the eyebrows of many. Plenty more just like it and all dealt with by the same tweezer: me.

Right, let me take one last look in the mirror before I go. Got to admit, I've really scrubbed up well tonight. A twenty-five-year-old-looking thirty-three-year-old (I swear by Molly's Age Retracting cream – it's an exclusive at Jarrod Jones). Five foot six (and a half) with long, black shoulder-length hair, which I really must make a hairdresser appointment for to get these raggedy ends done. Slim-ish (well, size twelve can hardly be called fat, can it?) and adorned in my favourite Chanel gown. You can't just wear a Chanel dress; you have to adorn yourself in it. It's the one major designer dress, that I ever paid full price for. It cost me an arm, a leg and a big toe, hence why it's my favourite. I don't usually do pastels, but something about this shade of light blue just called out to me.

Oh my gosh, look at the time! It's nearly seven thirty and my reservation is in an hour. Have I really been staring at my reflection and resurrecting memories for the past thirty minutes? I recognise this as a stalling tactic. I read about them in a self-help book. It said '... recognising is the first step. Recognise, then overcome ...' Now I've recognised, I can overcome by just getting this show on the road. By feeling the fear and doing it anyway. I can do this. I can *do* this, unless I suddenly break down mid break-up. That might bring on some tears, which will probably make my mascara run, and then my nose run, which will probably lead to me smudging my lipstick and ... Enough! Now is so not the time for panic. Panic could put another eighteen months between now and when this moment arrives again. I have to do this today.

Take that man downstairs to the restaurant and somehow tell him that we need to go our separate ways. Deep breath, Jess. You will be strong. You will be cool. Like that Nike advert says, 'Just do it.'

2

Bobby

Jess must really be pulling out all the stops tonight, Bobby thought, as he carefully smoothed out the newspaper to ensure no wrinkle hid any life-changing sports news. He glanced up at the anniversary clock Martell had bought them for their tenth anniversary. Jess thought it was hideous but their son was so proud of his gift that she hadn't had the heart not to hang it up. Bobby leant ninety degrees to the left so that he could get a better view of the staircase and also see if he could get some sort of view of Jess. No such luck. She'd been getting ready for this dinner for hours now. There was no football on the box and he'd already read the whole newspaper twice. His latest trawl through the newspaper was to commit all the facts to memory – well, the sporting facts anyway.

His stomach gave a gentle growl, further reminding him just how hungry he was. Jess had booked them a table at some apparently posh restaurant he'd never heard of – Galleon something de something or another. As long as there was chicken on the menu and he could recognise that it was chicken when it was on his plate, he'd eat anywhere – literally. Right now he felt like he could eat anything. He couldn't help wondering, why such a fancy restaurant?

In fact, the more he started to think about it, the more unusual he found the way Jess had just sprung this dinner arrangement on him. As far as he could remember, and his memory wasn't the best at times, it wasn't a special occasion or anything. Or was it? He started to rack his brain to make sure he hadn't forgotten any of the majors like their anniversary, her birthday or even his own birthday. That, believe it or not, had actually been known to happen. Jess was used to both his occasional forgetfulness and his occasion forgetfulness. At least she always remembered every single occasion; it was good that one of them did. They were a good team, him and Jess. He loved her a lot.

He rested his chin on his fist thoughtfully. What if she'd had another promotion at work and that's what they were celebrating? That is, if they were celebrating.

No, it couldn't be that. He couldn't recall her talking about anything new that she was thinking of going for at work. Though, if she was talking to him while Eastenders was on, he would barely have recollection of her presence, never mind anything that she may have been talking about. He was a man and everyone knew men weren't the greatest at multi-focusing. You'd think that after ten years, Jess would realise that. Yet, every now and then, there would be times when he was watching Grant or Phil and could still vaguely hear Jess's voice in the background, suggesting that there was a strong likelihood she was telling him something that he was not going to remember.

Nope. It definitely wasn't a work celebration. Okay, time to checklist the possible occasions that might warrant a fancy restaurant. What was today's date? April 19th. Well, it definitely wasn't Valentine's and he knew that a whole year hadn't passed since he last gave her money so she could choose a gift for her birthday.

He got up and walked over to the window. Maybe Jess just didn't feel like cooking today. Yeah, it was probably something like that. He knew Jess liked to eat out now and then, and even though the way to his heart was with a good old-fashioned home-cooked meal, he didn't have a massive aversion to it being cooked outside the home on occasion. He wasn't too proud to wolf down a McDonald's once in a while. In fact, right now a Chicken McFillet would be Nirvana, he was so hungry. Besides, Jess getting a break from the cooker every now and then was a good-mood maker – it always put him in a good mood if he didn't have to hear Jess grumbling at him to wash the dishes if she'd cooked. Cooking had never been his forte, though he had given it his very best shot, albeit only once. The once was when he'd surprised Jess and Martell by cooking a chicken curry with a little rice on the side. It had looked so straightforward when Delia did it.

★ ★ ★

'Okay. Tuck in people. It's not every day you get to sample my culinary skills.' Bobby looked proudly at his creation on his family's plates.

'So Martell, how was football tryouts today?' Bobby turned to his son. Instead of a description of his day coming out of his son's mouth, rice grains flew everywhere.

'Martell! What have I told you about speaking with your mouth full!' Bobby instinctively raised his voice and was shocked when he saw water streaming from his son's eyes. Martell wasn't normally this sensitive!

'Hot... Dad... HOT! Water!' Martell was fanning his mouth and frantically reaching for the whole jug of water. 'Okay, maybe my hand slipped a little with the curry powder, but it can't be that bad, Martell.' Bobby stopped short. His son's sodden cheeks told him that it was indeed that bad. Bobby looked over to Jess for help. Jess was

spooning the rice high into the air and letting it plop back onto her plate.

'Okay Jess, maybe my hand slipped a little with the water in the rice too, but soft rice grains are easier to digest.' Bobby couldn't look Jess in eye.

'Bobby, this rice looks more like porridge.' Jess scooped up some more rice, and again let it plop onto her plate.

'Not everyone can make porridge, so it's not all bad then.' Bobby smiled at his spin on the situation.

'No, it wouldn't be all bad at all if the meal was supposed to be Superhot Chicken Curry and Porridge.' Jess smiled, Martell downed some more water and Bobby just looked deflated.

'But hey, you tried, right?' Jess smiled encouragingly at him. 'Tell you what, let's strike a deal. I'll do the cooking as long as you do the washing up. How's that sound?' Bobby had to admit the offer sounded very appealing.

'And Dad, I'll help you wash the plates if you promise I'll never have to eat your cooking ever again.' Bobby laughed. Martell's offer had just sealed the no-more-Bobby-cooking deal.

* * *

Bobby moved back towards the sofa, resumed his spot in front of the football pages and switched the TV over to Sports One for added back-up. He smiled, having managed to convince himself, somewhat semi-certainly, that he was over-concerned over nothing. They hadn't had an argument or a disagreement for ages. Or had they, and he just hadn't realised it? He tended to be very laid back and there had been the odd occasion when Jess was upset at him and he hadn't even noticed. There was that time when, apparently, they hadn't been speaking for two days. He'd thought she was being quiet because she had work stuff on, or was thinking about the next episode of 24 or something. Jess was indeed the biggest Jack Bauer fan and would toss and turn the whole night after a particularly tense episode.

They hadn't done the 'Do' for a couple of weeks either. Could that be what this dinner was about? Normally, he'd freak out about that, but he knew Jess had been studying for some management exam and was a bit stressed. That was probably the cause of her recent bout of headaches too. He'd been nothing if not understanding. How understanding he'd still be after three weeks without 'it' was a whole other matter. Explicit magazines and movies were no substitute for the real thing. But he didn't want her to feel any extra pressure for not performing her conjugal duty, so right now Ms P Anderson was his best pal. He just needed to relax. It was just a little difficult to do that because he couldn't remember them going to such a lavish place before, not even on any of their past ten anniversaries. Apparently this restaurant was in Park Lane. Park Lane! Maybe she wanted the Talk? Every so often Jess would arrange the Talk, usually at some local restaurant. It would be about itemising what they'd done lately. Or more recently, what they hadn't done.

* * *

'Bobby, did you realise that we haven't been to a social gathering for five months?' As she spoke Jess crossed out a line on the imaginary list she held.

'We've been food shopping together three times in four weeks, but you've eaten plenty more than three times.'

Bobby nodded in acknowledgement. He wasn't about to

challenge her; her list was legendary. It was usually cinema visits that came next.

'Blockbusters have never seen us so regularly as in the past two months, but we can't make it to the cinema. Okay, maybe you can't pause the film when you go to the toilet, but the cinema experience is the cinema experience!'

Bobby managed to stifle a yawn. If Jess saw that, he'd get another earful about how he was always tired except for things he liked; an exaggeration he was too tired to defend. He needed his energy to watch the boxing later.

★ ★ ★

The format of the Talks didn't deviate much. He actually found it quite endearing, the way Jess got animated during a Talk. She really turned him on when she was animated. Her nose crinkled in that cute way he liked, her eyes sparkled, her bosom heaved. He was getting turned on just thinking about how much she turned him on! The only time he fancied her more was when she was angry. Their arguments started heated and always, absolutely always, ended with a different kind of heat. He smiled at a memory. Luckily they didn't argue too often because Jess also liked to throw things. He would usually try to manoeuvre her near the sofa, not just because you got more damage control from cushions than vases, but because that was where most of their arguments ended, where her eyes sparkled and her bosom heaved. His smile widened even more, exposing all of his teeth.

The Talks of late seemed to have a recurring topic. Jess thought they'd become too routine. He preferred to think of them as comfortable.

★ ★ ★

'Bobby, there's no pizzazz in our relationship anymore. We need some pizzazz.' Jess always found sound effects better when describing what their relationship was lacking.

'Jess. Jess. We have pizzazz. But it's impossible to have it all the time.'

Jess opened her mouth to tell him, he was sure, how it was possible to have it all the time, but he was ready with his pre-emptive strike.

'Jess, relationships are like businesses; they can't always be booming. You inevitably get slow periods.'

Jess opened her mouth to speak again, but this time paused of her own accord. The business analogy got her every time.

'Jess, in relationships like ours that have stood the test of time, it's not because of fireworks everyday ...' Bobby knew one wrong word, one out of place inflection and Jess would pounce on it. Right now she was all ears, so he knew he was holding his own. '... it's because we have the comfort and security of being settled, with fireworks thrown in on special occasions. And that's what the pizzazz really is.' It was a rare day that Jess didn't have a comeback. Looked like today was a rare day.

* * *

Bobby was a man who was proud to say he'd settled down. Most women were crying that this was what they wanted in a relationship and then, when they got it, they suddenly wanted something else. Women! Never satisfied! That's what the Talks should really have been about.

Luckily he would just calmly listen to whatever she had to say. Calming and charming, that was him. Or so he'd been told. In college he'd been voted most likely to be able to stop a female catfight without being scratched! He'd always been really laid back, more a listener than a talker, which was ideal around Jess. That was actually probably ideal around most women. It was a good thing he was that way inclined too, because Jess, as well as being your typical female conversationalist, was also a leader. She liked to be in charge of a situation. She liked to talk and talk everything through. Dotting the i's and crossing the t's she called it. Fortunately for him, Jess's way was usually the best way to go, so he didn't really have a problem going along with whatever she decided.

A lot of men were scared of strong-minded women, but that was one of the very things that had attracted him to Jess. She was still very American in her ways, even though she'd already been living in England for several years. You could still hear tinges of her original accent when she said certain things. She was also very confident, as everyone knew Americans could be, as if they were born with it, as if, in the delivery room, the doctor said, 'Your baby's got ten fingers, ten toes and a lovely head of confidence.'

Bobby frowned at where his thoughts had turned. He was sounding like a walkover even to himself and that was definitely something he was not. What he was, was one for an easy life. He'd learnt early on in their relationship that in order to have that kind of life, it was usually just best to go with the flow. He did that by simply avoiding getting into debates. Jess had this uncanny ability to get her point across in such a way that if you tried to argue against it, you'd end up losing your train of thought and wondering why you'd wanted to disagree in the first place.

Sometimes, he thought, and he knew this made him a chauvinistic swine, that when freedom of speech for all was introduced, there should have been extra conditions attached for women – ones that they would have to agree to before they were granted the right to it. For example, they should have a time limit on how long they could talk at any one time on any subject. Without it women would continue to make a whole conversation about something that could be covered in a sentence.

But Jess wasn't your typical woman. She was different. Not in an extreme way like in her views, or dress or anything like that, there was just something about her, other than her obvious attractiveness, that made her stand out in a crowd. She was an original. Yeah, maybe original was a better word to describe her. Original in the way she spoke and original in her sense of style. If you were certain that most woman would generally act in a certain way in a certain situation, then Jess was certain not to. The first indication of this was on their first date.

★ ★ ★

'Jess, you'll never guess where you're going tonight!' Bobby rubbed his hands gleefully, barely waiting for Jess to step through her front door.

'Hmm … cinema?' she guessed.

Bobby stopped in his tracks and looked at her, slightly deflated that she had so quickly hit on exactly where they were going. Determined not to have his surprise ruined, he tried a different angle.

'Aww, who couldn't guess the cinema? That's where ninety three per cent of first dates are.' He could see a question forming on Jess's lips and lest it be to question his unfounded statistics he swiftly continued: 'But can you guess what we are going to see?'

Jess smiled at him blankly, indicating that she didn't have any idea worthy of mentioning.

'Okay, I'll give you a clue. The tickets were sold out a week before it was released and it stars every woman's heartthrob.' There. He'd practically told her what movie it was.

'Hmm ...' Jess looked up in the air, closing one eye and scrunching her mouth. 'Nope, can't think.'

He looked down at her again, to see if she was kidding, but she really didn't seem to have an inkling. This should have rung warning bells in his head. Every female he knew, and even a few he didn't, had been going on about this film for weeks. Maybe she'd been busy. Or out of town.

'Well, I won't spoil it for you then. We should have good seats. I bought the tickets in advance to make sure we weren't lumbered with seats so close to the screen, that people would mistake us for being in the film.'

Jess laughed at his joke. The film was going to be a hit with Jess and therefore a hit for him with Jess. Early had never been his most reliable time so he'd made a good move getting the tickets a few days ago. He shrugged off the spot of doubt before it even had time to form a thought in his head. How could he go wrong? After all, all women liked romantic movies, happy endings, a good cry and all that, didn't they?

★ ★ ★

Whoever said that hadn't encountered anyone like Jess. Less than twenty minutes into the movie that myth was completely dispelled. For Jess, a good cry was equivalent to a good snore, and the happy ending the same as happy dreams. She'd fallen asleep! And at a particularly moving part of the movie, when George Clooney looked softly into Jennifer Lopez's eyes! Bobby had taken that as his cue to turn and look softly into Jess's eyes.

★ ★ ★

'Jess ... Jess? Erm ...' Bobby stared at her closed eyelids. This was meant to be the best bit of the film. He gently shook her. No response. He tried again. Still no response. This time he gave her a slightly harder nudge. Jess jumped – no, leapt – out of her sleep! Her unfinished popcorn flew out of her lap into the unfinished cup of coke belonging to the lady in the next seat, which then spilled onto the crotch of the man next to her. It was like something out of a Carry On film!

'Oh my goodness! I am SO sorry!' Bobby profusely apologised and took the blame all round for the incident. If he hadn't, the look that the wet-crotched man gave the popcorned-coke lady ... Well, good thing only sticks and stones could break your bones.

'What? Oh, has the film finished?' Jess mumbled groggily, totally unaware of the third world war she'd nearly been responsible for. 'Oh, I didn't fall asleep did I? I'm so sorry, Bobby! Romantic movies send me to sleep quicker than a glass of milk.'

★ ★ ★

Bobby shook his head, wondering how he'd made it through that date. He could smile about it now, but he had been so embarrassed at the time that even if the ground had swallowed him up, it wouldn't have rescued him. Jess never realised what had really happened because she still seemed to be half-asleep when they finally left the cinema.

After that, he'd decided to do no more pre-arranging. And from that day forward, he'd let Jess choose whatever films they watched. He knew it was a cop-out, but hey, the easy life was his motto. If the movie wasn't action packed, he'd just do what he now fondly called a Jess Special: take forty winks, though he always made sure that his popcorn was finished before his snoring started.

He chuckled at the memory and then sighed. He couldn't grasp why this dinner tonight had suddenly got him 'tripping', for want of a better word. He closed and folded his newspaper and walked over to the window for the second time that evening. Or was it his third? The neighbours would think he was a Peeping Tom at this rate. His mind was just all over the place because of this mysterious dinner and he couldn't understand why. Maybe it was because, if she had something planned, she'd usually let him know a lot sooner than the night before, because of sorting out a sitter for Martell.

Thinking of his one and only son filled him with pride. He loved Jess all the more for giving him that boy. Martell got good results at school all the time, which was a major achievement in itself seeing how a lot of kids his age couldn't even read properly. Of course, the little critter had been known to try and get a better deal from the other parent if the answer to his request for sweets or another fifty pound computer game from the first parent was not quite what he was hoping for. But that was kids for you.

Together they'd done a good job raising Martell. He wasn't for a minute saying that single parents couldn't do the right thing, because he'd always believed that one parent was better than none. He just also believed that two was better than just you. They were a good team. Jess took care of the finer details and he took care of showing his son how to be a man. So tonight couldn't be about Martell.

Bobby sighed and sat back down in front of the newspaper. This back and forth from the window to the sofa, especially on an empty stomach, was starting to make him feel nauseous. Why on earth was his mind working overtime like this? He closed his eyes and breathed in deeply. Everything was cool. They were just going out for dinner. The only thing he should be worrying about was just how Arsenal were ever going to replace Thierry Henry.

3

Jessica

I walk slowly down the stairs and my pace has got nothing to do with the five-inch heels that I bought in a Mui Mui sale two months ago. I get to the living-room doorway and stand there looking at Bobby. Just like I thought, he's reading the back page of the newspaper. I've often wondered if he even realises that there's news in it other than sport. I wonder, if he'd paid the finer details of our relationship even a little of the concentration he pays to working out whose goal difference will win which team the league, would we be here now? Why am I even taking him to dinner? It's like I'm trying to create a pleasant memory of something that is not going to be pleasant to say or hear. You know what? I'm not going to wait until dinner. Now is as good, or bad, a time as any. I straighten up and take a deep breath. Stomach in, wonderbra'd chest out.

'Bobby …'

'Jess, at last! I was starting to think you were making your outfit. Do you know …,' he starts.

'… I think we should call it a day,' I finish.

'… how long my stomach has been waiting…' He stops as what I've just said registers, and looks up at me from the sports pages.

'Huh?' he says, in a baffled tone.

He's looking at me blankly and, already, I can feel my confidence slowly ebbing away. I quickly continue. 'What I'm saying is, I don't want to do this anymore, Bobby.'

He looks totally non-expressive. Maybe I need to try and lighten up what I'm saying, if there is a way of lightening up bad news. 'To quote a famous Philadelphian phrase: We keep on trying, but it's still dying.' Okay, maybe it wasn't Philadelphian, or famous, or quoted, but it was definitely light. I can hardly believe this is me speaking so matter-of-factly about ending something I've lived in for nearly a third of my life. Bobby's still looking at me like I'm talking gobbledy gook. This is bad because that indicates that maybe I'm not getting my point across as directly as I think I am. But, it's also good because as much as I may have prepared my speech, that preparation didn't extend to what his reaction would be. What if he acts all hardman about it? That won't be good. But then again, what if he gets all emotional? Gee ..., I don't think that'll be good either. Damn! What if he cries?

Dealing with this is hard enough without dealing with tears too. I don't think Bobby's pride would allow that to happen anyway, but who knows? All I know is that I don't want to get into this crying thing. It'd probably only take me seeing his eyes well up to make me stop what it's taken me so long to finally start.

'Are we back on that again?' he says surprisingly patronisingly. I guess from that response, tears are not going to be an immediate issue. Phew. Still, something about his tone gets my back up.

'Jess, now is not the time. We should get a move on or we're going to be late for the restaurant. And if I get any weaker from hunger and you have to assist me there, we'll be later still.' He shakes his head at me as if I'm trying his patience, stands up and smooths down his pants, looking at me as if to say, 'Can we just go now?'

I shake my head in disbelief. Did he really just totally dismiss me?

'Bobby, I'm serious. This is it! I'm tired of doing this. No more going through the motions. I don't want to anymore.' I'm feeling drained by the second.

'Listen to yourself. What? You're saying you want to end having a family?'

His look of disbelief is not shifting. How can he even say that to me? Our family isn't going to change in the way that he's suggesting. We're still going to be the same old Mum, Dad and Martell. Just not in the same house. This isn't quite turning out the way I'd planned. He's twisting it all. I can feel my voice rising.

'That's not what I'm saying and you know that ...' He rolls his eyes at me like to say 'Whatever'. 'We've grown apart and I don't see how you can't see that the gap is as wide as the Grand Canyon!'

He's looking at me really hard now. 'Jess,' he says, all traces of patronisation now gone from his voice. 'Jess, I know you've had something on your mind for a while. Maybe I've been a bit blind in not realising it might be more than just a work problem.'

Acknowledgement. Damn! He always starts with acknowledgement because he knows I can't challenge that.

'If this is about being more spontaneous, or more being more thoughtful, or being whatever it is this time, I'm trying. So far I seem to be getting it wrong, but I'm willing to put in the hours to try and get it right.'

Effort. Damn again. He's doing that you-can't-blame-a-man-for-trying thing because he knows I can't blame this man for trying.

'But Jess, it can't be done overnight. I can't suddenly give you everything you seem to think is missing on tap. Don't try to make me feel like I can.'

Expectation. I can't believe he's using the unreasonable expectation one on me! How did I forget how good he was at getting through the Talks with all this stuff? He is playing me like a violin and the tune is going to number one unless I hang onto my resolve.

'Jess, can't we talk about this properly over dinner? The table is booked already.' He cocks his head to the side and gives me that little half-smile he does when he's trying to get out of trouble. He looks like a little boy when he does that. I feel my heart waver a little. If I go to dinner now then my die-hard attempt will have done just that. Died. The thought of us sitting down and having a new conversation about the same old thing just makes me go cold because he'll manage to turn everything around. I'm usually so good at swinging talky things in the direction I want them to go, but with these kinds of Talks, I don't seem to be able to get the same result. It baffles even me. Bobby knows he has the edge over me in this. I can see this ending up like one of our regular Talks and us going full circle. I just can't do that again. It has to end now. He is right about one thing though: changing our situation is not an overnight process. An over-years process would be a better description. Am I being totally selfish in thinking if ten years hasn't been enough, then maybe it's not meant to be?

'Bobby.' I inhale and hold for five seconds. 'I don't want to talk about it over dinner. In fact I don't want to talk about it any more.' That little boy smile is slowly fading. I feel like a wicked witch, but I can't back down now. 'It's not you that needs another opportunity to change. It's us. We need to change. Somewhere along our journey, we stopped being a "we" and are now a "you" and a "me".'

35

The little boy smile is gone. I feel horrible, really horrible, but I can't let that show. It's for the good of us both in the long run. As long as I hold that thought, I'll get through this.

'We have been driving in different cars down the same road for a long time now. We've come to a junction and I have to turn off and go my own way.'

Wow. I said it. After swallowing that mouthful from me, there'd surely be no room for him to eat dinner anyway. We're both to blame for this, but even I'm feeling that he's getting the brunt. Well, actually no. He's still a bit more to blame than me. Where men can carry blame or carry the suitcases, they should. That's why they have stronger shoulders than women. Logic aside, I still feel like the villain of the piece here.

I'm amazed at my exterior calmness. No tears, no stuttering – an achievement, I assure you. Bobby's standing up now. For once not even the news about Fernando Torres or Torrid or whatever his name is, the so-called hottest thing in Spain, is holding his attention over me. He's pacing from the sofa to the window, window to the sofa. My head moves in unison, from the sofa to the window, window to the sofa.

'Is there someone else, Jess?' he asks. He sounds calm, but with Bobby, I don't know if that's a good sign or a bad sign. I mean what do I tell him? That I haven't met a new boyfriend, but I have made a new friend who's a boy? That's not going to help him accept this is something I have to do for me. It's going to make him think I want to leave him to run into the arms of another man, which isn't the reason at all. Well, not wholly the reason.

'No, there isn't.' There's no need to elaborate more

than that. I must admit that I'm struggling with the not-quite-a-lie but not-exactly-the-truth element of that statement. Bobby's not saying much, just staring out the window. He turns to face me and to say he looks upset is an understatement. This has got to be the turn-it-back-on-me guilt trip part. This is where I'd usually fold, but I didn't come this far for that to happen now.

'How can you be so blasé about this? This is our lives you're talking about ...'

I stop him mid-sentence. I'm ready to defend myself then I see the pain in his eyes and the words don't materialise. Suddenly I'm tired. I've been standing in the doorway this whole time and right now I need to sit down. I go over to the single seater and perch on the armrest. Bobby's still staring out of the window. Probably wondering what he can say to put the ball back in my court again.

'I want Martell.'

Well, that was a fifteen-love shot if ever I heard one. This has clearly affected Bobby more than even I could have thought. He's clearly lost his mind. He wants my child? I look at him and raise a single eyebrow.

'I'm not even entertaining that statement about my child, Robert.' Martell was always just my son, and Bobby always Robert when I needed to make a point. 'You will always be able to see Martell, but he is not next season's football kit. So no, you can't have him.' With that firmly spoken I slide from the armrest into the chair and cross my right leg over my left. I smooth down my dress over my knee and link my fingers through one another. This is my be-serious-now-Robert pose.

'You can have everything: the car, the house, whatever. Just give me my son.'

Oh my goodness! Have I made him certifiable? If I didn't know any better, I'd think he was serious. But I'm not going to think that. Or say that. In fact, there is only one thing to say in response. For emphasis, I rise up slightly from my seat, put both my hands on my hips and look him straight in the eyes. Then I say the one and only thing I can say. 'Not. Going. To. Happen.'

He stares back at me for what seems like eternity. I think I've hit a home run. If looks could kill, Bobby would be picking up a long wooden box for me and a new black suit for my son.

'I hate you.'

The words are so chilly, they have icicles on. He suddenly stomps towards me, past me, then out the front door. Without even having to turn around I know this, because the whole street probably heard it slam.

4

Bobby

Bobby stood outside the front door for several minutes. He felt stuck in indecision: should he go back and talk some more, or should he wait for Jess to calm down and come to her senses? He turned to walk down the street. He was having a hard time coming to terms with what had just happened. Did it really even happen? Walking down the street with his hands in his pockets and a frown on his brow, he concentrated hard, going over it in his mind.

Okay, Jess had come clickety clacking downstairs in possibly another new pair of shoes – no surprises there. The woman had hundreds of shoes and they were everywhere: under the bed, in the wardrobe, in the cupboard under the stairs, in black bags in the shed, simply everywhere. He had four pairs of shoes, including a pair of slippers, and they fitted the bill for every occasion. In fact, as he recalled, one pair hadn't even been worn yet. Bobby frowned a little more. Why he was thinking about Jess's shoes when he was in crisis?

Okay, thinking back. He hadn't looked up from the newspaper, but that couldn't have been what set her off because she knew what he was like when he was in the middle of a vital football article. It had to be finished – no interruptions. Besides, he'd been waiting for her for over two hours, so she could hardly begrudge him an extra five minutes reading time. Nope, all the bases checked out there. There was no way that football could have been what set her off. So where was the 'We should call it a day' coming from?

At first he hadn't even realised that was what she'd said. He'd thought she'd said: shall we call up today? But that didn't make much sense. She'd already confirmed the restaurant booking for eight thirty and it was only seven, so there was plenty of time to make it. No, something must have happened today. Maybe someone had cut in front of her while she was driving.

He'd refused to believe that Jess was serious at first. They were happy together. A happy couple with ups and downs like anyone else. It might seem like more downs than ups at the moment, but that was just the current route, not the final destination. When her words finally registered correctly, he'd looked up from the newspaper fully expecting to see a big joking smile on her face and to hear the word 'Gotcha!' Jess could be a real joker at times, and even though he wouldn't have thought much of her material on this occasion, he could have forced an appropriate reaction, an exaggerated roll of the eyes maybe. But there was no smile. Not even a crack.

'Hello there, Robert. You're looking deep in thought. Everything okay?'

It was Mary from number seventeen. 'Meddling Mary' was Jess's preferred title for her. Mary was the neighbourhood watch as well as the neighbour who watched. If there was something scandalous going on in the street, she was guaranteed to either know about it or be the cause of it. The last thing Bobby needed right now was to be the street's next bit of hot gossip.

'Hey, Mary.' Maybe a simple smiling hello would be enough to get her off the scent. 'Everything's great, thanks!' Maybe everything being fine would have been a more appropriate response than great. It was clearly obvious that he didn't look great or Mary wouldn't have felt the need to ask the question in the first place. Bobby mentally smacked himself on the forehead.

'Hmm …' Mary could convey so much with a simple sound effect. She was clearly suspicious. 'How's your young lady then? Haven't seen her for a while.' She was lowering her eyelids in that covert way.

'Jess has been really busy at work, late nights and stuff.'

Mary was squinting now. That was never a good sign. He really had to get out of this conversation.

'Hey, speaking of late nights, you had a bit of a late one yourself the other night, didn't you?' Bobby challenged Mary's squint with a big wink.

'I have no idea what you're talking about. I'm in bed by nine o'clock most nights,' Mary sniffed. She always sniffed in that affronted way when she felt her privacy was being exposed. For such a nosy neighbour she was fiercely private about her own goings-on.

'Not last Saturday night, though! I could have sworn I saw Ron from number forty two leaving your house, and it was more than a little after nine. But don't worry, your secret is safe with me.' Bobby gave her another big wink, accompanied by a double elbow nudge against the air.

'As I said, you are mistaken, young man. Anyway, Anita needs feeding so I must be off.' Stomping off, Mary glared over her shoulder muttering something under her breath that sounded very similar to '… people should mind their own business …'

Usually, something like this would tickle his fancy something rotten, but today Bobby couldn't even muster a smile for his victory against the biggest meddler the street had ever known.

He needed to focus on what could have prompted what happened. What could he possibly have ballsed up? Did he forget to take out the rubbish? Or was it that he left the toilet seat up again? He could never understand why that was such an issue. It wasn't like he made a big deal when she left the toilet seat down. Guess it was too much to think that chicken was all that was going to be on the menu tonight. He could've kicked himself when the words 'Look Jess, we're going to be late' spewed out of his mouth when he realised she was serious; the words of a desperate man who, in his desperation, couldn't summon something more sympathetic and unpatronising. It's a wonder Jess hadn't thrown the vase at him. She hated being patronised. She also loved the vase. That explained that, then.

Surely all this couldn't be the result of their not talking as much as they used to? Maybe they didn't have the marathon type conversations she had with some of her friends but then he wasn't the world's greatest authority on the season's newest bags. They talked, though; they talked loads. But come on, timing is everything. She couldn't honestly expect it to be a two-sided conversation when he was watching boxing, just like he wouldn't expect her undivided attention if she was watching Coronation Street. Though, admittedly, she would give him her attention if he wanted to talk, he didn't actually *expect* it. He loved Jess to death, he really did, but she could be a real Drama Mama at times. One of her favourite Philadelphian terms, that was fast becoming one of his too, for obvious reasons.

Maybe if he'd apologised straight away that would have stopped her in her tracks, given him a bit of time. He usually liked to know what he was apologising for, but given the end result he would have happily taken the blame for lack of world peace. Anything she wanted to hear would have gushed forth from his lips if it would have avoided all of this. And he could have ended it with his killer smile: not quite a beamer, more like a pose-for-the-school-photograph type smile. Jess usually couldn't resist it. That smile had got him out of many a past pickle with the love of his life. It might have got her to pause everything, at least until they'd got to the restaurant, buying him some time to think about what to do next. And then he'd have been in the right place to show her that she was over-reacting to whatever it was she was over-reacting to. Things always looked different by candlelight. Fine time for his brain to be all active and full of bright ideas now, wasn't it?

He flopped down on a nearby street-bin. It wasn't the most comfortable choice of seating, but his street was unfortunately one where the houses were step-less; sprawling out on the floor in the middle of the street would just draw even more attention to his plight and make him look like a crazy person. Actually, sitting on the bin wasn't the best image either, but image was really the last thing on his mind right now. 'How could you miss the signs, Dumbo? How could you miss the signs?' And as if that wasn't bad enough, he'd paced too. He groaned and closed his eyes, in his mind smacking himself on the forehead again. He always paced when he had to get something serious straight in his head. When he was confused he had to pace. When he was nervous he had to pace. But how pathetically gawky had that made him look on top of his lack of verbal skills? Then, just when he thought he

43

was making a good attempt at keeping his composure up, perspiration had let him down; his shirt was undeniable proof of this. He had just handled everything wrong.

It was supposed to be a simple dinner. How had it turned into this? How had he gone from being a happy, family man in a long-term, steady relationship to a single, sitting-on-a-street-bin bum? His head hurt, and his bum hurt. He'd gradually been sinking further and further into the bin without even realising. Hoisting himself out, he started walking down the street again.

His surroundings felt surreal. The cars, the trees – all just seemed like one big blur that he couldn't quite get into focus. Only one thing was consuming his whole conscious-ness right now: this situation with Jess. How could he not have had an inkling that something was up? He slapped himself on the forehead – this time literally. Why else would she go to all the trouble of a spur of the moment dinner if she didn't have something up her sleeve? And talk about impatience; she didn't even wait for them to get out the door! The way she'd sprung this announcement on him was very underhanded. Not like her at all, which meant someone else must be behind it. Yes! That would explain everything! That wasn't Jess talking. Clearly something was bothering her and no doubt discussing it with one of her Meddling Mary friends had forced her thoughts in this direction. He'd take interfering friends any day rather than some other guy. The glimmer of relief he'd felt when she told him there wasn't someone else washed over him again. He didn't know what he'd have done if she'd said there was. Bobby kicked a stone in the street and laughed as he recalled asking for Martell. Talk about grasping at straws! He could laugh now, but at that moment he was deadly serious. Jess had put him straight about that in no uncertain terms.

He stopped and stared up at the sky. Jess was everything to him. He couldn't hate her if he tried. Did he really say that to her? Just thinking about it made him cringe. He was supposed to be a man in control of his emotions and even if, at that second, he had fleetingly felt that he hated her, surely he didn't need to actually say it? He didn't hate Jess; what he hated was the situation she had put them in. He'd just wanted to hurt her the way she had hurt him. The front door had been the vent for his anger. He hadn't realised just how much force he'd used to slam the door until he saw that the thick shatter-proof glass, whilst staying intact, had actually shattered. Like his world.

5

Jessica

I look up at the clock on the wall. A whole five minutes has passed and I'm still standing in the same place, with my hands still on my hips. Only difference is, I am breathing again. I didn't even realise that I had been holding my breath until I started gulping in large amounts of oxygen.

I slowly sit back down on the sofa armrest. I feel different, but why? Then I know. The feeling is one of loss. I am at a loss. I'd done it; I have finally told Bobby I wanted to finish and now I have all sorts of questions swimming around in my head. What's next? What do I do now? Do I cry or should I be overcome with relief at the fact that I'd actually done it? Any normal woman who ups and ends a ten-year relationship should really shed a few tears, shouldn't she? Strangely enough, crying is the furthest thing from my mind right now. I'm sad, very sad about the whole situation, but not tearful. Does that make me a hardhearted bitch? Will people think that?

I can hear it now: 'But Bobby's so great! He's family!' and 'Will the real Cruella Deville please stand up?' By the time Bobby puts his slant on it, my name will no doubt be tarnished, like a priest who goes on a date with a hooker. I'll be labelled as scandalous. Everyone Bobby knows will be singing that hip-hop song by Missy Elliott when they see me, the one where she's singing about some girl being a bitch. In fact, I think that might even be the name of the song: She's a Bitch. They'll probably want to rename the tune in my honour to 'She's a Jess' instead. I hate playing the role of bad guy and it so felt like that. It's bad enough that I'm always deemed the bad guy with Martell (because I have to tell him, 'No son, you have to eat your greens,' where his dad gets to tell him, ''Course son, choose whatever bar of chocolate you want.'). Sod it. Who really cares what people think anyway? Me … a little … I guess. Well, it's not exactly nice when their thoughts aren't complimentary and you actually know they're not. I think I have a headache coming on now.

I slide off the armrest and into the seat of the chair. The imprint where my butt had nestled not ten minutes before is still there. I put my fingers to my temple. I didn't realise that this whole thing would take so much out of me.

I think back to the moment Bobby said he hated me. I'm really hoping it was just temper talking, even though it felt like he meant it. It was the look that did it. Like his eyes were butcher's knives and I was a piece of meat. Ooh, I shudder to think what must've been going on in his mind. Am I being naïve in believing that we could remain friends of some sort, for Martell's sake? Okay, and for my guilt-soaked sanity?

Bobby's so caught up in some hazy aura of how we used to be that he simply refuses to see that we aren't that couple anymore; haven't been for a very long time. I'm slowly shrivelling with the constant pressure to keep it all together for him and everyone else. Why can't he see that, just this one time, I have to do this for me first and fore-most?

★ ★ ★

'Jess, you and Martell are my only family.' Bobby looked like a lost little boy when he made statements like that.

'So, have your mum and dad been relegated to strangers

in the night then?' Bobby also had a selective memory when it suited him.

'You know what I mean. When my parents emigrated to Miami last year, that made you and Martell my only family HERE.'

'Okay, point taken … what was the point again?' Jess already knew what the point was, but it irked her to admit it.

'That you should always put your family first.'

Jess looked at him wearily, knowing full well that even though he said 'family' he really meant him. It was how his mother was with his father and so, for him, that meant that was how it should be.

'Yes Bobby, I know and I do. I just wish you would too sometimes,' Jess added quietly under her breath.

★ ★ ★

I so want him to understand that I'm unhappy, and if I'm not happy, *we* can't be happy. This time I can't put his feelings over mine, even though it's proved a hard habit to break. As far as I can think back in any of my relationships, family or otherwise, it has always been about putting everybody else first. Even when I came to land on British shores from Philadelphia some thirteen years ago, at the tender age of twenty, it was to please somebody else: my mother.

★ ★ ★

'Wake up, Honey, we're leaving.' Mrs Montrose forcefully drew back the curtains.

'Ugh, Mom! What time is it? What do you mean, "we're leaving"?'

'Just what I said: leaving. And if you don't leave that bed in the next five seconds, those covers will get the same treatment as these curtains!'

Jess could hear from her mother's tone that she wasn't playing. There was an edge to it that she hadn't heard before.

'Where are we going?'

'London.'

'What!' Jess jumped out of the bed. 'Are you serious, Mom? Why are we going to London?'

Mrs Montrose stopped taking her daughter's clothes out of the wardrobe and sat down on the bed.

'Sit down, Honey.'

Jess was nervous now. What was going on?

'Sweetheart, I know that you know your dad has had many friends for a while now. His indiscretions are too indiscreet when the neighbours start shaking their heads at me in pity. I can't turn a blind eye anymore. I need a new start someplace else, and I've chosen London. So chop chop, Honey. Tania has already packed two suitcases; you know how excitable your little sister can get. The plane leaves in three days and there's lots of packing to do.' Mrs Montrose got up and started clearing the wardrobe again as if the news she'd just divulged was a trip to the local super-market.

* * *

I'd always known Daddy had a roving eye. He was the original player. As he got older, the women he played with got younger, until jailbait would have been a more accurate description of them. I never knew it bothered Mom. They'd officially separated years ago, but stayed living in the same house for me and Tania. Keeping up appearances, Mom called it. She'd always been big on showing the world what she thought was the proper image. But when the world started seeing what she didn't want them to see, it was time for her to take control another way. And with Mom, drastic was not an unfamiliar word.

* * *

'But Mom, why do we have to go all the way to London? That's in another country! What am I going to do all the way over there?' Jess was wide-eyed with disbelief.

'With your business degree, you can get a job anywhere in the world, Jess. You've just finished college; you've not started working yet, so it's a perfect opportunity for you to experience life in a different part of the world. There is life outside Philly, you know.'

Jess wasn't convinced. Philadelphia was all she'd known. All her friends were there and she wasn't someone who made friends easily, unlike her little sister Tania who had always been Miss Popularity.

'I don't need to go too though, do I, Mom? I mean you could take Tania and I could stay with Dad.' Jess had always been her father's best girl even though there had been occasions when some of his ever-younger girlfriends seemed to want to battle it out with her for the title.

'What on earth are you saying? You can't stay here and leave your baby sister all alone in another country! You can hardly look out for your baby sister from the other side of the world, now can you?'

How many times was she going to emphasise that Tania was her baby sister? Jess thought. Five years her junior, at fifteen, Tania was hardly a baby.

'You know your sister has always wanted to travel. She sleeps with that atlas you bought her under her pillow. How can you deny her this dream?' When Mrs Montrose was organising a guilt trip, she sure could drive that bus smoothly to its destination.

'How am I to blame for Tania's dream just because it's not mine?' Jess could barely contain her exasperation.

'Because I will not separate sisters; it's like separating twins; it's just not right. We won't go without you. I'll just stay and live in your father's humiliation of me and Tania can learn to get over the regret. She's fifteen now, so only about a lifetime or so for the hurt to fade.' Mrs Montrose didn't even stop packing as she spoke. She knew she didn't need to. Especially after she drove the final nail in.

'Your grandmother must be turning in her grave knowing you could even think about leaving your baby sister to fend for herself.'

'FINE! Fine! I'll go!' Jess couldn't stand the thought of disappointing her deceased grandmother even more than her live family members.

★ ★ ★

Just to make sure there was no danger of me changing my mind, Mom got Tania on the bandwagon.

★ ★ ★

'You have to come Jess, you just have to! Please, Please, PLEASE Jess!' Tania was beginning to sound like a scratched CD.

'Okay okay, Tania. I'm coming to London too.' Jess sighed resignedly.

'Yay! We're going to have SO much fun! I've been reading

about different parts of England in my atlas. We can visit France too – it's not that far, you know.'

'Sure, whatever. I have to break this to Dad first, though. He's got to be okay with this or I might have to reconsider.' Jess was secretly hoping her Dad would suggest she live with him instead.

'Call him now, call him now, Jess!' Tania was beginning to make Jess feel nauseous the way she was using the bed like a trampoline. Jess picked up the phone and dialled her father's number.

'Hey Pops, it's me.'

'Who's that? Lucinda?'

Jess looked at the phone in her hand indignantly and rolled her eyes. 'No Dad, it's your real daughter, not your sugar one.'

'Jess! Hello, Sweetheart!' Mr Montrose bellowed happily.

'Dad. I've got some bad news.' Jess could hear her father draw in breath. 'Mom wants me to move to London with her.'

'Phew, Honeysuckle, I thought it was something serious!' He roared with laughter again. Jess didn't know if she should feel happy that he'd taken the news well, or unhappy that he'd taken the news well. 'Just make sure you keep in touch and come back to see me every so often. Sounds like a great opportunity for you to spread your little wings, Marshmallow. Well, I've got to dash, Sweet Pea; I'm expecting Lucinda any minute!' With that Mr Montrose blew Jess a kiss and hung up.

Jess looked at the receiver, then at Tania bouncing like an excited kangaroo. There wasn't the remotest chance of her getting out of this now.

* * *

And I do speak to my Dad. Every Sunday.

Anyway, I think that's what marked the start of a pattern of selflessness: in friendships, boyfriend-ships, work colleague-ships – any kind of ship. Today I've parked the selflessness and replaced it with some selfishness, just this once, just for me.

Damn, this headache just won't let go. I go over to the window and just stare out of it at nothing in particular. I look at my car parked in front of Meddling Mary's house – the nosiest neighbour in East London. I bet she saw Bobby slam out of the house. And I know that her sister now knows, the pastor's wife probably knows and, by tomorrow, very possibly the world.

She needs cleaning: my car, not Mary. I'll take her to the car wash tomorrow. Bobby usually hosed her down and hoovered her out. Bobby … Oh hell, here comes the barrage of doubts. Have I done the right thing? Is this decision really going to make me happy? I'm going to be single for the first time in this old house. No. Of course I've done the right thing. It's about the most right thing for my life that I have done in a long while. So why have I got this pounding headache? I need an aspirin or some-thing. Or … maybe just someone …

6

Bobby

Had he really walked up and down this same street five times already? Bobby was thankful for the gentle breeze that cooled his hot head. He had done the recrimination thing, the what-went-wrong thing and the why-didn't-I-see-it-all-coming thing. He now had to do the how-to-fix-it thing. It was not going to be easy. His easy life, as he knew it, had abruptly ended ten minutes ago. He hated emotional confrontations. He'd been known to go to extreme lengths to try and avoid them in the hope that they'd just eventually go away. Like just turning up the television volume or interrupting her saying he had an urgent call to make. He knew it made Jess mad, but he'd rather deal with her anger than anything deeper. Not this time. By blindsiding him like this, Jess had taken the situation right out of his hands.

Ten years. To be cast away like a pair of old holey socks. But hey, socks could be mended, and so could this. He didn't know how he was going to fix things, just that he had to. As long as there was no other guy lurking in the background there was a chance to sort everything out. He wouldn't, couldn't, give up on his family, even if it meant going back to basics: the dating, the flowers, the chocolates, all that malarkey. Whatever it took, he was prepared to do it. He acknowledged again how hard it was going to be. He was a man who'd been out of practice for a while; a good ten-year while. You just didn't think you'd still have to be doing stuff like that when you'd been with someone for as long as he had.

He thought back to when he'd first met Jess's grandma,

not long after he'd started dating Jess. It was at one of those get-to-meet-the-family visits.

* * *

'Hmm.' Grandma Pearl slowly perused Bobby from head to toe. Five minutes later, nothing other than the initial sound effect had passed her lips. Squirming wasn't something that Bobby was used to, but squirm he would if it meant making a good impression on this woman.

'So, Grandma Pearl, how are you today?' Polite small talk was usually a good ice-breaker.

'Good.'

Bobby waited for a little more elaboration. Five minutes passed before he realised that wasn't going to happen.

'So, Grandma Pearl, how are you finding the weather? It's been unusually warm for this time of year over here.'

'Good.'

Bobby had already been pre-warned that Grandma Pearl was a woman of few words, but this was putting a whole new definition on the term.

'Robert?' Something other than the word good! Bobby pricked himself up and puffed his chest out. This was the moment of truth.

'Yes, Grandma Pearl?'

'You've found a good girl in my granddaughter. Take care of the little things and the big things will take care of themselves.' Bobby waited again for a little more elaboration. Five minutes later he knew that was going to be his lot. He didn't quite know what she meant, but would rather stay in the dark than let her think her granddaughter was going out with an idiot. Jess was very fond of her grandmother, so getting her on side could only score him

points. He responded in the way that anybody trying to get the highest score possible would.

'Yes, Grandma Pearl.'

★ ★ ★

How mistaken could he have been about the little things? And of all the times for something from so long ago to finally hit home.

The breeze had suddenly turned into a stark chill which was beginning to seep through his shirt. It certainly hadn't been his best idea to fly out of the house without a jacket. It suddenly dawned on him that by slamming out of the house he might have made himself homeless. He still couldn't get past the fact that he seemed to have missed all the signs that now seemed so clear. How could he have been so ... so ... Mr Magoo-ish about their relationship?

Bobby took a deep breath. He needed to stop beating himself up about what had already happened. He had thought that giving Jess her own way was *the* way. Any other woman would have jumped at the chance to have everything their way.

So they were in a routine. Wasn't that what you were striving for in a relationship? To be in a routine? Okay, maybe he hadn't been the most attentive or helpful or supportive or thoughtful or ... Okay, maybe he hadn't been a *lot* of things, but they had history, a lot of history. And they had a child. Surely that made it worth giving him another chance? The more he thought about it, the more confused he got as to the best way to make things right again. His head was all over the place. The only thing he knew for sure was that he couldn't give up his family as easily as Jess seemed able to.

And what about Martell? He knew Jess'd never keep him from seeing Martell, but it would never be the same as seeing him every morning before he went to school or every night before he went to sleep. That was how often he'd want to see his son, and that couldn't happen if they weren't together. Martell was *his* son. For all the years he and Jess had been together, only his son shared the Phillips name, even if at the end of a double barrel. Martell Christopher Montrose-Phillips.

His name was attached to nothing else in their home. Everything, even down to contents insurance, was in the name of Jessica Montrose. Why was that? Well, when Martell came along they'd needed a bigger place. There hadn't been enough space in his one-bed council flat for a new baby *and* all of Jess's clothes and shoes. He'd been between contracts at the time and Jess hadn't yet risen through the ranks to be the manager she was now. To get a decent size mortgage she'd added a friend's name so she could use a joint income to get enough for a decent size property. Jess eventually took the other person's name off with the intention of eventually adding his, but they'd somehow never got around to it. There'd never seemed any rush and it hadn't seemed important. The new house had always felt like 'their' home even though Jess chose all the décor and furniture. He'd occasionally bought something for the house like a vase or a picture, but they'd always get damaged or mysteriously disappear.

★ ★ ★

'Jess ... I bought a vase yesterday.'
'That's great, honey.'
'So ... where is it?'

'Where did you put it, babe?'
'Right over there on the coffee table.'
'Isn't it there then?'
'Err … no.'
'Oh! … was it that spotted one with the jagged edging at the top?'
'Yes! That's the one!'
'Nope. Can't think where it could be, sweetie.'

★ ★ ★

Admittedly his additions didn't always go with the look of the place. He'd never really had an eye for furniture and stuff. So, when whatever he bought ended up where no-one could see it, he decided to make his contribution by cash in Jess's hand instead. He was actually happy that he'd got off the hook and would never again have to accompany her on furniture shopping expeditions when he could be home, watching sport. He'd never admit it, but he'd actually picked a couple of things that even he knew were hideous (his taste wasn't *that* bad) just so that they would disappear and justify him just paying for stuff instead of having to pick it too.

Not once did Jess ever make him feel that it was technically really her house. It always felt like their house: their home. The car too was officially a Montrose possession.

★ ★ ★

'I'm sorry Mr Phillips, but your car finance application has been denied.' The car salesman shook his head politely.
'Why would that be?' Bobby questioned.
'Could be too many loans outstanding.'
'I don't have any loans. I don't even have a credit card.'

'Ahh … that must be it then. No credit history.' The salesman shook his head as if this was rarely heard of.

'We need a car, Sweetheart,' Jess took charge smoothly. 'Ferrying Martell all over the place without one is going to be impossible. Shall we try the finance in my name? I've lost count of the number of credit cards I've had.'

Bobby nodded resignedly.

The salesman put in Jess's details, waited a few seconds, then smiled. 'Application accepted, Madam!'

* * *

It wasn't just physical possessions either. Even the car insurance couldn't be in joint names.

* * *

'How much?' Bobby spluttered. 'That's not far off the cost of the car!'

'I'm sorry, sir, but the points on your licence mean we have to put a premium onto your quote.'

Bobby sighed. Who'd have thought his boy-racer days would come back to haunt him like this? 'Can you hold the line a moment please?' He turned to Jess who was silently listening at his side.

'Would making me the lead driver and you as an additional driver make a difference?' she asked. Bobby relayed the question to the insurer.

'Hold on a moment, sir, let me just adjust the details. You'll be happy to know, sir, with you as an additional driver, your quote has just been reduced by nearly three hundred pounds. Isn't that great?' The insurer gushed.

* * *

He may have parted with the pounds to help pay for all these things, but technically none of it was his or in his name in the legal sense. Which reminded him of an additional reason for being particularly possessive over his son: Martell's birth certificate *did* have his name on it. Martell was all he had now and he'd be damned if he let Jess upset his son's life just because she had a bee in her bonnet about hers.

Going back to the house now to try and talk things over again wasn't going to be a good move. He needed time to think of a plan; Jess needed time to be receptive to said plan. Operation Get-Jess-Back. As long as there was no-one else in the picture then there was still a chance for them. As long as there was a chance then he had to go for it. Ten years with someone was a habit that would take more effort to break than to keep. He didn't have a clue where to start. It was going to take more than flowers and a pretty apology to fix things. He needed help. A woman's help. A woman like ... That was it! She would know! Suddenly he needed to make a call. Shit, he'd stormed out of the house without his mobile phone. Shit, shit, shit. He sure hoped that the phone box at the top of the road was working.

7

Gary Martin. How did I ever let that happen? He had been a crush of mine, from the moment I first laid eyes on him three months ago. He and Maddy were good friends. They had been for years. I first met him when Maddy and me were on one of our shopping expeditions, which were nearly always all day events, even if only a purse was the end result.

* * *

'Girl, this is just not any party – EVERYONE is going to be there. My outfit has to be on point with no chance of duplication by anyone else.' Maddy always liked to stand out, and woe betide anyone who wore the same outfit as her.

'The thing about shopping for outfits for a party where everyone is gonna be, is that you're likely to bump into some of those same people also buying their outfits for the party.' Jess smiled at her friend.

'Damn, WHY did you have to say that? It's like you saying it has made it happen!'

'What on earth are you talking about, Drama Mama?' Jess rolled her eyes.

'Look. Over there!' Maddy had already fixed a smile to her face even though it wasn't hard to tell she wasn't best pleased at being spotted.

'Hi, Madeleine. I'm guessing all these bags are for tonight?' A deep voice made me slowly turn to the direction it was coming from. There the source was – in all his magnificence.

'Actually, I'm merely holding these bags for my friend. Jess, meet Gary. Gary Martin.'

★ ★ ★

Madeleine did all the talking that day. All I could do was stare. He was *that* fine. I could barely squeak a hello when she introduced us. After he'd left, I kept looking backwards to see if I could catch one last glance of the mesmerising Mr Martin.

★ ★ ★

'So, who was that?' Jess's jaw was ajar.

'Close your mouth before you swallow a fly. It's just Gary. I've known him forever.'

'So, he's going to be at the party tonight?'

Maddy stopped mid step and swirled around, bags knocking anyone in close proximity. 'Now why would a practically married woman be concerned about that?' Maddy raised her eyebrow to emphasise just how unusual she found the question.

Jess shrugged, hoping to appear nonchalant. 'He's a good-looking guy. It'll be nice to know there'll be something to look at other than the four walls, is all.'

'Yeah, he's good looking and he knows it.'

'I was just making an observation, that's all.'

'That's not all, because that's not like you. He's my pal, Jess, but you're my best pal. Gary is a player. Trust me, you don't want any of his game.'

'Who says I do?' Jess's indignance felt forced even to herself.

'Well, he would love to add you to his list of conquests. Lucky for you, you've got a good man like Bobby. They don't

62

grow on trees. Ooh, look at that dress in Oasis's window, let's go there next!' Maddy didn't see the expression on Jess's face as she bustled off– it was one of intrigue.

* * *

And I did hear exactly what Maddy was telling me. I just didn't listen. I could see for myself that Gary was a definite ladies man. He reminded me so much of my father. He was fair of face, firm of body and fine of fine. All the F's you could want in one package. Gary even knew Bobby. Apparently they weren't friends exactly but if they met they could comfortably have a how-are-things kind of conversation. I later realised that not only was Gary a ladies man, he was also a lady's man as in belonging to somebody. He was engaged. All of these facts rolled up together always make me wonder how on earth I got into this situation.

Nathan's birthday party was where it all began. The same party that me and Maddy had been out shopping for. When Gary arrived, my tongue-tiedness of the shopping centre somehow disappeared.

* * *

'So, is this the sexy outfit you bought when you were shopping earlier today?' Gary smiled.

'This old thing?' Jess pinched her dress. 'No. The sexy outfit I bought is to wear another day.'

'Who knows? I may be lucky enough to have the pleasure of seeing you in that one too.'

Jess smiled back. 'Who knows indeed.'

* * *

We talked constantly throughout the whole party. Talked, laughed and clicked in a way that Bobby and I hadn't in a long time. It felt good.

★ ★ ★

'So, you've been friends with Maddy for a while then?' Gary handed Jess the drink he'd got her from the bar.

'Since school. But you know Maddy, knowing her even for a day feels like you've known her forever!'

'Ain't that the truth!' Gary laughed, mocking Jess's slight accent playfully.

'I can't believe you're a stepper!' Gary swung Jess around to the R Kelly classic tune.

'See these twinkle toes? Well, you ain't seen nothing yet!' Jess smiled and did a little intricate foot movement. Gary roared with laughter.

★ ★ ★

An exchange of numbers ensued at the end of the night – just as friends of course. Telephone calls followed, which led to long insightful conversations that sometimes lasted for hours.

★ ★ ★

'You wanted to be a dancer when you were younger then?' Gary asked.

'I thought ballet slippers were so cool – the way you could stand on your toes like that!'

'Chelsea are definitely the team to beat, I'm telling you!' Gary was insistent that his football team was the greatest.

All Jess's football knowledge had been gleaned from Bobby. 'Well, with the amount of star players they have, they should be unbeatable, yet Arsenal's young ones beat them two weeks ago!'

'No way! You like Seventh Heaven's last album? Me too! Track four – Living like Riley – is my favourite.' Gary couldn't believe he'd found a fellow fan in Jess.

'Wow, go figure. All my friends thought I was a looney tune when I said I had their album.'

★ ★ ★

A lunch here, a meeting there and then the proverbial 'one night it just happened' happened. In all my ten years with Robert, in fact in any of my relationships, I had never been unfaithful, was never even interested in being unfaithful. Yet within a couple of months of hanging out with this Gary guy, fidelity and devotion had flown out the window.

★ ★ ★

'But I like you Jess, a lot.' Gary sounded almost anguished.

'Just because you like someone in a particular way, doesn't mean you should do something about it.' It was hard for Jess to remain practical when she knew she felt similarly.

'Why?' Gary asked

'Because I'm with someone.'

'And …?' Did he really need her to spell it out?

'And you are too.'

'Jess, something that feels this right … Can you really, honestly, truthfully from the heart, say it's wrong?' Gary sounded incredulous.

Yes, was on the tip of Jess's tongue, the very tip – but somehow the word would not fall off the edge.

★ ★ ★

Gary took me to a complete different emotional plane, one that I could never have imagined I would visit. And sex hadn't even come into it yet! When sex did eventually come into it, I realised that me and Bobby had come to the end of the line. I knew I couldn't go back to what we had. The first 'it' happened a few weeks back. Since then Bobby must think I'm about to expire, the number of excuses I've given him to avoid sex.

★ ★ ★

MONDAY
Bobby reached over to Jess.

'I'm sorry baby, I have got the worst headache ever. Feels like I've been kicked in the head with a steel boot.'

WEDNESDAY
Bobby smiled slyly at Jess.

'Sweetie, I've started early this month. My river is running as red as a bottle of Sauvignon.'

FRIDAY
Bobby ran his hand up Jess's leg, she put her hand on his to halt it before it reached her knee.

'Did I tell you that I nearly put my back out at work this week trying to lift a batch of folders? It's been playing up so much since, at this rate I'll need a chiropractor.'

SUNDAY
*Bobby looked over at Jess. She winced at him. He nodded
understandingly. No words were needed.*

★ ★ ★

The idea of sleeping with two different men at the same
time didn't and still does not appeal to me. Some old-
fashioned values that fortunately didn't fly out the window
with the others. The next step couldn't have been anything
other than ending my relationship with Bobby.

You could tell that I was a novice at selfishness because
I didn't consider the consequences, or the history, or even
Martell, when Gary and me started out. I just knew that
the experience had made me recognise that something
very vital had gone missing between with me and Bobby.
That feeling, that passion … Now I'd had a taste of it, I
knew I couldn't be in a relationship without it.

So, I'd taken the step and ended things between me
and Bobby. Now I could consider the consequences.
Consequences like, just who was I forsaking a ten-year
relationship with child for? A guy who was already more
than a little involved in a big way with another woman?
Maybe Gary wouldn't be the One, but he was the one
who finally made me realise that my relationship with
Bobby wasn't going in the right direction. It didn't seem
a particularly pressing issue that Gary's direction wasn't
the right direction either. Did I really want to go from
being the woman to being the *other* woman? Anyway, I
can't think about that right now, especially with this headache. All I can think is that I need to hear his voice now
more than anything. I go over to the phone and call his
mobile phone number. Any woman who has been in a

relationship with someone who is already involved will know that landlines are off-limits. After a few rings he picks up.

'Hello?' I say.

'Hey baby, what's up?' He goes silent for a few seconds like he already knows that something's up. I know it's going to sound corny, but it's like he's in tune with me, as if he already knows without me having to say anything.

'Do you want to see me tonight?' he asks.

I stare into the phone. After a few seconds I respond. 'Won't wifey wonder where you are?' As the words come out of my mouth I instantly wish they hadn't. I hate it when I act all catty like that. Yuck. But I just can't help it sometimes. It's like jealousy, but not jealousy. More like annoyance with the whole predicament that is us. I can't explain it. I just hate it. He lets it pass as per usual. He hates arguing. I hate that he hates arguing; release is good for the soul.

'What are you up to?'

What do I tell him? Oh, just getting rid of my boyfriend of ten years because you've made me realise something's died with us and I need to let him go even though I need to let you go too?

'Nothing much. You crossed my mind, so I thought I'd call to see how you're doing.' Why couldn't I just say what was really on my mind to this person? He made me feel so needy sometimes. It was not a feeling I was used to. Bobby always needed me; I didn't have the opportunity to get to need anybody.

'Well look, it's Saturday. I've got a party to go to. Put on some glad-rags and meet me there?'

The idea of seeing him sounds appealing even though

I don't really feel in the party mood. Once again it's like he pre-empts my feelings.

'We can talk or I can just look at you. You know whatever we do as long as we do "it" together always works for me!' He laughs softly. He knows that works for me too. I can't believe that I can be so strong when it comes to Bobby but so weak when it came to this guy. Yuck. I really hate that. He gives me the address, we fool around on the phone for a few more minutes then we leave it at we'll-see-each-other-later.

What am I thinking of? Not even an hour ago I ended the relationship I've had for nearly a third of all the years I've been on this earth and now I'm contemplating going to a party! What exactly do I have to be partying about? Nothing. I just need a shoulder to lean on right now and I can't think of a shoulder I would rather lean on than Gary's, and if it means going to a party to get said shoulder then that's where I'm going.

With that now all rationalised, there's nothing stopping me apart from maybe a little bit of conscience? But you know what? I can soothe my conscience tomorrow; tonight, there's no more sitting and wallowing in thoughts of what-am-I-going-to-do-now. I'm already dressed up with nowhere to go and I made too much effort for somebody not to appreciate. My only immediate worry is who to go with? Part of the other woman protocol is that you can't turn up at familiar gatherings with the object of your desire. I'm certainly not bold enough to walk into the party alone. I'm not for equality THAT much. I'll ring Maddy. She is always up for a party. She answers before the phone completes one ring.

'That was quick! Are you expecting a call?'

'Yes, Janine's being dropped off; I said I'd drive tonight. She's supposed to ring when she's outside.'

'Oh.'

'Why, what's up?'

'I was hoping to go out tonight, that's all. Didn't fancy a night in, staring at the walls.'

'Thought you were out this evening with Bobby?' I could hear the cautious tone in her voice.

'That's another story for another night.'

Maddy was silent. She was one of the most astute people I know when it came to my feelings. A lot like Gary. Eventually she offered, 'So you should come tonight. It's a housewarming. Trevor won't mind.'

'Housewarming?

'Yeah, Trevor's sister bought this great place ...'

Maddy continues but my attention has lapsed as I'm trying to come up with someone else to go to Gary's party with. Maddy is in full flow about her party and clearly not worried about Janine trying to get through on the line, and some of her conversation starts to seep into my subconscious. Then she comes out with something that suddenly makes me tune all the way into what she's saying.

'Sorry, where did you say the party was again, Maddy?' She could not have said what I thought she said.

'I said it's at number twelve Bourneville Street. It's just up the road from me so no miles of driving in heels; you know how I hate that. I'll even come and pick you up. So do you want to go?'

Right now, all I want to do is go and look at the piece of paper that I wrote the address of the party Gary told me about. So I do. Just as I thought, it is the same party! How much of a coincidence is that? Now, I'm a horoscope fanatic and firm believer in signs. As far as I am concerned it's a super-size sign if two people give me the same address for the same party on the same night. That can only mean that I'm supposed to be there. Oh shit, what if Bobby finds out? We only broke up about an hour ago. How heartless will that make me seem? Still, I haven't even had a chance to tell anybody yet, I mean I've barely told Bobby. It's unlikely he's told anyone yet either.

I know, I know, really and truly I shouldn't be out partying tonight, but it's not like I'm going to be throwing my hands in the air and waving them like I just don't care, for goodness sake. I just need to get away from these walls for a while. It feels like they're closing in on me. Even if Bobby does know this Trevor guy, he definitely won't be in a partying mood. At least there's no chance of seeing him again this evening. With that all rationalised, I am after all already dressed and ready to go somewhere …

'Maddy, come and pick me up when you're ready.'

8

Bobby

Bobby had to restrain himself from bashing his head against the phone box, the way he was bashing the handset. The phone number had either one nine three two or two three on the end of it. His memory was straining to assemble Melinda's phone number correctly. Problems like this were born from the mobile phone age. You got so used to using the phone memory to store numbers that you ended up not being able to use the memory you were born with.

He hadn't spoken to Melinda in ages. It had to be at least six months since the last time she'd called. He hoped she wouldn't think he was taking a liberty calling her out of the blue like this. No. He didn't think she would. He truly believed that despite everything, they had managed to strike up a genuine friendship over the years. Bobby knew a lot of people thought that men and women couldn't really be friends, and a few that may even have thought that he and Melinda had more than just a regular friend-ship. But it wasn't like that, well, not really. They'd only ever overstepped the mark once. Just the once. It was after a huge argument with Jess.

★ ★ ★

'Sometimes, just sometimes I feel I could just strangle Jess. I love her to bits but she can really try my patience to the maximum.'

'I know exactly how you feel, except for me with Don it's more like all the time.' Melinda had a faraway expression on her face.

'Things not so good between you and your fella?'

'I'd say that's the understatement of the century.'

'Well, to put a positive spin on it, sounds like things can only get better then. I'm sure they will, Mel.'

Melinda looked deeply into Bobby's eyes and smiled softly. 'That means a lot to me, Bobby. You mean a lot to me.'

Bobby felt hypnotised. The two moved their heads towards each other, until there was nothing between them – not even air.

* * *

Melinda always maintained that she and Bobby were friends and friends should make time for each other. He wasn't blind to the fact that after all these years she'd maybe still got a soft spot for him. He wondered if he was trying to take advantage of that fact. He was certainly thinking of himself and how to fix his predicament. He was also feeling the need for some attention, and he needed it now. It had taken less than an hour for his whole world to cave in before his eyes and he felt like a shell, empty and of no use to anyone. Melinda would be able to change that. She could always make him want to beat his chest like Tarzan! Even in a ten-minute conversation, she could make him feel that his thoughts and opinions were the most important in the world.

* * *

'If they gave people more incentives to not be unemployed, the economy would be in much better shape.' Being self-employed, this was an issue Bobby had always felt very strongly about.

'You make a valid point, Bobby. I never looked at it like that before. What sorts of things would help, do you think?' Melinda placed her elbow on her knee and cupped her chin, fully concentrating on his response.

'More grants, more entrepreneur training – stuff like that.'

'You know what, Bobby? You should have been a politician. I think you may have missed your vocation!'

They both laughed.

★ ★ ★

It wasn't that he didn't think his opinion mattered to Jess, he was sure it did. It was just that where Jess might challenge it, with Melinda it was simply good enough. Bobby couldn't explain it; Melinda just seemed to understand him, sort of how Jess used to in the beginning. He could never understand how, in the six years he'd known Melinda, she hadn't been snapped up by someone decent. The guy she was with obviously didn't appreciate her. He certainly wasn't complaining though, because as selfish as it might sound, he needed her, and he wasn't in the mood to tiptoe around some deadbeat boyfriend.

No, her number wasn't one nine two three so it had to be the other way around. It just had to be. Damn, for leaving his mobile at Jess's house. You didn't realise how reliant you got with those things until times like this. He suddenly realised what he'd just said: he'd left his mobile at Jess's house. Look at that. He was already thinking about the house like it wasn't his home. In all of ten years that feeling had never crossed his mind, yet within an hour it was as if it was his most natural thought ever. He was momentarily shaken to feel that he no longer had the right to push his key through what was their front door.

He quickly shrugged off the thought and redialled. Yes! The phone was ringing. He was confident he'd finally got the right number.

'Hello?' Melinda answered after one and a half rings. She must have been sitting by the phone waiting for a call. As women do. Bobby was half-expecting the answer machine and didn't speak immediately.

'Hello?' Melinda said again

'Hi, Melinda. How are you?' He didn't even know what to say. He could hardly just launch into his troubles, but it was all he could think about.

'Bobby? Is that you? Hi!' Melinda sounded so happy to hear his voice that his spirits lifted almost instantaneously. These couldn't be tears welling up in his eyes right now? He needed to compose himself, fast. He couldn't let this break him. He decided to play safe and not say anything in response to her welcome.

'Are you okay?' she asked.

Bobby was still silent. Her welcome now had tinges of concern in it. He was sure that she must already sense something was up. Not that it would be very hard to guess in his current state.

'Do you want to talk about it?'

Ah, the magic words he needed to hear. 'Are you busy right now, Mel?'

'I've got nothing going on that can't wait. I've always got time for you, Bobby, you know that.'

It was almost as if she was scolding him for even asking the question. He wasn't going to make any assumptions though. His assuming days were over. He'd assumed him and Jess were fine and look at the outcome of that.

'Is it okay, if I pass round?'

'Of course. Let me give you my new address. I moved recently.'

As she said the words, he realised that he didn't even know her old address. He'd never wanted them to get too comfortable during their brief personal liaison.

★ ★ ★

'Bobby are you sure you want to do this?' Melinda asked quietly.

'Right now I am. I don't know how I'll feel tomorrow, but today I've never felt more sure.' Bobby held Melinda's face between his hands.

'My place or yours?' Melinda asked. They both frowned, their thoughts aligned in that somewhere neutral would be preferable. A thought suddenly struck Melinda.

'Barry's on holiday for a couple of weeks. He's given me the keys to his place to water his plants.'

Bobby smiled at this revelation. 'So, let's go check his plants are being taken care of. And while we're there we can see what other business we can take care of too.'

★ ★ ★

Bobby didn't have any paper to write down the address she was saying but somehow the details stayed in his head on top of everything else.

'I'm on my way. I'll see you soon. Oh … and thanks Mel.'

He was already starting to feel better. Nothing had changed and nothing had been resolved, but just knowing that he had someone in his corner shone some light on the saga that was now his life. It wasn't that he didn't have other friends who would be there for him; he just wasn't ready for their kind of support just yet. What he needed was Melinda type support, where he could talk if he wanted to or not talk if he didn't want to. No pressure and no explanations expected.

He started to walk towards the cab station. Funny, he thought, how Melinda had come to mind after all these months as the one person who could help him. It wasn't that he didn't know a lot of people. He'd never understood the concept of being surrounded by people yet feeling lonely. He did now.

The cab station looked deserted, indicating he was going to have to wait a while. He hadn't even been sure that Z Cars would still be in operation, it was that long since he'd had to take a cab. Even on his worst drinking binges with the boys, they'd never taken cabs Just thinking about alcohol made him want to down a whole Martell, and he wasn't talking about his son. Like he could down his son. He chuckled to himself, amazed that he could find some light humour in this day. He pushed open the cab station door.

'How long, mate?'

'About five minutes.' The controller didn't even look up from the crossword he was doing. Bobby took a seat and waited. Five minutes passed quickly and still there was no sign of any wheels approaching the shack fronting as a cab station. He'd forgotten that cab stations always said that the cab would be 'about five minutes' but in real time that could mean ten, fifteen or even half an hour. By the time the car finally arrived, his five minutes had turned out to be more like twenty, but it was here now so he wasn't going to fuss. He just wanted to get going. He gave the cabman Melinda's address and off they rolled.

Mr Cabman must have sensed that he was in a hurry because they'd hardly driven fifteen minutes before they'd arrived. Bobby paid him from a wad of notes in his pocket. He might have forgotten his mobile, but he never forgot to line his pockets with cash.

Bobby walked down the street looking for the right door number twenty eight … sixteen … twelve … yep, he'd found it. He stood looking at the door for a few seconds before ringing the bell. He wasn't sure why he delayed. Maybe he was hoping that as the door opened all his troubles would disappear. Melinda answered the door. He looked at her; she looked at him. She didn't say a word, just gave him a warm hug and pulled him inside the house.

'Nice place,' he commented. For crying out loud! Surely that was not the best he could come out with after not speaking to this woman for nearly half a year?

'Thanks. Excuse the mess and all the boxes. I only moved in about two weeks ago. Welcome to my dream home! Well, what will soon be my dream home after I've done some decorating.'

He nodded approvingly. Melinda had always talked about buying herself a nice big house. Looked like she'd finally done it.

Bobby pointed his chin in the direction of a couple of crates full of beers, wine and a whole assortment of alcohol.

'Is the decorating theme going to be an off licence? Either that or you're a very thirsty woman.'

Her eyes followed his. She turned back to him and gave him a playful push.

'Ha de ha ha. Very funny. I'm actually having a house-warming party tonight. Another reason why I've been stalling with the decorating! Just a few friends over to help celebrate the purchase of my new home.' Bobby was happy for her, he really was, but his bad day was stopping him showing the happiness just yet. He would tomorrow.

'And it's a good thing that you're always as well turned out as you are because now you can't use the excuse of needing to go home and change to get out of staying for it.' Melinda rubbed her palms together gleefully.

A party was the last thing on his mind right now. Melinda's idea of a few friends was drastically different to his. She'd once held a surprise dinner party for her best friend that was supposed to be for a few close friends. There had been at least twenty-six people, all eating and talking at the same time over music played by a hired DJ.

However, the more he mulled the idea over in his mind, the more it started to grow on him. What better way to temporarily distract himself from his problems?

His silence made her give him a concerned look. 'Are you up for a party tonight, Bobby?' She looked so forlorn, as if she was torn between carrying on her plans or putting her celebration on hold to tend to him.

Even though he wasn't in a partying mood, he couldn't spoil Melinda's night. He might be feeling selfish, but not that much. Besides, there'd be plenty of time for them to talk after the party. If Jess ever saw him shaking a leg after just breaking up, she'd be even more convinced that her decision was justified. Especially since the last few times she'd wanted to go out – he hadn't. Thankfully, bumping into her wasn't likely to happen. No doubt she too was going over and over what happened. But he needed a break for tonight. There'd be more than enough time to go over it all again tomorrow, and the next day until … he didn't know until when. Melinda's concerned look had now changed to one of expectancy. Expecting him to say something, as it appeared he'd been lost in thought for at least five minutes. He looked at her, gave her a smile and a reassuring hug.

'Mel, if you're up for it, then I'm up for whatever is happening at Bourneville Street tonight.'

9

Jessica

Wow, this is some party. And some house. Gary's friend, whoever she is (only a 'she' would pick out somewhere like this), has really got it going on with this place. It's absolutely gorgeous. Very spacious. Good thing too, because there are a lot of people here tonight. Clearly the lady of the house is somewhat popular.

Looks like I'm going to be busy scanning everyone. When you attend shindigs like this, it's almost an unwritten requirement for you to observe who's wearing what and, most importantly, whether they should be wearing it. I'm not being catty if that's what you're thinking! It's the essence of woman-ness (inherent in most women, not just me) to notice the attire of others.

So who's here tonight? Ahh, there's Barry. I haven't seen him for ... wow, it's been a good few years. We used to be quite good friends back in those days. I swear he was a sexaholic back then because if it moved, he moved to it. Big, small, tall, short, he could never get enough. I'd even had to rescue him a few times by pretending to be his main squeeze when one of his ladies started coming on too strong. He catches me looking at him and comes straight over to envelope me in the biggest hug.

'Jess! How have you been? You look great!'

Barry is genuinely happy to see me. This greeting alone has worked wonders for my mood already. While I'm basking in all these glorious compliments, Gary Martin walks into view. He's looking super sexy as always, and acting like the local celebrity, as always, slapping backs here and kissing cheeks there. No doubt, after he's done lip to lip with every other female in this party, he'll want to plant those lips on me. And will I complain? Unlikely, except it'll be like I've kissed everyone in this party too. He hasn't seen me yet and I refuse to go over to him. I don't want to seem too eager, even if just being here has probably already given that away.

While I'm waiting for Gary to see me, I take the time to observe what else is going on around me. Well, what do you know! Teresa is here. Teresa Peter, the Man-eater or Teresa the Teaser. Take your pick of nick-names; she has so many and you couldn't say she didn't earn them. She scored a home run with Gary's little brother, Devon, knowing he had a pregnant girlfriend. Okay, the girlfriend wasn't exactly pregnant but she was trying for a baby, which makes you wonder who was more canine – the dog Devon was or the bitch Teresa is. If she'd *dared* to even look at Bobby ... Well, let's say I would have been reaching for my earrings. Lucky for her, she knows better. I wonder who she's seeing now? Someone of her own by now, one would hope.

Memory lane is a long road tonight. I can see old school-friends galore; some have changed, some haven't. The music is really pumping, though. They are playing my songs. I know usually you would have just 'a' song. A single song. But there are so many good ones, so I figure having a few isn't really a big deal.

Okay, now who is that guy who just keeps staring at me? He's studying me like I'm a reflection in a mirror. His face is not familiar. At first, I thought our eyes were just meeting because I was in his line of vision, but for the past twenty five minutes? I think not. No, he's definitely staring.

Well, I'm going to stare him out this time so that he knows that I know he's staring. Hold on … wait a minute … he is surely not coming over? Oh, please no. No! No! No! I can't be caught up in a conversation with a stranger when Gary finally comes over to me. Oh, where is Barry to save my skin for a change? Still yakking to that female. 'Time standing still for no man' doesn't apply to Barry. He's clearly still trying. Oh shit, too late for anyone to rescue me now. The starer is right in front of me.

10

Bobby

It sounded like the whole world was at the party. Bobby could only go by what it sounded like, because he had yet to venture downstairs. All his earlier enthusiasm had started to subside the minute Melinda's first guests walked through the door. He'd thought he was ready to put his problems on hold but now he wasn't so sure he could. Mel really had done herself proud with the house, though. It really was a nice house. Though he didn't think he'd want a whole load of people tramping through it if it was his, party or not. Still, he could see why Mel wanted to celebrate her house purchase and show it off. She'd worked really hard to get it. Ambitious lady. Same as Jess. Looked like he was drawn to ambitious women.

He was beginning to feel conscious that perhaps he was being a bit unsociable. Then again, he was still composing himself; it wouldn't do his street cred any good if someone said some trigger word or other and he suddenly broke down. He hadn't realised Mel knew so many people. Come to think of it, he hadn't realised so many people that he knew, also knew Mel. Now that was food for thought; if they hadn't been so very careful, their short fling could easily have been flung right back in their faces. Mel kept coming upstairs every few minutes to see if he was okay so he really should go downstairs now. It wasn't fair for her to be worried about him … yet. She was the hostess and the only thing she should be worrying about tonight was whether there was enough ice for the drinks. Oh, and enough brandy. Martell brandy. He could do with a drink.

It was Mel's night and he should be helping her celebrate, not hindering her. They'd have plenty one-on-one time tomorrow.

Time to make his entrance. He crept downstairs and peeped through the gaps in the banister. He felt like a little boy who'd been told to go to bed but couldn't resist taking a look. He'd barely gotten halfway down the staircase when he was spotted.

'Hey, Bobby! Hey, man, what's happening?' It was Peter Piper. That was his real name too. No need to explain how cruel the kids had been at school, especially when they had a name like that to work with. Bobby gave him a hearty slap on the back and solid shake of the hand.

'Pete! Look's like life has been treating you well. How's Linda?'

'We just celebrated our 11th anniversary yesterday.' Peter smiled proudly. Bobby smiled too, but it was a bitter smile. He and Jess were never going to reach that milestone now. Damn, was everyone's life suddenly going to reflect back onto his? So much for this party helping to put everything behind him for a few hours. He hadn't even managed two minutes. As Peter continued to reminisce, Bobby suddenly felt a tap on his back.

'Hi, Bobby.'

Hopefully the person would keep his mind focused on something other than Jess. He swung round with a big smile that he wanted to remove as soon as he saw who it was. Good manners forced the smile to stay on his face. Of all the times to see Teresa Peter it had to be today.

'You wouldn't happen to know where the toilet is, would you?' She smiled that vixen smile that he and every other guy in the area knew so well. 'Upstairs, second door on the left.' It was getting harder by the second to keep the smile pasted onto his face.

'Thanks. So Bobby, how are you?' She cocked her head slightly to the side. A sure sign that she was homing in on him. He knew the minute he uttered the words 'I'm single' she would disappear like sale goods in Primark. But for some reason, he couldn't say it. It wasn't because he didn't want her to disappear; he just wasn't ready to publicly acknowledge that his relationship was over.

'I'm fine, Teresa. And yourself?' Again, politeness compelled him to respond. If Jess ever saw Teresa fixing her radar on him, she'd have a fit. Or would she? Recent events painted a different picture.

'I'm good, and I must say that you're looking good. Jessica must be treating you well.' The words slid slyly off her tongue.

Bobby smiled. 'Mm hmm. So what have you been up to?'

'All sorts really. I could tell you … or I could show you if you want.' She gave a suggestive little laugh.

In a not-even-five-minute conversation, this girl had already managed to play her first card and he hadn't even realised the game had started. Teresa was lethal. Her reputation really didn't do her enough justice. If he showed fear then he'd lost the round.

'Well, there is a saying: It's good to talk.' He laughed. She didn't.

'There's another: Actions speak louder than words.' She lowered her eyelids, looking at him pointedly through the slits.

'Loudness only applies if hearing is an issue.' At least his melancholy mood hadn't affected his quick wit. He sure needed to be quick with this woman.

'Oh, so you'd rather I whispered to you what I've been up to?'

Damn, the girl was good. He had to get the conversation back on track. 'Not today, Teresa.' He smiled to soften the words.

'Another day perhaps, then. Second door on the left, you said?' As she walked up the stairs she looked over her shoulder at him and returned the smile to show that his response had not even fazed her. He watched her until she was out of sight. He felt he had to make sure she wasn't peeping to see where he was going. He needed a drink. There was no reason why he couldn't accept Teresa's offer. It would be the perfect opportunity to check out for himself the difference between fact and fiction when it came to Teresa. It would also let Jess know that even if she didn't want him, someone else did. Thoughts back to Jess again. It was definitely time for that brandy.

He moved through the throng of people towards the bar, nodding and smiling greetings as he went along. He noticed a lady with her back to him in a blue dress. The dress looked familiar. Did Jess have one like it? Damn, not again with thoughts of that woman. It looked like there was only one thing to do: he had to get her back.

He finally reached the kitchen bar. It wasn't hard to see that Melinda was in her element playing hostess. She caught his eye, winked and held up a finger as if to say 'Wait a minute'. Still smiling and talking to one of her guests, she poured him a brandy and passed it to him over the guest's shoulder. He smiled back at her in amazement. Not only did she appear to read his mind but the fact that he hadn't seen her in months, didn't seem to have affected their relationship a bit. It was as though Melinda had seen him only last week. She was a true friend. If anyone could help him get his head around this situation with Jess, she could. He raised his plastic cup to her in salute and went back to his spot at the bottom of the stairs. He'd seen Teresa go into the living room so he was safe here. He looked around again to see if there were any more familiar faces.

11

Tyrone

He could do it. He could talk to her. He was Tyrone Powers, confident and assertive. He could achieve anything he wanted to and he was going over there to talk to her. The positive thinking mantras didn't seem to be working for him today. It was probably too late to take his own affirmative advice anyway. She probably thought he was some kind of freak by now, the way he'd been staring at her for the last half hour. She must have noticed. He'd hardly been discreet about. He couldn't help it. There was something enticing about her.

Looked like she knew a few people at the party too. He knew a few, but he'd never seen her before, that was certain. He would have remembered her. She definitely must think he was a weirdo. That's what he would think if a stranger kept looking at him like that. He wasn't weird; he was just shy. But not always. His shy gene only seemed to kick in with women. At work he was Powers by name and a Powerhouse by occupation. His job demanded it. In certain circles he was considered an up-and-coming director of short films. He'd won an award at the Cannes Film festival just this year for a short film about life in the inner city told through the eyes of a ten-year-old boy. Directors had to be firm, so that everyone on set knew who was in charge.

He was hoping he could draw on some of that firmness, with a bit of charm of course, to talk to this lady. That was another thing that caught his attention about her. She looked like a lady. She reminded him of the star in his first film, back when he was in university studying the art of film-making. He couldn't stop staring at her either, but he could only dream about approaching her because, back then, he really would have been considered a weirdo. He had that dorkish look of big framed glasses with double thick lenses that covered half his face, magnifying his acne and making it look worse than it really was. He was a geek. The girls he liked were never interested in him and he was never interested in the ones that liked him (few that there were). Being a director, having to talk with authority to people he normally couldn't say boo to, eventually kick-started his confidence. What also helped was advice he once got at lunch from a new actress.

* * *

'How do you think that scene went, Tyrone?' Janine was always eager for feedback.

'Better. A lot better.' He liked the way she nibbled on her sandwich as she waited for his comments. 'Aim for the camera to be in your side view. You'll know you're always in frame then.'

'Gotcha. Ty, you don't know how much you've helped my acting. I feel my knowledge expanding under your tutelage.' Janine smiled.

'And I under yours. How do I look today?' Tyrone gestured towards his attire.

'Better. A lot better.' She spoke in the same manner as he had addressed her. They both laughed. It had become a running joke between them. In exchange for his feedback on her acting, she gave him tips on his image. Janine was very trendy; Tyrone was not.

'Hey, have you ever tried contacts, Tyrone?' She cocked her head to the side.

'Ooh no. I've always been a bit squeamish about putting things in my eyes.' Tyrone shuddered at the thought.

Janine sat up bolt straight. 'I promise you, Ty, after the initial slight discomfort, you'll get so used to them, you won't even remember they're there, honest. Oh and ...' She started to rummage in her bag and pulled out a fancy jar of face cream. '...I got this for you as I was getting new mascara. It'll work magic on those spots, I promise you. You'll be looking like a male model in no time!'

Tyrone smiled as he took the jar and held it in the air. Could it be in a more feminine container? Rather than thinking, 'My acne days could soon be over,' all that came into his head was, 'How am I going to explain this in a bathroom cabinet full of men's aftershaves?'

* * *

Janine had been right. Taking her advice was the beginning of Tyrone's transformation. But though he may have been transformed on the outside, the inside transformation took a little bit longer; his confidence was still lacking. He was still painfully shy, which was a real downer since the woman across the room was the first that'd caught his eye in ages.

Why was he so nervous? He looked pretty decent today. His daughter had told him so before he'd left out.

* * *

'Daddy, you're not really going to wear that tonight are you?' Tyrone's daughter, Jenny, looked at him in disbelief.

'Why? What's wrong with it?' Tyrone responded cautiously.

'Well, Daddy, your shirt has stripes going across and your trousers have stripes going down. It looks weird.' Jenny shook her head and started colouring her book again.

Tyrone looked at his reflection and frowned. His daughter had a point.

'So, what do you think would look … not weird?'

Jenny abandoned her colouring and walked over to his wardrobe. 'Lift me up, Daddy, so I can get a better look.' Tyrone obliged, and Jenny started sorting through his hangered clothes, taking out a shirt, looking at it then replacing it, taking out a jacket and giving it the same treatment. Finally she'd decided.

'This one, Daddy. This top and these pants and those shoes. You can put me down now.' Jenny wriggled out of his arms, went straight back to her colouring. Tyrone looked at the items she had picked out. Plain navy trousers, navy striped shirt, brown shoes. He went into the adjoining bathroom and changed. When he looked in the mirror again he had to admit he looked hot. Well, at least a lot better than before.

'How do I look?' Tyrone gave her a twirl. Jenny grinned and gave her father a big thumbs up!

* * *

He'd forgotten what a little fashionista his daughter was. At eight years old she was a dedicated follower of fashion – definitely her mother's daughter. Enough daydreaming! His thoughts were moving away from the point which was to go over talk to that lady. Okay, he was going … wait! Not yet. She'd started talking to somebody. Oh crumbs!

It was Barry. Barry was renowned for chasing anything in a skirt. What if he was chatting her up? Please, don't let him have stalled so long that he'd lost his opportunity. Tyrone hoped – no, prayed – that Barry wasn't hitting on the potential mother of his next child. Something was funny because they were laughing and joking, having a thoroughly hearty time over there. They seemed a little too familiar with each other to have just met. Maybe they were friends. Familiar, platonic friends – that would be perfect!

A thought suddenly hit him. What if the girl was Barry's girl? He needed to get a grip; he was being silly and panicking for no reason now. He'd seen Barry when he arrived nearly an hour ago, and only now he was tending to her? You didn't leave a woman like that standing on her own for too long. At least Barry's conversation had given him a bit more time to think about what he was going to say to her. She looked like a classy lady, so no point in even attempting any of those lines from that film he'd watched last night.

★ ★ ★

'Welcome to THE Dating school where we make sure your first impression lasts!' The teacher did a flamboyant twirl in front of the class. 'Question, anyone?'

Student one: 'Well, there's this lady that I see at my local bar every Thursday. I swear I've seen her looking at me when I've walked past, but I can never think of what to say!'

'Hmm ...' the teacher responded. 'Howabout when you walk past her next Thursday, you say to her "Do you believe in love at first sight, or should I walk past you a second

time?" How about that?' Student one nodded enthusiastically.

'Any more for any more?' The teacher did another twirl.

Student two: 'At my drivers' education class there's a woman that I like. What can I say to break the ice?'

'Hmm ...' the teacher answered. 'If it's an icebreaker you want, try "Hi, I'm Mr Right, someone said you were looking for me?" How does that sound?' Student two grinned happily. The teacher gave another twirl and staggered a little because he'd made himself dizzy. He recovered his composure quickly and gave the class a big smile. 'Remember folks – you never get a second chance to make a first impression!'

★ ★ ★

The advice had seemed really cool when he'd heard it yesterday, but not so clever in the cold light of tonight. Then again, she was laughing with Barry so she seemed to have a sense of humour; she just might think his lines were amusing. Speaking of funny, maybe he should tell her a joke. If you could make a girl laugh you're half-way to her heart. He'd read that on a bumper sticker once. But what joke could he tell her? He didn't know her well enough to tell her a dirty joke. Besides, dirty jokes were for the lads. A corny joke maybe? Then she might think he was corny. So what kind of joke? He'd heard a good one the other day. He tried to remember it the way he'd heard it. It was all about the way you told them. It could be the funniest joke in the world, but if you didn't tell it right ... He ran the joke over in his mind as if he were telling her ...

A woman woke up in the night and saw that her husband was not in bed with her. She put on her dressing gown and went downstairs to look for him. He was sitting at the kitchen table with a cup of coffee in front of him, lost in thought and just staring at the wall. Suddenly she saw him wipe a tear from his cheek.

"What's the matter, dear?" the wife asked. "Why are you down here at this time of night?"

"Do you remember twenty years ago when we were first dating and you were only sixteen?" he asked.

"Yes, I do," she replied.

"Do you remember when your father caught us in the back of my car making love?"

"Yes, I remember."

"Do you remember when he shoved that shotgun in my face and said either I marry you or spend twenty years in jail?"

"Yes, I do," she said.

The husband wiped another tear from his face and said "You know ... I would have gotten out today."

It cracked him up every time! He wiped a tear of laughter from his eye. If he still found the joke *that* funny, it probably wouldn't be the best idea to tell her that one just yet. He'd be in fits of laughter before he got to the end and would just spoil it. He'd save it for another time, when he knew her better. Why was he planning what he would say to her in the future?! He couldn't even decide what to say to her now. Maybe that was the problem. He shouldn't be pre-composing what he was going to say to someone like her. He should be natural and just say 'Hello'. In fact that's exactly what he would do. He took a deep breath. The way he was jittering about, anyone would think he'd never said hello to a girl before. Now was as good a time as any to use some of the tips he'd gained from the confidence seminar he'd gone to.

* * *

The lecturer spoke with conviction. 'Not everyone is born confident, but you can attain confidence. The trick is to act! Act like you are confident, and soon you will be.'

Tyrone looked sceptical. 'Can it really be that simple? Just act and it will be?'

'Yes, it really is!' The lecturer nodded eagerly. 'Try it; just try it at the very next social event you are at. I guarantee you'll be surprised how effective simply pretending to be a character can be!'

* * *

He would put himself on the other side of the camera and act his socks off in the part of Mr True Confidence. All he had to do was wait for the right opportunity, which looked like now. Barry had turned away and was talking to someone else and the lovely lady was all alone. Not for long though.

12

Jessica

'Hi, my name is Tyrone,' the starer says.

'O...kay.' I just agree with him. I'm not quite sure how else to respond when a staring stranger comes over and introduces himself out of the blue.

'How are you enjoying yourself?'

'I'd be enjoying myself a lot better if I knew why you keep staring at me.' He gives me a little smile and has the good manners to look shame-faced.

'I apologise ...' He pauses for a while as if deciding what he should say next '... but not for staring.'

Well, that was unexpected. I raise my eyebrow and say, 'Then why are you apologising?' Why am I even entertaining this conversation? Where *is* Gary?

'Because I should have said hello before staring, because then it wouldn't have seemed rude, not that I was being rude.'

Okay, now he's babbling. Do I have a sign on my head that says I'm a babble zone? Before I can excuse myself to the ladies room he gets to his point.

'What I'm trying to say is that I didn't mean to make you uncomfortable. So, I'm apologising for any ... uncomfortability I may have caused you.'

Uncomfortability? Is that even a word? I look at this Tyrone guy, for a few long seconds. He'll soon think it's retaliation for him staring at me. I can see he's nervous. Just who is he anyway? I decide not to say anything, even though I'm intrigued. I wonder what he's going to say next.

'I didn't catch your name?' He looks expectantly at me. I soften a bit. He's been polite enough, so it'd be just plain mean to be rude in response. I go for a cheeky answer instead.

'I didn't throw it.' I revel in my witty retort. By the time he comes back from that one, I'll have made my move to move on. But I have barely finished my sentence when he comes back at me with an unexpected response.

'Well, I'm ready to catch it anytime now, so, whenever you're ready.'

He crosses his arms and smiles down at me (he's actually quite tall), checks his watch, looks at me and smiles again. It must have been the little look at his watch that made the first crack in my shell of resistance. It did, grudgingly, make me smile, enough for me to allow him to know my name.

'My name's Jessica'.

'I'm pleased to meet you, Jessica'.

I wait for him to expand on this, but moments later we are still looking at each other in silence. Now, I'm confused. This guy has been eyeballing me all night, just to know my name? Surely not? Wait … I can see that Adam's apple quivering. I do believe there might be more to come.

'You really like this DJ don't you, Jessica?'

Okay, not sure what direction this is going now. Musical tastes maybe?

'I swear I could hear you from where I was standing, trying to sing along,' he continues.

Did he say 'trying' to sing along? He clearly doesn't have an ear for music or he'd recognise that my singing transcended the bathroom.

'Oh please!' I say and we both laugh. Well, any 'uncomfortability' he was feeling earlier seems to have gone.

'Who are you here with? I've only heard you singing solo so far. Is there no duet to follow?' He laughs again.

Got to hand it to him. That's got be the smoothest way I've ever heard of finding out if I'm here with another man. I'm actually beginning to think that maybe this Tyrone guy's okay, even though he looked like a quivering mass of ... something standing by the bar. What a transformation two metres of hallway can make. Before I can answer him, someone he knows comes over and slaps him on the back.

'Hey, Tyrone! How are you man? Where've you been hiding?'

He turns to acknowledge the friend and gives me an I'm-sorry-I-can't-get-out-of-this-but-I'll-be-real-quick-look. Milliseconds later, over to my right, Barry has finished his conversation and decides to resume his conversation with me. Over to my left, Mr Gary Martin appears to have finally seen me and is also coming over. No time to fix anything; I just have to believe that I'm looking my best. I'm feeling unusually anxious. Barry, Tyrone and everybody else have faded out of my consciousness. This will be the first time that I've been in a situation like this with Gary, with so many people that we both know. Today's been a day of debuts for me it seems: breaking up, immoral partying out.

'Hey, Jess,' he says as he reaches my side.

'Hey, Gary,' is my reply.

This is the kind of chatter you have to make in public places like this. I'm sure that instead of 'Hey, Jess' he really wanted to say 'Here I am, Jess' and my reply, instead of

'What's going on?', would have been more along the lines of 'Let's get it on'.

'May I have this dance?'

Does he really need to ask that question? But then I must keep remembering that this banter is for the sake of our audience: Barry. Barry! He abruptly springs to mind again. I turn my head and sure enough, there he is, a definite third party to our surface conversation.

'Sure.' I say. I pat Barry on the arm to indicate I am going as Gary and I walk towards the living room. And that is the end of our conversation. Well, our conversation in words anyway. The way his body glides against mine, well what can I say? There is a whole different kind of conversation going on.

So we're dancing, and I am in that zone to which only Gary seems to be able to take me, when some guy behind nearly knocks me into next week. Gary winces and who can blame him; I can only imagine the indentation my heel has just made in his foot.

'Sorry!' I whisper to Gary. Seconds later, the same guy bumps me again, and I whisper something a little more profane under my breath as I step on Gary's other foot.

My assailant and his dancing buddy are so close that we're almost dancing like a quartet. The dance floor is quite crowded, but come on now! To alert this buffoon to the fact that I'm not his dancing partner, I try creating more space for him and his big behind. Clearly not the best move as this means less space for myself with Gary's foot paying the price yet again. If it wasn't so dark I'd give this strictly-don't-come-dancing idiot such a look, he'd have no problem reading what was in my mind. What's more, his aftershave smells like MuskOne, the same one that Bobby had on today. So, not only is this bumping not helping my heels, it's not helping me to forget today's earlier events, which was the whole point of being at this party.

Damn, this dance area is getting hot now. At least big-behind guy has made a teeny bit more room with his sudden quick exit. Good thing too because the heat was beginning to make that over-familiar aftershave of his bother me – for reasons other than the obvious. He sure was in a hurry to get away, though. Left his partner mid-record. Toilet emergency perhaps? Who knows.

Me and Gary are making a major contribution to this heat problem. I need a drink so offer to get us some. I meet Maddy by the bar; she's sipping on her usual non-alcoholic beverage of lemonade.

'And who's that you've been dancing with? Very closely, I might add.' Maddy missed nothing, even in a room that was as dark as hell itself.

'That's my friend, Maddy. You know … my friend?' I emphasise and give her an all-revealing stare. As it sinks in, her look turns into one of complete shock. She looks at me real hard, eyes ajar and jaws open.

'You mean … the friend that you were telling me about?' I'd vaguely mentioned Gary (though not by name) a few days ago.

* * *

'You've been very chipper lately. Bobby been doing some new moves on you?' For Maddy, something sexual had to be behind anyone being in a good mood.

'No. Actually it's some new conversation with a new friend. Didn't realise how stimulating a fresh point of view could be.' Jess smiled at her friend.

101

'A new friend?' Maddy looked surprised.

'Yeah.' Jess had temporarily forgotten how sharp Maddy was.

'I wonder what kind of conversation you and your new friend must be having to put a smile like this on your face. I know it's good to talk, but hey, maybe I need me a new friend too.'

Jess looked seriously at her friend. 'I like him, Maddy, I like him a lot.'

Maddy looked up from what she was doing. 'Define "a lot" Jess. Is it like a little self-indulgent bar of chocolate a lot, or I can't really afford Jimmy Choo's a lot?'

Jess thought carefully before she responded. 'Anything is affordable if you budget carefully for it. That way it doesn't need to infringe on your other expenses.'

'Hmm …' Maddy looked back down at her magazine, suddenly reluctant to get involved in this line of conversation, '… just be careful you don't end up paying more than it's really worth.

This time, Jess didn't respond at all.

* * *

I nod at Maddy's question. She looks at me in disbelief, over in his direction in disbelief, and then at me again with – if it's possible – twice as much disbelief as before.

'Has he got something to do with why you're not out with Bobby tonight?' she asks solemnly. I nod in the same way that she asks.

'You do know that he's …' she trails off. She doesn't finish her sentence because she knows she doesn't have to. I half-smile to acknowledge what she hasn't said – that Gary is a soon to be married man. Maddy just shakes her head, looks at me again with a frown and shakes her head again. She sips her lemonade and shrugs her shoulders as if to say she just doesn't understand but whatever. And who can blame her for being confused? Hell, I'm confused. Here I am seeing a guy, who is seeing me and somebody else. I mean, I'm sensible Jess. I'm rational Jess. I am not supposed to be in this situation; I'm supposed to advise everyone else not to be in this situation. Because that's what sensible and rational people do. Until now.

I can feel my headache coming on again and I know it's down to thinking about all of this coupled with remnants of big-behind-guy's aftershave. Solution? Stop thinking about the current situation and start thinking about getting Gary the drink I promised him about five minutes ago.

I take the drink back to Gary, sipping mine along the way. He puts one arm around me, slowly draws me close and takes the drink from me with his other hand. He downs it in one go. He then takes my drink and finishes it in the same manner. His eyes don't leave mine for a second.

I turn to Maddy, who at this point just so happens to be dancing right next to me. And after being at the party for not even ninety minutes, I tap her on the shoulder and whisper in her ear.

'I'm going to leave now. I'll call you tomorrow.'

13

Bobby

Same old faces, same old music. Bobby just couldn't seem to get into the swing of things. Melinda was giving him a wave from the bar every few minutes. He knew she was focusing on him a lot more than she should be right now. It was time to make an effort to at least look like he was having a good time, for Mel's sake if not for his. The last thing he wanted to do was spoil her big night.

Down the hallway, he could see Gary Martin doing his celebrity thing as per usual. There was something about that guy that he didn't like. He had no reason for these thoughts; as far as he knew Gary was an okay guy. Maybe it was the way he'd caught him looking at Jess once: a little too lecherously for his liking. Gary's reputation with the ladies preceded him. No one had ever thought he'd settle down. Even Barry had been surprised when he'd heard Gary was getting married later on this year. He'd never seen him out with his fiancée, funnily enough. A leopard like Gary would never change his spots. If the wife-to-be believed that she'd be the one to change him then good luck to her, Bobby thought. She was going to need it.

Maybe a dance would loosen him up. He moved towards the main living room. The party was in full swing now. It was really dark in the room so it didn't matter who he asked to dance. It wasn't like he'd be able to see what they looked like, like that mattered. He could feel Jess consuming his mind again, but the girl standing right next to the doorway might be able to nip that little problem in the bud.

'Excuse me, may I have this dance?' He hoped she didn't think that sounded un-cool. He hadn't asked anyone to dance for years, hadn't had to. Luckily for him, this appeared to still be the way it was done because the girl didn't even answer, just wrapped her arms around him, quite tightly, actually. He clearly wasn't going to get a chance to see if he could still do his urban Fred Astaire moves on this occasion.

★ ★ ★

'We can do that Jess, it doesn't look that hard.' Bobby said the same thing each week he watched Strictly Come Dancing.

'Bobby, they make it look easy because they are professionals.' Jess shook her head.

'Come on, I'll show you how easily it can be done. Come on!' Bobby pulled Jess to her feet and started to dance.

'Well, well, Bobby. You're actually not that bad! Have you been taking secret lessons?' Jess narrowed her eyes at him playfully.

'It's natural talent, Baby, all natural talent!' To show her just how Fred Astaire-ish he was, he spun Jess around, unfortunately a little more forcefully than he'd thought. As he pulled her back to him, she stumbled.

'Yow, Jess! I think you've decapitated my toe!' Bobby hobbled on one foot, holding the damaged one in the air.

'Ooh, I'm sorry! You might think you're Fred, but I'm definitely not Ginger!'

★ ★ ★

That certainly taught him to check that Jess didn't have on one of those ice-pick-heeled sandals she so liked wearing before pulling her to dance. Thinking back to those days, how on earth had he handled dancing cheek to cheek at parties in the past? Surely it couldn't have been like this? Everyone one was just so close to everyone else. He'd swear the lady behind him was hinting, by way of shoving, that this dance area wasn't big enough for both of them. He turned his dance partner slightly to get a glimpse of this person and see if maybe they were of a size where the extra dance floor space really was a necessity. He couldn't make out what the woman looked like due to the darkness of the room, but from her faint silhouette he could see she was about Jess's height and size. She even smelt of Jess-like perfume. If he let his imagination run riot he could even start to think this woman was Jess. Okay, he was officially losing it. A perfect stranger who just happened to be Jess's height, size and smell was suddenly morphing into her. The whole thought made him stand his ground a little more firmly than he might normally have which in the process inadvertently caused the woman to stumble forward. The last thing he wanted to do was battle for floor space. It was so dark and hot in the room; his own aftershave had started to turn his stomach. MuskOne was supposed to make you feel like you could run the world. All he wanted to do was run to the toilet.

Suddenly he'd had enough. Why was he even dancing with this girl? What was he trying to prove? That he could put Jess out of his memory? He already knew he couldn't because in his heart he didn't want to. All this jostling was just reminding him why he was really at this party, and it wasn't for dancing. It was clear to him what he had to do and he didn't want to wait a second longer. Bobby apologised to his dancing partner, saying that he could see someone signalling for him urgently. The fact that the darkness of the room made it impossible to see past his nose was irrelevant. Anyway, he didn't care. All he cared about was that he needed to speak to Melinda right now.

As he forced his way out of the room, he saw Melinda straightaway, leaning against a wall, talking to some guy. She saw him after a few seconds. He didn't know if it was the stricken look on his face that turned her smile into a frown, but he saw her pat the shoulder of the guy she was talking to as an excuse to leave the conversation, and then she came over to him.

'Are you okay?' She looked so concerned that he felt like a prize heel. He was about to spoil her night, but he needed to get what was on his mind off it, before he went out of it.

'Can we talk, Mel? Now? I don't mean to take you away from your guests,' he lied 'but I just need to ...' He didn't get a chance to finish as she interrupted him.

'Don't be silly, Bobby. You need to talk? Come on, let's talk.' She ushered him upstairs like a child. Maybe she could sense he felt as helpless as one. They went into her bedroom, where she sat him down on the bed, then dragged a fancy cane chair up close to him. Picking up his hand, she waited in silence for him to speak.

'Me and Jess finished today.'

Melinda looked at him with a blank expression. 'Finished what?'

'Finished with each other. Well, she finished with me.' He saw the penny drop. To her credit she recovered quite quickly and the shocked look was soon replaced with one of sadness.

'I'm so sorry, Bobby.' Melinda looked like she was willing to do anything to help. He wondered how long that look was going to last when he sprung his next bit on her.

'I want you to help me get it back.'

Again, the waiting-for-more expression cast over her face. 'Get what back?'

'The relationship me and Jess just ended.' Again the penny dropped, and this time Melinda pursed her lips into a silent O.

Shit! Had he gone somewhere that was out of bounds with a female friend you had once had a brief affair with? Had he asked the unaskable from someone who had always assured him he could ask her anything? Melinda let go of his hand, stood up and slowly walked over to her bedroom window. All sorts of thoughts ran through his head as he tried to guess what could be running through Melinda's. It had to be a toss up between "How could you ask me something like that?" and "Well, this is what I would do if I was you in this situation." It really could go either way. It all depended on whether he'd offended her or not. He knew he'd feel offended if she asked the same thing of him. It wasn't that he wouldn't want her to be happy. It was just that they had a special friendship and he wouldn't want to play a part in her finding some man that would likely change it. That wasn't him being mean, just him being a man. Several minutes passed and Melinda still hadn't responded. It seemed like no answer was going to be the answer and he felt even worse as the seconds dragged by. Time for Plan B, which was:

Apologise to Mel for taking her from her party to listen to his problems;

Put on the fakest smile to distract her from his heart laying in bloody blob on floor;

Make as graceful a getaway as he possibly could without looking like a total loser.

A three-step plan B. Not bad considering he'd only just thought of it. He opened his mouth to instigate step one, but before the first word came out, Melinda turned and looked at him.

'Well, this is what I would do if I was you in this situation …'

14

Tyrone

An Oscar-winning performance of the All Confident Man (just like on the DVD) and he still didn't manage to get the girl. It was now Sunday morning, several hours after the party and Tyrone still couldn't understand how he had managed to blow what was probably his only opportunity to speak to Jessica. In those few moments, when he had been acting like nothing could faze him, he had actually started to believe it. He had even sensed from Jessica that she believed that was really him. He felt like kicking himself. He'd been staring at her like some love-struck idiot, gathering the courage to say something, and when he finally did, he'd said little more than his name. He'd turned his head for a few seconds to speak to a friend and the next thing he knew, she was being waltzed off to dance by Gary. Bloody Gary Martin. Did he never miss a trick? Now he might never see her again. Even though she knew a few people at the party, he'd never seen her before so she probably didn't go out that much. She probably had someone anyway. How could a woman like that not already be snapped up?

It was probably a blessing in disguise that he didn't get further with her anyway. Why get all his hopes up just to find out that she wasn't available? Everything happened for a reason and that was probably the reason: she was already seeing someone. Anyway, if she wasn't and they were meant to meet again, fate would make it happen. Who did he think he was kidding with this fate crap?

He should have gone straight in with the joke. If he

had, she'd have been laughing and he would have been half-way there. He could just imagine it …

'That was a really funny joke, Tyrone.' Jess wiped a tear from her eye.

'If you found that funny, wait until you see my dance moves!' Tyrone suavely drew Jess close then dramatically bowed her over his arm. Jess laughed even more. Three dances later, she was still laughing.

'You've been the highlight of my night, Tyrone. My face aches from laughing!'

'You haven't heard anything yet, but you could if you gave me your number; I could call you tomorrow, when your face has had a chance to rest.' Tyrone winked, hardly able to believe that this was him flowing so naturally with this woman.

'I can't wait to hear what else you've got! You can call me on …'

Tyrone smiled happily and took his mobile phone from his pocket to record the number.

So simple, yet he still hadn't managed to do it. So much for his confidence act! He was probably never going to see Jessica again and it was no more than what he deserved.

Nope. He couldn't allow that to be the end. She'd really piqued his interest. Jessica. Not a very common name in the circles he moved in. First Jessica he'd ever met, in fact. She probably thought he was a fool anyway; if she was even thinking about him at all. Why did the Gary Martins of this world always get the girl?

Tyrone sighed. Was there really any point in dwelling on what could have been? He was hungry. It was Sunday morning and he felt like having pancakes for breakfast. He wasn't sure why. Maybe having something American to eat would make up for the American he couldn't have. He'd noticed a very slight tinge of an American accent when Jessica had spoken. It made him feel unusually sad to think of not seeing her again. He didn't know how, but he *would* see her again. He just had to make sure he was prepared. He was officially going into chat-up training. He was going to dig up all his best jokes, chant his affirmations and dig up his confidence DVDs. He would not mess up the next time he met her. He'd be ready. He had managed to get her to tell him her name despite staring at her like a psychopath, so surely, with a bit of work, he could persuade her out for a drink or something? He just had to find her. It would be a mission: mission not so impossible. They had been at the same party, so knew some of the same people. How hard could it be to track her down?

15

Jessica

Oops, I did it again. Now why does that line sound familiar? Oh, I know. Didn't Britney have a song called that? I don't have a clue what the song was about, but the title sums up last night perfectly. How can something so bad for me, feel so good? My head is remorsefully screaming: How could you? What about Bobby? My body is defensively retaliating: Why shouldn't you? What about Bobby? Right now, my body's winning.

I'm sitting up in bed, leaning against my headboard, reviewing last night's events. Usually, this would be the moment when I'm supposed to gaze down at Gary, still sleeping by my side, and sigh at the wonder of this morning after the night before. And I probably would too, were he still here to gaze at. But as he left about half an hour ago that'd be a bit difficult. I have one basic rule: Gary has to be out of my house before sun up or before my son gets up. At this time of year, that makes his curfew six-thirty sharp. What if somebody like Meddling Mary saw him creeping out of my place at ten in the morning?

My clock radio is showing that it's nearly eight now. I know I should feel guilty, but my dominant feeling at this moment is something else as I reminisce on what is now precisely an hour-and-a-half-old memory. I hug my pillow close and shut my eyes so that I can recall how he softly stroked my hair, so that I can remember how he cleverly caressed my neck, so that I can think back to how tenderly he touched my ...

Who is that banging the front door like I'm wanted by

the police? It's Sunday morning so it can hardly be the mailman. My reliving of that moment is now totally ruined so I may as well just get my ass out of bed. Just because it's Sunday does not mean my child doesn't have to have breakfast. I robe up and shuffle down the stairs to investigate the source of what dared to horn in on my horny mind replay, and at the damn best part too; nothing worse than when your climax is cut short, whether in reality or in your dreams. As I approach my front door I see the source of the racket. Pizza leaflets. Pizza leaflets! At eight o clock on a Sunday morning? As I shake my head in disbelief, I hear noises coming from the living room; more precisely, the noise of rockets being blown from the sky. I'm not sure all the sound effects are coming from the game either. Martell is up playing with his Playstation.

Sometimes I think he thinks he's actually physically part of the game, the amount of hissing and swerving he does in front of the screen. I'll be the first to confess I don't know much about these computer games, just that they seem to change like calendars. Annually. One year it's Sega Dreamcast and another year Nintendo something or another.

Thinking about my baby playing his game, reminds me of another even more important reason why I had to sacrifice my lie-in with Gary. Children should not see an unfamiliar face in bed with Mummy before you've at least told them that the familiar face of their father is not going to be so familiar around the house anymore.

My initial joy at seeing my son totally oblivious to all except Lara Croft – just like every other male – has turned into apprehension. The thought of telling him that his daddy won't be joining him in his game today is threatening to ruin our precious Sunday morning. How do I tell him there'll be no father for him to leer at Lara with this Sunday, or any foreseeable Sunday for that matter, depending on how soon it takes Bobby to adjust to our new situation? It was kind of a ritual between father and son to kill bad guys first thing in the morning, last day of the weekend, a ritual that, by way of consequence, is now broken.

I walk towards the living room and stand in the doorway. A feeling of déjà vu comes over me. Wasn't it from this same spot not even twenty-four hours ago that I broke some similarly upsetting news to his father?

'Morning honey,' I say softly.

'Hey, Mum! Did you have a good time last night? Has Angie left yet? When's Dad getting up? I'm really gonna bust him up today!' Martell fires back at me without looking away from his game for even a second.

That's my baby! One question at a time was never his thing. Yes, I answer to myself, I had a good time last night and this morning too. And yes, Angie already left discreetly this morning a little after I arrived somewhat indiscreetly.

* * *

Jess pushed her key into to the door as quietly as jingly keys permitted.

'Now Gary,' she whispered, 'be very quiet. Don't stand on the third step, it creaks. Go straight up to my room. I do not want Martell to even turn in his sleep.'

Gary nodded quietly and walked through the door. They both crept up the stairs and stopped dead as the third step creaked. Jess swung round and gave Gary a hard stare. He mouthed a 'Sorry!' to her while she jabbed a finger against her lips in a silent 'Ssh!' Just as Gary reached Jess's room door, Martell's bedroom door opened. Jess shoved Gary through the door and swung round nervously with a big smile on her face. It was Angie, the babysitter.

'You're back, Miss Montrose.'

'Err … yes Angie. Was everything okay?'

'Yes, Martell is never a problem.' Angie looked at the strained expression on Jess's face. 'Are you okay, Miss Montrose?'

'Err … yes! Of course! I'm fine … just a little tired.' If Jess smiled any harder, she was sure her face would crack. She began to play with her bedroom door handle.

Angie smiled as if a light bulb had flashed over her head. She winked at Jess. 'I'll just say goodnight then, and let you … rest. Say goodnight to Mr Phillips for me.'

Jess's relief could not be hidden, unlike her guilt-ridden face in the darkness.

* * *

God bless a son that sleeps like a mummy in a tomb. Not even an earthquake can wake Martell when he's tired, a great thing considering how the earth moved for me last night. All the tension with what happened with Bobby just seemed to culminate into something seriously explosive.

I walk into the room and sit down in the armchair. My choice of seating is solely down to the fact that Martell is spread out all over the larger sofa like a blanket.

'Can I disturb you for a minute, sweetheart? I've got something on my mind I need to talk to you about.'

My child must have heard something in my voice that not even I realised was there because he turned from his game almost immediately. To get him to do that on any other day is a feat not usually accomplished so easily.

'What's the matter, Mum?' He looks questioningly at me. He also tilts his head to the side and raises his left eyebrow, a trait he obviously inherited from me. I open my mouth to say something, but nothing comes out. The words are literally caught in my throat. I must look like someone who is talking on TV but with the sound turned off. There are a few people I wouldn't mind wishing this affliction on – myself not included. What a moment for my voice to take a vacation. I start again. This time I take a deep breath first, clear my throat and close my eyes for about six seconds.

'Martell.'

From that alone, I'm sure that he has automatically picked up on the fact that this is going be a talk of a serious nature. It's a rare day that I address him so formally. Baby, Honey, even Sweetie are my usual titles for him. He probably thinks he's in trouble as calling him by his birth-certificated name is the usual sign of this. When I finally untie my tongue and get my speech going, he'll know that he's not and then he should feel a bit more relaxed, maybe even relieved, and that should take some of the punch out of what I've got to tell him.

'Your dad isn't here.' Phew! There, did it!

Martell looks at me expectantly as if to say Is that it? He shrugs his shoulders patiently at me. 'Okay. So what time is he coming back?'

What's with all the questions, questions, questions! What is it with kids today? Why do they have to question everything? What happened to the days of blind accept-ance in what your mother says, for goodness sake? Martell is really forcing my hand so I'm just going to have to spill it. I take another deep breath. Oxygen has never before felt so difficult to inhale.

'Well, Honey, he's actually not coming back. Not like forever so that you won't ever see him again or anything ... because you will ... whenever you want to ... except on Sunday mornings for your video games ... Unless he comes back on Sundays just to play the games with you ... Or if he takes you out to play someplace else ... Or if you're already with him.'

At this point I realise that I'm babbling and so I stop. Martell is looking at me with both eyebrows raised now as if to say 'Are you losing it, Mum?'

Was this garbled, jibber-jabber really coming out of my usually articulated mouth? It was so not like this when I was talking to Bobby last night. Oh no, then the words were tripping over themselves to get out. So what was wrong now? Why can't I just tell my son? I need to try again. I'm counting on third time lucky. I inhale deeply again because this time I'm just going for it.

'Your dad and I, me and your dad, have decided not to live together anymore.'

Miraculously it finally comes out the way I want it to. Clear and calm and all in one breath. I silently brace myself for tears or anger or ... something. Seconds pass and ... nothing. Martell is just watching me in a kind of thoughtful way. Right now, I'm just hoping that those thoughts are ones that we're going to be able to talk about without the accompaniment of a box of Kleenex – and I mean more for my usage than his.

'Does that mean that I get to stay sometimes with you and sometimes with Dad like Ricardo does?'

Ricardo was Martell's school buddy whose folks had broken up about this time last year when his mother found out that Ricardo had a new baby sister.

'Yes ...' I slowly answer.

He nods his head, still looking somewhat thoughtful, and then turns back to his game. I'm beginning to wonder if he actually really heard me. Surely he can not be this unfazed about me and his dad separating? How can he possibly be so calm about the news?

'Are you okay, Baby? Is there anything else you want to ask me? Anything you want to talk about regarding this?'

He briefly turns round from his game again and gives me a reassuring little shake of his head. 'No Mum. I'm cool.'

And with that, Lara has his attention again. The surprise is all on me now and I think I'm in denial about his reaction. Is the breaking up of parents so commonplace nowadays that my baby thinks it's the norm and therefore requires no more explanation than whether he gets the privilege of two beds? I open my mouth to say more but before any words come out I close it again. A question has just crossed my mind. If you break some news to your child that unexpectedly does not break his heart, do you then try to break it down some more in order to get the expected reaction, or do you just thank your lucky stars for the reaction you got? After giving that thought some consideration, I decide that the only thing I need to question my baby about now is what he wants for breakfast, and I already know it's going to be pancakes.

I shuffle towards the kitchen and look over my shoulder, just to reassure myself that Martell has really taken the news okay. It's also at this precise moment, that he breaks his previous highest score and starts doing a dance move that he learnt from one of those music videos on MTV. His personal improvisation must be swinging the console in the air, and waving it like he just doesn't care. I reckon that that's all the confirmation I need to feel comfortable that Martell's okay with the news. Only time will tell, but I think my baby's going to be alright about this. He's going to be okay.

Speaking of okay, I hope that Bobby is. I don't even know where he is right now. He didn't take any clothes with him and it doesn't look like he came back last night when I was out. No doubt he's somewhere hating me. I hope that we can at least be civil about this before too long, for our baby's sake. I know I hurt him, and I honestly feel terrible about it, but no matter how it was said, there wouldn't have been any way of saving his feelings. Thank goodness I won't have to go through that with him again.

That just leaves Gary. I know what I've got to do about that. Just need to catch my breath from breaking up with Bobby before I do the same with Gary. Too many nights like last night are not going to help, that's for sure. I think what I need is a male time-out for a while to re-focus. Good thing there isn't anyone else in the picture. Just dealing with the Bobby and Gary situations is more than enough for now.

16

Gary

Gary was preening like a peacock. What a night! He had rocked Jess's world, as always. There had been something abandoned about her performance last night. He'd always felt she was holding back a bit, but last night there was no sign of that. He must be getting better. What other explanation could there be? He laughed to himself. He wasn't even surprised at the blockbuster news she'd given him.

* * *

'Gary. Something happened tonight. The real reason why I called you.'

'You mean it wasn't just to hear my voice, then?' Gary smiled.

Jess nudged him softly. 'Be serious a minute, will you?'

Gary held her hands in his. 'Talk to me, Jess.'

Jess took a deep breath. 'Me and Bobby are over. It ended tonight.' Gary was silent. Jess looked up at him, expecting … something.

'How are you feeling?' he asked.

'I don't know. I really don't know.' Her voice cracked slightly, but no tears came. Gary hugged her, tightly. Over her shoulder a sly smile crept over his lips.

* * *

He'd known it would happen eventually. Bobby was never going to be a problem for him, but now that he was officially out of the picture … Well, that simply made the road ahead traffic free and he was all for a smooth ride!

Naturally he had to show serious concern and hide his elation as Jess was clearly struggling to deal with her new situation. It was a shame he had to leave so early, but he had to respect her wishes in regards to her son. But if he'd had his own way, he'd be there for the whole morning, and even some of the afternoon. There was something about that woman that he just couldn't get enough of. So he was in a relationship already. So what? His lady at home was happy. She was getting everything she needed from him, which was him. Whenever she needed him, he was there. He didn't sneak out or make silly excuses. He didn't need to. He went out a lot, and it had always been like that from the day his fiancée met him. That was part of the parcel that was him: unwrap him and accept him as he was. She was getting hers, so why shouldn't he get his? With Jess. He had needs too and he simply didn't think that one woman could fulfil them all. He was being honest. Good luck to the guy that could find all he wanted in one package. That was great for him, but as far as he was concerned, you had to know when to go back to what worked for you.

You couldn't fight what was natural to you. It was natural for a man to need more than one woman; that was nature's law, not his. How many other species in the animal kingdom were truly monogamous? According to the last Survival programme he'd seen, it was foxes and birds. And birds didn't really count. A million species and that was it.

Some would say it was wrong and morally it probably was. But you had one life to live and you couldn't live it trying to make everyone happy. He'd tried that by settling down and denying himself what was so frequently offered.

★ ★ ★

'Hey Gary, fancy hooking up sometime?'
    'Sorry Sarah, I'm already hooked up I'm afraid.'

'Gary, how would you like to take me out for a drink next week?'
    'I'd love to, Lisa, but I don't think my fiancée would.'

'Gary, any chance of a nightcap tonight? I'm free ...'
    'Ahh Sheila, If only I were free too. But alas, a fiancée has ensured that is no longer the case.'

* * *

He'd really tried at first; for three long years he was absolutely faithful. But it was all too much for a red-blooded male like him. Inevitably, he gave in.

* * *

'Suzy! What a surprise.' Gary beamed down the phone.

'Hey, Gary. Saw you the other day while I was driving. You look good. Thought I'd call and see how you were doing.'

'I'm doing good, too,' Gary replied with a self-satisfied smile.

'Ha ha! Gary. Ever the confident one. Some things don't change do they?' Suzy laughed huskily.

'Nope.'

'But apparently some things do. Heard you're off the market, so to speak.'

'Didn't your mother ever tell you not to listen to rumours?'

'So it's a rumour that you're engaged?'

'It's a rumour that I'm off the market. I came back on

the minute you called.' Gary decided that a man could only resist temptation for so long.

★ ★ ★

He was human. It was just harmless, insignificant one-nighters at first. They didn't even really count as far as he was concerned. And then Jess came along. He didn't plan for it to happen. It wasn't like he went looking for another woman. From the moment he'd first seen her, he'd known that his three-year female-fast was over.

★ ★ ★

'Pleased to meet you, Jessica. I see you've got Maddy holding your shopping. Is that to keep your hands free for ... other things?' Gary could never miss an opportunity to flirt with a pretty woman.

'That's right. Other things like more shopping.' Jess smiled.

'I take it one of the purchases in the many bags is an outfit for the party tonight?'

'Possibly.' Jess found herself strangely tongue-tied around this man.

'Hopefully.' Gary amended. 'And I hopefully look forward to seeing your purchase later.' He winked.

Jess kept her expression bland even though the thought of seeing this man again wasn't an unpleasant prospect. Maddy broke into her thoughts.

'Righty-o Gary. So many shops, so little time, so see you later!' Maddy smiled over-brightly at Gary, linked her arm through Jess's and turned them both on their heels.

★ ★ ★

Jess made him realise just how much he missed his natural calling. He really had intended to give up that Mr Lover life but when Jess came along, the old him came flooding back. He'd seen Jess a couple times before with her boyfriend. Bobby had made it clear, in that way that guys do, that he was not going to let him get anywhere near his girl.

He could honestly say he'd never been responsible for breaking up anyone's happy or unhappy home. Contrary to popular belief, he'd never actually gone out hunting for women. He wasn't so conceited as to say he was God's gift, but he was confident enough to know he was a good-looking guy. Women liked him and the truth of the matter was he'd never had to chase them. They nearly always came to him. There were only two occasions he could remember where he did have to work, and work damned hard to get the prize. Once was for Jess and the other was for the woman who was now his fiancée. His brother had always told him his charm wouldn't work on a good girl because she'd see right through him. He'd always thought his brother was jealous, but with Tia he had started to believe that maybe his brother was right.

* * *

Gary walked past the law firm window for the fourth time this week and for the umpteenth time; he was going to try his luck again.

'Good afternoon, Tia. And how are we today?' He gave the lady at the reception desk a wide smile.

'I am well, thank you. You're in a good mood.' Tia smiled softly.

'Seeing you does that to me. my dear.' Gary did a little

bow. Tia shook her head and laughed. 'Anyway, I brought something for you.' He passed her a white paper bag.

Tia looked into the bag and frowned. 'Gary, you really didn't need to bring me lunch again.' She reluctantly accepted the roll from her favourite bakery.

'This I know, but I wanted to. I live in hope that I can bring you to lunch one day instead of bringing lunch to you.' Gary sighed dramatically, then cocked his head to the side. 'So how about it, Tia?'

Tia narrowed her eyes at him. He'd been bringing her lunch a couple of times a week for months now, as well as asking her out to lunch on the other days.

'It's only food. What could be the harm?' Gary cocked his head to the other side.

He had a point, she supposed. What would be the harm? He seemed a decent enough guy. It was probably time for her to start socialising again since her break-up. Still, she wasn't sure. 'Hmm … I don't know.'

'What's to know? You get a menu, you choose, you eat and I foot the bill!' He smiled again. Tia could feel her reservations evaporating. He had a cute smile. And it was just going to be a harmless lunch …

* * *

Seven months after that lunch, they were seeing one another. All the hard work he'd put in to just get Tia to come out with him had meant he'd actually taken the time to get to know someone properly. He realised he didn't want to hurt or disrespect this girl in any way, just protect her. With Tia he was going to put his playing days behind him and really try to make this relationship 'the one'. It wasn't as hard as he thought it would be. He'd managed it for three whole years. It was weird. He was content with Tia and knew that he wasn't going to leave her, but when the opportunity came up for a chance to get to know Jess better, he couldn't let it go to waste.

★ ★ ★

'Hi Jessica, everything okay?' Gary noticed the far-away look on her face as he sat next to her on the bus stop bench. She looked up in surprise.

'Gary! Oh, hi. Yes, I'm fine. Just got a few things on my mind.' Work was hard, and at the moment home was hard too.

'Anything I can do?'

'Not really.' Jess laughed without humour.

'Anything a drink can do?'

Jess laughed again, this time with genuine mirth. 'Oh, I don't know.'

'What's to know?' Gary gestured with his arms. 'You sit at the bar, you order, you drink and I foot the bill.'

Jess thought about it. Gary seemed a nice enough guy. And it would just be a harmless drink ...

★ ★ ★

Tia was the person who had helped transform his reputation. No one thought that he could do it. No one thought that Gary Martin would ever settle down. His relationship with Tia had changed virtually everyone's opinion of him. He liked it. He liked the fact that people took him more seriously. It was like he'd been elevated to a different status. He received a different kind of respect now, and all just from being in a settled relationship. He didn't want to let that go. So if it meant keeping two relationships on the go, one a lot less publicly than the other for obvious reasons of course, then so be it. He'd thought it was going to be really difficult and surprised even himself that his skill of juggling between women had come back to him so easily. Proof that it was in his blood.

He loved Tia, but there was just something about Jess. He couldn't put his finger on exactly what it was, but it was something he didn't want to do without any time soon. Jess had been amazing last night, but he could also sense her withdrawing from him slightly. He was uncannily susceptible to her moods. He knew she wasn't happy with their situation so he'd have to pull out all the stops to keep her enticed. He knew what buttons to press to convince her that something that they both enjoyed wasn't wrong, especially with Bobby now out the way. He'd plan something special for her. What was his trademark saying? 'If she's fine, make her dine, then make her mine.' He'd have to start thinking of some serious excuses at home for the time it was no doubt going to take to persuade Jess that they should keep going. Nipping her reservations in the bud was going to be a challenge even for him, but he'd never failed to rise to a challenge yet.

17

Bobby

Bobby woke up feeling groggy. He hadn't felt this bad since the drinking binge he'd been on when he turned twenty-one. It must have been some party last night. His head was pounding as if a meat tenderiser was beating against it. He looked at his watch to see what time it was. Nearly midday. He looked around to catch his bearings and caught his breath instead. He was not alone. He jumped up from the horizontal position he was lying in and realised his shirt was also unbuttoned all the way down. He took a deep breath, trying hard not to hyperventilate. Okay, he wasn't going to panic. This was real life and not some corny film where the guy wakes up after a heavy night out drinking and finds he's in bed with some strange woman.

He peeked under the quilt so he could get a better look at who he was sharing it with. Oh shit, oh shit, oh shit! Now he was panicking because this woman didn't look so strange. Oh shit, oh shit, oh shit! How the hell did he end up in bed with Melinda? He had barely finished with one woman and here he was in bed with another. What was worse, he couldn't even remember how it had happened. Curse that brandy. It wouldn't block out thoughts of Jess that he actually wanted to forget, but now he wanted to remember something, it had knocked his memory bank for six. He needed coffee. Urgently.

Bobby slowly drew the quilt back to make a quick exit. He was even more baffled when he saw that he still had his trousers and socks on. Melinda was still sleeping and right now he was loath to wake her. He turned away from the bed but before he could get to the bedroom door, the decision as to whether to let the sleeping Melinda lie was taken out of his hands.

18

Bobby

'Hey Bobby,' Melinda said softly. Not in a lovey dovey way but in a gentle try-not-to-startle-somebody way.

'Morning Mel.' Bobby's discomfort at this moment knew no bounds. Neither of them said anything for the next few seconds and even though it was his turn to speak next, he was more than happy for Melinda to take his turn.

'Nothing happened, Bobby.'

The relief at hearing those three magic words spread across his whole body like wildfire. He must have done a good job of hiding it because she continued. 'I talked, you drank, we fell asleep. In that order.' She looked at him with a half-smile that couldn't even begin to compare to the one that was now on his face. Suddenly coffee didn't seem so important. He leant over and kissed her on the cheek. Not a regular peck, but one of those raspberry type ones. She laughed and he left the room, mouthing, 'See you later.' She nodded understandingly and snuggled back under the quilt.

Walking down the stairs and seeing empty plastic cups littering the place just confirmed that Mel's party must have been a blinding success. He closed the front door and started walking down the street. Breathing in the Sunday morning air his head started to clear and refresh his memory.

★ ★ ★

'You need to go back to basics, Bobby.' Melinda folded her arms in an official manner as she spoke.

'I know that, but just how basic are we talking about?'

'Chocolates, flowers, phone calls first thing in the morning and last thing at night basic.'

'Okay, I can do that. That's pretty standard.' Bobby nodded repeatedly.

'And you need to do some stuff off your own back that she can look at as helpful.'

'Like?'

'I don't know … like picking up your son from school, something like that.'

'But I do pick him up from school sometimes!' Bobby felt quite indignant.

'Without Jessica asking you to?' Melinda raised her chin.

'Well, if she doesn't ask me, how would I know he needed picking up?' Bobby had to stop himself from adding 'Duh!' on the end.

'How about you call her and tell her you're picking him up BEFORE she asks you?'

Bobby opened his mouth to protest again, then closed it again as he thought about what had just been said. 'What does that do?'

'It shows that you're being thoughtful of her time.'

Bobby digested these words a little longer. 'You're saying just picking up my son on my own initiative could earn me points?' He was almost incredulous at the simplicity of it.

Melinda smiled. 'Every time.'

* * *

Last night had definitely been an educational conversation. Who knew picking up his kid could make an impression? Or packing away the shopping or hoovering the house?

It hit him that Jess really did a lot around the house. And at work. And with Martell. He didn't really do that much at all, other than be there. He'd really thought that was enough. He was sure that he must have done stuff at some time, but he also knew that if he didn't do anything, even though Jess might moan for a bit, it would still get done. He now realised just how unmercifully he'd played on that. No wonder Jess was fed up with him. He'd be fed up with him. Was it really too late? He shook the thought from his head. He refused to dwell on that possibility.

There was no time to waste. He needed to put some of his new-found revelations to use asap. Operation Get-Jess-Back was now under way. It still needed a bit of fine tuning, so he couldn't go back home just yet. He needed a couple of days preparation at the very least. Shit. It hit him again that he didn't have his mobile phone on him. He still couldn't get over how he could have left home without it. He could barely remember his own number without it. Luckily he could remember the number of the one person who happened to be a similar size to him, so that should solve the immediate clothing problem. This was one of the few friends who, along with Melinda, Jess didn't know about so wouldn't think of calling if she was concerned about his whereabouts. He didn't make a habit of having secret friends from Jess; he just didn't think that every friend should also be 'their' friend. He was sure she had the odd friend or two that he didn't know about either. He just hoped David's shift work at Jarrod's didn't include Sundays.

David was an expert with women: a lethal weapon in Bobby's Operation Get-Jess-Back. If David couldn't fill in the blanks about how to get a woman back, then he was well and truly stuffed. He couldn't bring himself to wake Melinda again just to use her telephone. For the second time in days, he was having to beat the streets for a public telephone box.

19

Jessica

It's not that I don't like Mondays, Tuesdays, Wednesdays or even Thursdays for that matter. It's just that out of a possible seven days in a week, if I had to vote, none of them would come out as the hot favourite. I particularly think that Thursday should be called Tease-day, because that's exactly what it is. It's far enough away from Monday to not be considered the beginning of the week, but not close enough to the weekend to be considered a part of that. Teasing you with the end of the working week, but just not quite delivering the goods.

It's Thursday today, twenty minutes past ten and Friday can't come soon enough. I've been so busy this week I can barely differentiate one day from another. Whoever said hard work never killed anybody wasn't doing hard work, that's for sure.

I'm a little pre-occupied this morning for some reason. Something's in the air. I don't know what to start working on and believe me it's not through lack of choice. Maybe I'll start with the Karen Jameson account. She's a new glove designer. Who'd have thought gloves could be anything but a winter thing? But somehow she's made them the fashion accessory of the moment.

So now I know what to start on. Then why don't I just start? I push out my chair and get up to gaze out of the window at the car park. It's just beginning to show signs of cars other than the employees' ones. It's times like this when I miss my old job. Choosing outfits for young people was so much more straightforward.

'Okay guys, what's the focus this season for our thirteen to eighteen range?' Jess went to the front of the long meeting table, non-permanent marker poised over the white board for suggestions.

'Jeans' answered one of her staff members whilst busily sketching on a pad.

'Well, that shouldn't be too hard. The smallest kids want the biggest jeans and the kids that think they're big want the smallest. So, Baggies and Skinnies?' Jess looked around the table at her staff, busily scoffing the cream cakes she'd bought for the meeting. Murmurs of approval came back at her. It was anyone's guess whether they were nodding for her cakes or her suggestion. She decided the latter, only because it meant an early end to the meeting and she could go meet Maddy for a long lunch.

'Right then, people, that's a wrap.'

★ ★ ★

Teens are a lot less fickle when it comes to fashion than grown-ups. They just want to wear whatever the celebrities are wearing in a size contrary to their own. Following that basic format you couldn't go far wrong. Adults were another ball game. Much more mental effort involved there. Ordering jeans for adults meant considering baggy jeans, tight jeans, long leans, longer length jeans, shorter length jeans, straight cut, boot flare, wide leg. The list was endless. And that applied to almost everything including, unfortunately, bloody gloves: leather, suede, hand, driving, long … ugh.

I'm too distracted to work. I sigh and focus my attention back on the car park to see if there's any action going on down there. There's always something going on there. Last week it was a staff versus customer argument, both fighting for the same space.

* * *

'Oy!' shouted the delivery driver. 'If you park there, I won't be able to get in, will I? And if I can't get in I can't deliver, can I? And if I can't deliver then there'll be nothing for you to buy, will there? Think you need to park somewhere else, mate.' The delivery driver chewed his gum to accentuate every sentence.

'Oy, right back at you!' the customer answered back testily. 'If I can't get in to spend my money on what you're delivering, there'll be no need for your delivery, will there? I see you didn't get the customer is always right memo!'

While driver and customer stared moodily at one another, neither wanting to be the first to move and so give the other access to the prime parking space, a young man sped through the car park in his Mini. He shot neatly between the two vehicles, parked in the space of contention, got out of his car and whistled as he strolled into the shop.

* * *

I really must be distracted if a stupid incident from last week is more prevalent in my mind than top of the range gloves. Sigh. Oh, that looks like David's Monty just pulling in. David works in lingerie. Monty is what he calls his Mazda. David has a reputation for being a bit of a love 'em and leave 'em type of guy. Knowing him, he's probably creeping in from one of his conquests' apartments right now. It's still early and he doesn't usually start until about midday.

I have never met a person more suited to a job than David is to lingerie. He has that outrageous but smooth sales talk. It's not hard to see why ladies everywhere, staff and customers alike, can't resist him. That is, all the ladies except this lady. Gary's enough to make me avoid guys like David, like I avoid platform shoes. My ankles are delicate and so is my heart. So no matter how many times he asks me to lunch, I always decline.

That's what's in the air today. Gary-ness. After last weekend I've been questioning myself every night, wondering how I ever allowed Gary Martin to infiltrate my safe little world. He caught me at a weak moment; immaculate timing on his part, I must say. I don't remember a time when I've felt this vulnerable. I never felt like this with Bobby. I felt for him, of course, but never felt vulnerable like this. I don't think I like it very much. It's almost as though the outcome of my current state of happiness lies in someone else's hands. And that's never a good thing.

I have been conversing with David a little more than usual these past few days though, purely on a non-lunch basis of course. I just needed someone to bounce some of my mess off of. You know, like when you run a hypothetical situation past someone when really it relates to you, but you don't want them to know that.

* * *

'So David, say a person liked a person, but was already involved with another person, would that make them a bad person?' Jess always ended up sounding cryptic when she had to replace actual names with an impersonal noun.

'Hmm ... depends.' David looked thoughtful.

'On what?'

'On why the person who is already with a person suddenly likes another person.'

'Okay.' Jess nodded like she understood, then shook her head to indicate that she actually didn't.

'Is the person unhappy?' David perched his leg on her desk as he prepared to elaborate.

'Which person?'

'The person who is with a person but likes another person?'

'I guess, or they wouldn't suddenly like another person, would they?'

'Hmm ... depends.' David looked thoughtful again.

'On what?'

'On the motives of the person.'

'Which person?' Jess was starting to confuse herself with all these persons.

'The person who is going with the person, knowing she is with a person already.'

'Why? What does motive have to do with anything?' Jess was intrigued. She'd never considered that angle before.

'Unhappy people are easy to take advantage of because they will often seek to not be unhappy without considering whether their methods will hurt the person they are with already, if that person finds out.'

'So, that makes them a bad person, then?' Jess had come full circle to her original question and was very interested in what the conclusion would be according to David.

'Hmm ... depends.'

'On what, now?' Jess was getting exasperated.

'On whether the person feels remorse.'

'Which person?' Jess asked patiently, even though she felt like throttling David.

'The person who is already with a person. It doesn't make them a bad person – because they are human. But it doesn't make them a good person either because the person they are with would be relying on them to make the right decision in regards to them.'

'O...kay. Thanks, David ... I think.' Jess didn't know if she was confused or enlightened.

'Anytime, Jess.' David turned to leave her office.

'David?' He turned back around to face Jess.

'What made you think the person already involved with a person was a "she"?'

'Wasn't it?' David winked and turned to leave the office again.

* * *

David, considering the womaniser he was, actually had a good take on my situation from a male perspective. Oh, there goes my phone.

'Good morning, Jessica Montrose speaking. How may I help you?'

'Hey Jess, you can help me by going to lunch with me today. How about it? My treat!' It's none other than David himself. Whoever said speak of the devil and he will appear, knew what they were talking about.

'Hi, David. What's on the menu today?'

'Well, there's always me. As you know I'm an acquired taste. Taste me and you are going to want to acquire!'

'Hmm ... anything else?' As I said, the guy never quits.

'If your palette is not that adventurous, there's always a choice of Burger King or the Sandwich Bar. The staff canteen is out. I'm sure the new cook there used to work at a prison, the slop they've been serving lately.'

I chuckle. 'The array of choices that you have presented before me is simply mind-boggling. Unfortunately I'm going to have to pass on them all. I already have lunch in the form of a ham and cheese sandwich lovingly prepared for me by my son. He would never forgive me if he found out that I blew his sandwich out for yours.'

'Aww, you're breaking my heart, Jess!'

'I'm sure you are more able to deal with disappointment than my son.'

'You'd think so with this constant rejection from you. Yet I'm still crushed every time you turn me down.' He gives the biggest mock sigh.

'Sure you are.'

'Guess there's no persuading you today then, is there? Think I might try my luck again tomorrow.' He really has the staying power of bad aftershave.

'Bye bye, David.'

'Bye bye, Jess.'

As I rest the phone back into the cradle, I smile to myself. I just might take him up on that lunch date one of these days. I mean, as long as I stay in a loud, crowded place I won't be able to hear his whispered sweet nothings in my ear. I don't know if I'm just imagining it, but I'm beginning to think that since I split from Bobby there must be some sort of change in me. I mean, David asks me to lunch every so often, but these last few days, it's been like every day. And if I'm not mistaken, that Philip guy from Menswear has been double friendly of late, and that new guy from the canteen, Errol or Ferrol whatever his name is, asked me to lunch yesterday. Even Shirley from haberdashery, who everyone knows has a liking for females, has been awful smiley with me these past few days.

Something is going on. I don't now if single people give off some kind of signal, but if that's the case, I need to know what it is because I don't want to be giving it to Shirley that's for sure; she wouldn't be my type even if I was that way inclined.

My phone rings again, a welcome interruption to my train of thought.

'Good morning, Jessica Montrose speaking. How may I help you?'

'Jess. It's me.'

Shock temporarily cuts my voice box off. It's Bobby. I haven't heard from him since last Saturday. I was worried because I couldn't contact him; he'd stormed off with nothing but the clothes on his back. But I know that Bobby knows a lot of people who'd readily put him up if need be. My concern was more that he hadn't been back for anything, not even his mobile phone, which, for Bobby, is usually an extension of his ear. Not even Martell has heard a peep from him, which really is unusual. Even if I'm not in his world anymore, Martell still is. I suddenly feel awkward. I don't know how to respond. I know a 'Hi' would probably be the logical reply, but I just don't feel that's going to cut it. Maybe I should ask him if he's okay? But then that could get me anything from a calm 'I'm fine' to a not so calm 'What the hell do you think?!' and I don't think I'm ready for the not so calm option.

'Jess? You still there?' Bobby's voice makes me realise that I haven't actually said a word yet.

'Yes! Bobby ... Hi.' Damn, surely that is not the best I can do? Still, it might be a good thing that I'm lost for words on this occasion. I can just leave it to him to do the talking and say what's on his mind.

'Jess, can we meet up? To talk?'

Oh, oh. So much for me thinking I'd gotten off lightly with just a slammed door and crazy demand for my son. Now he wants to talk? Now, when I don't want to? I may have passed the finish line before, but I honestly don't know if I can do it again. Wait up, get a load of me. Why am I even assuming that this talk is a let's-get-back-together one? I mean, he could want to make arrangements to get his stuff, even though he has a key. Or he might want to see Martell. Yeah, that could be it. Yeah.

'Okay Bobby. No problem. When? Tonight?'

'No! Not tonight and not at the house.'

Okay, well this conversation is clearly not going to be about getting his stuff or seeing Martell.

'How about tomorrow evening?' he continues. 'We can talk over a meal or something. I'll sort it out. Eightish be okay?'

I had plans for tomorrow so should really say 'I'll get back to you' but seeing as I don't know how to get back to him that would be a little difficult. And I'm not feeling comfortable enough in our new, as yet unestablished relationship to ask him exactly where he is. Easier to just cancel my other plans, I think.

'Okay … well just let me know where to meet you.'

'Will do. See you tomorrow, Jess. Wear something nice.' With that he rings off. I'm still looking at the receiver in my hand wondering if I just heard what I thought I heard. Did he tell me to wear something nice?

20

My watch – a favourite and extravagant Cartier from Bobby – confirms that thirty whole minutes have gone by since I last looked at the time. The list of what I have done today comprises of three telephone calls, two of which had nothing to do with work and one of which, if I give it any more thought, will mean I won't be able to do any work.

I can't wait for the day to be over because Tease-day will be over and it'll be Friday, which I have got booked off. Why did I book it off, though? I know I booked it off for a reason … Let me look in my diary. Oh my gosh! How could it have slipped my mind? How could I have forgotten my date with Gary tomorrow afternoon? It was all I could think about a few weeks ago. I know I'm supposed to be sworn off men for a while, but this so does not count. This plan was made way before my swearing. I mean what if Gary's planned a surprise? How out of order would I be to ruin it at the last minute? I simply have no choice but to go with the flow. Sigh. The sacrifices I have to make.

It's most likely going to be my last date with him anyway because I'm serious about breaking it off. So what kind of spoilsport would I be if I didn't at least make the effort to enjoy what is possibly our last outing together? It makes sense to at least create a pleasant memory of the day so that the focus will be on the good time we had and not on the good times we're no longer going to have. Bless my logic. Oh, please. I can't believe my phone is ringing again.

Has my extension been mixed up with the call centre or something?

'Jessica Montrose speaking.'

'Hi Jess.' It's Gary! That speaking of the devil thing is really freaking me out today. I know I shouldn't feel happy to hear his voice, but damn it I am.

'All set for tomorrow?'

'Of course. I haven't been able to think of anything else.' For the last couple of minutes.

'Good. It's going to be a special day, Jess. A memorable one.'

Hmm, but maybe not for the reasons you're hoping for. What I say is, 'Can't wait!'

'I'll pick you up at midday?'

'See you then.' I hang up with a grin as big as all outdoors. A five-minute conversation with Gary, and I feel as relaxed as if I'd had a massage for two hours. Oh oh ... tomorrow ... *shit!* What have I done? My efforts to put Bobby out of my mind were so successful that not even a shadow of our earlier conversation crept back to remind me that I've agreed to see him tomorrow too! And there's no way for me to contact him to re-arrange. I take a deep breath and focus on my semi-dilemma. I'm off all day tomorrow so I've got from midday 'til early evening to be with Gary. It's supposed to be an afternoon date anyway, so I reckon I can get out of seeing him in the evening too. My alarm immediately subsides. I just may be able to pull off meeting them both.

This brush with panic seems to have given my button the push it needed to buckle down to some work. Before I can say Jack Rabbit, the next time I lift my head it's already lunchtime. I need a drink. Nothing alcoholic, just a little something to wash down Martell's sandwich. A trip to the shop is warranted, I think.

As I leave the building, I can hear someone tooting a car horn like their finger is stuck on it. I don't usually turn around for such things, but for some reason this horn is being tooted so persistently that the nosiness in me makes me swing my head to see where it's coming from. As I gaze toward the driver, he starts to wave frantically, apparently at me. I don't recognise the car and without my glasses can't see the driver clearly. I turn my head from left to right as you do – to make sure that it really is me he's waving at and not someone beside me and also to make sure that if I do wave back and realise it's not for me, I can readily style it out by turning my wave into stroking my hair. Nope, it's definitely me this person is waving at. The driver erases my doubts by jabbing his finger rather aggressively in my direction. I stop walking and the driver pulls over. To my surprise it's the starer from the party.

'Hi. Jessica, isn't it.' The way he spoke, it was more of a statement than a question.

'Hi, how are you? Tyrone, isn't it.' I figured I'd follow his lead with the confirming identity thing.

'Just popped down here on the off chance and saw you. Can hardly believe my luck! Are you at lunch or shopping?'

'I'm on my lunchbreak. I work at Jarrods.' Now why did I tell him that? It was not like me to volunteer unrequested information.

'Really? I was in there a few weeks ago getting a gift for my daughter. Got in an argument with one of your colleagues in the car park.' I nod at this and smile knowingly.

'Jessica, believe me when I say this is very out of character for me, but would it be possible to speak to you again? You sort of vanished from the party before I could get a chance to talk to you.'

'Ah, yes … Something came up and I had to leave early.'

'So, may I contact you again?'

How ye olde world polite is he? 'Well, I have a rule not to give my number to people I don't know.'

'How about people you do know? It's not like we haven't been introduced?' He smiles shyly. Rather beguilingly too, I might add.

'An introduction doesn't mean you're not a stranger.' What is it about this guy that holds my attention?

'Well, how will I stop being a stranger if I can't contact you to get to know you better?'

'That's a good question. I'll think about it when I'm eating my sandwich back at work. And, if I happen to bump into you again, I'll tell you what answer I came up with.' With that I give him my prettiest smile and turn to head back to my building.

'Okay,' he calls after me. 'I'm going to hold you to that!'

I look over my shoulder to give him a little wave and point at the approaching traffic warden. He smiles at me while using the same smile on the warden, trying to buy himself some time to get his car back in motion. It's quite a nice smile. Heading back to the office, I feel like I've got a spring in my step. That is until a thought hits me like a punch from Mike Tyson. Not only do I have to meet Gary and Bobby tomorrow, but I also noticed that this guy Tyrone had a nice smile. That can't be good. The last person that prompted that type of personal observation from me was Gary, and look how that turned out. Another thought suddenly strikes me. This one makes me turn up the pace and literally race back to the office. I don't even think to acknowledge Errol or Ferrol whatever his name is who tries to catch my eye as I zoom past the canteen. I literally greet Shirley in haberdashery with a grimace, such is my focus to get to my destination.

I get to my office, throw down my bag and hurriedly try to compose myself. Still breathless from rushing, I reach for the phone because there is no doubt in my mind that I now need some professional help with this situation.

'Hey David, glad I caught you. I'm still a little peckish. Is that lunch invitation still up for grabs?'

21

Tyrone

Tyrone couldn't believe his luck bumping into Jessica like that. It was so worth the cost of the parking ticket. He'd only popped up to the West End by chance. Who'd have thought that would be where he saw her again? He'd only managed to stop thinking about her for a total of about two hours since the party, and that was only with the help of a football match. It had been a great game, what could he say? After she had vanished from the party, he had spoken to Barry, hoping he would be able to help him contact her.

* * *

'Hey Barry, can I ask you something?' Tyrone was still craning his neck, looking around for a glimpse of Jessica. Where could she have disappeared to so suddenly?

'Sure, T, what's up?'

'You see that lady you were just talking to?'

'Be specific, my man,' Barry smirked 'I've been talking to a lot of ladies tonight!'

'Jessica?' It took all his self-control for Tyrone not to roll his eyes.

'Jess? Good friend of mine. Known her for years. She's taken, though. Actually I'm sure I saw spotted her guy earlier, no doubt they came together.' Barry pursed his lips to emphasise to Tyrone that he was out of luck. Tyrone's heart sank a little even though he wasn't surprised to hear that Jessica wasn't single. A woman like that had to already be hooked up. Still, it would have been nice to know a little

*more about her. No harm in hoping her relationship was
on the rocks, was there?*

* * *

He had been so surprised to see her and it had taken him
so long to think of what to say to her that he nearly lost
her in the crowd. Honking his car horn at her like some
demented duck had seemed to be the only way to get her
attention before she disappeared again.

He didn't care what anyone said; this was meant to be.
Be what exactly he didn't know, especially if she was
already with someone. Whatever it was about Jessica that
held his attention, he hadn't felt in a long, long time. He
didn't meet women that interested him that often. She was
one fish that was not going to escape his hook just yet.

22

Bobby

Bobby could see his work was going to be cut out for him. He couldn't quite gauge anything from Jess. She didn't have much to say, which was unusual from someone who usually had a surplus of words. Still, he wasn't going to let that faze him. Operation Get-Jess-Back was underway. She'd agreed to go to dinner with him without too much persuasion, and that was a good sign; a very good sign indeed. Jess had probably been so quiet because she hadn't been expecting his call. She worked better if she had a chance to prepare and he worked better if she didn't.

* * *

'Your woman seems like a she's a planner.' David nodded his head wisely.

'A planner?' Bobby was confused.

'Yeah. Whenever she's got something significant on her mind, she plans her conversation ahead. Like when you have those talks, she already has a list of to-do's, doesn't she? And the break-up? No way that was a spur of the moment thing. She's a planner.'

'Okay ... So is that bad?' Bobby's face dropped. His Get-Jess-Back plan was stumbling at the first hurdle.

'Not necessarily, my friend, not necessarily.' David smiled cheekily. 'Not if you catch her off guard.'

'And how am I going to do that?' Bobby was becoming convinced that his plan was doomed to failure; so much for David helping him.

'Hit her with something she's not expecting.'

Bobby raised his eyebrows to David signalling for him to elaborate.

'Okay.' David leant his elbows on his knees. 'When you call her, the chances are she'll be expecting you to be mad or upset or something, right? Well, next time you call her, do something she won't expect – like ask her to dinner at short notice. She'll never expect that so won't have planned her response.'

A smile slowly crept over Bobby's face. 'I'll have caught her off guard.'

'Exactly! And as long as you've planned what you want to say, she'll be stunned into just listening, maybe even agreeing with you.'

Bobby could almost picture the conversation in his mind. It might just work!

David blew on his knuckles and rubbed his chest. They looked at one another and laughed.

★ ★ ★

Time to put Melinda and David's tactics to the test see how they fared in the real world. Having both a woman and a man's perspective to work from had really helped him cover all the bases – he hoped. Jess was going to see a Bobby that she hadn't seen in a long time. They had been okay once and he was full of fresh determination to get them back to that point. She still cared; her agreeing to have dinner with him proved that and made him even more determined not to give up on her without one hell of a fight. And he was going to make her fight too – with her conscience, exactly as David had advised.

★ ★ ★

'Okay, so I kind of know what I want to say. I'm just not sure where to start.' Bobby wanted to make sure that when he finally spoke to Jess, it was pitch perfect.

'Start where it will make the most impact.' David was busily changing TV channels as he spoke. And they said men couldn't multi-task.

'Like where?' Bobby couldn't believe how much coaching he needed. He had taken out of practice to another level.

'Her conscience. Women generally hate to make people feel bad, unless they hate the person then hell hath no fury. So sock her with anything that will plug at her conscience.'

Who knew that his friend was such a Google of information in this area? Bobby reached for a pen – he needed to take notes.

* * *

Jess always had a well-developed conscience about making anyone feel bad. Bobby hated the thought of making her feel bad too, but all was fair in love and war. And if making Jess feel guilty was what was needed for him to get her back, then so be it.

23

Gary

Gary rubbed his hands together gleefully. His date with Jess was still on track for tomorrow. He had been ready to obliterate any attempt on her part to cancel, but she seemed to still be looking forward to it. Maybe his Jess-sensor was a little off after the party. Even though the night had ended just like he'd anticipated, he'd still had the feeling that something was up with her, like she was trying to distance herself from him. Still, it served as a reminder that he couldn't let his game slip with a woman like her. He couldn't believe how invigorating the challenge of the chase was. He'd almost forgotten that, in his attempt at being the monogamous partner.

He wanted to make sure that their date on Friday afternoon went like a dream so that if she was thinking about thinking what he thought she was thinking, she would think again. If he knew anything for definite about Jess, it was that she was attracted to him. Most women were and, luckily for him, as different as Jess was in other aspects, in that area she was similar to most other women. If he needed to concentrate on that attraction to keep Jess in his world, then that was just what he'd have to do.

24

Jessica

Friday and my day off. Two wonderful things rolled into one! And it's not just any old day off either. I need to make myself look spectacular for later. According to David – that's what I need to do. The man should write a book. Lunch with him yesterday after seeing Tyrone was easily my best decision of the day. His insight into relationships in uncanny. Who'd have thought that all that wisdom could have evolved from being a … well, a male slag really. I mean, I go to him with my dilemma with three different people and he gives me his one solution fits all advice.

* * *

'Okay David, you can tell my plight by the mere fact that I'm not doing the "what if a person liked a person" thing again. This is serious and I can't afford to be confused by the answer.' Jess finally stopped for breath.

David looked surprised at what he'd heard, but only fleetingly. He'd heard more sordid tales than that in his time. How could she get around this situation, though? Jess could see the cog wheels of his mind turning as he processed the information she'd given him. Ten minutes later he was still sitting in silence.

'David, did I tell you that this is all happening in less than 24 hours?!'

'Be cool, Jess, you can't rush genius.' David leaned back in his chair smugly. Jess rolled her eyes.

'Right then,' David suddenly sat up straight. "Go shopping and buy something so you'll look sensational. The

ex-boyfriend will see how great you look without him on the scene and realise that you're blossoming without him. So he will understand that he shouldn't hold you back. The guy who is involved with someone else will see this power-fully sexy, confident woman who knows her own mind. So, when you say it's over he'll know there's no point in chal-lenging your decision. And if you happen to bump into the new fella again, you'll look so hot that he won't want to leave your next meeting to chance so he will let you know what his intentions are – even if you are only curious. So, shop in heels until then.'

This time it was David's turn to stop for breath and Jess's to sit quietly – in amazement.

★ ★ ★

It all made so much sense, except for the shopping in heels. That must definitely be a David fantasy. I mean, who does that? I'm apprehensive about meeting Bobby later, but looking forward to my afternoon with Gary. It should be the other way around and after today I need to restore the natural order of things – somehow.

I still don't know where Gary's taking me, but he's confirmed for about the fifth time that his afternoon off work is booked in stone (he couldn't take the whole day – too suspicious) and he can't wait. Sad to say, neither can I. This has to be one of those other woman dates that take weeks of planning to make sure the fiancée at home won't suspect anything is amiss. Even though I feel deceitful, the fact that I'm doing wrong is not concerning me as much as it should and this worries me. I know I have to deal with this one day soon, but it's clear even to me that that day is not to be today. I might as well put David's advice to good use, and take the morning to shop around so that the afternoon is free to fool around. It's got to end, this Gary thing, so for today, why fight it?

So, what exactly do I need? Stupid question really. What would any girl need for a special date? A new outfit of course, from head to toe-showing shoes. Yeah, I think a nice pair of strappy sandals with very high heels is a must on my morning's to-get list. My hair is not looking its best though, so the third thing I must do when I get back home, right after dancing in front of the mirror in my new stuff and checking my answer phone for any better-not-be-cancelling-on-me messages, is give it a good wash. I just hope I have time.

First stop Oxford Street. I'll start my trawl from there. Faith shoes are nearly always a safe bet for a pretty pair of sandals. I've already got a last resort dress in mind in case I don't find one; it did feel a little tight when I tried it on last night. Proof that I can no longer be in denial about my current addiction to Magnum ice creams. Crap. I'm never good at clothes shopping under pressure. Something for my feet last minute: no problem; something for any other part of me: always the opposite. Well, if I don't find anything, it'll just have to be a toss up between holding in my stomach and something with lots of Lycra from my wardrobe. Better get my butt in gear if I want to get all the shops in. I believe in giving every shoe store an equal chance, from high end designers right down to bargain Betty's. You'd be surprised where you can find something half decent these days. I went into a pound store just two weeks ago and bought some pretty clip-on earrings; I saw the same earrings a week later in the accessory section of a department store for fifteen bucks! I turn my nose up at no shop.

Tottenham Court Road. This is where I get off. Good thing I've started early. I've only got the morning to get what I need. It's not busy yet so it almost feels like I've commandeered the whole street for my personal shopping pleasure. Without further ado, first stop: Faith shoes. Well, it would be my first stop if someone wasn't yelling at me. I've only been here two minutes and already I've been spotted. Can't a girl shop without interruption, especially when she has limited shopping time? I can't see who it is, but I sure can hear them yelling my name at the top of their voice. My ear drums are vibrating, but I'm loath to turn towards the sound, which would make the whole street aware that I'm the person being targeted by this human loudspeaker. In fact I'm not even going to break my pace. I keep walking like I'm hearing impaired. Whoever it is, let them catch me up and tap me on the shoulder to get my attention like any sane person would.

With my nose in the air I continue walking until suddenly I feel myself hurtling forward! What the hell …?

25

Tyrone

Tyrone loved his jeans. They were his most favourite jeans in the whole wide world, holes and all. God forbid if his mother ever saw him in them. She'd have a coronary and haul him out for shaming the family, walking the streets looking like that. His mum refused to acknowledge the concept that holes and pre-creased clothes were actually on the catwalk these days. So, as much as he loved his wonderful, comfy, live-in-them-if-he-could jeans, he loved mommy dearest more. This trip to Oxford Street was to get a new pair just to prove to her that he had discarded the old ones.

It was such a trek to come all the way to the West End just for jeans, but experience had shown him that the local men's shops (not that there were many where he lived) just didn't have quality high on their agendas. He'd bought his last pair from The Jeanstore on his local high road. The denim was so stiff that it made him stiff. In fact, the one and only time he'd worn them for a full day, the coarse cotton had actually bruised him. Good thing he hadn't been seeing anyone at the time. Local cotton had shown him just how delicate he really was.

He really needed to update his wardrobe. Shopping wasn't his favourite pastime. He regarded clothes as a basic necessity, like food, and didn't derive any pleasure whatsoever from adding to his collection. He'd been quite fortunate that a few of his past girlfriends had actually been happy to shop for him. He made a mental note to ask Jessica her thoughts on shopping for men, just in case.

He smiled ruefully to himself; like he was going to see her any time soon. He looked at his watch, and quickened his step when he saw the time. He needed to get a move on if he wanted to be finished before the lunchtime hustle and bustle. It was Friday so everyone would be using their lunch break to buy clubbing clothes for later. Getting caught up in that would definitely make his quest for jeans even more of an ordeal.

It was funny the way shopping had made Jessica spring to mind, maybe because this was where he had bumped into her yesterday. How crazy would it be if he bumped into her again today? Every time he saw her she looked good, from top to lovely bottom. And what a lovely bottom. He'd gazed at it for longer than political correctness allowed. He couldn't seem to help himself; whenever he saw her he just stared. Looking through a camera all day gave you a habit of having a bit of a fixed stare which was embarrassing if the stare-ee happened to catch you. What was good, though, was that it also made you aware of all the little details; things that other people might not notice: earrings with unusual patterns, shoes with the same shimmer as the straps on her dress, the slight lacy imprint of her thong. He smiled. That particular observation showed that she preferred sexy lingerie to the functional type of underwear that men usually hated. How had his train of thought gone from earrings to her ripe little derrière again? From a director's point of view, Jessica was the full package. Her outfit was the background scene, her accessories, the props. And Jessica herself? Naturally the starring character.

If even a day off, intended solely for purchasing denim, couldn't take his mind off viewing everything as if through a camera lens, he definitely needed a holiday. Enough daydreaming. Back to the task at hand: where to buy a new pair of jeans. Denim & Co. That was an interesting title for a shop. It suggested that there was hope that he just might just get what he was looking for without having to spend the whole day going from shop to shop.

He wandered slowly into the road, looking left and right with the natural intention of completing the journey to the other side, until a sight made him stop dead in his tracks. Not to take a phrase too literally it could actually have come to that if the taxi man hadn't slammed on his brakes and beeped at him angrily. Tyrone hastily put his hand up to apologise and trotted to the other side of the road to get a better look at what he thought he'd just seen. Jessica? That woman looking in the window of Dolcis shoe shop really looked like Jessica. He knew he could be prone to daydreaming about this woman, but hallucinating too?

'Jessica!' He shouted her name. The woman didn't turn around or acknowledge the shout in any way, making him wonder if he had made an embarrassing mistake. He squinted, trying to get a better focus on the person who was now walking ahead of him. It wasn't her. It couldn't be … Could it? He yelled her name again, but she didn't even falter in her step. He sighed. The best thing he could do right now instead of hunting down strange women was to hunt for the jeans he'd come for. He turned and walked away in the opposite direction, but he couldn't stop thinking that there was still a possibility it might have been Jessica. Did he want to chance missing out on seeing her again? Maybe she hadn't heard him. She had long hair after all so it could have muffled her hearing. Anything was possible when you were grasping at straws! Anyway, there was no harm in making sure.

He spun on his heel in a way that would make a ballet teacher proud, and started to jog back in the direction of Dolcis, hoping the woman was still browsing the windows; he'd never be able to guess what shop she might be in. Luck was on his side because he saw her looking in the Faith's window. It really did look like Jessica. He'd nearly caught up to her. The woman did look good from behind; the way she was tottering in those heels looked hot. It would be worth risking talking to her even if she wasn't Jessica. Why did he always dither whenever he thought about talking to Jessica? He seemed to get butterflies in his stomach to the point where gibberish threatened to spew from his lips if he spoke to her. He had an idea! He would accidentally on purpose, bump into her. That way, if it wasn't her, he could apologise; and if it was her, he could say something witty like 'Fancy bumping into you!' Yeah, that's what he'd do.

As he tried to discreetly sidle up next to the woman, his nerves took over and he bumped into her a little harder than intended. He had to grab hold of her arm to stop her falling over. He took a good look at her face and it was her! It was Jess! He quickly blurted out his pre-prepared line in the hope that she'd forget he had nearly knocked her into next week.

26

Jessica

'Well, fancy bumping into you!'

It can't be! Again? My shock at seeing this Tyrone guy again silences the profanity that he was going get for nearly knocking me over. This is way too spooky! Until a few days ago I'd never seen this guy before in my life, and now, everywhere I turn he's popping up like a waffle from a toaster.

'Have you figured out an answer to how I could get to know you better? You said you would after you had lunch, yesterday?'

I'm still speechless, but luckily I look okay. Good thing I took David's advice over my better judgement and wore heels to come shopping today. I compose myself quite quickly.

'Hello again. Tyrone, isn't it? I don't recall giving you any date for my response.' Is this me flirting? Why am I flirting?

'Well, you said when you next bumped into me, which is now. So, technically, today is the date on which you should have an answer for me.'

He smiles, disarmingly. I'm disarmed. I can't even think of a witty comeback. I put it down to the fact that my shoulder was nearly dislocated a few moments ago. I bow my head slightly as if to say touché.

'What are you doing down here anyway? No work today?' I ask. I start walking again and he falls into step with me.

'Can you believe I took the day off to look for a pair of

jeans!' He laughs and I smile. I seem to do a lot of smiling around this guy.

'Yeah, I can believe that. I've been known to call a shop in another city to send me a pair of shoes that I couldn't get anywhere closer.'

'Well, we seem to be going the same way. Mind if I walk with you?'

I didn't mind, so we walked together. In and out of every shop that we could see, from Tottenham Court Road to Oxford Circus, then down some side roads and nearly to Marble Arch. Our trek takes us off the beaten tracked main road to venture down both Bond and South Molton streets.

'Hey, can we stop in here?' Tyrone points to the Levi store on Regent Street. I'd almost forgotten he was searching for something too. There's a lot to choose from in here so he should definitely find something.

'Hmm, these look interesting,' he says, stopping by a pile of dark blue denim. I can't believe my eyes when he holds up a pair of jeans that look tight enough to be stockings. I figure for a minute that he's picked them up as a joke, until he starts studying them up against himself in the mirror. I just hope he doesn't ask me for my opinion.

'What do you think of these, Jess?'

Now what do I say? They're like denim leggings, more suited to a lady of the night than a man in the day. I know we've had a good time today, but I don't think we're close enough for me to tell him that those jeans could possibly prevent him from carrying on his family lineage someday.

'Hmm … well … you know …' I end on a non-committal shrug-shouldered half-smiling shake type nod of the head and hope that he gets from that, that I hate them. He clearly got something because he puts them down and signals that he's ready to leave the shop.

We end up going down a road that I've never been down before. It has a couple of cool shoe shops on it. How could this place have escaped my radar? It's in one of these shops that I see the snazziest pair of sandals. The heels must be five inches at least. That's a little higher than I'm used to so I hope I don't break my ass when I wear them out later. They have these long laces that tie around the whole leg, right up to the knee with a single diamante-covered strap going across the toes. I twirl in them in the shop and nearly make myself dizzy in the process.

'My turn to ask your opinion, Tyrone. What do you think of these?' I don't get an immediate response from him so turn to see if he heard me.

'Err …' he croaks.

If I didn't know better I'd swear he was starting to salivate a little at the mouth. He also seems to be breathing heavier. Too much walking and not enough water perhaps? 'Are you okay?' I'm a little concerned.

He swallows hard, nods and mumbles, 'Yeah. It's a bit warm in here.' He walks outside and starts looking at the shoes in the window. I just shrug my shoulders and do a little dance in the shop in my soon-to-be new footwear. When I leave the shop, swinging my shoe bag, Tyrone smiles at me. At least he's looking better. There's something to be said for fresh air.

'So you bought them, then?' he asks.

'How could I leave them? Don't you like them?' Now why'd I ask him that? I mean, it's not like I care if he likes them or not. Do I? Of course I don't. These sandals are sex on stilettos, the sales person said so.

'Erm … yeah, sure,' he mumbles again.

It isn't quite the answer I was hoping for and once again I find myself wondering why I'm bothered about what he thinks. It's what Gary thinks that counts; after all, I bought them with him in mind. I know I shouldn't have, but come on, it may be my last date with him, remember? Sigh.

Tyrone's phone rings and at that same moment a different ringing goes off in my head. The time! Shit! It's nearly midday. Gary's supposed to be picking me up at two. What the hell am I still doing down here? I don't want to focus on why time didn't cross my mind when Tyrone was showing me tight jeans.

'Tyrone, I've got to go. It's been real cool hanging with you today. You sure you just came shopping for men's jeans? I've never met a guy who was so willing to come into just about every shop that only sells women's stuff. You're not a bad shopping partner. I could actually trawl shops with you again.'

'Well, don't be surprised if I hold you to that and give you a call on the number you owe me, to do the men's shops next time!' He laughs and once again manages to make me laugh too.

For that alone he deserves my digits, so I give them to him. I am in far too much of a hurry to think about any possible consequences.

All I can think about now is that I've got to hustle and get home to get ready for my date. Gary hates it when I'm late because he's always on time, which doesn't always work with the fact that I'm not. And it's not like I can give him an excuse of, 'Sorry, I got carried away shopping with another man.' I need to get my behind down to the train station now if I've any hope of getting ready in time. If I'm late it'll set everything back and the last thing I need is for Gary's time to gatecrash into Bobby's. My day is complicated enough already.

I do that run/walk thing back to Oxford Circus tube station. A train pulls up straight away. Praying really does help in times of crisis, it seems.

Thirty minutes later I'm at my stop. That's not bad going. I'm still on track to be ready on time – just about. As soon as the doors open I fly off the train and do that run/walk thing again, only to get the damn heel on my shoe stuck in some grate in the floor. I don't care what David says; heels are not for shopping in, especially when you're in a hurry. As I struggle to get the heel out of the grate, I come to the decision that it's easier to just slip my foot out of the damn thing and try to pull it out with both hands, well actually one hand while I hold my bags in the other. With a huge unladylike tug, I finally get the shoe out. No time to even put it back on since every second counts. Running down the street with one shoe on and the other off is really not a good look for me.

27

Gary

Gary couldn't believe that he was being held up at work today of all days. Last-minute urgent deliveries just had to happen on a short-staffed day when he was meant to be off, didn't they? He had no choice but to personally deliver the parcel himself. Being in charge of a courier service with a guarantee to ensure that every parcel was delivered meant that, every once in a while, you had to get your hands dirty and actually do a delivery. Luckily it rarely happened. Unluckily it had today. One good thing was that the address was only down the road so it shouldn't take too long. In fact, if he jumped on the bus, he should be there and back in no time.

It had been a long time since he'd taken the bus. It was actually quite relaxing, not having to pay any attention to anything other than the stop you had to get off at. He could let his thoughts enjoy anticipating what he was going to get up to in the next few hours. Jess was probably at home right now, thinking of him and prettying herself up. She couldn't resist him, try as she might. It wasn't a brag; it was a fact. Right now she needed him. And with no Bobby for her to guilt trip over, it should be easier to persuade her that he was there for her in any way she wanted him; maybe not at any time, due to his circumstances, but definitely in any way. After this afternoon, she was going to want him in that way even more. He'd make sure of that.

Oxford Street was getting busy. He hadn't realised that people started shopping so early on a Friday. He would have thought the streets would be bare at least until lunchtime. He looked at the shoppers. That couple over there looked like they were having fun. The woman looked like she was very happy with her purchase. If she swung her bag any more she'd knock someone over. Hold on … No, it couldn't be … could it? That looked like Jess. He quickly moved from his seat to one closer to the front of the bus and leant over the passenger sitting there to get a better look. It *was* Jess! Laughing and shopping with Tyrone Powers!

'Hey!' said the man whose head, without realising it, Gary had been using to keep his balance.

'Sorry, mate,' Gary quickly apologised. He didn't have time for an argument. He needed to get off this bus. Now! Either the bell wasn't working or the bus driver was deaf because the bus didn't stop at the next stop. Shit! He'd never catch her up now. Phone! He'd call her. He reached into his pocket for his phone and speed dialled her number. The phone rang … and rang … and then … voicemail? Voicemail! Why the hell wasn't she answering? Too busy giggling like a schoolgirl with Tyrone. He speed dialled her number again until it went to answering machine again. And again. And again.

He was getting annoyed. Very annoyed. Was she really ignoring him? So many women out there dying to have him ring them, and this one was ignoring his calls. After all he'd risked for this relationship, he certainly wasn't going to lose her to the likes of Tyrone Powers. He took a deep breath. No need for panic. He had to stay cool. He had no need to be jealous. Who was Tyrone after all? He would casually mention it to her when he saw her later. Her reaction would allow him to assess just what was going on. All he needed to worry about now was making this delivery before midday like the company guaranteed, but he couldn't seem to shake the picture of the two of them happily shopping away when she should have been home getting herself ready to meet him. He frowned to himself. The last thing he needed was a fly like Tyrone in his ointment.

28

Jessica

The piercing ring of the phone penetrates my concentrated efforts to get into this damn dress. If I had concentrated on shopping instead of flitting in and out of shops looking for men's jeans with Tyrone, I might have been able to come away with more than just a pair of sandals. Even Lycra isn't on my side right now. I glance at the caller ID and it is he for whom all this effort is being made.

'Hello?' I answer like I don't know who it is. Having caller ID is not something that you want to broadcast to the world, especially when you're prone to having the odd I-don't-feel-like-talking-to-you moment.

'Jessica, it's Gary.'

Now, those do not sound like the dulcet tones I'm used to. I'm as perceptive to his moods as he is to mine and I know, even before this conversation starts, that he's in one.

'Hey, Gary, what's up?'

'Fine. How are you? How was shopping? Get what you wanted, did you?'

Well, he's clearly not trying to hide his sarcasm. How did he even know I was shopping? And where is this attitude coming from? Could this be a ploy to get out of our date? As much as I've been looking forward to today, it really won't take too much of an excuse for me to abandon my struggle with this dress.

'If you've got something on your mind, Gary, just say it, okay?'

'I'm just asking you how your shopping trip was. Did Tyrone help you choose an outfit then?'

'Tyrone?' Oh oh. Actually, no oh oh. I've done nothing wrong.

'Yes, Tyrone. I saw you and him shopping together down Oxford Street earlier today. You've never mentioned that you knew him.'

'Was I supposed to?' He remains silent, but the silence says so much more than words could. 'Not that I owe you any explanation, but we happened to bump into each other and as we were walking in the same direction we decided to walk together. Is that a new crime that I'm not aware of?' My voice is rising slightly. I'm not sure why I'm getting worked up. I haven't done anything wrong, yet I'm feeling unusually defensive. He must sense my temper rising because he immediately backs down.

'I'm sorry, Jess. I didn't mean to sound like I was interrogating you. It's just I saw you, and you were both so engrossed, you couldn't even see me trying to catch your attention from the bus. I even phoned you and you didn't answer so I thought you were deliberately ignoring me.'

'Did it occur to you that maybe I didn't hear it? Contrary to popular belief it's not glued to my ear at all times, you know. It was probably at the bottom of my bag and with all the other stuff buried in there, most of the time I can't even feel it vibrating.'

'I know, I know. I'm just being irrational.'

Who's he telling! 'You have no reason to be. As I said, we met by chance and I gave him my opinion on a pair of jeans. Besides, you know what I'm like when I go shopping, Gary. Would you have wanted to trek around with me?' I can hear the cogs in his head turning as rationality starts to take hold and the picture of me trying on a zillion outfits while he patiently watches forms in his head. 'Exactly.

So jump back out of my throat because there really isn't room for you and my tonsils down there.'

He has the good grace to sound like the sorry idiot he must now feel like. 'Jess, I'm an idiot.'

I'm glad we agree on something.

'Let me make it up to you later. I promise you'll like the way I beg for forgiveness.'

I'm still annoyed with him for trying to give me the third degree and part of me wants to tell him to take a hike. But the part of me that just can't throw away an opportunity to spend time with him has the stronger hold. I take a deep breath and curse myself under it for continuously being so pathetically feeble when it comes to this guy.

'Come on, Jess … Pretty please?'

It's the pretty please that does it. 'Okay, Gary. Just get your butt down here before I change my mind. You've got just over an hour to think of the best way to get your begging groove on because, believe me, I will make you beg.'

He laughs that soft laugh that never fails to make the hair on the back of my neck curl to attention. He blows me a kiss down the phone and we both hang up.

What was that all about? I'm not talking about the cross-examination from Gary – I can understand jealousy getting people a little riled. I'm talking about why I got so indignant rather than just spilling the whole truth. Not that I lied about Tyrone and I walking in the same direction, but I didn't make it clear that it was the same direction down several streets. I gave the impression that I just went into a shop with Tyrone to give him an opinion on jeans, but conveniently didn't elaborate on the fact that he then returned the favour by accompanying me into several others. I didn't even stop to think about my evasiveness with Gary, I just evased. You know what? I should just get ready instead of wasting time trying to figure out why Gary didn't cross my mind once when I was with Tyrone shopping for an outfit to go out with Gary in.

Anyway, I don't have to answer to Gary; he has a fiancée. And before she turns from fiancée to wife, we will be over. I will find the strength so help me. I will not be involved with this man after he takes those vows. I know I've already crossed the line getting involved with an 'involved' man, but the line where the involved man is married, is one that not even my little toe will cross.

I must admit, his reaction surprised me. I've never thought of Gary as the jealous type. He always seems so confident and self-assured, like no woman can get to him. More likely he's pissed because he thought I should have been at home prettying up for him. That's makes more sense actually. At the moment my life with men seems like a dodgem car ride: no particular direction, just all over the place. I'm going to roll with it for now and see how it goes.

Now, back to more pressing matters of the moment. The note for Martell and the babysitter are done. The gas is turned off, the hair tongs are unplugged. I hope I look okay. The dress I was determined to wear was just as determined not to be worn. When the split in the back split even more I knew there was just no more fighting the fact that I had to choose something else. I'm sure my whole wardrobe is on my bed right now. I'm not sure where he's taking me so I have to take into consideration warm yet cool yet comfortable yet sexy. Difficult as it was, I think I made the right choice when I found this little number lurking in the dark recesses of my wardrobe. It certainly goes with the new sandals. I think Tyrone liked them but I know Gary is going to love them. Actually, where is he? He should have been here at two; it's now ten past. It's not like we can spend whenever we want together so the least he could do is get to me on time. Why am I so agitated? Please don't tell me this is excitement I'm feeling because of a little afternoon out? Who am I kidding? Of course it's excitement. The shame of it. I can barely sit still. I need to calm down. Maybe a cup of coffee will help. I sure hope so, because the last thing I need right now is for him to know how his little visit is making me feel.

29

Gary

Gary slapped his forehead. Hard. He'd put his foot in it and had nearly spoiled the day before it had even started. He couldn't think what had come over him. He had acted like a jealous fool and it wasn't like him to let a woman see she could get to him like that. Seeing Jess up Oxford Street earlier with that guy had taken him by surprise. Made him a little bit schizoid; that was his only explanation for his behaviour. He'd only intended to casually mention he'd seen her.

He didn't do the jealousy thing. He was, after all, Gary Martin. Women were supposed to be jealous of him, not vice versa. But the minute he'd heard Jess's voice, he just couldn't keep the sarcasm out of his. He could kick himself for losing cool points. He hoped he'd managed to redeem himself by saying he'd make it up to her. He knew just how he was going to make it up to her, too. A holiday, just for the two of them, had been on his mind for a while. Now might be the perfect time to turn the idea into reality. Jess may have said that she and Tyrone were just harmlessly shopping, but it hadn't looked harmless to him. It had looked like Tyrone was staring more at Jess than in windows for jeans.

Gary even had the perfect reason for going away for a week: Pete Piper's wedding! Pete was finally tying the knot; after seven children he was doing it in Jamaica. He would tell Tia it was an all-lads-supporting-the-groom type hol and that would leave him free to take Jess along. He'd still have to find a way to persuasively pitch it to Jess, but luckily he knew which of her buttons to push. He'd ensure he pushed them all later. It was a skill he was pleased to know hadn't deserted him after three years dedication to one woman.

It was ironic that he'd seen Jess earlier. He had been taking a chance doing that last delivery because Tia, who thought he was out of London today, had a nosy friend who worked in the area.

Tia's friends were always telling her he was no good and that he'd never change, but she trusted him. Even more so since so many years had gone by and they hadn't found a single thing to back up their talk.

* * *

'Tia, why are you with him? Haven't you heard the stories about him?' Tia's friends chorused in unison.

'No, I haven't. What are these stories?' Tia sighed.

'Apparently he's got four different women.'

'Have you seen him with these four women?' Tia questioned patiently. This wasn't the first time her friends had told her a 'story' about Gary.

'Well ... not exactly,' replied friend one.

'Okay, with three of these women then?'

'Well ... not quite,' answered friend two.

'Have you seen him with even one of these women?'

'Well ... maybe not, but my friend works with a receptionist who knows the receptionist at his company who is the sister of the assistant who sits in the office next door to his and she said that he is constantly on the phone! All day!' friend three finished triumphantly.

'Hmm ... now let's see, he works in a delivery firm, people phone in delivery requests ...' Tia looked at her

177

friends who should have had the good grace to look shame-faced at their unfounded gossip. They did not. For them, the gossip mill was the foundation of all that was juicy. Truth was irrelevant.

★ ★ ★

Tia's trust was not something he wanted to lose but he was prepared to jeopardise it a little to counteract what was happening with Jess. The last thing he expected to see was Jess strolling happily along, swinging no doubt another pair of shoes, with another man. The urge to jump off the bus, run and wrap his arm around her shoulder and casually say something like, "What a surprise seeing you down here, Tyrone," was strong. Tyrone would definitely have got the not-so-subtle hint that Jess was not available. Damned bus driver. He had a good mind to report him for not stopping even though the bus stop had been empty and he'd rung the bell twenty times, but only after the bus had already passed the bus stop.

He knew he had no right to feel like that about Jess because he already had a woman, a fiancée to be precise. It was just that Jess was one of those women that had always seemed unattainable – like Tia. He could never resist that type of challenge. And now that he had attained her, he wasn't about to let the likes of Tyrone Powers steal her from under his nose. Call him selfish, he wouldn't argue.

Traffic! Why the hell was there still so much traffic on the road? Shouldn't lunchtime be over by now? Shit. He wasn't going to make it on time. It was bad enough that he'd upset Jess, but to make it worse it looked like he was going to be late. Jess knew that being late once in a while was unavoidable because of his situation, but it didn't stop her giving him the cold shoulder when it happened. Still, he had to admit, he liked the challenge of having to thaw out her chilly moods.

Tia was calm and uncomplicated; Jess was fiery and passionate. They were total opposites, which was why he had to have them both. The contrast between them complemented and satisfied him completely. The thought of giving either of them up didn't bear thinking about.

He was nearly at Jess's home now. Luckily he wasn't too late. Jess would be looking stunning as always. He hoped she would wear something high heeled. He was getting hard just thinking about her in a pair – and nothing else. There was no space outside her house to park up and do a grand gesture of sweeping her off her feet and kissing her senses away when she opened the door. Plenty of time for that later; for now, tooting his car horn to let her know he was waiting would have to do.

30

Jessica

Where oh where is he? Agitation seems to be bringing out the Shakespeare in me. It's a quarter past two now. Maybe drinking this coffee will help more than just constantly stirring it. I want to be composed when he gets here. I want to be ... Wait, is that the tooting of a car horn I hear?

I nearly spill the coffee all down my dress in my haste to rush to the door. I sprint to the door as fast as one can in five-inch heels and yank it open with unleashed anticipation.

'Can you hold this parcel for your neighbour, love? Tried ringing a few bells, but no answer. Figured if I honked me horn enough someone would come out to see what the ruckus was!'

ParcelForce guy's laugh sounds like a honking horn too. My heart nosedives into my stomach. I could happily kill the delivery man for raising my hopes. As I sign the delivery note, I hear another car horn. Not to be fooled twice, I don't even raise my eyes from the paper. The tooting becomes a little too persistent. It's him! Instinctively I know without even looking up. A big smile lights up my face. It's only when I see ParcelForce guy smiling back missing-front-toothlessly at me that I realise what my grin must be conjuring up in his mind. I shove the signed delivery note back into his hand and raise my eyebrow at him. As he turns to leave, I race back inside my house, grab my purse, take one last look in the mirror then I slam the front door behind me.

I can feel Gary's eyes undressing me as I waltz towards

his vehicle. As I slide into the passenger seat and turn to clip in my seatbelt, Gary's lips connect with mine. For the next few moments I feel like waterlogged bread, all soft and squishy. You know when you read those romantic books and the hero kisses the heroine and she's supposed to get all weak at the knees? Well, I can confirm that it's all true. Gary's kisses can really do that. The man makes me melt: the shame of it. When I open my eyes (yeah, somewhere along the line they closed) he's staring deep into them.

'That's the first part of my apology for earlier. I really am sorry, Jess.' For a moment, blindsided by the kiss, I don't know what the hell he's talking about. All I know is that he's forgiven. I smile back hoping that he'll think I'm smiling in acceptance of his apology rather than because I'm lost for words.

'So. Where are we going?' My voice sounds a little faint even to my ears, but I'm hoping Gary hasn't noticed. He's cocky enough as it is without knowing his kiss has knocked me for six.

'Ah ha!' he says gleefully and then we're off.

After that, the day turns out to be pretty much a blur, we have so much fun.

* * *

'That turn off sign says Richmond. That's where we're going, aren't we!'

Gary doesn't answer, just smiles mischievously and revs the car engine to go faster.

'Dancing Queen! Dancing Queen! Oh yeah!' Gary and Jess hit the high note together. A dog looking out of the window

of a passing vehicle jumps off the seat onto the floor and starts to whimper in fright.

'Ow, Gary, that hurt!' Jess shouts as Gary playfully hits her with a picnic tea towel. She throws a twig at him in retaliation and squeals as she runs off with him hot on her high-heeled heels.

'I'm tired now, Gary.' Jess plops down onto the grass short of breath.

'Up you get.' Gary pulls her back to her feet. He bends and hoists her onto his back.

'And to our left we see a big ... tree!' Gary commentates in an official voice as he carries Jess around the park.

'Kew Gardens, by piggy back – I like!' Jess giggles.

★ ★ ★

We end this most amazing afternoon, rolling around in a secluded grassy area doing adult stuff, and boy, do the sandals do the job! Gary takes his punishment, and me, like a real man! It's times like these that keep me in this thing even though I know it's the wrong thing to be in. He holds my hand as we walk back towards the car three whole hours later.

'Did I tell you that you look amazing? And those sandals! Are they what you bought today? Did you buy them for me?' All I can do is nod as he draws me near and rubs against me to emphasise again just how much he liked my shoes.

'You know what, Jess? You've put a spell on me. You must have. I don't normally do things like this.' He takes my hand and we start to walk towards the car again. I can see, as he squints up to the sun every so often and shakes his head slightly, that he really can't believe what we got up to today. I can just about believe it myself. I didn't know I still had it in me. Somewhere in my relationship with Bobby that side of me had been suppressed, to the point where I thought it had totally disappeared. Bobby would never chase me around the park or give me a piggyback ride. He'd probably say he was too tired or that I'd put on weight and was too heavy or something. Isn't it funny? When you ask a man whether you've put on weight because you're concerned, they don't want to tell you, but the minute they think your weight is going to concern them, then as free as a man from jail, the opinions just roll off their tongues. Thinking of Bobby, I've still got to meet him later this evening. Well, that's brought me back down to earth with a bump.

While we're cruising through traffic, I look over at Gary who's still looking thoughtful while trying to avoid a motor biker who's trying to manoeuvre past the car. I wonder what's going on behind those beautiful eyebrows.

'Jess. Come on holiday with me.'

'Holiday, Gary?' Now I wish I hadn't wondered. Talk about be careful what you wish for! A holiday? Together? I don't think that's a good idea.

'My friend is getting married in Jamaica in a few weeks. Why don't you come with me? It'll be just like today except, instead of just for a few hours, it'll be for a whole week. Doesn't that sound tempting? Come on Jess ...'

As he's talking, he's taken the opportunity of a traffic jam to put his arm over my shoulder and put his head next to mine, as if I'm supposed to imagine the scene as he must be picturing it in his head. The vision in my mind is not so much a sandy beach as a film credit roll which instead of listing actors is listing questions. What am I going to tell my son? What is Gary going to tell his fiancée? Why didn't he ask his fiancée? What happened to this being our last date? So many questions slowly moving down the screen in my head.

'Think about it, Jess.'

If only he knew just how much I've thought about it already in these past few seconds.

'We can work out the details; we can make this happen. Please just don't dismiss it, okay? All I ask is that you think about it.' He pushes out his bottom lip and gives me those puppy-dog eyes. Not that that's the reason for me not telling him 'No' right now. I just figure that a little time between his suggestion and my answer might at least soften it a little. I just smile at him. He obviously takes my response as positive instead of the delaying tactic that it is. I'm prepared to live with the mis-assumption. For today, anyway.

As we near my house, I'm thinking of the dash I've got do up those stairs to sweep the messy pile of clothes off the bed into a messy pile at the bottom of my wardrobe. Temporary fix, of course. Gary's phone rings. Instead of answering it straight away, he's staring at the screen like he's contemplating whether or not to let it go to the answer machine. Curiosity is killing me and also seems to get the better of him because he decides to answer. From the vague 'yes, no' answers he's giving, I can tell he's talking to the fiancée.

'Something's come up, Jess.'

From a man to a wimp in a matter of seconds. He hasn't even got the balls to tell me it's her. My first reaction is to fire all sorts of questions at him, just to see him squirm like the worm he has become, but I know how upset I'll get. I've got Bobby to see later, and I don't want to take the chance that my mood won't be back to normal in time. My second reaction to act nonchalant is the one I go with.

'Whatever, Gary.' I turn to climb out of the car intending to slam the door real hard behind me, but he gently holds my neck with one hand and kisses me. Hungrily. Angrily. Then softly. For a second my mind goes blank and I have to make a conscious effort to remember why I wanted to slam the car door.

'Don't be mad, Jess,' he says staring deep into my eyes 'If I didn't have to go, you know I wouldn't. Think about the holiday, okay?'

When he eventually drives off, I linger on the kerbside, inhaling the fumes that he left behind.

Wearily I go into my house. First place my eyes go to is the phone table, where my note to Martell has been replaced by a note from Angie, the babysitter. She's taken Martell to McDonalds, and then they're going to see a movie.

I walk upstairs and flop down on the mountain of clothes on my bed. I've got an unexpected couple of hours to kill now before Bobby gets here. My usual choice for a few hours in a child-free house would be to watch some mindless TV while soaking in my bath, but this holiday seems to have a strangle-hold on my concentration that not even Jerry Springer can distract. I know that this was supposed to be our last date, but I have to admit that I'm tempted by the idea of spending more than just a few hours at a time with Gary. But a whole week away? Out of the country? It just feels like we'd be going into a whole different realm of deceit. And what a tangled web that would start weaving. I can't seem to summon up any enthusiasm for it. Gary seems really keen on the idea. It's not going to be easy to get it across to him that I am not likeminded. Anyway, I told him I'd think about it and I will: tomorrow.

Right now, I need to find another pair of shoes to wear later. Not only are these sandals not appropriate for dinner with Bobby, but, if I wear them for even another two minutes, I will forfeit being able to wear any shoes at all for possibly the rest of my life. I've definitely got to come down a couple of inches if I want to get through the evening. Five-inch heels are so not for frolicking in the park. It would do me good to remember that in future. I think my red, padded-soled mules will do nicely, providing both comfort and less heel-ache. Only an inch and a half less, mind you, but three and a half inches compared to five is like putting on a pair of flatties. Perfect. It's amazing how a shoe can totally transform an outfit. As soon as I find the other one then I believe I'll be suitably de-sexyised for tonight.

Finding this shoe is not going to be as simple as just looking under the bed. Must remember to gather up some of Martell's school work too, so that Bobby knows that he's still a part of the decision-making process regarding his son, even though he rarely makes any decisions. I'll put it in my bag to whip out at a moment's notice. I don't know what Bobby's plan is for tonight, but I'm sure Martell will be high on the agenda, as well as various derogatory remarks about me being the ruination of his life. Actually, I'm being unfair. He didn't seem hostile on the phone the other day. In fact, he was quite amenable;

he even told me to wear something nice as I recall. That was an unexpectedly civil thing to hear him say since our previous conversation had ended with him hating me. Oh, there's the door. It's too early for Bobby and I'm not expecting anyone. It'd better not be Martell getting Angie to bring his little behind back here to ask if he can have toffee popcorn. He'll never sit down for the whole film if he eats it. There's something in the toffee that makes him hyper, because plain popcorn he's fine with. He and Angie always seem to end up doing that child-adult battle thing.

* * *

'But toffee popcorn is my favourite, Angie!' Martell whined.

'Thought hotdogs was your favourite.' Angie continued reading the film reviews to decide which one to get tickets for.

'It's toffee popcorn.' Martell fixed his mouth obstinately.

'Well, you can't have it. It makes you hyper.'

'But it's a new type of toffee in the popcorn.'

'You can't have it. It makes you hyper.'

'But it didn't last time!'

'It did.'

'No, that was just me being excited.' Martell folded his arms.

'It wasn't.' Angie paid for their tickets without even looking at him.

'It was!' Martell stamped his foot.

Angie looked at him sternly. 'Martell, you can't have it.'

'I want to ask Mum.' Martell folded his arms again.

'She'll say no.' Angie pursed her lips knowingly.

'She might not.'

'Okay. Call her.' Martell took Angie's phone and dialled his home. Jess picked up the phone almost immediately.

'Mum, can I have toff...,' Martell started

'No,' Jess replied before he finished.

'But ...'

'No. And do not dial this number to ask me about anything toffee-related again.'

Martell handed Angie back the phone. 'Can I have a hotdog, please, Angie?'

It took a great effort for Angie not to smile in triumph over a nine-year old.

* * *

When did 'No' stop being 'No' to these kids? It would be just like him to twist Angie around his finger and get her to bring him all the way back so he could ask me about that stupid toffee popcorn but technically not via a phone call. Hmm, no. Not even he would be that stupid. Whoever it is can wait. My shoe is my priority right now.

31

Bobby

Bobby couldn't recall a time when he'd felt this nervous. Maybe his first job interview when he was sixteen. Tonight everything had to go perfectly. Restaurant booked – check. Shirt crease free – check. Nails not bitten down to the cuticle – check. This dinner was the perfect opportunity for a fresh start with Jess. If everything went to plan she'd soon forget he'd ever said he hated her. Well, if not quite forget, maybe relegate it to a vague memory.

He wasn't sure how he was going to handle this; it would be the first time seeing her since her break-up speech. The restaurant was a really nice one so that should help the atmosphere anyway. Melinda had suggested it, said it had ambience. He'd wanted to book the restaurant that he and Jess had never quite managed to get to – Galleon something de something or another – but not knowing the proper name made that difficult. Probably a good thing too. That dinner was clearly never destined to be a good one, and he really didn't want anything bad to happen tonight. In fact just the opposite was what he was hoping for. Melinda's restaurant, a Thai restaurant called Chic, sounded ideal.

So the venue was taken care of. Now, what to do when the waiter took their order and went off to get it cooked? Did he launch straight into apologies and declarations of doing better next time?

Bobby looked deep into Jess's eyes and reached across the table for her hand. 'Jess, what can I say? I'm sorry. I'll clean the house from top to bottom with a toothbrush, I'll give Martell Mandarin lessons on the weekends and I'll build you an extension with a glass ceiling with my bare hands. This I promise to you.'

Or did he style it out with some polite general chit chat?

Bobby leaned back in his chair and surveyed his surroundings nonchalantly. 'So Jess, how've you been? Cool? I read an interesting book the other day about caterpillars.'

Whichever direction the conversation took, he wanted to be able glean from it how receptive Jess would be for a reconciliation. He had finally realised the magnitude of what Jess had put up with him for years. It was going to take an amazing feat to banish those memories.

Martell would actually be the perfect starter – after the shrimp, of course. Their son was a neutral conversation piece, not only important to both of them, but the most important link between them too. Martell was going to help him and Jess get back together and didn't even know it. His eyes softly glazed over as he thought of his son. He couldn't wait to see him. It had only been a few days, but he missed him so much already. He'd have to spend some time with him as priority. He was beginning to feel really guilty for not having spoken to him since he walked out of the house nearly a week ago. He didn't want his son to feel like he was in the middle of his parents' issues. With any luck, those issues just might be sorted before it had any effect on him at all. He just had to stick with David's plan.

* * *

'Now,' David instructed as he leaned forward to emphasise the point he was about to make. 'There's no need to come down too hard on yourself when you're apologising. She already knows why she thought it had to end, so dinner's not the best place to remind her by spouting off declarations of being a selfish idiot.'

Bobby made a mental note to scratch that out of his conversation. The whole first thirty minutes of it would need to be re-written.

'You've got to big yourself up,' David continued. 'Remind her of all the good times you had.'

Bobby made a mental note to add that to his conversation. The whole last five minutes of it now needed to be looked at again.

* * *

Melinda, on the other hand, advised something completely different.

* * *

'If I was you in this situation, I would acknowledge my faults. You're only human. Let her know that you underestimated the extent of the issues, even though she'd told you time, and time, and time ...' Melinda turned and winked at him when she emphasised this bit, '... again, you foolishly brushed it under the carpet.' Melinda paced up and down with her hands clasped behind her back as she spoke, quite similar in manner to Bobby when he paced. He nodded and repeated to himself '... foolishly brushed ...'

'Let her know you're ready to clean under that carpet now, so don't hold back on what you didn't do.'

Bobby repeated to himself, '... don't hold back,' and

wondered whether a note pad at this stage would serve him better than his memory.

★ ★ ★

Between the two of them he was either going to spurt out stuff like an agony uncle for a magazine or get so confused that he'd be all tongue tied. Then Jess would really think yep, he was an idiot and that her decision was the best one after all. He figured he should just lay off too much talking about the past and let his future actions speak for themselves. Words hadn't worked too well for him so far, so not much logic taking that route again.

There were still two hours to go before he was due to pick Jess up. He doubted he'd be able to sit still for that long. He'd nearly worn a pathway in David's carpet with all his pacing up and down so far. He'd been staying there since he'd walked out, even though Melinda had offered to put him up.

★ ★ ★

'You can stay here if you want, Bobby, as long as you need to. There's plenty of room as you can see.' Melinda smiled and made a sweeping gesture to show all the space around her.

'My mate David is putting me up, but if he gets fed up of me borrowing his aftershaves, you just may hear from me.'

Melinda nodded understandingly. If only she knew how hard it had been for him to decline the offer. He wondered again if he wanted Jess back for the right reasons, and again he put the thought aside, reaffirming to himself that any reason was the right reason.

★ ★ ★

Waking up in Mel's bed, as innocent as it was had been, had nearly given him a coronary; a bit too close to Going Too Far for his comfort.

Temptation might not let him off the hook so easily next time. He was, after all, a man, and she was, after all, all woman; best to limit nights at her house to the one of the party.

Too much time on his hands was responsible for the tawdry path his thoughts had taken. He should just go and pick up Jess, because that's where his thoughts needed to be. He wouldn't even call first in case she told him she wasn't ready. That would give him no choice but to pick her up at the arranged time and leave him wearing an even bigger path into his mate's shag pile. Transportation was sorted in the form of David's rental.

* * *

'Course you can borrow my courtesy car, mate.' David threw Bobby the keys.

'A courtesy? Where's Monty?'

'In the garage, mate. I only went and reversed into a bollard, didn't I?' David rolled his eyes.

Bobby laughed, 'That wasn't too clever. How'd you explain that plonker move to the insurance company?'

'Told them I was hit and run from behind. I'm fully comp anyway.'

Bobby thought about this explanation and frowned. 'If you're fully comp why not just tell them about the bollard? Wouldn't make a difference, would it?'

David grinned. 'If you'd heard the sexy voice of the insurance assistant that took my details, believe me mate, the story made a difference!'

Now where were those car keys? David had been a saint for him throughout this situation, but payback was going to be a bitch. He was a good friend, but with him it was always a favour for a favour. So far, favours he'd be indebted to David for involved his home, his wheels and his on-tap tailored advice. His repayment of these favours would, without doubt, have to reciprocate fittingly, and, if he knew his friend, it'd be a big one. Still, if it got him back with Jess, he'd happily repay his debt twice.

A Citroen ZX. Not bad for a courtesy car. At least he wouldn't have to squeeze himself into a Corsa, which meant he'd be crease free when he reached Jess. Traffic wasn't too bad either for a Friday evening. So far, the elements of fate seemed to be on his side.

It didn't take him long to get to Jess's. In his efforts to be fashionably early, instead of nervously early, he'd stuck to the speed limits all the way. He'd even stopped to buy some spur-of-the-moment flowers from a man selling them on the roadside. Unfortunately it hadn't significantly delayed his earliness. There was still over an hour to spare and that could definitely be classed as nervously early. Maybe he could say he came early to see Martell. Yeah, that sounded ideal, even though Jess had already told him he'd be with Angie, his babysitter. He could just use the universal excuse of forgetfulness. Or would that be too lame? There was no way he could sit in the car for an hour. He'd go crazy. At least at David's flat there was space to pace, not just sit and switch radio stations. Fuck it. He'd made a decision to come early, so he'd deal with whatever that meant to Jess when he had to.

He got out the car and walked up to the door. It was

weird not to feel free to just push his key in the door like he normally would. The doorbell hadn't been working for months. Something else Jess had been on at him for ages to fix that he'd never quite got around to. Now that he had to use it to attract her attention inside, he could appreciate her annoyance with him. Good thing you didn't get such mechanical problems with doorknockers; that had always been in good working order, or should he say banging order. Jess always got pissed when people banged it too hard. He hesitated. This had been his home just a few days ago; it felt too strange. Maybe he should phone her to let her know he'd arrived instead. That was as good as ringing the doorbell or knocking the door these days according to David.

* * *

'Making a call is the way to let them know you're outside, my friend,' David said matter-of-factly. 'Actually, I can't remember the last time I met a date at her front door. Scratch that; I can't even remember when I left my car to meet a date!'

With the amount of dates David had and the number of calls he probably had to make to announce his arrival, it wasn't a surprise that he had a spare mobile to lend Bobby.

* * *

Bobby made a mental note to remember to collect his own mobile from Jess before they headed out. Luckily he'd not been in a talking mood for obvious reasons, otherwise he didn't know how he'd have managed to survive the last few days without it. He was being silly. He would just do the normal visitor thing and knock; technically he was now a visitor. A vision of Meddling Mary from next door peeping through her curtains, watching him knock at what used to be his own front door, flowers in one hand, mobile phone in the other, filled his mind. She would put two and two together and correctly come up with four. He quickly knocked the door again. Because having to wait for three seconds made his vision of Meddling Mary even stronger, he knocked again. And again. After five more seconds his agitation, which was speedily reaching crisis point, made him reach for the knocker again. Before the metal could connect with the wood, the door suddenly swung open.

32

Jessica

The doorknocker again? Give a girl a chance to get to the door, can't you? I look out of the window and nearly fall out of it in surprise. That can't be Bobby already? He's not supposed to be here for another hour and I'm still looking for this damned shoe. And what's with that constant knocking? If I don't answer that door for no other reason than to stop that infernal knocking, I may just knock him out to stop it instead.

I limp to the door; wearing only one shoe has left a four-inch difference in height between my right and left foot. I wrench open the front door with such force that the breeze created gives me that haven't-quite-found-the-time-to-drag-a-comb-through-my-hair-yet look.

'Bobby. Hello. You're early.' I just about snap out my acknowledgement before turning on my heel. I don't mean to be curt but I really need to find my other shoe.

'Hi. How are you? And nice to see you – to you too.'

'Sorry. I'm looking for my other shoe. I hope that son of yours hasn't been playing "I'm a tall basket-baller" in my shoes again or you are so going to be childless. He nearly broke his little neck playing ball in a pair of my heels last time.' Martell was always Bobby's son when I felt he'd been up to no good. 'I've been looking for this shoe for the past twenty minutes. Where the hell can it be?' I'm starting to uproot furniture now. Cushions are going to be next to fly across this room.

'How come you're here so early anyway?' I ask with my head buried behind the sofa for the third time.

'I thought I'd hang out with Martell for a bit, but remembered just before I knocked the door that you said he wouldn't be here. Jess? Jess!'

As his shout penetrates my concentrated search, I stop with the armchair cushion in mid hurl and look over at him.

'Here's an idea. Might it not be quicker, not to mention tidier, if you maybe just put on a pair where you've got both shoes to hand? Get it? Shoes to hand?' He gives a nervous laugh. As I drop the cushion to put my hands on my hips and turn to tell him that it might also be an idea for him to help me look, I notice the bunch of flowers. My words come to an abrupt stop on the edge of my tongue. Instead I raise my eyebrow to ask the silent question.

He understands straight away. It is uncanny how a man can get a silent message, but when you tell him something out loud he acts like he doesn't have a clue.

'The flowers? Oh, they're for you. They caught my eye and I thought they'd look nice in the living room.' He shrugs his shoulders nonchalantly, but I can see the half-smile and the little beam in his eye. Please don't tell me that he thinks this dinner is something more than just catch-up? Okay, damage control.

'Thanks Bobby; you shouldn't have. Dinner was a good suggestion, we can catch up about family stuff. We both know I hate cooking on a Friday so eating and discussing at the same time ...' I give a little half-smile.

'Yeah, yeah, of course. I know that. What other reason could there be?' He makes a screwy face and shrugs his shoulders.

He always does that when he's trying to pretend that something is nothing to him, when really it is.

I go into the kitchen to look behind the cooker for the shoe and casually continue, 'Yep, just food. Just eating and catching up about current affairs. No celebration for winning the lottery, or even something way out there like me becoming the president's wife or us getting back together.' I'm hoping that will register and stick in his mind for later. I force a laugh as I walk back into the living room and try to budge the bookshelf so I can search behind there for my shoe. Thinking of food has made me realise that I'm actually quite hungry. I didn't get much eating done today. It just may be a good thing Bobby's here early after all.

I continue my shoe-hunting process with an exaggerated sigh, hoping that he'll get the hint to join in the search too. And if more searching will help distract me from my ever-growing hunger pangs then it's all good. Seems like Bobby's taken the hint because he starts looking behind the small armchair. I don't mention the fact that I've looked there three times already.

'But it's not that way out, is it?' he says thoughtfully. I give him a muffled, 'Huh?' as I am now on my knees trying to reach deep behind the cabinet. At this point, any normal person would give it up and throw on another pair of shoes. But for me it has become more than just looking for a missing shoe. It's a case of, hungry or not, I will find this shoe and wear it tonight or die trying.

'Is us getting back together such a way out idea? I mean, even now we can go out together and enjoy a meal, just like we used to. In fact maybe ...'

I can feel him gathering momentum. I know exactly where this little speech is going and before he can move it into second gear I cut into his sentence with an alternative ending. '… maybe I should just get another pair of shoes. I am feeling a little peckish now. Give me two minutes,' I blurt out, turning and limping out of the room.

It's probably for the best that I couldn't find that shoe. Just from waltzing up and down the house in this single shoe, my foot is killing me. The near stilettos I wore earlier have finished me in terms of heels for tonight. It's got to be flats. Well, two inches flatter at least; got to think of the whole ensemble and any less than that will not work. If only Bobby knew how starved I feel right now, he'd be scared because I am likely to eat his wallet away. I am so going to be a pig tonight; I don't care who sees me. Just the same, if I'm going to be a pig, it's got to be in appropriate shoes.

Upstairs, I kick off the one mule and slip my feet into lower sandals. I sigh as comfort caresses my feet. Trying my hardest not to let my enthusiasm for food get ahead of me, I force myself to walk back downstairs in a ladylike way, instead of taking them two by two, and calmly say to Bobby, 'I'm ready. Where are we going?'

'Aha!' he says.

What is it with all the mystery locations today? First Gary, now Bobby. I really hope that this sudden similarity between them is where it starts and ends. I am too hungry to deal with anything more than that. In response I just smile, one of those all wide lips and no teeth smiles, and grab my keys from the side table.

As we walk down the street, I automatically walk towards my car. Not because I particularly want to drive, but because Bobby doesn't have one and with the amount of food I intend to pack away this evening, I don't fancy waddling in search of London Transport when I'm done.

'I'll drive,' he throws over his shoulder.

With what keys? I silently throw back. Then, there it is, the bright lights indicating the remote unlocking of what looks like a Citroen. A really nice Citroen ZX to be precise. I am itching to ask where it came from. At the same time I'm wondering whether I am allowed to ask him his business. Will the question be a prime opportunity for him to tell me it's none of mine? It's going to be a complicated evening if I've got to question every question I want to ask with a question.

'Nice car, Bobby.' I compliment him instead.

'Thanks. Borrowed it from a friend.' He answers the question I didn't ask. 'Hope it's okay, me turning up early.' If only he knew just how okay it is. I'm so hungry that if I talk it'll get worse. I want to open my mouth as little as possible until the moment I'm stuffing food into it, so I nod and smile.

We drive in silence. Not because of any awkwardness (well, not on my part anyway) but because Bobby doesn't say anything to me, and I gladly go along with that. I thought it'd feel a bit weird, but for some reason it doesn't. I sneak a look at Bobby and he's got a small crease on his forehead. He always gets that little crease when he's thinking hard about something. I'm not about to ruin his concentration, I'm just thankful for it. I take the opportunity to turn up the music slightly, not because I like the tune but more because I want it to drown out the sound effects coming from my abdomen. Hopefully it's not so loud as to break into his train of thought, but loud enough to cover anything I might 'break out'.

I'm beginning to feel faint for want of food. How could I let the day pass by and have only eaten one ice-cream cone? Half of one ice-cream cone actually, because Gary had his fair share of it: mostly the ice-cream, mostly off me. I know now that woman can not live on loving alone. Frolicking in the park takes energy, and energy takes food. I hope it's not some dainty restaurant where the food is just plate decoration. I'll die if it's a sea food restaurant. I don't think my stomach could handle the time it would take to delicately make sure I don't swallow a fishbone. I made that mistake once when I went to a fish restaurant with Maddy and ordered Skate.

* * *

'Maddy, I am so hungry! I can't even remember when I last ate!' Jess gobbled the fish dish down, hardly chewing it as it passed her lips. Skate was her favourite.

'Chew, girl, chew!' Maddy shook her head at her friend, as she delicately placed a tiny morsel of food in her mouth.

Suddenly Jess started to point frantically to her mouth.

'Yes, I can see your mouth is full; everyone can see that.' Maddy shook her head again and cut another morsel. Hunger was no excuse for bad table manners. Jess started to bang the table and point to her throat. When Maddy looked up she noticed her friend was an odd shade of blue. Something was stuck in Jess's throat!

'Help! Someone help my friend! She's CHOKING!!!' Maddy dropped her knife and fork and started running all over the restaurant waving her arms above her head in panic. The diner at the next table jumped up and grabbed Jess around her chest and lifted her up repeatedly.

'Hgh … huh … HGH!' A bone flew out of Jess's mouth and onto the plate of her saviour. The whole restaurant went silent, then burst into a rapturous round of applause.

People were slapping the diner on the back in congratulation and fanning Maddy with menus, as if it were she that had nearly lost her life.

'Waiter,' Jess said breathlessly after gulping down a few pints of air. 'And another plate of whatever he was eating – hold the fishbone.'

* * *

An expensive night that had cost me more in embarrassment than anything else. I shudder just thinking about it. Fish is not going to be on my menu tonight, even if it's the only thing on the menu. Tonight I just want meat and plenty of it. I'm so hungry I can't think of anything else.

'Are we nearly there?' That's more words than I intended before eating. All this motion on an empty stomach is making me feel queasy. I hope I didn't sound too snappish. I offer another all lip no teeth smile to take off any edge that might have been on my abruptness.

'Yes, I'm just looking for parking.' My heart, along with my belly, immediately lifts. It's good to know Bobby wasn't just placating me because, sixty seconds later, he's pulling into a parking space. As we get out of the car he waits for me to walk around to his side and then puts his hand in the small of my back to guide me in the direction of the mystery restaurant. I raise my eyebrow at this because normally he'd just slam the car door on his side, wait for me to slam mine, then wait for me to fall into step with him. This hand on my back thing is not the norm, but not wanting to rock the boat before it sets sail, I don't say anything or move away. I'm actually glad of the support because this hunger is liable to take the strength from my legs.

Chic is the name over the door we go through, but the décor is definitely oriental. Hallelujah, we are eating Chinese! I literally have to restrain myself from grabbing his hand from my back, swinging him round and hugging him. I mean, everybody knows that there is nothing like a Chinese meal when you're hungry. The menu always has just about everything you could ever need to keep your jaws going indefinitely. Please, please let it be a buffet: an eat as much as you like buffet. Oh, there's the magic sign! Eat As Much As You Like – One Price (Drinks Not Included). My pace quickens and before I can stop myself, I have walked straight to the little reception desk and blurted out, 'Name of Robert Phillips – table for two.' As the words trip over my tongue in their haste to get out, I can feel the shame of what hunger has just made me do. I don't even have to look up because I can feel Bobby raising his eyebrows at my blatant disregard of being-taken-to-a-restaurant etiquette. I slowly turn to face him, do a little two-step dance, and mouth the word 'Toilet' to him. He looks at me for a few seconds and then smiles and nods his understanding. Saved by the little ladies room, that universal, all-encompassing, excuse to excuse a variety of behaviours.

I turn and run off to the toilet. All I do when I get there is look at my reflection, twiddle my earrings and wash my hands to take up some time. As I'm as hollow as an Easter egg, that's the best I can do. When I think enough time has passed to make it look like I genuinely had to use this facility, I speed walk back to the main eating hall and do a quick scan of the room. First thing that catches my eye is the selection: vast equals good. I also see that it's busy, a good indication that the food is good, which is a good indication that my hunger issues will soon be resolved. I see Bobby over on the edge of a group of tables, conveniently close to the buffet. He waves a plate at me to get my attention. I don't need any more encouragement to make a bee-line towards him, nearly knocking a massive bowl of rice from the hands of a lady who, by the size of her, looks like she's maybe had enough already.

'I thought I'd wait for you to get back so that we could go to the buffet together.'

I barely notice his smile and his attempt at togetherness as I grab the plate from him and proceed to load my plate like this is my last chance before a famine. Singapore noodles, special fried rice, a few spare ribs, a couple of chicken wings and some strands of seaweed on the side. I definitely need another plate specifically for the duck and pancakes. I look wildly around and underneath the food counter I see a stack of plates. I lay my filled plate in a gap in the serving area, hoping that nobody makes the grave mistake of mistaking it for part of the selection on offer. Onto my second plate goes some duck, four pancakes, some sliced spring onion and a huge dollop of plum sauce. Hmm, there's still some space on this plate and it seems a shame to waste it so I add a couple of mini spring rolls and a pork dumpling with batter.

I can feel Bobby staring at me, but I'm not concerned because this is a Chinese buffet so piling my plates mountain high is totally allowed. I know he's mumbling something at me in the background, but I can barely make him out due to the sizzling pan of some kind of fried beef that has just been brought over. I'm definitely going to give that a try second trip.

I look at Bobby and nod and smile like I really know

what he was just talking about. I'm still nodding and smiling as I head back to the table to tuck in.

That's about as far as I went with contributing to the communicational aspect of the night. I did most of the eating and Bobby did most of the talking. I can't truthfully say I heard all he was saying because my ears were full of my own munching. Crispy batter is really crunchy stuff.

I assume that some of the conversation somewhere along the line was about Martell, and I think that may have been during my second helping of Singapore fried rice and lemon chicken. I figure this because I particularly remember saying 'mm hmm' and nodding quite a lot. Only talking about our baby would make me do that to the extent that I was doing it. In all honesty my concentration was wholly taken by food; Bobby's conversation really only just grazed the periphery of my consciousness.

By the time I finish my fourth plateful, consisting of beef in black bean sauce, sweet and sour pork and plain steamed rice, Bobby is looking at me in astonishment.

'I forgot just how much you can pack away when you're hungry!' he laughs and, because I actually took in what he said this time, I laugh too. So far, all I've been taking in is lots and lots of food. I swear Chinese food must be water-based or something. I'm amazed that you can just eat and eat, be full, and then, ten minutes later, be good to go again.

Six platefuls later, we're sipping on coffee and indulging in general chit chat. Bobby seems even more friendly and receptive now than when we first got here. He really must have enjoyed the meal because I haven't seen him behave like this since we first met and he was trying to impress me. All in all, it's actually turning out to be a nice night. Not tense and uncomfortable at all. The only thing that's gotten heavy is the weight of this food, which is now beginning to take its toll on my gut.

Bobby looks at his watch, which prompts me to look at mine. Eleven thirty pm! Oh my gosh! Time sure flies when you're at starvation's door. We look at each other and I know he's thinking what I'm thinking. It's late.

'Shall we go or do you want to get a doggy bag first?' he smirks.

I give him a dirty look to let him know that I know that was his not so subtle dig at me trying to single-handedly eat the restaurant. Like I care.

'The sign virtually instructed me to eat as much as I like, and I liked everything,' I justify myself haughtily.

He laughs and puts his hands in the air indicating surrender and then points to the door.

Outside, the first thing I do is deeply breathe in the slightly chilled night air as I wait for Bobby to pay the bill. I did offer to contribute – as you do – but he just wasn't having it. I'm still surprised how nice this evening's turned out to be. I had serious doubts that we'd be able to go out and have such a good time so soon after The Break-Up.

He soon joins me and puts his hand in the small of my back again. As we walk to the car, there's a thoughtful silence between us. His silence is probably due to the fact that he got a lot of talking in tonight without interference from me. Mine is due to the fact that I think I overate.

We get into the car and the silence continues. I turn up the radio slightly to once again camouflage any potential sound effects from stuffing my face. In addition I also wind down the window slightly, just in case I create an excess of air due to excess eating. No point in taking chances. The journey home is much quicker, for which I am thankful.

My stomach is playing up again. Gee, when I go to pig out, I really make a sow out of me. I wind down the window a little more, so I can get more air. I'm beginning to feel a little nauseous.

'You okay?' Bobby looks over at me, a little concerned, probably more for the car than me. In fact, this is very reminiscent of the last time I felt queasy on our way back home from somewhere. A concert, I believe it was, and the cause of quease? A not so hot hot-dog.

★ ★ ★

'Bobby … I don't feel so great.' Jess groaned holding her stomach.

'I told you not to eat that sausage. The seller himself didn't look too healthy either.'

'I think we need to stop.' Jess practically had her head out of the window.

'We'll be home soon. Just keep taking deep breaths.' Bobby sounded annoyed. It was mid-winter, his team had just lost and he just wanted to get home.

'Ooh … Bobbeee …' Jess swayed in her seat. Bobby recognised the cry instantly and slammed on the brakes. As the car halted with a screech, he jumped out and hauled Jess out with him. The shock of the cold air immediately made Jess's nausea subside.

'I think I'm okay now, we can go.' Jess shivered and attempted to get back into the car. Bobby, who was now warmly sitting inside, pushed down the lock to prevent her entry.

'Nope. Not yet.'

'Huh? Why not? I'm feeling better.' Jess was confused and started tugging at the door handle.

'You haven't been sick yet. I just spent nearly fifty quid getting this car valeted three days ago. Let's just be sure before we take off again, eh.' Bobby was adamant.

Jess looked at him incredulously. 'What? Let me in, Bobby!' She angrily shook the door.

Bobby shook his head and refused to budge. It was twenty minutes, and a dramatic act of up-chucking from a frozen Jess before Bobby was convinced his gleaming seats would not be soiled.

★ ★ ★

It was two weeks and four chilblains before I spoke to him again. Well, I'm certainly not freezing my behind off tonight.

'I'm fine, just a little full.'

'Just a little!' he laughs. I turn my back on him and pretend that the view out of the window is one of panoramic splendour.

'Okay, a lot. Just step on it, please.' I can feel the seat vibrating with the soundless humour that he's obviously trying to contain. So I ate a little too much. It was an honest miscalculation that any very hungry person could have made.

We finally pull up outside my house, and not a minute too soon. I jump out before the car even stops properly and head determinedly to my front door. All I'm thinking is that as soon as my key turns and opens the door, I'm heading straight to the kitchen to down at least a gallon of water and hope that settles my stomach a little. As I push the key in, Bobby calls out to me.

'Jess?' I take a deep breath, turn and look over my shoulder showing my toothless smile in answer.

'Thanks, okay. You won't regret it. I'll call you when

I've got some details.' Then he blows me a kiss and drives off. Huh? He blew me a kiss …? Suddenly I'm dumbstruck and really nervous because I don't know what the hell he's talking about or what has happened between leaving my house and returning for him to be blowing me kisses. He really must have had a good time tonight. What won't I regret? What details? Oh damn, what did I not hear but nod to because I was busy munching? I need to think, I need to think. I quickly turn back to the door, finish turning the key and head straight to the kitchen as originally planned. Fridge for water; freezer for ice. Got to settle this stomach so that I can think clearly.

Three glasses of ice-cold Evian later, something is vaguely coming back to me. I think he must have said something in between the plate of sweet chicken balls and the chicken with mushroom. If it wasn't at that point then it had to have been in between the chicken noodles and the chicken chop suey. Those are the only times I can think of where I really zoned out, because I love Chinese chicken. Those dishes had my full attention. Shit, shit, shit. I need to remember. Okay, this calls for something a little stronger to get my memory cells going. This calls for vodka. It's not my favourite drink but it should shock my taste buds back to the dinner table and hopefully back to whatever the hell was said. On second thoughts, maybe I should just ask him? Actually, on third thoughts, maybe I should just stick with the vodka idea.

I go to the drinks cabinet, well, actually, it's more like a little see through box in the corner of the room, and struggle to break the seal on the unopened bottle of vodka. Anyone could see that I am not a practised drinker by my fumbling attempt.

Okay, bottle now opened, I pour and down it in one gulp like an alcoholic. I nearly spit it back out in one gulp too, because it burns my throat. I give it a couple of seconds to settle into my system as if it's some secret memory enhancer. I'm even squinting with concentration, waiting for … for … something. Oh gosh … oh gosh … Something's happening alright. So much for nearly spitting this stuff out, I think it's going to come out all on its own, and with company too. I sprint up the stairs two by two and throw myself over the toilet seat just in time for it to catch the vodka and various regurgitated parts of the buffet menu. This upsurgence of food continues for about ten minutes, making a mockery of the hours it took to eat it. As I sit, sprawled listlessly on the bathroom floor, like magic, just why Bobby said what he did, pops straight into my head.

* * *

Jess was busily chewing on a crispy chicken wing, and boy was it crispy! Bobby was staring at her intensely but she barely acknowledged this as she concentrated on tackling the wing.

'Let's have a go again. It'll be better this time.' Bobby smiled.

Jess gave him a big smile and nodded enthusiastically. She couldn't agree more!

* * *

Food being the only thing on my mind at the time, I thought he meant we should go back up to the buffet table, because the second helping of food was going to be even nicer, which is why I said, yes. And I agreed to it. There was I thinking I'd cut that idea off at the jugular earlier on; thinking that it was plain old let's-be-friends that got us through the night without the slightest disagreement when all the time it was because he believed it was the start of let's-be-more-than-friends again. I've done the thing that I was so sure I wouldn't do: agreed to a reconciliation.

33

Jessica

I've been getting a bad vibe about this holiday since Gary first mentioned it. The day is now here and I still don't feel any better about it. After my double-date night with Bobby and Gary, I should have called my sister instead of Maddy. I just know Tania would have re-affirmed what common sense was already telling me.

* * *

'Sis, do NOT board a plane with that man. It'll be more than jumping from the frying pan into the fire; it'll be from the pool into the ocean. Mark my words, if you go no good will come of it.' Tania fancied herself as fortune teller at times. Jess could just imagine her wagging her finger and shaking her head at the other end of the phone.

* * *

But oh no. I had to have a second thought and I speed dialled Maddy's number instead.

* * *

'But you said you wanted to go to Jamaica ages ago! You said you needed a holiday. The Lord answers your prayer and now you want to tell him "No thank you?"' Maddy really had a way with words and looking at it like that, she had come up with a significant point.

'I suppose it would be churlish of me to deny what is clearly the will of a higher power, wouldn't it?' Jess rubbed her chin thoughtfully.

'Ask and ye shall receive. It's right there in that Great Book, chapter ... chapter ... The point is, it's there in black and white!'

'By Jove, you're right! Who am I to refute my holy destiny, if it leads to Jamaica?' Jess was now caught up in Maddy's fervour.

'Hallelujah!' they both shouted in unison.

★ ★ ★

All the holiday plusses that seemed to override my initial objections have now faded into oblivion. The negative vibe that I first felt is back with a vengeance. Even Martell's been hinting nearly every day for the past week that he doesn't want me to go.

★ ★ ★

'But why do you have to go, Mum?' Martell looked at Jess with sorrowful eyes. It didn't seem appropriate to use to use the holy justification that had seemed so apt with Maddy.

'I just need a break, sweetie. You know holidays are a good way to relax and rejuvenate.' Jess hoped the big word would sound official enough to throw her son off questioning her much more. She didn't want to sink to the depths of lying to her son.

'But you went on holiday a few months ago. Didn't you relax and rejuvenile then?'

Jess began to feel a little guilty. She had no choice. She had to use her trump card. 'You'll get to stay with Auntie Tania.'

Martell's ears pricked up.' For the whole week?'

'Yep. All seven days.' Tania always spoiled him so rotten

that after staying with her, if Jess didn't love her son so much, she could easily throw him away like gone-off veg.

'Cool!' Martell yelped, punched the air with his fist and ran upstairs to start packing.

* * *

Martell was never usually like this when I went away, but for some reason he didn't want me to go on this particular holiday. It's another bad sign. I know it is.

This whole holiday thing has been conceived in dishonesty from the start, right down to getting the time off to go on the damn thing. Usually, to get a few days off in my workplace you've got to give a couple months notice. To get the time off with just a week's notice I had to commit the ultimate sin. Okay, okay. The second ultimate sin.

* * *

'This is awfully short notice Jessica. You know the rules about time off.' Jess's boss looked at her over bi-focalled spectacles.

'Yes, I know. It's my grandma in Philadelphia. She's passed away …' Jess trailed off and looked sadly to the left, hoping the added dramatic content wasn't too much.

'Oh, you poor dear. Of course you can take the leave. Take extra time if you need it. I remember how I felt when my grandmother passed …'

Thirty minutes later Jess was still sitting in the office, consoling her boss who it seemed might need professional counselling to get over the death of her 'Nana Juniper'.

* * *

Well, it wasn't exactly a lie; my grandma has passed away! It's not like I actually clarified when. I just didn't know what else to say. I couldn't say someone was sick if they weren't, could I? That would be too much like wishing it on them and I'm superstitious like that. It just didn't feel so terrible saying my grandma was dead because she already is. If I'd used that excuse with my mother instead, well, my plane would probably crash and I would burn in hell.

Grandma must be turning in her grave to know that I'm using her name to support me in going away with another woman's husband to be. My workplace would bury my job right alongside her if they ever found out that I lied to get the time off. I think lust may be turning me certifiable. I could have told them the real reason for the holiday – a friend's school friend getting married – but somehow it just didn't have the same sense of urgency. And then there'd be all the questions like who was getting married? And who I was going with? The answers to which I wasn't about to divulge to my work colleagues.

Strangely though, despite my negative vibes and reservations, the chance of a holiday with just me and Gary was an appealing idea.

Gary, obviously more used to concocting sordid stories than I, apparently has all his bases covered as to why he isn't taking his fiancée.

* * *

'Tia, would you like to come to a wedding with me? It'll be mostly the lads all binge drinking, being rowdy and staying out all night. The bride will be really busy sorting stuff out, but I'm sure she'd welcome a hand as pretty as

yours.' Gary reached for Tia's hand and kissed it before continuing.

'Apparently she's been really stressed and snappy. I heard she threw a pot of boiled broccoli at the caterer,' Gary chuckled, 'but I'm sure she'll be happy for a bit of female company to sound off with, since most her friends can't get there until the day before. So, what do you say?' Gary rubbed his hands together and gave her a big expectant smile.

Tia was horrified. A few days of being a sounding board for the tears and cursing of a stresed-out bride who was a virtual stranger did not sound tempting at all.

'Oh … erm … things are crazy at work at the moment. I don't think I'll get the time off … wouldn't want to cramp your lads' hol. We can go another time.' Tia babbled every excuse she could think of to not go.

Gary gave a dramatically sad frown. 'Sure, Tia,' he sighed. 'It won't be the same without you, but I understand. But promise we'll go away together soon?'

'Definitely! I'll start hunting for packages right away!' Tia breathed a sigh of relief and went into the kitchen to fix the most considerate boyfriend in the world his favourite meal. As she turned her back, Gary patted himself on the shoulder and slyly grinned. He loved it when a plan came together.

* * *

It has crossed my mind that whatever he told her is exactly the type of fabricated tale he'd spin for me if I were in her shoes. It is one of the many things I'm storing as ammunition to shoot him with when I finally come to my senses and leave this thing he calls a relationship. I call it straight up craziness. Don't think I haven't tried to get out of going on this holiday, but Gary had those bases covered too.

* * *

'Gary, I don't think it's a good idea us going away together.'

'It'll be our first chance to have some significant time alone. We've got the blessing of the significant others: Tia for me and work for you. How can it not be a good idea?'

'Gary, I'm worried about this trip. What if someone sees us?'

'Baby, we're staying in our own private villa. Everyone else is staying at the main hotel. You'll have total privacy from all prying eyes – except mine.'

'Gary, I think I should cancel going on this trip.'

'You're telling me you'd rather stay in drab, rainy London and throw away the opportunity to unload your stress from work by spending seven glorious days on a Caribbean island, in a luxury villa, with on-tap sun, sea and sand, and being pampered in every way by moi?'

* * *

In the end I resigned myself to the fact that there were some things you couldn't fight; getting out of this holiday was one of them.

It's now five in the morning. Gary's picking me up in half an hour. I'm still throwing bits into my suitcase and I can't find my passport. Things feel far more stressful now than they ever do at work. Feelings of déjà vu are replacing ones of panic because the doom and gloom I initially felt about this holiday never entirely disappeared. Like my passport. Its mysterious disappearance is just the start, I know it.

Okay, let me concentrate properly. It's not like you leave a passport just any place now, do you? I just don't need this tension right now. It should only be in this drawer or this box, but it's not in this drawer and it's not in this box. Shit! Where is the damn thing? The shrill ring of the phone takes my attention. It's probably Gary calling to say he'll be here in about ten minutes.

'Hello?'

'Jess, I'll be there in about ten minutes.'

See. 'I can't find my passport, Gary!'

'What! Come on, Jess. You wait until you're ready to go to the airport before you decide to look for your passport?'

Well, that makes me feel reassured. 'Sarcasm is not going to help me find my passport, Gary. This is a sign, Gary. A sign we shouldn't be going!'

'Jess. Jess. Calm down. Of course we should be going and we'll have a great time. Don't panic. I'll help you look when I get there. Hey, we may even have time for something else too.' I can hear the smile in his voice.

'See you in a few minutes then.' That's what I'm talking about; he always manages to calm my fears with minimal effort, such is his effect on my emotions.

Things are already going wrong and we haven't even left the country yet. I decide I may as well wait for him to come and help me look for my passport and put a few extra things in my hand luggage: a book in case there's a lousy movie showing on the plane; my iPod so that I have an excuse to cover my ears if Gary starts talking too much about himself – his favourite subject. I'll put it in this compartment here and my purse in this one here so that

I don't have to rummage around the whole bag for them if I need them.

Wha… What is this?! My passport! I must have left it in this bag from when I went on holiday last time. But that was more than six months ago! I can't believe it. Gary will be relieved. That must be him knocking on the door now. Talk about timing. I plod heavily downstairs to go open the door.

'Jess, I'm really sorry. I didn't mean to be off with you about your passport. Let's not start our holiday like this. I'll help you look now. We've still got a few hours before we have to check in.'

He apologises before I even get a chance to say good morning. I'm being unfair. Just how much so is apparent from just how stricken he looks. It's not his fault I'm feeling like this about the holiday. Well it is … and it isn't. All the same, it doesn't give me the right to spoil his holiday. He's gone to a lot of trouble for us to have a good time so I should try, at the very least, to make a decent attempt at looking forward to it.

'I'm sorry too, Gary, for putting a dampener on our vacation. I just got a bit panicky about my passport. But guess what? I've found it now!' I hold it up with a bright smile and hope he doesn't see how much of an effort it is to keep my jaws that way. 'It was still in my travel bag from my last holiday.' As I speak I walk over to my case, already at the bottom of the stairs, awaiting transportation. Gary's eyes are suddenly bulging.

'Jess. I'm going for a week. How long are you going for? Never mind. I'll just take your portable wardrobe to the car and pray I don't do myself an injury.'

Men. Any opportunity to exaggerate, they just jump at

it. My suitcase is standard size for any woman going away from home to a whole other country, for more than just a weekend. Doesn't he realise that we have to take into account clothing changes for the weather, clothing changes for the various places one could go to in a day, the various perspiration-induced clothing changes … I could go on but I'm not going to. Whatever I packed is necessary. Necessary for all possible eventualities. I look around at the home I'm not going to see for a week, quickly checking that all the lights are turned out. Nothing left but to lock the door behind me. As we drive off, I turn my head and see him smiling at me.

'What are you grinning at, Cheshire cat boy?'

'I'm excited about this trip, Jess. A whole week, just the two of us – nearly!' My face would hurt if I grinned as hard as he is. Maybe somewhere along this journey to the airport I'll catch some of the excitement from him. Then again, seeing what I see now – maybe not.

'That's a lot of traffic up ahead.'

Gary stretches his neck to see what's going on over the roofs of the other cars. 'Looks like there's been an accident; traffic is moving at snail's pace.'

Great, that's going to put time we haven't got onto our journey.

'Good thing we left early,' he responds perfectly to the comment that I made only in my head.

'Oh no, Gary! I've forgotten my car sickness tablets,' I say all panicked again.

'It's okay, Jess. If you start feeling a bit nauseous, sit in the back. I've heard that helps and you won't feel groggy from the tablets.'

He smiles at me with confidence. Confidence that I

won't turn green by the time I get to the airport, and confidence that everything is going to be fine. I, on the other hand, am seeing all these incidents as my punishment for giving my grandma a second death.

Two hours later on a journey that would normally take half the time, I am about ready to heave all over Gary's back seat.

'Open the windows, that should make you feel better. I'll speed up. The sooner we get there, the sooner we can get you out of the car and ease your car sickness.' Gary shifts the car into another gear. So, the windows are wide open and we're on the motorway, driving at speeds that must be touching one hundred miles per hour. I'm not even going to talk about the state of my hair or the fact that Gary whizzing in and out of lanes may be more for his benefit than my needs. He's right about the car sickness though. By the time we get to the airport, I'll be Gary sick instead. I horizontally grimace a smile. Signs to Gatwick are showing twenty-three miles. My last thought as I close my eyes is thank God we are nearly there.

34

Gary

Gary looked in the rear view mirror to see Jess lying across the back seat. Looked like she'd dozed off. He could relax for a minute. He was beginning to feel like the hired entertainment. Jess had been in two minds about this holiday from the start. He had been using all his charms and persuasive skills to keep her in a frame of mind that would get her on that plane.

* * *

'Jamaica has great hot springs where the mud will do wonders for your skin. Celebrities pay hundreds of pounds for a little for their faces. You'll be able to bathe your whole body in it for a hundred Jamaican dollars – that's less than a pound!'

'Holiday-ay! Let's Celebra-ate!' Gary's impression of Madonna had volume, but unfortunately no tuning.

'The beaches near the villa are amazing, Jess. You'll get a fantastic tan in no time, and look even sexier than you do now, if that's possible!'

* * *

He wouldn't put it past Jess to get to the airport and then say she didn't want to go. He really wanted them to get away together. Who knew when they'd get another opportunity like this, so he wasn't about to mess up this one. So, if it meant being Mr Happy non-stop to the airport and then on the seven-hour plus flight, just to keep her mind positive, then that was just the game he'd have to play.

35

Jessica

I must have drifted off again because it looks like we're pulling into the airport car park. I don't even remember coming off the motorway. I look at Gary in the rear view mirror. He's looking a little more relaxed. I think I've been making him feel a bit tense even though he's trying not to show it.

We find a space surprisingly quickly. I get out of the car first to look for a luggage trolley. I really could do with a trolley for my luggage alone, but I'm not going give Gary the chance to make another crack about the size of my suitcase. He'll just have to find a way to balance both our cases on one set of wheels. The thought of how he's going to do that makes me smile to myself. My first genuine one of the day. Hopefully not the last.

There's no queue at the check-in desk, one of the benefits of not arriving quite as early as you're advised to. This morning, however, the reason there is no queue is not because all the other passengers have checked in early, it's because the damned flight is delayed! For four hours! My breath catches in my throat and I turn to Gary. He gives me a soothing don't-panic type smile.

'What happens now?' he asks the desk attendant.

She gives him two refreshment vouchers. 'Just wait for the announcement, sir.'

My response is two sagging shoulders and a sunken heart. Gary's response is to give me a hug.

It takes me precisely two hours of our four-hour wait to accumulate six shopping bags and spend two hundred and twenty-five pounds and eighty two pence in Duty Free. I've already delved into my allocated spending money and I haven't even left the country yet. I can already see that this is going to be a really expensive trip. Before the end of it Visa will want to marry me. Gary's looking at up at me from the pages of his newspaper like I've lost my mind, but he doesn't say a word. I arrange my new additions prettily around him, sit down, lean silently on his shoulder and close my eyes.

36

Gary

Gary looked over his shoulder at Jess. She'd turned mad, he was sure of it. Somehow she'd translated the delay into shopping time. How was she going to persuade the cabin crew that all this shopping was part of her hand luggage? Hopefully if they got on the plane last, they wouldn't make too much of a fuss in their eagerness to take off. Crazy or not, if shop until she dropped asleep on his shoulder helped Jess get through the flight delay, then it was all good. Must be a woman thing. He was sure she didn't need another summer dress, another pair of sunglasses, another bikini ... well, maybe another bikini was okay, especially when you looked as good as he knew she would in it. He'd get locked up for doing something indecent in public if he didn't stop his imagination running away with him.

Luckily, taking advantage of an unconscious woman was below the belt even for him and there was enough going on below there right now without him working himself up even more. Saved! By the announcement that their flight gate was now opened. Jessica was snoring heartily. She didn't believe she snored, but she did. And it usually meant that she was out of it, so it was going to be like trying to wake the dead to get her up.

37

Jessica

'Alright, *alright* already, Gary, I'm up, okay!' Does he really have to shake me so hard just to get me to open my eyes? If he's trying to release some sort of pent-up frustration for me not being one hundred per cent about this holiday, by shaking the life out of me, he sure as hell is doing a good job.

'They're calling our flight. Our gate is open. I've been trying to wake you for about ten minutes. Was beginning to think you'd passed away on me!' he chuckles.

Another reminder of the excuse I gave to go on this bloody holiday. My guilt over that clearly isn't going to diminish any time soon. I help him gather up the rest of my bags, trying not to think of the state my hair must be in right now and hoping that he'd be thoughtful enough to inform me if any excess saliva has escaped my lips.

The flight is all that you'd expect from economy class. Crowded, lousy food, not enough leg room and a restricted view of a tiny TV screen suspended in the air. I don't care what anyone says, I think that those TV screens that are on the back of the seats should be standard on every airline by now. This airline needs to move with the times. It's not right to have to hold my head at some unnatural angle for hours at a time to be entertained. Guess that leaves me a choice of either reading or sleeping instead. One day my dream of travelling first class is going to come true. I don't care if I have to save for it, beg for it or marry for it. One day I will travel first class. Just because I wasn't born with a silver spoon in my mouth, doesn't mean I shouldn't taste the good things in life.

Gary is sleeping, with his mouth slightly open. I look at him and wonder, as I do every spare moment I get, just what kind of spell this man has cast over me. Okay, so he's alright looking. Good looking even. Hell, he's down-right handsome and I still feel that Wow! when I look at him. But it's never really been about looks for me, so what can it be? It doesn't even really matter what it is. All that matters is that I figure out what to do about it. After the holiday, though.

The closer we get to Jamaica, the less apprehensive I feel about it.

'Ladies and gentlemen, we will be landing in approximately twenty minutes,' the pilot announces.

I need to fix up. I'm going to the sunny Caribbean isle of Jamaica with a virile, handsome man. I am the envy of hundreds of women, or I would be if I were allowed to tell them. This is a memory that I'm not going to be able to share with anyone. Except Maddy. And Tania. I mean I have to be able to gush over it with someone, that's all part of the whole experience! I've bought the sexiest slip of a nightgown. Gary is going to freak for sure when he sees me in it! That probably won't be for very long though, because as soon as he sees me in it, he's guaranteed to want to see me out of it. And, as an added accessory, the same strappy sandals from our last date. You know what? I can get into this holiday. Gary's right. I'm worrying for no reason. All I have to do is relax and enjoy the ride. Just like he's doing now. Is that a little smile I see on his face? He sure must be having a good dream. It had better be about me.

38

Gary

Of course I'll come for a drink with you, Ms Berry.

What was that, Halle? You want me to come for that drink in your room?

Of course I'll come for a drink with you in your room.

This is a nice room you've got.

Where? You want us to sip it in your bed?

Of course I'll come for a drink with you, in your room, & sip it in your bed. This is a nice bed you've got.

Oh look! Clumsy me, I've spilled it all over your soft, silky night-gown. Please. Allow me to remove it for you. Ahhhh yes. Allow me to dry you off. Ahhhh yes. Allow me to ...

Gary awoke with a jolt. Either they'd just crashed or that was some serious turbulence. Didn't these pilots have any consideration? He was in the middle of a dream about Halle Berry, for Pete's sake, and he was just getting to the good part, the best part. He felt like crying.

'Gary, you okay? You look like you just woke up from a nightmare.' Jess sounded concerned.

He quickly refocused on his surroundings and hoped he hadn't been talking in his sleep. He knew it was just a dream, but he couldn't be left like this. He hadn't felt this horny since he saw Tia in those stiletto thigh-high boots she rented for a fancy dress party. And nothing else. Okay, that was it. He and Jess were about to join the mile high club. Right now. Suddenly an announcement came across the loudspeaker as he started to unclip from his seat.

'The seatbelt sign is on. Please can you return to your seats and fasten your seatbelts.'

He couldn't believe what he'd just heard. She couldn't have said that!

'You've got to fasten your seatbelt, Gary. The way this plane is shaking, you're liable to fly out of your seat and into someone else's while they're still in it. I don't think travel insurance covers that.' Jess reached over his lap to check his belt. This must be what they call a rude awakening. He called it a frustrating one.

Poor Halle.

39

Jessica

Gary looks really strange. It must be the flight. I didn't think he would be someone who was nervous about flying. Either that or he must just get in a bad mood if he's woken up out of his sleep. I've never seen this side of him before because he's never been able to fall into a deep sleep at my house; he's never been there long enough to. Did I say he was handsome before? That's not quite an accurate description for when he's just woken up. I wonder if he's got any other hidden phobia apart from flying. I hope bugs isn't one of them because if I see a cockroach or other creepy crawly in the bathroom, he will have to get over it.

Okay, we're landing now. Geez. Did someone slip some rum in the pilot's orange juice? That was more like a crash landing than anything else. I cannot get off this plane soon enough.

Luckily it doesn't take us too long to get off the plane and through passport control.

'Checks done, check.' Gary sings.

How can he be so chipper after that long flight? I feel I could sleep where I stand.

'We just need to get our luggage now. Belt five, which is over there!' Gary grabs an empty trolley and wheels it in the direction of the belt.

'I hope we don't have to wait too long for our luggage; I could kill for a shower.' Okay, maybe that was a little dramatic, but I really need a shower!

I did say I hoped that we wouldn't have to wait long for our luggage, didn't I? So how come that worked for Gary and twenty minutes later I am still at this freakin' belt? Why is it that your luggage is always the last to come off the plane when you're in a hurry? Okay, Grandma, how many times do I have to say I'm sorry for saying you died again? Wait a second … Where is everyone else from the plane? I look around again. Yes, I am the only person from our plane still standing here. I turn to look at Gary to find him looking at me. That telepathic thing we've got must be going on because it's like we're thinking the same thing. He walks over to what looks like an information desk. I trail a few steps behind, that feeling of foreboding suddenly coming back to haunt me.

'Excuse me, we've been waiting an awful long time for my girlfriend's case. Everyone else from the plane seems to have theirs.' Gary sounds a lot calmer than I am. I'm just trying not to break my fingers; I've got them crossed so hard.

'Do you have your baggage tags, sir?' says desk lady with a faint Jamaican accent. 'Hmm … hah … oh, hmm … aah,' she continues.

I am fascinated at the fact that it's possible to do sound effects in local lingua.

'Oh dear, I'm afraid there's been a problem with your luggage, Miss Montrose.'

Did I say that foreboding feeling had come back to haunt me? Scratch that and amend to it has come back to consume me.

'Your case was accidentally put on another flight and has gone to Puerto Rico.'

Normally this kind of news would make me want to scream or shout or something. But I'm calm. The significant fact that in my suitcase I have at least six pairs of shoes that are yet to have their soles smudged, as well as several still-price-tagged garments and, most importantly, my favourite jeans, doesn't even seem to be quite registering in the proper manner. Even the fact that Gary said I was his girlfriend has bounced right off me. I think I'm in shock. The worst thing I could have imagined happening has actually happened, and I just don't think my brain is ready to absorb it. I turn to Gary and say the only words that could possibly come forth at a moment like this.

'I want to go home.'

40

Gary

Gary refused to believe this was happening. His holiday was falling apart before his very eyes. Jess was unusually calm, which, if he knew Jess, was her way of freaking out. Her calm was the one before the storm. Her storm was what he needed to put damage control on fast, because if he made the wrong response to the delicate fact that she wanted to go home, then the holiday was over. He had no doubt she would wait right in this airport for the next flight home. Drastic measures were needed. He had to dig deep to reach the place where he could affect her most. He reached over to her and gently pulled her to him.

'Baby, it's going to be okay. It's upsetting, but they will find your suitcase. In fact I'm positive that you'll only be without it for a day or two at the most.' Jess wasn't looking convinced. He whispered in her ear, 'And I'll make sure that for that day or two you won't need anything to wear.' He started to nuzzle her neck in that way she loved. He could feel her whole body getting a little less tense. He looked intensely into her eyes and could almost see the struggle inside her. He pulled her closer to him so that she could feel exactly what he was going to pre-occupy her with until they found her luggage. It seemed that was what was needed to tip the scales in his favour. She sighed and gave him a little half-smile that said okay, but she still wasn't happy. He gave her a long soft kiss on the forehead and turned back to the desk to sort out the finer details of the missing luggage.

41

I can't believe this man just used seduction on me to change my mind about not going home. What I can't believe even more is that it worked! Once again I'm reminded that Gary's persuasive powers are growing to crazy proportions. This trip cannot end soon enough to get my plan of action into action. I need to make me Gary-less as a matter of urgency before he turns me into some kind of slave to his whim. I have to keep reminding myself that I couldn't settle for what Bobby couldn't give me and I won't settle for what Gary wants to give me, even if I have to chant that like a mantra.

I take a deep breath and hope that he's right and that they find my suitcase soon. I don't know how I'll survive without my favourite jeans. They have true sentimental value in that they make my behind look like no other jeans can. Gary puts his case on the trolley and with one hand wheels it towards the taxi rank. His other hand is holding mine tight. Probably afraid that I'll run off if he doesn't keep a good grip of it. He may not be far wrong.

During the taxi ride it's obvious that Jamaica is a beautiful place. The streets are bordered with flourishing palm trees and I glimpse some of the most glorious sun-kissed beaches I have ever seen. In the distance are the majestic peaks of the infamous Blue Mountains from which the coffee I drank just this morning is named. But somehow not even this plus the dazzling sun are enough to distract me from thinking about my missing case, or the events of this vacation so far. It really has been one unlucky incident after another from the very millisecond this holiday began. Surely it can only get better? I'm going to hold onto that thought like a life buoy.

When we arrive at the guest house, my first thought is that it is very nice, but ... 'It's a little out of the way, isn't it, Gary?' I know he said it was going to be away from everyone else, but I thought he was talking seclusion, not exclusion. I can't see more than a handful of buildings in the immediate vicinity and the road doesn't look as if it's the kind that a local bus frequents.

'It's for privacy, Baby, total privacy.' He turns, pushes the door and wheels his case inside.

I look around the villa wordlessly. Kitchen's nice. Living area's nice. Bedroom's nice. I sink heavily onto the bed. It wasn't supposed to be like this. Is coming away like this so terrible that it deserves all of this misfortune? Before I know it a tear escapes from my eye. Dammit, that's the last thing I want to do. I wipe it away quickly, before Gary sees it.

'I'm going to the bathroom,' I call out to him. While I'm in there looking at my reflection through blurry eyes, Gary slips some of his toiletries around the door.

'Here you go, Baby.'

Everything I need to take a shower – so I do. Even after I've dried off, I'm conscious that I've barely and unfairly said more than a couple of words to Gary, and I think they were thanks, and thanks again. I glide my naked body under the cool sheets and promptly fall asleep.

When I next open my eyes, it's a little duller outside and Gary is nowhere to be seen.

42

Jessica

No! Could he really have gone and left me by myself in the back of beyond with all sorts of creeping creatures? I jump out of the bed, grab the sheet and wrap it around me in a panic. I shuffle to the door as quickly as my sheet-shrouded legs will carry me and poke my head outside. A little way down the road, I see Gary in conversation with some local person who suddenly starts pointing and nodding at me. Gary looks over and waves. He pats the guy on the shoulder and starts walking back.

'Hey, Baby, did you have a good rest?'

'Funnily enough I did. I thought you'd gone off and left me.'

'As if!' he laughs. 'You were sleeping, so I took a walk around and met that guy who was telling me a little bit of what goes on around here.'

I can't imagine what that could be, the area looks deserted.

'He says it's about a ten-minute walk to the main road where the buses run. Oh, and I got some good news!'

Great, I could do with some of that kind of news right now.

'While you were sleeping, the airport called your mobile and said they've found your case. We can collect it tomorrow.'

I want to *scream*, I'm so happy to hear that! Maybe, this is where my holiday luck is about to take a U-turn. 'That is music to my ears, Gary, it really is.' I'm so relieved that I don't have the energy to be my more dramatic self.

'I told you it wouldn't be missing for long, didn't I? I also told you I'd keep you occupied until you got it back, and I can think of no better time to be a man of my word.' He reaches over for the sheet, and the rest, as you say, is history.

The next morning is pretty much fun all over the villa.

* * *

'Hey, the bedroom looks different in daylight. Maybe "it" will be different too. Let's try!' Gary smiled and rolled on top of Jess.

'Hey, I think we should christen the dining area, the same way we christened the bedroom.' Gary smiled and reached for Jess.

'Hey, don't you think the veranda will feel a little left out if we don't do a little something something out there too?' Gary wrapped his arms around Jess from behind and gently turned her to face him.

* * *

We even did it, to my shame, behind some bushes on the edge of the roadside! The roadside was a definite first and last time, though only because I'm sure a mosquito took as much advantage of my behind as Gary did.

'Shall we go to the airport now?' Gary asks whilst feeding me a forkful of scrambled egg – our choice of late lunch. My big smile says everything.

An hour later we have picked up my case and are back at the villa.

'What do you want to do now?' Gary raises an eyebrow

at me and I can't help but smile back because I know what's on his mind. All my reservations about this trip just may have been for nought.

'Well, now I've got a bikini, how about the beach?'

'We have our very own secluded stretch, you don't really need a bikini,' Gary growls and plants a big kiss on my lips. 'Let's go to the beach!' He revs up the car engine and we hang out for the rest of the day, getting some sun, getting some sand and getting even more of something else.

That's pretty much been the formula since we've been here. Gary's friend's wedding, the so-called main purpose of this vacation, is on Thursday. It's strange; even though I'm not having a bad time, I'm not exactly having a glass-half-full time either. Yeah, we've had some fun, but it always seems to be tainted within hours by one thing or another. Every day I get up determined to make a memorable trip out of this, then something crops up to make it memorable for the wrong reasons. Like fate is reminding me to not get too happy out here because I've still got unhappy things to do when I get back. There's been the missing passport, missing case and uppity mosquito, and that was all by Monday, all within two days of leaving the country. On Tuesday we caught the wrong bus back to the guest house.

* * *

'Gary, are you sure this is the right bus? Nothing has looked familiar for a while now.' Jess strained her face against the window.

'I told the driver we needed to get to Caribe Villas and that he should let us know when we got there.' Gary walked towards the front of the bus to speak to the driver. After a

short discussion, the bus stopped and Gary turned to get off, beckoning to Jess to follow him.

'What's going on? Why are we getting off here?' Jess was confused. Nothing around looked recognisable and where they'd gotten off didn't look particularly touristy either. Locals sauntered past, looking them up and down in a lazy fashion.

'Apparently, we should have gotten off a while back.' When he saw the panic on Jess's face, Gary knew he had to look calm even if he didn't feel it. Another couple of locals walked past.

'English?' one asked.

'Yes, we need to get to Caribe Villas,' Gary replied non-chalantly.

The two men looked at one another and shook their heads. 'You far away, Sah!'

'How far?' Jess asked apprehensively.

'About two hours away far!' The two men shook their heads again.

* * *

It actually took us nearly two and a half hours to get back, by which time my sun tan lotion had expired (twelve hours before topping up needed, my eye!) and I got sunburn on my nose. Not really really bad, mind you, but enough to make it very uncomfortable when I repeatedly had to wipe my nose after the constant sneezing brought on by my allergy to a local dog that patrols around the guest house like it's its daytime job. Today, Wednesday, we hired a car for the rest of the week to avoid a similar wrong bus incident, only to have another incident instead.

* * *

'Gary, this looks like ...' Jess was searching for a diplomatic word for banger, '... a pretty old car and they still use leaded out here, look at the pumps. Maybe you should check before you refill?'

'Don't worry; I know what I'm doing.' Gary brushed Jess off agitatedly. What did she possibly think she knew about cars, that he didn't? He pulled the unleaded pump, filling the tank to the brim while tutting to himself, 'Women should stick to looking pretty.'

'Right,' Gary replaced the pump nozzle.' I think we're ready to go now.' He gave Jess a smug look as he turned the key. Kaput ... puff ... PHOOT. The car stalled. He turned the key again. Nothing. Jess leaned back in the seat, arms folded, not saying a word. Gary got out of the car and walked over to the petrol station attendant who was leaning lazily against another pump surveying the scene.

'I tink you put in de wrong petrol.'

Gary looked over at Jess and motioned to the man to speak a little lower.

'You gonna need a mechanic, for real.'

Gary turned around and smiled at Jess, giving her a thumbs up. Under his breath he mumbled, 'She's gonna kill me!'

★ ★ ★

We had to wait an hour for a mechanic to come from another village and drain the car so that we could put the correct petrol in. After that, I just wanted to go back to the villa. For all I knew a pig falling from the sky could be next! I don't think that anyone alive can convince me that there isn't some kind of mojo on this vacation. I have now resigned myself to the fact that these mishaps are my punishment for being out here with another woman's man. Basically, until I go home, I may as well sit tight and wait for whatever's going to happen next. Negative I know, but it's not like I can fight my deceased grandma, can I? I am convinced she's behind all this, all the way from the Other Side.

So far, nothing life altering has happened, but tomorrow is the wedding. It would just be my luck to sneeze (from my newfound Jamaican dog allergy) at the precise moment that the minister says that bit about speaking now or forever holding your peace. Ooh, just think, everyone would go silent and stare at me and my red nose. The bride would burst into tears, screaming that her day was ruined and everyone would accuse the groom of some unfounded misdemeanour. He would then helplessly plead his innocence while holding me by the neck and near throttling me. Ooh, I couldn't forgive myself if I had anything to do with ruining someone's wedding day. You know something? I think the best thing for everybody would be for me not to go. I know Gary will be disappointed, but once I explain, I'm sure he'll understand. May as well tell him now. No time to break bad news like the present.

'Gary.' I take a deep breath. It is not as easy as I thought it would be to just come out and say it. I hope he doesn't put me on some kind of guilt trip. 'Gary, would it be really terrible if I didn't go to the wedding tomorrow?' I don't exactly hold my breath, but I quit breathing for a few seconds.

He looks at me with no other expression other than a raised eyebrow. 'You don't want to go, Jess? Are you sure?'

'Yeah, Gary. With everything that's gone on, I'm not really feeling it.'

He looks at me in silence, a little bit too tensely. He must be so disappointed. It's going to come now: the guilt trip; the persuasive tactics. Better brace myself in preparation.

'Okay, Jess. If that's what you want.'

Huh? That's it? That's not what I was expecting. He gets up and goes outside. I'm baffled. I mean, is he upset? He doesn't seem upset. I don't know if I'm unhappy that he doesn't seem upset, or happy that he's putting on a brave face for me. Dear fellow. He's actually more considerate than even I would have given him credit for.

43

Gary

Gary couldn't believe it. Ask and you shall receive. How true was that! He'd been racking his brains from the minute they'd arrived to find a way to not take Jess to the wedding. Then, voilà! Like magic she put the solution right in the palm of his hand. Unbelievable. What a stroke of luck, and about time too. Something was due to happen to restore balance with all the strangely unlucky stuff that'd been happening this trip. He had actually started believing Jess was right about everything that'd gone wrong.

Now, everything had worked out perfectly. He knew the whole point of this holiday, as he had put it to Jess, was to come for this wedding. The thing was, all his friends that would be at the wedding knew Tia. How was it going to look if he turned up half-way around the world with another woman on his arm? The old reputation he'd fought so hard to re-invent, the changed man image he'd been striving to live up to these past few years, would all be wasted. Three years of effort down the drain in the space of a twenty-minute ceremony.

It wasn't coincidence that he'd found a villa so far away from the wedding hotel and everyone else who'd flown out for the wedding. It had taken him ages to get something that equalled decent and distance. He didn't want to imagine what it would have been like if they'd stayed near the rest of the wedding party or, worse still, at the wedding hotel, with people feeling free to come to his room at all hours, asking all sorts of questions. Being this distance away from it all, no one would bother to travel so far just to hang out. There was nothing out here. They were happy for him to come to them and he was happy to do that. And when he was ready, he could come back and have Jess all to himself. It had worked out perfectly.

He'd been careful not to show any reaction when Jess said she didn't want to go. At first he had been so shocked that he hadn't known how to react. As it sunk in, he figured that if he pretended to be too upset, she might change her mind and reconsider, to spare his feelings. Then again, if he appeared too happy about it she'd no doubt have cursed him out and changed her mind, this time to spite his feelings. Not giving any reaction at all would confuse her, but would hopefully sway her towards thinking that he wasn't best happy but didn't want to stress her about it. He hoped that by leaving the house, she'd think that he was either giving her space because she didn't want to go, or that he needed space because she didn't want to go. Either way he could go to the wedding tomorrow and have a good time, then come back to Jess and have a good time, all with his reputation intact. This was a win-win situation, the best kind.

44

Bobby

Bobby tooted his car horn again to let his son know that he needed to get a move on. Tania came to the window and waved her hand, splaying her five fingers to indicate that was how much longer Martell would be. Bobby gave her a thumbs up in acknowledgement.

He leaned back into the seat. With Jess on holiday for the week, this was a good opportunity to spend some quality time with Martell. That had sadly been lacking the past few weeks. He looked out the window and smiled widely as his son came bounding towards the car.

'Hey, Dad!' The hug Martell gave him winded him slightly as he flung himself onto him, but Bobby held him tightly for a good minute.

'Hi, Son, I think you've actually grown – your head anyway!' Bobby playfully rubbed his son's head.

'Whatever, Dad.' Martell rolled his eyes in a manner very much like his mother.

'So, where are we going?' Martell questioned as he buckled himself into the passenger seat, then reached into his rucksack for his Gameboy. No car journey was complete without his trusty hand-held time-filling device.

'Has your Dad got a day planned for you! Bowling, which should work your appetite up for McDonalds, which you can then relax off in the cinema. And if you're really good, I may even buy you that video game you've been going on about for the past couple of months.'

'Time Crisis?! Oh Dad, I promise I'll be the goodest son ever!' Martell could hardly contain his excitement.

Bobby laughed as his son put a little extra zeal into his Gameboy play. Now would be a good time to test the waters, while his son was in a state of near euphoria.

'So Mart, how'd you feel?'

Martell answered without looking up from his game. 'Fine, Dad.'

'I mean about me and your mum not being together like we used to?'

'Fine, I guess.' Martell shrugged his shoulders, still concentrating on his game.

'So, would you still feel fine if it went back to how it was? Me and your mum? Us all living together again?' Bobby asked cautiously.

This time Martell paused his game and looked over at his Dad. 'Really?'

'Well, me and your mum still have to iron a few things out, but our Sunday morning video game challenge may be back on sooner than you think.'

From the big toothy grin on his little face, Bobby knew what his son's answer was. As they pulled into the bowling alley Martell looked thoughtful.

'Last time we came bowling, Mum did a double strike. Do you remember, Dad?'

'Well next time *we* all go together, I will personally beat her record!'

Martell grinned excitedly again. It was one of the best sights Bobby had seen in weeks. It made Operation Get-Jess-Back all the more vital. There were a few more days before she was back and he had to make every second of every hour of every one of those days count.

45

Jessica

I'm not sure that yesterday was the moment for Gary to show his considerate side. Or for me to have had the martyrish idea of not wanting to go to the wedding. I'm having a change of heart, but I know it's too late to change my mind; place settings have now been set in stone. Gary called up the bride to inform her it would just be him before the suggestion had barely left my lips. He was just a little too raring to go for my liking.

* * *

'I'm going now, Jess. How do I look?' Gary opened his arms wide in front of Jess.

'Good,' Jess half-heartedly mustered a positive reply. She plumped up the cushions as an excuse not to meet his eyes.

He came over and wrapped his arms around her. 'Baby, you were the one that said you thought it best if you didn't go. Do you want me to stay here with you instead?' Gary cocked his head to the side.

'Of course not. You HAVE to go. I want you to go. Have a good time.' Jess gave him a weak smile. Gary gave her a penetrating stare. She slapped him playfully on the shoulder.

'Really! Go, have a good time!'

Seeming more satisfied with that response, he pecked her on the lips and spun on his heel.

'I won't be too late!' he called over his shoulder. Then, with a slam of the villa door and a rev of the hired car's engine, he was gone.

* * *

It's not that I don't want him to enjoy himself. Well, that's not exactly true, I don't want him to have a bad time, but I don't want him to have as good a time as he would have had with me there. That selfish streak in me rears its ugly head again, and boy is it ugly. He's been gone a good few hours now. About as long as I've been wandering around this place touching furniture. I feel a bit ... a bit ... abandoned. I understand that Gary must be busy helping out or pigging out or just all round having a whale of a time, but I thought he'd have at least called me to see what I'm up to, or at least to tell me what the bride's dress looks like.

Sigh. I don't know what to do with myself. The day just seems to be dragging. I've already read both the books I brought, one of Gary's, a magazine that I stole from the plane and some kind of 'All about Jamaica' newsletter type brochure that the last people staying here must have left behind. Not even sunbathing is appealing to me and usually nothing but a thunderstorm can keep me out of the sun. Gary ate the last bag of crisps we bought from England last night so we've run out of nibbles, and a ten-minute walk then a fifteen-minute bus ride is simply too much effort for a snack. I'm feeling homesick. I miss my baby. I miss Martell. I think I'll call, see how he's doing without me. It's early, it's overseas, and it's on a mobile phone so this call is going to cost a fortune, but my little sweetie pie is worth it.

The phone barely rings twice before Martell picks up. His aunt Tania can never beat him to the phone. You'd think he lived there the way he controls that phone when he stays over.

'Hi, Baby.'

'Hi, Mum! Are you having a good time?' That's my son.

Other kids would be asking what present I'd bought for them, but Martell is always concerned about my welfare first. Querying his present won't be far behind though.

'It's nice out here, Sweetie, but I am missing you though. And before you ask, your present is taken care of, okay!' He chuckles. 'So what you up to, Son?'

'Just playing computer games. Dad bought me a new one. It's called Time Crisis. I'm already on level four!' Ah, how easily the young of today are entertained.

'That's great, Baby, but when I get back you know I'll kick your little butt back to level two don't you? Give me a few days to see what it's about and you know I'll have you, because your mom rocks at all those games!' More like I suck at those games.

'Whatever, Mum!' He laughs and to hear the sound instantly lifts my spirits.

'Hey fella, how did hooking up with your dad go the other night? Is that when you got the game?'

'Yeah, we chose it together. We went to the cinema, then bowling and then McDonalds. It was really cool, but it would have been cooler if you were there too. Dad said that when you got back, we'd all do it again together and probably lots of other stuff too. He said that him not staying at the house might only have to be for a short while too. Oh, and we went to …'

It's obvious my child is missing me, that's why he's having to keep himself so busy. Poor Honey. Hold on! Did I hear right? I think I did! He just said that Bobby said that him not staying at the house may not be for long. What on earth is Bobby playing at? Why would he tell Martell something like that to give him the impression …? Oh no. He gave Martell the same impression that I gave him by not explaining his wrong assumption that night we went Chinese. Oh, I *knew* I should have sorted that out before I came out here! Maddy managed to convince me that it could wait until I got back because Bobby couldn't pursue anything with me out of the country. Maybe not, but telling Martell that, he's still managed to create an even bigger mix-up for me to sort out.

I admit I may have left him with the slight impression (through the total fault of pure hunger) that we were going to try again, but not even I thought he would take it to mean that it was practically a done deal. To think I believed that problems at home stayed there until you got back. Now not only does Bobby think we're definitely on our way back to togetherness but it looks like Martell does too.

'Mum? Mum!' Now my son has to scream across the telecommunication system to get my attention. This gets worse by the second.

'Sorry baby, my attention just went AWOL for a second. Thought I saw a beetle and you know your mom can't stand creepy crawlies. If ever I needed you it's now, Mart!' He laughs. I join him and hope it doesn't sound as false as it actually is. 'Okay Baby, I just thought I'd call and check in with you, see how you're doing. I'm glad you're having fun. Be good and miss me okay!'

'I will and I do!'

'Bye, Baby.'

'Bye, Mum.' He hangs up, yet I'm still holding on to the phone and the fact that my life has just become very messy. My head is hurting with my emotional entanglements. Hopefully the three days I have left on this island will not add to that. A nervous breakdown so far from home would really take its toll on my travel insurance.

46

Gary

Gary was bemused. Jess had been in a strange mood since the wedding. He could usually read how she was feeling, but either his radar was blocked or he'd suddenly lost his touch.

* * *

'Hi, Baby, I'm ba-ack!' Gary folded his arms around Jess to give her a big hug. She was unresponsive in his arms and after a few seconds determinedly disentangled herself.

'O...kay.' Gary wasn't sure what mood Jess was in, but he knew her well enough to know she was in one.

'So, I took note of everything!' If he responded with enthusiasm, it might just win her over. 'The bride's dress was okay, but the big bow at the back made her behind look big. Oh, and the cake! Four tiers, it was huge! But a little bit dry ...' Gary trailed off as he observed Jess paying more attention to a magazine he was sure she'd already read twice, than to his conversation. As his eyes met hers, he noticed her giving him a thoughtful stare. He shook his head and looked at her again. The stare was now replaced with a beaming smile. Had he imagined the look?

'I'm going out to the pool. Glad you had a great time at the wedding.' With that, Jess placed the magazine back onto the table and walked out, closing the door unusually quietly behind her.

* * *

He was beginning to wonder if maybe going to the wedding for the whole day had left her alone for too long. Too much time to think about things that he didn't particularly want her thinking about. He'd had all the best intentions to call her from the reception, just to let her know he was thinking about her.

* * *

'Cheers!' All the guys roared as they slammed their champagne glasses together. It was a surprise that the floor wasn't littered with broken glass. Gary surveyed his surroundings as he sipped the champagne. The bride and groom were busy greeting their guests and everyone else was either swaying on the dance floor or still eating and drinking themselves into a traditional stupor. Now would be a good time to call Jess and see how she was entertaining herself.

'Hey, not dancing, Gary?' one of his fellow revellers asked.

'Of course! It's an occasion for dancing! Just got to do something first.' Gary grinned, gave him a hearty slap on the shoulder and turned to exit the hall. It was too loud in there to hear himself speak. As he reached for his phone to dial Jess's number, he saw the low battery signal flashing, and then the phone went dead. Damn. He hadn't charged his phone for days.

'You have got to be shitting me!' he said to himself. 'She will never believe this!'

* * *

There was absolutely no point telling her why he hadn't called since that was possibly the most used excuse in the world, even if, in this instance, it was genuine. He'd hoped instead that when he got back, his undivided attention would show her how much he had missed her. Yet she'd barely spoken to him. Something was on her mind, something that had gotten there somewhere between him leaving for the wedding and arriving back, and it was something more than him just not calling.

This trip wasn't turning out the way he thought it would. Even though it was a great opportunity to have Jess to himself for more than a few hours at a time, he would be glad to get home. Tia had called a short while ago and he was surprised to find that he was actually missing her.

* * *

'Hey, Honey! Just calling to say hi.' Tia's voice crackled on the line. 'Oh, and I picked up a new raincoat for you. The weather's been fit only for ducks here and I don't want you getting drenched and catching a cold before your little body has had time to get re-acclimatised to our grotty weather.'

'Hey, less of the "little body"!' Gary growled fondly.

'So, go on. Gloat. Is it really as hot and beautiful as all the holiday brochures picture it?' Tia rolled her eyes as she played with the telephone wire.

'Yeah, but nowhere near as hot and beautiful as you.'

Tia laughed.' Gary, you are just too corny for words sometimes!'

'Ahh, but it's one of the many things you love about me, isn't it?' Gary responded cheekily.

'What. Ever. Gary,' Tia smiled, 'but what I'd love most right now is for you to get back safely. Call as soon as you land. Enjoy the rest of your break.' Tia blew an exaggerated kiss down the phone and hung up.

* * *

Yes, he had missed Tia, quite a bit in fact. It had been trying, having to constantly keep Jess in the holiday spirit, especially since she'd been on this bad luck trip. Even more now than ever, he realised just how much he needed the contrast between the two of them to keep his needs in balance. He knew he had a good woman in Tia, a very good woman. A woman many men wouldn't want to risk losing. But what was life if you didn't take risks? And Jess was the type of woman worth taking a risk for.

Still, despite all that had not been happening in the day, it was still all happening at night. Jess had been really intense, almost as if she had been trying to lose herself in him. It made for some mind-blowing love-making. Somewhere, he'd gone from just wanting Jess to needing her, and it wasn't just for the ecstatic sex either. It was like she completed him. He had to have her presence around him in some form or other.

Tia alone could not fulfil him as a man, as a person. He had to have Jess too. It was almost turning obsessional. Bringing her to this isolated part of the island was essentially a good plan, but it didn't give him much to work with in terms of grand gestures. That was what was needed to keep Jess content. Straying too far from the villa was out of the question in case they bumped into any of his friends so he'd wait until they got back home for the grand gesture thing. And boy, would it have to be impressive to banish all the negativity from this holiday.

Meanwhile, for the time they were still here, he'd just have to maximise the use of his night-time skills to make the days pass a little easier. Time for some real fun in the sun, and on the veranda, and in the bedroom, and in the shower …

47

Bobby

Bobby was feeling good. His plan was coming together nicely. He'd been putting all the tips David gave him to good use.

* * *

'Mate, get in with her peeps. Once you've got her people in your corner, you're onto a sure thing. A glowing compliment here, a favourable passing comment there never hurts, especially when it's coming from the peeps.' David gave Bobby that know-all nod. Bobby smiled back and nodded too. He knew exactly where to start.

* * *

Bobby was already back in regular contact with Martell. Even though that wasn't to score points, if it did, who was he to turn them down? With everyone else the points came from doing that one good deed that mattered.

* * *

'Hey, Tania, didn't you mention the other day that your garden was turning into a jungle? I saw some special strength weed killer on special offer at B&Q, so I thought I'd pick some up for you.'

'Oh Bobby, I dreamt just the other night that one of those weeds climbed through my window and tried to strangle me! Thanks so much. Now I can kill them before they kill me!' Bobby smiled at the relief and gratitude in Tania's voice.

'Mrs Montrose? I fixed the lock on your back door. Jess mentioned a while back that it needed doing. Better secure than sorry, eh.'

'Why, thank you, Bobby! That was very thoughtful of you. I was reading just the other day that burglaries in the area had gone up by ten per cent!'

'Maddy? You know the shoe shop that you and Jess live in? Well, I just saw a sign in the window saying they've got a one-day half-price promotion tomorrow, in case you didn't know.'

'Are you kidding me? How did I not know about that?' Maddy screamed down the phone. She took a deep breath to compose herself. 'Bobby,' she said solemnly, 'I think I love you. And all the shoes I'm going to buy tomorrow will love you too!'

* * *

Yes, he'd put his best foot forward with Jess's family and friends at every opportunity he could. She'd be back soon, and he'd made sure that he was one of the topics in her catch-up conversation.

48

Tyrone

Tyrone couldn't stop thinking about Jessica. She'd given him her number. The woman had actually given him her telephone number. A result that, deep down, he hadn't felt was possible. Weeks later he still hadn't used it! Well, technically he had. He'd picked up the phone and at least partially dialled the number before, just as quickly, replacing the receiver. He'd managed to do this several times, but before he could finish tapping out the number his mind would go blank. Whatever he had planned to say would just run out of his mind like a convict who'd found his cell door open.

He could slap himself for being so indecisive and dithery, a legacy from his nervy nerdy days. It was definitely time to break out the confidence DVDs again. If he'd needed them just to talk to her in person, then he needed them even more now to talk to her over the phone. And even to his own ears that sounded weird.

49

Jessica

Nine days since I've been back from the vacation of a life-time, meaning that it shouldn't be repeated in my lifetime. Nine whole days and I still haven't managed to break it off with Gary, even though the plan was to do it the minute the plane landed back on British concrete. The holiday made it even easier to see that we had to stop; it was the holi-nights that were difficult. They were good; too damned good.

★ ★ ★

'Gary, I think we should practise abstinence for the rest on the holiday.' Jess said determinedly.

'Okay, Babe.' Gary nuzzled her neck.

'We should never … have come on this holiday … it's not right …' Jess was starting to struggle to think straight in the face of Gary's distraction.

'Sure, Babe,' Gary stroked her thighs.

'And so … erm … and … ahem …' Jess was closing her eyes tightly to concentrate.

'And?' Gary asked before his lips closed over hers. Jess resisted for precisely three minutes, her longest record against Gary to date.

★ ★ ★

I think the sun and heat intensified everything, but I was clear that things couldn't continue down that road when we got back. I planned to tell him as soon as we landed; I'd been preparing exactly what to say for the whole flight.

★ ★ ★

'Okay, Gary, there's no time like the present,' Jess said determinedly.

Gary looked at her longingly, but didn't say a word.

'Just let me speak okay, Gary? I just need to get this off my chest.' Jess felt herself wavering slightly under his gaze. Gary still didn't say a word, just kept staring at her intensely.

'Right ... okay ... so ... right ...' Jess blinked to try and refocus on the speech she'd planned during the past nine hours in the sky.

★ ★ ★

His eyes were filled with longing and my mind was filled with the images from the holi-nights. The words just stuck in my throat. Since then I've only seen him once. and spoken to him little more than that too. Voicemail has never been such value for money. He knows something's up; it's too obvious for him not to. I shouldn't need to clarify what the something is. He should know. I was picking up the phone at least seven times a day to call him for a holi-night before putting it back down. Nine days later, it's down to twice a day. Absence is definitely making the heart grow harder. Plus work's been super busy, so that's helped; I've barely had time to think. One could almost think my punishment for going away continues.

I haven't quite managed to set the record straight with Bobby either. So much for my holiday resolutions. In my defence (as feeble as it may sound), Bobby has just been so sickeningly charming every time he's called that there's never been the right moment to pop in, 'Oh and before you go, I just wanted to confirm that a reconciliation is not on the cards any time soon.' Somehow, that just doesn't seem to be the appropriate conversation closer. I've been avoiding his calls too. Not the best example of a grown woman handling her business. Luckily, Martell hasn't mentioned anything about us all being together again. I think I got carried away thinking my baby was waiting with baited breath for some big family reunion.

I actually think I need another holiday just to sort out all of this. Now I know I didn't properly follow through on my last holiday declarations, but I don't have a choice now. I *really* need to get shit sorted asap or the Mental Health Institute will be using me as a case study. Besides, it can't be that wild an idea if Maddy agrees with it.

* * *

'A holiday? Most definitely. Best medicine in the world, except for milk of magnesia, which, according to my mother, is a cure all for every ailment.'

Jess could imagine Maddy already compiling her holiday wardrobe as she spoke.

'So, you don't think the fact that I've just come back from holiday makes another one seem ... well, like an extreme solution?'

'My dear friend, no solution is extreme for stress. You did say you were stressed, did you not?' Maddy questioned

'Well ... yes, a little.'

'And did you know that stress can lead to ulcers, unwanted pregnancies (because you'd be so stressed you'd forget to take your pill) and possibly even a nervous break-down? I saw that just the other day in an episode of CSI.'

'Err ... no, I didn't know all that.'

'Well, now that you do, don't you think another holiday in comparison to medical consultancy fees, prescription fees, and hours off work for doctors' appointments, not to

mention around the clock child care assistance for Martell, since you'll be in no fit position to capably look after him full time in your stressed condition, is a cheaper and preferable option?'

Jess was amazed at her friend's ability to apply logic in even the most complicated situations.

'Err … well, yes of course it would be preferable … I guess.'

'So. Acknowledging that, there's only one thing left to think about really, isn't there? Do I need to buy another bikini?'

★ ★ ★

That confirms it then. Another vacation will be where I find my inspiration to finally sort out my relationships crisis. I know it's been said that when it comes to men, we can't live with 'em and we can't live without 'em, but after the few weeks I've had, if I don't speak to another one for a year it will not be long enough.

50

Tyrone

Tyrone took a deep breath. No more putting it off. He was going to call Jessica today. Stalling for all these weeks might mean she'd already met someone. Maybe while she was on holiday. It was sheer luck he'd even found out that she was away.

★ ★ ★

Tyrone stood looking up at the shop sign. Surely there would be no harm in going into Jarrods just to say hello? What the heck, he was going in. He pushed open the heavy glass door and looked for a member of staff.

The lingerie department caught his eye immediately. He wasn't sure if it was because of the nearly indecent display of sexy underwear or because there was actually a guy selling it! Tyrone walked over to him.

'Hi ... excuse me?' As the staff member turned around, Tyrone could see David on his name tag.

'Yes, Sir! And how can I help you today?' David rubbed his hands together gleefully, looking as if he'd just found his next victim. 'Something for your lady? Or something for you, for the benefit of a lady?' David winked.

'Oh ... er no!' Tyrone felt a flush of embarrassment. 'I'm actually looking for someone who works here? Jessica?'

David looked Tyrone up and down curiously. 'And you are?'

'Oh, I'm just a friend! I was passing by and thought I'd pop in and say hello. A quick hello. That's it. Just Hi.' Tyrone found himself starting to babble.

'Sorry mate, she's on vacation at the moment, won't be back for a week or so. On the bright side though, I'm here with some bee-ootiful lingerie so why waste an opportunity to impress someone? That's what I say.' David went straight into his hypnotic sales spiel and Tyrone was hooked. Ten minutes and eight sets of underwear later, Tyrone was swinging a gift-wrapped set of lacy underwear. He hadn't even realised he'd reached for his wallet until David pressed the receipt into his hand.

'Well worth the price, mate. Your loved one's gonna love it!' David patted him on the shoulder. Tyrone nodded solemnly in agreement. His mother would indeed love it. She'd probably think he'd lost his mind too, but she would definitely love it.

★ ★ ★

That was nearly a couple of weeks ago so Jessica must be back by now, unless she had extended her stay, or her flight had been delayed. He was nervously digressing again. He hadn't even considered who she'd gone with. She wouldn't have given him her number if she was with someone, would she? He'd know for sure just as soon as he called her. What if she wasn't available? Or upset that he hadn't phoned sooner and gave him the cold shoulder? He was being ridiculous, she barely knew him so why would she be upset? He sighed. Why did the thought of speaking to this woman make his stomach jitter so much? For Pete's sake they'd been out shopping together. They'd already bonded. Well, sort of. Okay, enough dithering. He inhaled deeply. He was going to call her right now.

This was it. He was dialling … the phone was ringing … his heart was beating … She wasn't answering. Should he hang up? Or wait until it rang at least more than once?

'Hello, Jess speaking.'

Shit. She'd answered! He didn't know what to say.

'Erm … Hello?' Jess answered again.

If he didn't say something soon she was surely going to hang up.

'Hello. Is that Jessica?' He cringed as the words left his mouth. She just said she was Jess! Stupid, stupid.

'It is.' Jess paused, waiting for further elaboration that didn't seem forthcoming. ' And you are?'

'It's Tyrone. From the party … and Oxford Street … a few weeks ago. You were looking for shoes and I was looking for jeans.' Tyrone sounded like a blustering fool even to himself.

'Okay, I think that's sufficiently jogged my memory. How are you?'

He could hear the smile in her voice. Maybe she was glad to hear from him. This phone call might not be as hard as he'd thought.

'I'm fine. Thought I'd give you a bell, see whether your shoes went with your outfit.'

'Not quite,' Jess laughed, 'but they had the desired effect on something else so it was all good!'

He'd made her laugh! He was *so* in there!

It had taken only that icebreaker for the conversation to go from strength to strength. By his Sekonda, they'd been talking for over two hours. Tyrone was dying to go to the toilet, but didn't want to interrupt the flow of the conversation. In the two hours that had passed, he'd not only found out quite a bit about Jessica, but also that he could be quite a witty guy when he was at the other end of a phone line.

* * *

'I notice a very slight accent? Am I correct or do I need to look for a hearing aid?'

'No, the hearing aid can wait! I'm originally from Philadelphia.'

'Like Will Smith in the Fresh Prince of Bel Air?'

'Yup. Guess that makes me a Fresh Princess then, huh?' Jess joked.

'What do you do in Jarrod's? Are you some high flying exec?'

'Hardly, more like I execute sales to those who want to look fly, get it?'

Tyrone thought for a minute and then burst out laughing. 'People who want to look fly! That's an Americanism for looking cool, isn't it? You sell clothes!'

'Wow, wouldn't want to challenge you at charades on a dark night!'

'So Jess, put me out of my misery. Are you betrothed to another?'

'You are nuts!' Jess laughed. 'Well, I am sort of single. I've just come out of a long relationship – ten years to be exact – so I'm still dealing with that I guess.'

* * *

He wanted to ask what had happened, but felt it might be a little too personal a question so early in their telephone acquaintanceship. Surely, it wasn't too early though, after all that talk-time, to ask her out for a drink? There was only one way to know for sure: to ask. Tyrone inhaled deeply again and opened his mouth to speak.

'Tyrone, it's been great talking to you, but I've got to put my son to bed. He will stay up all night if he get's a chance and then start whining that he's tired in the morning.'

'Oh, okay. But, Jessica I wanted to…'

'Martell, you'd better turn that TV off!' Jess shouted. 'Geez, I'd better go before I end up strangling him. Great talking to you, Tyrone.'

'Hello? Jess, hello?' She was gone. Another missed opportunity. But there'd be other conversations, he'd make sure of it. This had been enough to make up his mind that one man's loss was going to be his gain.

51

Jessica

What a surprise that was, and quite a pleasant surprise at that. Tyrone seems like a really nice guy. Not that he wasn't a nice guy at the party and Oxford Street, but this conversation showed consistent nice guyness. And a real live director too? I'm a little bit impressed, I think. He was easy to talk to, no major gaps or long silences, just continuous yapping. For two hours. Wow. I don't think me and Gary have ever had that lengthy a conversation. I shouldn't criticise though, conversation was never really our thing.

It was nice to have a nothing-expected conversation with a guy. I haven't had that since all my trauma started. Talking to Tyrone just felt so unpressurised and normal. It's actually given me a new lease of ending-relationship-life. I can actually visualise the end of me and Gary. Maybe not the exact end date, but at least it's in view.

A good kick to my conscience to finish things – like wedding bells or some other life-changing, decision-altering event – would help. And if not, then I'll just have to woman-up and do it, because it's clear to me that Gary will not. If I so much as broach the topic he verbally or sexually changes it. No points as to which method of topic change works the best. I'm almost ashamed to admit it. And, I know his determination to hold on is because I'm fighting against it. He can be such a sadist.

This Tyrone guy seems funny and sensitive. Not that I'm falling for it or him. I mean, how crazy would that be with everything I've got on my plate already? Besides, I'm not very trusting of myself in these situations at the moment. Look how things have turned out after meeting Gary. Need I say more? Nice as Tyrone may be, telephone contact has got to be it.

Though I say the words with conviction, I know the echo of I'm-a-glutton-for-punishment will come back to haunt me. I wonder if we'd spoken for longer, if he'd have wanted to meet up or something? Luckily I had to go to sort out Martell, so I don't have to think about what I would have said if he had asked. I don't think I'd want to tell him no, and my love life is in too much of a muddle right now just with Bobby and Gary. And out of those two even more so with Gary. I should just be able to tell him it's over. I mean it's not like he's going to leave the person he's with for me.

* * *

'What exactly are you offering me, Gary?' Jess expressed herself angrily.

'A part of me that no-one else gets, Jess. Look, I wouldn't be able to slot perfectly into your life. There's your son to consider, not to mention the fact that our families and friends know each other.'

'Oh please, Gary! You can't live your life for everyone else; you can't please everyone all the time!'

'Maybe not, but does it mean that you have to do the opposite and possibly alienate a lot of innocent people? Maybe permanently?'

Jess balled her fists in frustration. He was telling her nothing and giving her nothing, and presenting it like he was giving her the world. She just wanted to scream at him, 'Get lost!' but the words just kept twirling around in her head with no escape route.

'Jess, what we have is special. It may not be ideal, but isn't something this special worth preserving? And if we don't have to hurt anyone else in the process ...' Gary trailed off.

Jess suddenly felt weary. 'All these secrets, Gary,'

'Hey. Everyone has secrets, Jess.' Jess stared at him, wondering what secrets he had from her.

* * *

I should go tuck in my son. I walk up to his room and it's unusually silent from the outside. No TV and no radio. I quietly open the door hoping to catch him in the middle of some sneaky deed and find my baby peacefully slumbering on the bottom mattress of his bunk bed. He had an athletics tournament at school today. High jump and long jump. My little kangaroo took second place in both events. Looks like all that activity has wiped him out. I smile and close his door. As if by immaculate timing my phone rings again. Gee, I'm popular tonight.

52

Tyrone

Tyrone knew that from an etiquette point of view he should wait at least a few days to call Jessica back. But he couldn't. Twenty minutes was more than enough time to tuck in a nine-year-old boy. Kids weren't really interested in bedtime stories at that age if his own daughter was anything to go by. Just goodnight, a hug and lights out.

Just before the clock struck ten he pressed the redial button. Even he knew that calling someone after that time went beyond the realms of respectfulness. Jess answered nearly straight away.

'Hello?'

He simply couldn't tire of hearing her voice. 'Hi, Jessica. It's only me again. Tyrone? I remembered there was something else I was bursting to ask you and it couldn't wait for another day.'

Jess laughed. 'Well, I wouldn't want to be responsible for you exploding, so ask away!'

Part two of Conversation with Jessica ended after midnight. She liked him, she had to. In what capacity he didn't know yet, but he was going to look forward to finding out. You wouldn't sacrifice Big Brother highlights on TV unless you enjoyed talking to the person you were talking to. He'd hate to think that the monstrous phone bill he was going to get had all been for nothing. Mobile to mobile was never going to be cheap, but cost hadn't even crossed his mind when he was talking. They just talked. The on-coming bill seemed to concern her more than it did him

★ ★ ★

'Wow Tyrone, we've been talking for a while. would you like me to call you back?'

'Out of the question. I called to talk to you, so I'll pay for it. Anyway, you saved me from bursting, that's payment enough!'

★ ★ ★

When the bill did drop in he might regret making that decision, but for now, speaking to her had been worth every penny he was going to have to pay. Even when his phone started to get hot, he didn't want to end the conversation. He'd been ready to risk irreparable ear damage for this girl he'd only just met. He didn't mess up this second opportunity to ask her out either.

★ ★ ★

'So, Jess, would it be possible to continue this conversation in person? I don't want to deny you any more beauty sleep.' Tyrone asked apprehensively.

The question tumbled out before he'd had a chance to think about it. He couldn't believe the words had actually come from his mouth. He couldn't believe it even more when 'Sure, okay,' came out of hers.

53

Tyrone

It hadn't fully hit Tyrone that he had a date with Jessica. Maybe it would when they were face to face and breathing the same air. It could so easily have not happened. He'd just taken a chance and asked, completely on the spur of the moment. He was expecting her to say no, so why would he have had anything prepared in case she said yes?

* * *

'Okay, another time hopefully?' Tyrone smiled sadly into the phone.

Jess was confused. 'Why? What's wrong with this time?'

Tyrone blinked hard, 'Huh?'

'I said Yes. I'd be happy to continue our conversation in person. We could do lunch.'

Tyrone was in shock. He couldn't speak. She'd said YES!

'Hello? Are you still there?' Jess shook her mobile phone to make sure the battery wasn't dead – like that would tell her.

'Yes … Yes! Sorry, Jess. I thought I heard wrong. Ignore me … no, don't ignore me! I'm an idiot, but I won't be when we go to lunch.' Tyrone recovered quickly.

'So, do you have anywhere in mind?'

'In mind?' It was Tyrone's turn to be confused.

'In mind for lunch?' Jess took a patient breath. This guy was a character indeed.

'For lunch … of course for lunch! Sorry, it's a little past my bedtime, so I get a little slow but I'm catching up with

*myself!' Tyrone was babbling again. He'd gotten a date;
there was no way he could blow it before he'd even gone on
it.*

'So?' Jess questioned again.

*'Well … ahh … yes, actually I did have a place in mind.'
Tyrone answered slowly, racking his brain at the same
time, trying desperately to think of somewhere impressive.
Not that he thought Jess had expectations of him, he just
had expectations of himself. At that moment his stomach
growled giving him the inspiration he needed.*

'A restaurant!' he ended triumphantly.

*'I gathered that it might be somewhere that sold food,'
Jess laughed. 'Any particular restaurant is more what I was
getting at.'*

*Tyrone had nowhere particular at all, but he knew he
couldn't tell her that. Eating out for him usually consisted
of a KFC burger en route somewhere. He could feel his
forehead getting hot and started to loosen his collar. He
hadn't felt under this much pressure since his driving test
and that was years ago. Suddenly he remembered a restaurant one of his production assistants had been raving
about. Damn, what was the name of it? Something de
something … Nope, it wasn't coming. He'd have to call a
bluff. It was a long shot, but anything was worth it at this
point. 'I'll give you a clue. It's a fancy restaurant and it
begins with Galleon.'*

* * *

He'd thought it was a great instant suggestion under
pressure. Jess suggested a more local alternative after pointing out things he hadn't even considered in his haste to
simply think of somewhere. He was glad that he'd agreed

with Jess's suggestion in the end. He'd have agreed to anything she wanted because she'd agreed to a date!

He'd arrived a little early, if an hour could be considered a little. Besides, a good thing about getting there early was if she happened to arrive early too, she wouldn't have to wait by herself *and* he'd get to spend even more time with her. He poked his head in the restaurant and there was no sign of her, or of anyone else for that matter. He didn't know if it was a good sign for a restaurant to be so empty. It did look quite cosy though. There was a buffet area, so it was probably Eat As Much As You Can. He hadn't seen an Indian Eat As Much As You Can before; he figured the Chinese had cornered that market. The place looked familiar. Why did it look familiar? Suddenly he remembered. He'd been there before.

★ ★ ★

'I've heard its fab here, Tyrone.' Serena nodded eagerly.

'Well, if you say it's been recommended, and you trust their judgement, then I trust yours.' Tyrone smiled. 'Shall we order?'

Tyrone beckoned to the waiter who brought over their menus. They didn't have to wait very long for their choices to arrive. Tyrone didn't know whether that meant really good service or indicated that maybe not everything was being cooked to order. Tyrone popped an onion bhaji into his mouth. As he chewed, he had to physically stop himself from spitting it out again.

'Ugh ... this is tangy. A tangy onion bhaji!'

Serena looked at him and took a bite of her one. She screwed up her face in agreement.

'Yes, a very unusual taste.'

Everything else they tried had some problem with it: the prawns were too chewy, the samosas too bland, the tenderised lamb too tough. The mild chicken curry Tyrone ordered nearly melted the roof of his mouth.

'Hah! Water, water!' he gasped.

Serena, in panic, threw the glass of water his face! Tyrone spluttered in shock. 'Oh! ... I thought ... I thought it would cool you down quicker.' She explained as she tentatively began dabbing his wet nose and cheeks with a napkin.

★ ★ ★

It hadn't been a buffet restaurant back then, which had initially thrown him, but the décor – in particular that three-headed duck on the back wall – had brought it all back. A few things had been nearly brought up back then too, if his memory served him correctly. He'd hated everything he'd ordered. The big difference this time was that he really liked his date. So, if it meant sitting and pretending to lick his lips, then so be it. He wasn't going to let a little matter like food spoil the evening.

Tyrone turned away from the restaurant window to see Jess walking towards him. He had to stop his mouth from falling open. She looked so good that it was a shame that she wasn't on the lousy menu. He hoped she'd mistake his watering at the mouth as desire for the food and not for her. He had to appear cool and cheerful at all costs. He didn't want to blow this opportunity to gaze discreetly at her. The last time he was caught staring at her at that party he'd felt like a right plonker. He definitely didn't want to make that mistake again.

'Hi. I got off work early, so thought I'd just come straight here.' Jess smiled as she offered her cheek to Tyrone. He greeted her with a cordial peck, quick enough for her not to think he wanted it to be more, even though he did. He linked arms with her in a chummy way. She gave him a surprised look then broke into a wide grin.

'I hope you're hungry. I may not be able to talk as much with my mouth full.' Tyrone beamed at Jess. He felt as if he'd been in her company a hundred times. He pushed open the restaurant door to let Jess walk through first and gave a little bow. She playfully poked him in the stomach. He gave a discreet outrush of breath and made a mental note that if that was a playful poke then he'd better not get on her wrong side.

'Sitting in or takeaway?' A thickly accented waiter asked them as soon as they entered the building.

'Sitting in, please.' Tyrone looked around as he answered. He could already foresee that they were going to be seated quickly. Nearly every seat in the restaurant was empty. The waiter didn't have to give much thought to placing them.

Handing them a menu each the waiter explained, 'Sitting in is for menu; buffet is for takeaway.' He gave a little bow and walked off.

'I already know what I want. Lamb.' Jess quickly perused the menu.

'What a coincidence, me too!' laughed Tyrone. As he turned to beckon the waiter, he suddenly appeared at his elbow as if by magic, order pad in tow.

'The lamb biriyani twice please.' The waiter jotted the order down, gave a little bow again and disappeared. Before Tyrone could ask Jess about her day, the waiter was back with their orders. Jess and Tyrone looked at one another; the same thought evidently passing through their minds.

Tyrone didn't know whether the food didn't taste that bad this time around or whether it was the conversation that made it taste better. As the evening progressed he barely noticed that the place was filling up because his concentration was totally monopolised by the woman in front of him. They talked and talked, and it flowed as easily as it had on the phone.

★ ★ ★

'No way! Right in the middle of a crucial meeting, the sprinklers went off?' Tyrone roared with laughter.

'Yes! Absolutely soaked my flip chart presentation!' Jess wiped a tear from her eye.

'Yes, I always wanted to have something to do with television. As I wasn't pretty enough to be in front of the camera, I figured why not behind it?'

'Aww, shall we get the violins out?' Jess laughed.

'I think if I wasn't a director, I'd maybe have tried singing. I tried out once.'

'Where!? In your bathroom, with your comb as a microphone?'

★ ★ ★

It wasn't until the hovering waiter started to do the most hacking of coughs that Jess and Tyrone got the hint: the restaurant wanted to shut. When they looked around, they were the only customers still in the restaurant. They looked at each other in amazement, then both drew up their sleeves to look at their watches.

'Wow, it's eleven pm!' Tyrone shook his head in wonderment and reached into his pocket for his credit card. At the same time as Jess reached for her purse. 'Don't you dare. I asked *you* out to dinner, ok?' Tyrone gave her a slitty eyed look.

Jess lifted her left eyebrow in surprise. She'd thought she was being the modern woman by offering. There was only one way to smooth out this awkward moment.

'Did I ever show you the DKNY purse my ex-team bought me?' Jess gave a giant smile as she modelled the bag on her arm. They both laughed at the way she disguised her faux pas.

As the night drew to a close Tyrone walked Jess to her car. As she stepped into her vehicle, she wound down the window.

'I'll call you, Jess.' He gave her cheek a second peck and walked off with an evident spring in his step.

Tyrone was on cloud nine. Tonight had been perfect. He couldn't wait to ask Jess out again, and had barely restrained himself from doing so straight away. He wanted to take things slowly. He could see potential with Jess, and as much as he liked her, he wanted to be as sure as he could before taking things further. One pigeon step at a time. If he'd done that in previous relationships instead of rushing in, they might have turned out more successfully.

54

Gary

Gary was concerned. So the holiday with Jess hadn't been the dream one that he'd imagined it would be, but it hadn't been all bad. Well, not for him anyway, and it wouldn't have been all bad for Jess if she hadn't kept going on about all the bad luck that was apparently besieging her. Even he had to admit though, if only to himself, that she had been unusually unlucky. But hey, shit happened sometimes.

Now they were back, she was being as elusive as the Scarlet Pimpernel. It was never a good sign when Jess was difficult to get a hold of. He'd only seen her once since they'd got back. It was over a week since they'd even spoken. Surely she couldn't be that busy? Her moods weren't usually a problem for him; he only had to see her in person to smooth out any issues in his special way. His difficulty was how he could get to see her in person if he couldn't even speak to her on the phone.

55

Bobby

Bobby's agitation was growing. Jess was always busy since she'd got back from holiday. Every time he called she seemed to be in the middle of something or other. He was eager to hear whether she had heard about all his good deeds to her family and friends. When she brought it up, he knew he had to act nonchalantly, as if his help had been no big deal. However, it was going to be a bit difficult to get his 'act on' if he couldn't even get to speak to her on the phone.

56

Jessica

I replace the phone receiver after yet another conversation with Tyrone. The second today. He's about the only guy I am speaking to on the phone at the moment. The more I speak to him the more he grows on me. Since we went out to dinner we've been talking regularly. Not quite every day mind, but it looks like it's heading that way. I thought he would have asked me out again after we went Indian the other day. Even though we're purely platonic friends (emphasis on the platonic) for some odd and very strange reason all the concerns of a first date had flooded my mind – even though our dinner wasn't a date. Even though it definitely, no way, no how, was a date.

* * *

'I know we're only friends, but I still feel a bit apprehensive, Tania!'

'Of what exactly?'

'Well, what if I get food stuck in my teeth? Friends or no, I would die a thousand deaths of embarrassment!'

'So take a small mirror with you and when you're eating anything stick-in-your-teeth-ish, just discreetly take a look. Next concern?' Tania didn't even stop filing her nails as she spoke.

'Would you let him pick you up or would you meet him at the restaurant?'

'Definitely meet him there.'

'Because?'

'Because if he pisses you off, you don't have to rely on

biting your tongue to make sure you've got a lift home.'
Tania didn't even have to think about her response.

'Okay, Miss Know it all, what if while we're waiting for
the starter, we run out of things to say?'

'After your marathon conversations? Hardly!' Jess went
to interrupt but Tania continued. 'Eastenders,' she ended.

'Eastenders?'

'Yes, Eastenders. Everybody watches it, everybody has an
opinion on it and you can talk about it 'til the cows come
home, or at least until the samosas arrive.'

Jess shook her head in amazement. How did her baby
sister get so clued up on the protocols of dating?

★ ★ ★

I know I'm nuts to be encouraging whatever it is that's
happening between me and Tyrone. It's as if the dilemma
keeping me up at nights with the other two isn't enough.
Oh, enough of these men. I need to call back my girl.
Maddy has left me three messages so far today saying I
need to get back to her as soon as humanly possible. As per
usual she's left no clue as to what the urgency is. Might as
well see what's up while I'm still in chatter mode.

'Maddy, it's Jessica. What's up?'

I'm greeted with some loud background music. I
wonder if Maddy can actually hear what I'm saying when
I call her sometimes. She's got her music turned up so loud
I'm surprised that she even heard the phone ring. It's like
a party twenty four seven at her house. Her neighbours
would probably throttle her if she didn't keep them in
discounted theatre tickets.

'Hi Jess! You know you mentioned in passing that you
needed another break to sort your head out? Well, you'll

never guess what?' Before I attempt to hazard a guess she continues, 'I saw a bargain flight to Barbados today. Wait for it ... one hundred and seventy five pounds, self-catering, for one week! It's in a week's time. How's that for the cheapo of the century!'

'Wow! That really is a true bargain.'

'And with my charm I managed to get the guy to hold two seats without a deposit until they open at ten tomorrow morning. So what sayeth you? Fancy it?'

'Yes.' I don't even need to think about it. Work shouldn't be a problem. I'll just say I have to go back for the reading of my grandma's will because she requested it. It's another lie and I hate the fact that I seem to be getting so good at them, but it's one that makes a lot of follow-on sense due to the fact that I went to her 'funeral' a couple weeks back. Sorting out my relationships is priority as of now and this holiday is going to be where I create the grand plan of exactly how I'm going to do that. A plan that's going to be so much better than the current one of dodging Gary's calls like a professional hockey player.

★ ★ ★

Jess picked up her ringing phone and saw Gary's number. 'Maddy, quick. Answer this for me. Tell him I've got diarrhoea and my hands are full of toilet paper so I don't have a spare one to answer my phone!'

Gary's number was flashing on Jess's phone.

'Martell, Sweetie, do Mom a favour and answer this call for me. Tell the man that I'm in the bath.'

Martell looked confused and was about to question his mother.

'I'm going into the bath very soon, so it's not a lie. You're just telling him in advance, Honey.'

Jess looked at her phone screen to see Gary's number again.
'Tania, tell this guy that I'm on emergency jury service and am not allowed to take any calls for a few days in case I hear something that might influence my judicial opinion!'

★ ★ ★

A plan that won't require a fresh batch of excuses as to why I can't go out with Bobby.

★ ★ ★

'Bobby, no can do tonight. I've got to watch a Survival episode about spiders in the wild. It's to help Martell with his homework.'

'Shucks, Bobby. The laundry basket is overflowing. If I don't do some washing tonight, I'll run out of clean underwear!'

'Oh dear, Bobby. Can't meet tonight, I'm afraid. Banged my little toe and now I've taken off my shoe, I don't have a clue how I'll get it back on.'

★ ★ ★

My excuses are now ranging from scraping the bottom of the barrel to bordering on the fantastic. I need to tell Bobby the truth. I need to tell both him and Gary what time it is. And like that's not enough, the head honchos at work can't seem to agree on a simple matter as to what theme they want the sale window to have. Lord only knows how much I need to be in an environment where none of these problems exist. When I'm back, and revitalised, I'll be able to tell not only the boys where to go, but the bosses too.

Gary will definitely be my first project. This holiday will be the perfect place to prepare my leaving speech. Just thinking again about what happened makes my temperature rise. It would make anyone get hot under the collar. And he wonders why I won't take his calls.

★ ★ ★

'Gary, aren't we supposed to be meeting up today?' The incredulity in Jess's voice was clear. This was their first opportunity to see each other since they'd got back.

'Were we? Oh, I must have forgotten,' Gary replied nonchalantly.

'Forgotten? You forgot!'

'Sorry, Baby. I've been swamped. We can just reschedule.'

Jess envisioned him shrugging his shoulders as if forgetting was no big deal. He'd probably had to specifically plan, possibly rearrange and probably lie to make it happen because she'd had to do at least two of those. Now, after all that, he was suggesting rescheduling as if it could happen at the click of some fingers. Jess's frustration started to simmer.

'We should just reschedule? That's what you're saying, right?'

'Sure, let me just look in my diary. Got a meeting then … picking up Tia there …'

Jess couldn't believe what she was hearing. He was just trying to slot her into some gap in his diary. He wasn't bothered in the slightest. How she wished that she felt that way too. Tears of anger pricked at her eyes: anger at herself.

'You know what, Gary? Forget it,' Jess stated, then imme-diately hung up the phone.

★ ★ ★

That was the first time I felt that I could actually do with-out this guy in my life. Something must have clicked for him too, because he immediately called me back. I picked up the phone and promptly slammed it back down again. He called again. This time I couldn't even be bothered to pick it up. I could hear his lame ass apologies as they were being recorded on the answering machine.

★ ★ ★

First message: Jess, what happened? The phone just went dead. Call me back.

Second message: Jess, can you please call me back?

Third message: Jess, I'm sorry. I shouldn't have forgotten. I'll make it up to you. I can only do that if you please pick up the phone.

Fourth message: Jess PLEASE pick up. I'm sorry. I'm sorry. I'M SORRY!

★ ★ ★

As I stared ahead of me, my anger was slowly being replaced by a sad hopelessness and then I started to cry. I cried like my whole heart was breaking – but the tears weren't over Gary. It was over the whole big mess my life had become. I had to sort it out, for my own sanity if nothing else. Later on that evening, when he'd called for about the tenth time, I decided to answer it. Mainly because the machine was so full of the messages he'd been leaving all day that it couldn't hold any more.

* * *

'Gary, it's over.' There was no emotion in Jess's voice. It was evident that Gary was shocked because he didn't answer straight away.

'Jess. You're being a tad ridiculous. Don't you think you're over-reacting just a little bit?'

'No. I don't.'

'I forgot, for crying out loud! I forgot! I'm human!' Gary shouted down the phone. He was met with Jess's stony silence. The gravity of the situation hit him. Jess was serious. She wanted out. Panic suddenly overwhelmed him. It was not a feeling he was used to.

'Jess, I love you. Don't do this to me, to us,' he said urgently. Jess still did not respond. Gary continued softly. 'Jess, if it was so simple to be with you, don't you think I would be? I love you, Jess!'

'If you loved me, you would let me go.' Jess could not disguise the sadness in her voice.

'It's because I love you why I can't.'

* * *

After that I couldn't speak any more. I felt drained. He said he was coming around, and for all my protesting that he shouldn't, he did. He came, we talked, we did it, he slept, I couldn't. I knew then that that was my farewell performance.

'Alrighty then!' Maddy's exuberance breaks into my thoughts.

'The travel agent is open 'til ten, so may as well call him back now. No point in waiting until tomorrow. I'll pay on my credit card and you can sort me out later. Is that okay?'

'Yes.' I couldn't seem to add more to my responses than that.

'Alrighty then, speak to you tomorrow!'

No sooner do I put down the phone than it rings again. I jump from the surprise of it and answer it before the first ring finishes.

'Hello?'

'Hi, Jess, it's me, Bobby.'

Oh no, not now. 'Hey Bobby, I'm just on a call, so I'll have to get back to you. Bye!' I hang up before he can respond. I won't be able to get away with using that excuse for much longer, but right now I've got nothing else. I sigh, just in time for the phone to ring again. This time I scrutinise the caller ID because I really am out of reasons not to talk to my child's father. I look in surprise at the number flashing and pick up.

'Hello.'

'It's me.' I smile in recognition of Tyrone's voice.

'Hey, wasn't I just speaking to you?'

'You were, but I thought that a paltry two hours of conversation with you just wasn't up to our standard.'

We both laugh.

'Guess, what? I'm going on holiday! In a week, and not a moment too soon I might add, I am bidding England another temporary leave of absence.'

'Lucky you, where're you off to?'

He sounds genuinely interested. Like he does about everything I say. Even when I'm talking about hairspray. 'My friend has seen some knock-down flights to sunny, sea-ey and sandy Barbados and is booking it as we speak.'

'I think I'm jealous! I've been thinking about going on holiday for a while now. It's been a few years since I was last away.' For a minute Tyrone seems lost in thought.

'So, what's stopping you? If you can go and you want to go, then go.'

'You make it sound so simple.'

'It is! Stop thinking and get going, that's what I say. That's what I'm going to do.'

'You know what? I just may do that!'

We both laugh as I add a little 'Hurrah!' on the end. Our conversation then moves on to places we've been and places we'd like to go and in no time another two hours has gone by.

'Oh, oh. There goes my cordless. That beep means it needs re-charging I'm afraid. You've talked my battery out!'

'I can call you in ...' Tyrone continues, but I interrupt.

'I have a few things to do, so the beeping is also a reminder for me to stop yakking and get on with them.'

Tyrone sighs dramatically. 'Okay. Parting is such sweet sorrow. I'll call you later, on the morrow.'

'Look, you're a poet, and don't even know it!' We both laugh at my wit and on that note I manage to end the conversation. It's not that I couldn't have talked to him all night because I'm sure that I could have (in fact I nearly did one night last week) but I'm going to Barbados in a week. That date will be here before you know it, therefore I need to start packing. Now.

57

Bobby

Bobby knew he was a changed man just from the patience he'd been exhibiting in the face of his continued non-contact with Jess. Even today, when she'd more or less put the phone down on him, he wasn't upset. He wasn't worried. Not at all. He knew that no matter how busy she was now, they'd have to meet up soon enough; he'd have to see her eventually. How did he know that? How could he be so sure? Martell was how. Bobby smiled to himself as he replaced the receiver.

58

Jessica

We are here! Barbados! The girls are here! I can't believe what was just a booking a week ago is now a reality. Here at last and not a moment too soon. I need this holiday like I need air. The stuff that's been happening has been unreal. I'm still confused by Bobby's reaction when I called him up to tell him I was going away again.

★ ★ ★

'Bobby, I'm flying away again for a week. In a week actually. Is it okay for you to look after Martell? I know it's short notice, but it was one of those deals that was too good to miss.'

Bobby didn't answer.

'Bobby? ... You still there?'

'So, you're off again are you?'

'Erm ... yes.' Jess wasn't sure how to take his response.

'I see. Your "friends" like to get away, don't they?'

'Erm ... yes. It's no secret that Maddy likes a holiday.'

Suddenly Bobby's whole tone changed. 'Of course she does! Everyone knows how hot-footed old Maddy is! And who can blame her? You'll have a great time on holiday with Maddy! No probs. I can have Martell for as long as you and Maddy are on vacation.'

Jess held the phone away from her ear and looked at it, wondering if it really was a sane Bobby talking on the other end.

★ ★ ★

The man practically bent over backwards to accommodate me with Martell. Hmm … guess I'll have to think about that along with everything else while I'm on the beach.

Good thing I started packing as soon as Maddy told me the news about the holiday. The time flew quicker than even I imagined. When I finally decided to call him, Gary couldn't believe that I was going away so soon again either.

* * *

'In two days? You're going away again in two days?' There was no hiding the shock in Gary's voice.

'Yes Gary. I'm going to Barbados in two days.' Jess's response was calm. She didn't want anything Gary might say to get her worked up before she left.

'Okay. Well, let me give you a lift to the airport. I should be able to sort something out. Let me just get my diary and swap a few things around.'

'I don't think so, Gary.' Jess was firm. 'It'll be easier for me to get a taxi. Listen, I've got go, I've still more packing to do. Bye.'

Jess hung up quickly without waiting to hear what he had to add. She took a deep breath, this was just the start. By the time this vacation was over, they would be too.

* * *

I was hoping for an uneventful trip to the airport (travel sickness tablets … check, traffic update … check) but that soon proved to be wishful thinking on my part. From the minute I got to the check-in desk, it was clear that surprises were in store for me.

After struggling to get my case on the luggage belt, I wait patiently for the check-in lady to stick all the tags on. I glance around, as you do, to see who else was going on vacation and who was trying to persuade their check-in person to turn a blind eye to their overweight pieces. My jaw and my passport drop to the floor when I see who I see, standing as carefree as you please, three check-in desks down.

I start to squint (as if that's going to make the vision clearer) to make sure I'm not mistaken. Mid-squint, the person turns, catches my eye, gives me a Queen Elizabeth-like wave and a smile. They then turn back to their check-in desk like it's the most natural thing in the world for them to be there. By now, my own check-in lady is getting a little antsy with me.

'Madam! For the third time, may I see your passport?'

'Oh … Sorry! It's right here!' I quickly pick my passport off the floor and give it to the lady and lean back to look three desks down again. The surprise is now on me, because they are no longer there. I now know the pitfalls of not eating breakfast before a road trip. Hallucination by hunger appears to be one of them. I shake my head and the image of who I've just seen out of my mind, and make my way to McDonalds – the agreed meeting point.

* * *

The shrill ring of the phone jerked Jess out of her sleep. Eyes half-closed, she fumbled to pick up the receiver.

'Hey, Jess, can you believe I'm still packing?' Maddy doesn't preamble.

Jess struggled to open her eyes a little wider to look at

the clock beside her. It was three am. THREE am! 'Maddy, do you know what time it is?' Jess croaked.

'Yes. Time for me to make some final decisions about what I'm taking. I am twenty kilos overweight at the moment.'

'Twenty! That's almost another piece of luggage!' Jess would have sounded more shocked were she more conscious.

'I know this, and my time to fix this is limited. So, my friend, I will meet you in McDonalds if I don't meet you at check-in. I sorted out our seating on-line already.'

'Mm ... mmm ... okay.' Jess mumbled. The word 'McDonalds' was the only thing she recalled as her eyes closed again.

★ ★ ★

It just so happened that Maddy wasn't at McDonalds but in Sunglasses City. I found her just as they were doing last calls for our flight.

'Come on, Maddy!' I grab her and we run, wheeled hand-luggage and plastic carrier bags flying behind us. I see the air hostess up ahead pointedly looking at her watch with a constipated smile on her face.

'Boarding passes, please,' she says stiffly, making me wonder if it's just her smile suffering from the dreaded affliction. I quickly hand her my pass, buying Maddy some time as she rifles through several pockets in her bag before finding hers.

'36D and 36E. To your right, ladies.'

We walk towards our seats, head angled upwards checking the seat numbers as we go along to find that we have an aisle separating us. Before I can holler at a member of the crew at the unjust travesty of having two friends separated on an eight-hour flight, I remember that it was actually Maddy that chose our seats. I put my bag in the overhead locker and then my mouth clamps shut in shock when I see who is see sitting in 36C. This time I didn't even attempt to squint like I did at check-in.

'That is you, isn't it? Tyrone?' I say, pinching him to make sure he's real. A piercing 'Ouch!' soon told me he was no figment of my imagination. The 'Ouch!' that came from him was considerably softer than the one that came from me when I broke my fingernail on his jacket.

'No way!' I exclaim again, nursing my broken nail. He smiles and nods while rubbing where I pinched him.

'What the heck are you doing here? Did you stowaway?'

'Not exactly. I just decided to take your advice and go on holiday. I know Barbados is a small island, but I figured it could probably hold me too, so why not there?'

Well, what could I say to that? Tyrone talked for the whole flight: all eight hours of it. I put it down to excitement and the fact that he'd already had a lot of practice back on the ground. Okay, so I spoke a lot too. But at least my excuse is I'm a woman so talking a lot is very likely programmed into my genes. We did go for broke, though. We even talked while we watched the movie, which starred Jennifer Lopez as a battered wife. We managed that by using one earphone each so that we could listen to the film and listen to each other talk at the same time. At one point, Tyrone got so involved in the film that he actually started yelling at the little screen in front of him: 'Watch out!'; 'Look behind you!'; 'Aww, man I can't believe you *did* that!' There were a few times when I had to look at him and blink to make sure it wasn't Martell sitting next to me. I don't think Maddy was too put out by me sitting and chatting to Tyrone for most of the flight. Normally she'd try to hold it against me.

* * *

'No. It's fine. Of course I don't mind sitting with a perfect stranger for eight hours. It's not like I really wanted to sit with the friend I came on holiday with. I mean, why would I?'

Maddy had conveniently forgotten that it was actually her that had booked the seats and clearly hadn't looked at the picture that would have shown her that an aisle separated them.

* * *

How Tyrone managed to wangle a seat next to me, when my own travel partner couldn't, will forever remain a mystery. It wasn't like Maddy was that far away either, I mean, I could still see her dinner selection. My eyes nearly popped out of my head when I saw the hunk that was sitting next to her. Some stranger! He was the kind of hot guy you end up sitting next to in romantic novels, where he spills his drink on you, you get mad and by the end of the flight you're practically engaged.

The irony is, Maddy doesn't even like making small talk on flights. I remember one where a little old lady started to make conversation with her.

* * *

'So, my dear, what do you do?' The lady smiled intently at Maddy. Maddy did not acknowledge her but continued looking straight ahead, a little smile on her face.

The lady looked puzzled. 'Excuse me, dear,' she addressed Maddy again.

Still no response from Maddy whose expression hadn't changed.

The lady touched Maddy's arm. Maddy looked at the lady and gave her a big smile then turned to look in front of her again. The lady, confused now, touched Maddy's arm again to get her attention.

'I asked what you do for a living, my dear.'

Maddy screwed her eyes at the woman's lips and then pointed to her own and shook her head. She then started simulating hand movements covering her ears. The lady concentrated hard on the hand-signalled message her neighbour was trying to relay, then clapped her hands in recognition.

'Oh, I understand! You can't hear me!'

Maddy gave the woman a thumbs up and pointedly pulled out the airline magazine to scrutinise the duty free perfumes on offer.

★ ★ ★

Admittedly it was a tactful way to get some peace, but some of Maddy's hand signs were very, very questionable.

Eight hours ten minutes later we have finally arrived in beautiful Barbados. Even though we broke conversation records on the plane, me and Tyrone didn't make any plans to meet up when we touched ground. He's probably made his own holiday plans anyway and chances are, even though it's a small island, I won't see him again while we're here. Hmm ... Then again, I may see nothing but him because it's a small island. Whatever anyway. I've just landed in sunny Barbados for crying out loud. Plenty of time to think about who and what I'll see when I start working on my sun tan.

We step off the plane into glorious heat and Maddy, the hater of small talk, is still talking to that guy. They're walking in step, like they're a couple! I hope she doesn't forget that, even after an eight-hour conversation, that guy is still a stranger. He could be some kind of serial killer for all she knows.

Grantley Adams International Airport is nice. You can see everything almost at once. The line for customs, all the exits, the toilets. In fact, from here I can even see the belt where they're unloading the luggage from our plane. There's already a suitcase with a 'very heavy' sticker on it that looks very much like mine.

The queue where the customs officers are looking at everyone's passport is moving pretty quickly which is always a good thing. Before I can count to ten, okay maybe count to fifty, I'm at the front.

'Passport please,' asks the customs lady.

I'm hoping she doesn't scrutinise my passport too much. The picture in it is a constant reminder of a freaky hair phase I was going through. I've battled with temptation to report it lost, just so I can get a new one with a new picture before it expires in three years' time.

I can clearly see now that that case is mine. I exhale in relief, knowing that this time my clothes have arrived at the same destination as me, at the same time as me. Now, all I have to find is Maddy. As I thought, she's still yapping with that guy from the plane. Is that scribbling I can see being done on that piece of paper he's just given her? Is that a smile I can see on her face? I think my girl has scored a touchdown and we haven't even been in the country for half an hour. I shake my head in disbelief. She looks up and sees me, so walks over.

'Jess, I've sorted out some places for us to go to tomorrow night and Friday. I didn't bother about tonight because I figured you might be tired from all that talking you did on the plane.' I open my mouth to speak in defence but she raises her palm to my face and continues, 'Yes, don't think I didn't hear you. And don't think that the fact that I didn't get any of that talktime, considering we are on holiday together, has gone unnoticed.'

Indignant now, I open my mouth to attempt to speak again, and again she raises her palm. '… or that my sacrifice will go unrewarded. Hmph. Anyway, just in case you do manage to muster up a little energy, I took Trev's number. Can you believe he's staying just up the road from us?'

I wonder how she knows where 'up the road from us' is when she's never been to Barbados before.

'Trev?' is what I actually ask. That is some fast familiarity going on when you're already syllableising a man's name when you've only just met him.

'Oh yeah, Trevor. The guy next to me on the plane. He comes here every year to see family, so knows all the places to be. And since I've got his number, we know all the places to be too! Hey, that looks like my suitcase right there.' And with that, off she jets to get her stuff off the belt. I'm sure her suitcase must be dizzy by now, the amount of times it's probably gone around that belt.

I smile to myself. With Maddy around, trying to have a restful holiday is going to be an interesting challenge.

Tyrone is still over by the luggage belt sorting out his case. Having him around is going to be interesting too. I should see about getting a taxi to take us to the hotel. I would kill for a cold shower right about now. I'm about to swivel on my heel to the direction of the taxi stand when out of the corner of my eye I see somebody waving. It's Tyrone. Not a wave goodbye either, but a wave to say hold up a minute. I wonder what's on his mind? He finishes talking to what looks like a holiday rep, and comes over.

'Hey, Jess, how are you getting to your hotel?'

'With great difficulty if Maddy doesn't get a move on with those cases. Everyone from our plane is already queuing at the taxi rank. We'll have to wait for ages by the time we get over there.'

'Would you like a ride?' he smiles.

I'm sure he got his cases only just before Maddy. He wasn't in the taxi queue so how'd he manage to sort out transportation already? Hired car, maybe? Can't see him holding any keys though. Hope he's not offering the use of his back because comfort, even a little bit, has to come into the equation. Oh, and naturally Maddy too, of course. All these thoughts going on in my head yet 'Huh?' was all I managed to get through my mouth.

'Do. You. Want. A. Ride?' This time he says it really slowly, pronounced as if I'm somewhat hearing challenged. He cocks his head to the side with a cheeky grin. Suddenly I don't care if the ride is on his shoulders, as long as it gets me to that hotel. That cold shower is now calling me like an annoying customer.

'It is hot, I am sweaty, I am tired; and so I am not refusing. Thanks Tyrone. Let me just go hurry that girl up.'

I proceed, fully prepared if need be, to drag Maddy by her hair, away from the suitcase belt where she's surrounded by three native porters, all trying to help her find a suitcase that it takes me all of five seconds to find.

When we go back over to Tyrone he transfers all of our cases onto a trolley with his case and then starts to push it. I think to myself 'What a gentleman!' But what confuses me is where he's taking us. The hired car area and the taxi stand with its twenty-people-long queue is on the left, while we are clearly going to the right. Now I know all that stuff about not giving a man directions so I'm not about to go against the grain and challenge that, but there is nothing to stop me asking him where we are going.

59

Tyrone

Tyrone would never have guessed, if Jess hadn't mentioned it, that Maddy had only just met the guy she was avidly talking to. Anyone would have thought they'd known each other for years. He owed the guy a big favour for keeping Maddy occupied so that he could have Jess all to himself on the flight. If he saw him in a bar, he'd buy him a rum. He was just hoping that the guy wouldn't offer the girls a lift before he had the chance. He'd read about helicopter rides from the airport on the internet and figured why not do the whole touristy bit and cut out the taxi queue by travelling to his accommodation by air. He managed to catch Jess's eye when he was talking to the airport lady who organised the rides.

★ ★ ★

'So, can I get the advertised helicopter ride from the airport?' Tyrone asked.

'Yes sir, you can. The rides are very popular and as your flight is the first in, you're in luck! I'll radio over to confirm, sir.'

'Sorry, can I just ask what the cost per person is?'

'The cost is for the rental of the helicopter sir, it's not based on the number of occupants. The helicopter holds three people plus the pilot.'

A big grin came across Tyrone's face. Three people. Today, that was his favourite number!

★ ★ ★

He beckoned Jess over before the lady had even finished telling him all the details. It struck him, what better way to make a good impression on the start of Jess's holiday than to offer her and her friend a lift to their hotel by helicopter?

Jess's friend Maddy seemed to be having a problem finding her luggage and Jess had gone to help her. Turned out that was the best thing that could have happened; if it wasn't for that delay, Maddy's new friend might have got in an offer of a ride too. To make sure there was no mind changing, Tyrone quickly loaded all Jess and Maddy's suitcases onto his trolley. Where the clothes go the women go. He could see that Jess looked a little baffled, while Maddy was just following along, concentrating on what looked like a map. He just kept pushing the trolley without even glancing behind to see if they were keeping up.

'Where are we going?' Jess asked.

He'd known it would just be a matter of time before she wouldn't be able to contain the question any longer. He'd noticed she was very much someone who liked to know everything that was going on in advance.

'To get our lift to the hotel.'

'But the taxi rank is over that way.' Jess crinkled her forehead. Still without looking back he could imagine her pointing in the direction of the taxi rank.

'I know. Look at the queue,' he answered, smiling to himself. He was enjoying keeping her in suspense. He could see the helicopter ahead now, and the airport lady waving him in its direction. It was at this point that he looked back at Jess, just in time to see the I-see-it-but-I-don't-believe-it reaction on her face.

60

Jessica

I think we're walking towards that helicopter pad over there. What I don't understand is why? I open my mouth to shout the question to Tyrone, but I stop myself. Seeing the pilot hop off the thing and start to load the suitcases tells me all I need to know. I must be doing a great impression of a mosquito catcher with my mouth wide open like this. I look at Tyrone in disbelief as he walks over to me, takes my hand and pulls me gently towards the helicopter.

'If you just stand there, we'll miss the flight,' he says as calm as you please. I, on the other hand, can't seem to register that I'm about to be taken to my hotel in a helicopter. A helicopter! I look behind me at Maddy who seems to have decided she's had enough of the map she's been reading. She crumples it up and stuffs it into her handbag. When she finally looks up and sees the helicopter, she too does a mosquito catcher impression.

'Are we going for a ride in … that?' she asks in awe.

'Yes. Is that okay with you? There was a bit of a queue for the taxis so I thought this would be quicker.' Tyrone is so nonchalant with his response, I can almost believe that he's taking pleasure in the shock he's caused us. 'Especially as Jess told me that she is dying for a shower, and it wouldn't do for her die right at the beginning of the holiday because you'd be alone.'

He looks down at me and grins. I'm still lost for words so it's a good thing that Maddy seems to have enough for both of us.

'Well, bearing that in mind, let's board this bird without further ado! On both our behalves I accept your kind offer of transportation.' And indeed without further ado, the girl ducks her head so that the blades don't take it off and climbs into the helicopter. Tyrone and me follow. He climbs up first and holds out his hand to help me up. I nearly miss my step due to the wind from the blades blowing my hair all over the place. So much for my trip to the hairdresser yesterday. What a waste of thirty pounds. Luckily I recover my composure quite quickly. To fall at the feet of this man – literally – would have been embarrassing enough to make me turn right back around and join the end of the now thirty-plus-strong queue at the taxi rank.

I sit down next to Maddy; Tyrone sits next to the pilot and seconds later it's lift off.

Barbados by helicopter has got to be the best way in the world to get a ride to your hotel. The view is absolutely fantastic. Every few minutes the pilot tells us where we've just flown over. To the left is a place called Bathsheba village where King David's wife was supposed to have bathed in pools of milk that kept her skin soft. Nowadays, to get that result in the bath, I make do with the twenty-five per cent moisturiser in the Lovely Doveley Bath Wash. To the right is Cherry Tree Hill – a hill that now has no cherry trees. Hmm … that's all I can say to that. Up ahead is Hackleton's Cliff, one thousand feet above sea level, where some dude decided to commit suicide by riding his horse over it. All I can say to that is poor horse. Just the same, I am fascinated. Even Tyrone astonishes me a little with some pretty intellectual questions about the island. Like what's the native dish? And what's the island's main export? The responses I don't really take in as I'm still enraptured by the view.

Maddy is busy making the most of the texting facility on her phone and therefore missing most of the sights. This is so amazing. I still can't get over the fact that I'm getting a sightseeing ride to my hotel in a helicopter! If he wanted to impress me, he gets ten out of ten for this.

'We are approaching St James. We'll be at your hotel in approximately ten minutes.' All too soon, the pilot announces that the wondrous ride is about to end. I look at my watch and am shocked to realise that we've been in the air for over half an hour.

By the time we land, I've abandoned all efforts to save any part of my hair-do. We disembark the helicopter and retrieve our bags from the hold. What an amazing trick it would be if Tyrone was booked in the same hotel as us.

'Where are you staying, Tyrone?' Sometimes going for the jugular in your questioning is just as good a way to get to the root of something as subtlety.

'I haven't actually booked a place to stay yet. Thought I'd wait until I got out here and see where was most central.'

That's adventurous. Not sure I could fly so far away without knowing in advance where I was going to lay my head.

'The travel agent gave me a few recommendations when I booked. There's Sandy Lane hotel: that's meant to be quite popular and reasonable. Not too far from here either. I'll probably check that one out.'

I think it's at this point that I'm supposed to say, 'Why don't you see if you can get a room here?' The guy *did* just give us a ride in his helicopter. Could he have manoeuvred it this way? If he did then it's damned sneaky. If he did then I'm damned impressed, again. Well, I've decided that this is a holiday of decisions, so here comes the first one.

'If you haven't sorted out anywhere to stay yet, why not see if they've got any rooms available here?'

He looks at me quite strangely and doesn't answer for a few seconds. In fact the silence drags out so long that I wonder if he heard me.

'Really? Would you be okay with that? I don't want to cramp your style or anything.'

'Well, just make sure you don't then and that should solve that problem.'

He looks at me blankly which makes me think the joke hasn't quite registered with him yet. It soon will ... five ... four ... three ... two ...

'Ha ha!' he finally laughs. 'Okay! If you're sure it's okay, I'll do that then.'

'Well. I'm going to get that shower I've been dreaming of. Maybe I'll see you later.' I turn with my suitcase and wave at him over my shoulder. I hope I'm not going regret my decision to invite him to stay at the same hotel.

Turns out Tyrone staying at the hotel was a great decision. I'm hoping it's the first of many this vacation. Tyrone has just been the perfect host and it's not even his party. Even Maddy can't believe what a charmer he's been. And he's not made one personal advance towards me either.

* * *

'Hey, there's a great restaurant around the corner from here. If you're hungry, it would be my pleasure to take you and Maddy to dinner.'

'The hotel's got a neat little cocktail bar downstairs. How-about a "spirited" nightcap before bed, ladies?'

'Spoke to a local and they said there's a cool club just a few miles from here. If you've no plans, I've hired a car so can give you guys a lift to check it out.'

★ ★ ★

It's been a real battle to get him to allow either of us to so much as contribute to a tip. Maddy's hung out more than a few times with her flight buddy Trevor, so much so that the only time we've really had quality catch-up time together is during wardrobe changes.

★ ★ ★

'So Trevor took you to the famous Oistins Fish Festival?
    'Yes! Girl, I ate so much fish, I feel like a mermaid. Do mermaids eat fish?'

'Tyrone swam for a whole hour? So what did you do?'
    'Topped up my tan at the beach, what else?'

'Jess, Trevor knows the whole island, I swear. He took me to some off-the-beaten-track cove. It was really beautiful!'
    'Weren't you a little bit nervous, going to the middle of nowhere with him? I know you get on well and everything, but you still haven't known him very long.'
    'Girl, you know I don't go anywhere without my mace!'

'Enough of me and Trevor. What about you and Tyrone? You guys seem to be getting really close.'
    'He's a nice guy, Maddy. A really nice guy. I don't know if

that's a good thing considering what happened the last time I thought a guy was really nice. Look how that turned out.'

★ ★ ★

So much for a girly holiday. On the occasions when it's just been me and Tyrone, like now, he's still always been the perfect gentleman.

'Okay, we've talked about life, loves and life again. What's next?' I laugh.

I thought that we'd covered most topics back home, but this guy has layers like an onion. Gary's name comes up in a third-person-hypothetical-situation kind of way. I ask Tyrone his opinion of the Gary third-person-hypothetical situation. If I didn't know any better I'd have thought I was talking to Doctor Phil.

'An interesting one,' he begins. 'I think a guy like that preys on perplexed women. They seek out women that are in search of that missing emotional something in their life.'

'Missing emotional something?' That's a mouthful to say, never mind search for.

'Yeah, like affection or passion.'

'Ahh. I see.' I didn't.

'They grab the opportunity to play on these feelings and manipulate the situation to their own ends. Because the women are already troubled, they think the attention has some sort of genuine merit. It doesn't.'

'Ahh, I see.' I still didn't.

'It's about control, knowing they have power over the woman. If she's strong then, hopefully, one day she'll see the light and get out. But for those women who aren't, well

311

they could be left hanging in there for years. Or until he decides he's moving on.'

'Oh! I see.' This time I actually did see. And I cannot be in this thing with Gary for years! It's almost like Tyrone knows Gary, the way he described the predator. His insight into this stuff is deep. I think I have a new-found awe of this guy. And his wisdom doesn't just seem to cover third-person-hypothetical situations either. It transcended to hypothetical work situations, hypothetical family situations, even typical hypothetical girly situations. I know. I tested him! I mean, he even knew the significant difference between cream, off-white and ivory. Go figure.

Needless to say, this week has flown by. The days are blurred with chilling out, eating, beaching, partying, sunning, sea-ing and sanding. I now feel prepared to do what needs to be done when I get back. With Bobby and Gary that is. With Tyrone, I have no idea. During this time out here we, inevitably, got close.

★ ★ ★

'Jess, I've had an amazing time on holiday with you. You know that, right?'

'I've had a good time too. You've been a good friend. To both me and Maddy.'

'Oh.' Tyrone's face fell.

'What's up?' Jess looked concerned.

'I was hoping that by now you'd see me as a bit more than just a friend.'

'Oh.' Jess echoed Tyrone's previous response.

'So?'

'So ... what?'

'So ... do you ... could you see me as more than a friend?'

Jess sighed heavily. 'Tyrone, my life is complicated right now. I have lots to sort out at home without contemplating a new relationship ...'

Before she finished Tyrone pointed to her face with a huge grin on his. 'Aha!'

'Aha?' Jess was confused.

'You said "contemplating a new relationship". You wouldn't contemplate a relationship about someone you only saw as a friend!'

Jess quickly started to deny this, then paused. What was the point? As always he was spot on.

'Regardless of how I may, or may not, feel about you, Tyrone, it doesn't change the fact that my life is still complicated.'

'It doesn't have to be.'

'How do you come to that conclusion?'

'Like this ...' Tyrone reached for Jess and looked deeply into her eyes for several seconds.

Jess felt a struggle within, she wanted to move but couldn't. She wanted to breathe but couldn't. This holiday was to sort out her relationship messes, not add another one to the mix. He was still just staring at her. She wanted him to kiss her, and she didn't want him to kiss her. Tyrone bowed his head towards her and took the decision out of her hands.

* * *

It was just a kiss, but it could so nearly have been more. The scenario was almost a perfect match to when me and Gary first hit it off and I knew that I had to end things with Bobby. The difference here is the way I feel about Tyrone – it surpasses anything that has ever transpired between me and Gary. With Gary it was raw passion, but with Tyrone it was something deeper.

We didn't talk much about the 'incident' afterwards so I'm not sure what it signifies, if anything. I don't want to put a label on anything without mutual confirmation so I'll think of us as friends with potential. It's the potential that makes it a must to clarify stuff with Bobby. I just want to make sure that everything between us is as clear as spring water so that in the unlikely event that he should see me walking down the street with a male counterpart, he won't feel that he's within his rights to make a scene about it.

I sure have my work cut out for me when I get back, but I think I'm ready. Sunbathing in Barbados has definitely been the bullet of enlightenment. All I've got do now is put it in the gun of confrontation and point the trigger of confirmation at Bobby and Gary.

Better fill Maddy in on these latest developments. By my watch it's about time for a wardrobe change and what better time to do the catch-up thing than while organising eveningwear and topping up lip gloss.

61

Bobby

Bobby had now changed his shirt three times, he was sweating so much with nervousness. He hadn't done the whole plan-a-date thing from start to finish for years. He felt good that he hadn't lost the knack. David would be proud. Well, maybe not that proud seeing as he had helped him out a bit with the order of things: drink at a bar first to loosen her up, then dinner with more drinks at a fancy restaurant (not too fancy though to keep her in that comfortable vibe) and then maybe another bar and finish the night off at a salsa club to work off all that food. Naturally it was David's idea for the salsa bit.

* * *

'David, as great an idea as Salsa is, I can already foresee a problem there.'

'What's that then, mate?'

'I can't Salsa.'

'Okay, but what's the problem?' David appeared genuinely confused.

'Erm ... I can't Salsa!' Bobby emphasised.

David rolled his eyes. 'Mate. You want to show Jess that you've changed, right? So what better way to do that than by taking her somewhere she would never expect you to take her? You not being able to Salsa actually works in your favour because she'll see the lengths you're prepared to go to.'

* * *

Bobby would have been happy to go to a regular club where he was familiar with the music and with the moves required for onlookers to be satisfied that he could actually dance. But, as per usual, David's logic was way ahead of him in a-strange-but-made-sense kind of way. He wiped more excess moisture from his forehead. Why on earth was he so nervous about going on a date with a woman he'd been sleeping with for over ten years? Just thinking about it made him feel even worse. He couldn't believe it had come to this. He felt like he was at school with David and Melinda as his tutors.

* * *

Melinda: If you think you're going to stall on things to say, pre-plan your topics of conversation.

David: Breathe man, just breathe. You'll be no good to anyone unconscious!

* * *

Nervous or not though, he was determined to come out top of the class on this date, so he had taken note of everything. Jess didn't know what he had planned for her. In fact he hadn't even asked her yet, but he was confident she'd be available, even if that was the only thing he was confident about. Jess never really made plans when she returned from a holiday. Her first weekend back was ideal for this kind of surprise. He'd even arranged a sitter for Martell.

* * *

'Hi, Angie? It's Bobby. Martell's dad.'

'Oh … Hi, Mr Phillips. Is everything okay?' Angie sounded surprised.

'Oh, yes! Everything's fine. I just wanted to know if you'd be free to babysit Martell on Friday?'

Angie was silent.

'Hello? Angie? You there?'

'Yes Mr Phillips … err, Mr Phillips, is Miss Montrose okay?' Angie sounded concerned.

'Erm, yes she's fine.' Bobby was surprised at the question.

'Okay, phew. I thought I'd ask because you've never called me to babysit Martell before.'

'Oh Angie, you joker! I've called plenty of times!' Bobby laughed.

'Err, no, Mr Phillips.'

'Okay, maybe not plenty of times, but surely a couple?' Bobby smiled a little nervously into the phone.

'Err, no, Mr Phillips.'

'Once?'

'Afraid not.' Angie confirmed gently.

Bobby was silent.

'But, I'd be happy to babysit for you, Mr Phillips, as happy as I am to babysit for Miss Montrose!' Angie added chirpily.

★ ★ ★

The possible 'I have to stay home with my child' excuse was taken care of. That in itself would knock Jess's stockings off. A huge tick would be in his favour, simply because he'd made a call and arranged a sitter, something he could have sworn he'd done before until Angie insisted otherwise. He'd been quite shocked to know he'd never called Angie before. But that was all in the past. The new him was all about calling babysitters. Another indicator of his serious intent to be a changed man.

Failure to prepare was to prepare to fail. He made one last check of his emergency list of conversational topics for the night. It seemed to cover everything: politics, current affairs, latest celebrity gossip. It was likely he wouldn't need it, but the way he was feeling it'd be just his luck for his mind to go blank. He cringed at the thought of just staring at Jess like a ventriloquist's dummy, shovelling food down his throat. Everything had to go perfectly. The name of the game was Impress Jess. At the end of the night he didn't want to literally be crying into his beer, 'If only ...'

His list of topics was fine. Now to go over his agenda. He knew exactly how he wanted it to go:

Part one – First, a bar. General catch up on each other's health and well being: How are you? How's work? That kind of thing. Hopefully they'd be playing music really loudly in the bar, so by the time they'd taken turns in saying 'Pardon?' a few times, it'd seem like they'd caught up without him having to use too many topics on his list. That would be his cue to add, 'It's a bit loud here, should we go eat now?' To which she'd shout, 'Yes, please!' in relief. So they could then go to the restaurant.

Part two – the restaurant. Dinner would be a bit trickier because they'd have to move on to meatier conversation and there'd be no loud background music to use as an excuse if he got stuck for words. Hence, Martell would be the logical topic of conversation: what he'd been up to, school, witty comments he'd come out with lately, yada yada yada.

Just running through the agenda calmed him. Maybe he'd been panicking for no reason. Thinking back to their last few phone conversations, although brief, they'd been quite amicable – when they could talk that is. The last time they'd dined out at Chic, they'd had a good time. A very good time in fact because she'd agreed to give them another chance. He'd been gobsmacked that she'd agreed so easily. Maybe the way to a woman's heart was food too. It had taken something this major, for him to get the point that Jess had apparently been trying to get across to him for so long.

He'd never thought that choosing the restaurants, organising the bookings, taking more of an active interest in Martell's schooling would be a big deal, but the effect had been astounding. Sometimes he could actually hear the surprise in her voice at his response to something she said. Probably thinking that it was so un-Bobby like. So far his efforts were succeeding.

Saturday night was just going to be more icing on the cake. More icing would be the trip he'd arranged to Alton Towers for them and Martell and, if the weather held up, a romantic picnic at Hyde Park on Sunday. He'd even borrowed a real picnic basket. He didn't imagine Jess was going to be a walkover, even if she had agreed to see how things went with unusual diplomacy. But that was okay. Anything was okay if it meant them being a proper family again. Jess would likely want to take things as slow as humanly possible and would be looking for the slightest slip-up to call it a day again. He was ready for the challenge. He didn't care how long it took and how many Ps & Qs he had to mind, he was in for the long haul. His efforts were bearing fruit and that was encouragement enough.

He hadn't impulsively gone overboard with fancy stuff like chocolates, especially after the last time he'd bought her flowers. From her reaction, he'd felt like eating the bloody things. In hindsight, he'd probably not been very subtle and a little too soon. Concentrating on the less obvious things was definitely a better action plan. Stuff she had mentioned in passing that he'd picked up on. Stuff that showed he was paying attention to the details.

★ ★ ★

'Dad, that was cool! I never knew dolphins were so smart. Mum said she wanted a book about dolphins the other day.'

'Your mum is interested in dolphins?' Bobby was surprised. He'd never heard Jess mention this interest before.

'Yeah, for some fashion project at work. Hey, Dad, can I have a drink, please?' Martell asked confirming that nine-year-olds had the attention span of two-year-olds at times. The two made their way to the Dolphinarium general shop. As Martell went to select a drink, Bobby browsed the book section.

'A book on dolphins … hmm …' He picked up one that looked particularly dolphin-info packed.

As they left the Dolphinarium and got into the car, Bobby gave the book to Martell.

'What's this for, Dad?'

'Your mum. Tell her it caught my eye and I thought she'd find it useful. Don't forget, son. Give her that exact message.'

Martell nodded as he browsed through the pages.

★ ★ ★

When Jess called the next day, he'd made it go to voice-mail, just so he could listen to her gushingly thankful message over and over again. Nonchalance was the key.

Jess was noticeably more relaxed after that. Doing the small normally un-noticeable things in the hope that she'd notice was now a key strategy.

★ ★ ★

'Take care of the little things, mate, and the big things will take care of themselves. That's what I say, Bobbo my boy.' David nodded sagely.

Wise words indeed, Bobby thought, even though they did sound a little profound to have hatched totally unaided in his friend's brain.

★ ★ ★

The ultimate hope was that Bobby and Jess would eventually fall back into place. A small bunch of flowers in about another two dates should be about right to ensure he didn't get the reaction he'd got before. He could just shove them in her hand when she opened the door and mumble something about them matching the paintwork. Nonchalance again was the key. It didn't matter what you said as long you were cool about it. It was all about timing. It was all about precision. It was bloody hard work though. He couldn't wait until it became second nature like it was with David. He just hoped it didn't take all the years that David always liked to say it had taken him.

★ ★ ★

'As natural as all this may seem, mate, it didn't just happen overnight.' David shook his head dramatically.

321

Bobby heard this little speech every so often and knew the best thing to do was just listen. Silently and with no added commentary.

'It's taken me years to learn all these dating trade secrets. Years, mate. I should write a book, I should. I'd make a million!'

Bobby silently mouthed, 'I'd make a million,' at the same time behind David's back. As David turned to face him, Bobby gave him a solemn thumbs up.

'When you're right, David, you're right.'

* * *

Jess should be back from lunch by now. He'd better call to confirm his plans with her, so that she could have her outfit prepared. A repeat of the lost shoe scenario could ruin the evening, and he wanted everything to go smoothly.

It was a wonder Jess didn't have a lost shoe problem more often. It was a testament to her organisational skills, which meant by logical deduction that it had to have been Martell who was responsible for disrupting that order. Bobby's concern was why his son found strolling up and down in his mum's stilettos more entertaining than his Gameboy. Maybe it was time for that father/son talk.

The ringing noise on the other end of the line stopped suddenly, interrupting his thoughts as Jess answered.

'Hi Jess, it's Bobby. Haven't really spoken to you about how your holiday was. Hope you had a good time. I've arranged a night out for us tomorrow. I know, I know, I'm being a little presumptuous, but I know that you don't usually plan anything for a couple of weekends after you come back from somewhere, and I've taken the liberty of planning something for us. Next week we can do something to include Martell. Don't worry I'll sort that out too ...'

'Whoa! Hold on a minute!' Jess interrupts.

62

Jessica

Talk about not giving a girl a chance to say, 'Hi, how are you?' What's with all this pre-scheduling of my time? I know it's my own fault for not nipping this in the pre-holiday bud, but even for Bobby, that's getting a little ahead of himself. This can't go on. This wrong has to be righted. Like now.

'Bobby. Bobbbyyy. Sounds like some big planning going on there.'

'Not really big. I just thought it'd be nice for us to go out, catch up, have a laugh, you know.'

Now he's trying to make it sound like it's no big deal, which means it's a whopper. I could smack myself for letting it come to this. In fact I will, but maybe later.

'Well, I'm glad that you didn't go to any real trouble because I can't do tomorrow. You were right though, I haven't made any plans to go out, but me and Martell haven't had a weekend just to ourselves for a while, so I thought this would be a good one for us to chill out together. You know, have some mother/son bonding time.'

'I called Angie and arranged babysitting if that's what you're worr… '

Once again I have to cut him off.

'Bobby. The babysitting isn't a problem. It's just that I want to sit with my baby.' He goes silent and I immediately feel horrible about dashing cold water on his plans like this, but needs must.

'I'm really glad that we've been getting along and it's been cool hooking up with you to get up to speed about

Martell and stuff, but … that's it, Bobby.' Still silence from him. Still, unfortunately needs must.

'I think I may have given you the wrong idea somewhere along the line and for that I'm truly, truly sorry. That wasn't meant to happen.' I pause for effect. 'And neither are we.' Did that sound cold? It's just a little hard to warm up something like that. I feel about an inch tall right now. It feels worse than the first time I broke it off, but I know I have to nip this in the bud. Bobby's been great these past few months, but I know it's just to get us back together. He'll be great for a few months then he'll go back to Bobby of old. Classic Bobby behaviour which I've experienced once, twice, countless times, and while his endeavours have changed, the structure definitely hasn't. Why, oh why, didn't I clear things up as soon as I realised the confusion? He's still not saying anything.

'Bobby? You still there? Are you okay?' He sounds kind of strange when he answers.

'Okay? Of course I am. Why shouldn't I be? It's not like it's the first time you've led me up a garden path. I should actually be used to it by now.'

This is not good. 'Bobby …' This time it's his turn to cut me off.

'What? *What?* You're sorry? You didn't mean for it to be this way? Sure you did. This is the way that you always meant it to be. Why though, Jess? Why won't you allow us to try again? Because I didn't follow through all those times? I *will* this time!'

He goes silent for a minute. Like a thoughtful silent. Oh oh. What if he's thinking of asking me if I'm seeing someone?

'Is there someone else, Jess? I know I asked you before,

but I feel I need to ask you again, because this doesn't make sense. Do you have another guy?'

I can almost feel him bracing himself at the other end of the phone for my response. Lord knows, I know what that feels like because I'm bracing myself for my response too. Just what the hell do I tell him right now? I think I've done enough for one night in just clarifying us; I can't deal with any more than that right now. I'm not ready to share Tyrone with the world just yet. What would I say anyway? I mean, I'm not even sure exactly what we are, so there's really no need to tell Bobby anything right now because technically there isn't anything to tell. I mean, the question was if I had another guy, and I can put my hand on my heart and categorically state that Tyrone is not my guy at this exact moment in time. He's a friend with the potential to be more. How much more is yet to be divulged, even to me.

'No, Bobby, I don't have a boyfriend.' Then I add in a whisper. 'And it's not that I think you don't want to change, I just don't believe that you can. And without that belief, there is no basis for trying again. I'm sorry, Bobby.' Next thing I hear is the dialling tone in my ear. Was that too much? I wince and take a deep breath. This sure as hell doesn't get any easier.

You'd think practice would make perfect. Instead it just makes me pissed off: with myself. I have to set the record straight properly, with everyone, including Gary. I'm not going to waste any more time waiting for the right moment to deal with him. I'm not about to risk Gary catching me off guard too.

Now is the right moment to phone him and break things off. I haven't spoken to him much since I got back from Barbados – so much for my preparations. This past week I've developed serious skills in avoidance: avoiding Gary's calls, avoiding Bobby's advances, avoiding sounding too happy every time I hear Tyrone's voice on the other end of the phone. Gary's been the hardest because Gary is the slickest. I don't know how he does it, but if ever he makes me mad, he can always find a way to turn it around and make me feel like I've got the wrong end of the stick or that I'm over-reacting. And I mean always – doesn't matter how prepared I am. I already feel like pure crap about hurting Bobby, so if I'm going to feel like that about Gary too, why spread it over more days than I have to?

Okay, deep breath. I've got to compose myself so that I say exactly the right thing. Luckily, I've already rehearsed my Goodbye Gary speech, albeit only to myself in the toilet mirror on the plane.

★ ★ ★

Jess looked at herself haughtily in the mirror. 'Gary Martin. We. Are. Done. Do you hear? It's OVER!' Too harsh.

Jess gave a semi-smile at herself in the mirror. 'Gary. We've just got to kick this habit that is us.' Too nonchalant.

Jess screwed up her face. 'Gary, Gary, GARY! I can't go on like this. WE can't go on like this!' Too dramatic!

Jess placed a serious but calm expression on her face. 'Gary. I think it's time to end this.' She smiled to herself. Simple. Perfect.

★ ★ ★

I know it's a cowardly way to break up, by telephone, and a complete waste of my practised facial expressions. A personal meeting would have been better: for Gary maybe, but definitely not for me. I'm not nervous about saying my bit, so the nerves are definitely coming from having to hear his bit. He has a certain way with words, as well as with other things that I'm not so sure my immunity can deal with face to face just yet.

'Hi,' I say as he answers the phone. It doesn't even ring twice. Probably the shock of seeing my number showing on his caller ID. Now I've said my greeting, my rehearsed word-for-word speech has suddenly deserted me.

'Jess! Are you okay? Where've you *been*? I've been calling, as I'm sure you already know from the amount of missed calls and messages I've left you! What's going on, Baby?' Now why did he have to end with Baby? The way that word rolls off his tongue does it for me every time, usually. This time I'm not going to let that throw me.

'I'm okay, Gary. I just needed some time to sort out some stuff in my head. I've had the time and I've sorted the stuff. So, this is where I'm at.'

'What's going on, Jess? Talk to me.' He sounds cautious. I suddenly feel a bit callous catching him off-guard like this.

'Gary, I needed this time to think about us and where we're going. It's to nowhere, Gary. It's to nowhere. You know it; I know it. And I can't do this any more.' Not quite how I'd rehearsed, but the message is still clear.

'Jess, come on …' He's ready to make that speech about the good time we have when we're together, and about just being happy to be with each other. I'm not even trying to listen to that right now. He's not going to twist me up this time. This time *he's* going to listen to *me*.

'Gary, please. I know what you're going to say. But the fact remains, you're going to be married soon and I don't want to be doing this when that happens. I shouldn't be doing it now. These are unchanging facts. Am I wrong?' I kind of hold my breath. Even though I know what his answer is going to be, somewhere deep down there's still a part of me that's hoping it's miraculously going to change. Hoping he's going to tell me I'm wrong, that things will change. He doesn't answer, which is an answer in itself. No miracles happening in my world tonight. I don't need to say any more.

'Gary, let me go.' I can feel myself starting to plead.

'I can't,' he says simply and ends the call.

That was *not* what I expected. I have practised a virtual response to every comeback that he could possibly have come back with, with mathematical precision … And he comes out with none? I drop on to the small armchair to re-think what just happened. Did I actually manage to finish with Gary or not? Somehow, it doesn't have that ring of finality about it like it did when I rehearsed it. Before I can really get down to analysing the conversation, the phone rings again.

'Hello,' I answer automatically.

'Jess, it's Bobby again. I'm sorry for putting down the phone and I'm sorry for trying to rush you into things. I've not been giving you time to think things over properly so it's no wonder you feel pressured,'

Huh? I don't remember telling him I felt pressured into making my decision.

'Listen, just forget that conversation ever happened,

okay? You just chill, and I'll speak to you soon.' He blows a kiss down the phone and hangs up before I can tell him that I don't want to forget the conversation and that I don't want him to either! He blew a kiss down the phone! This scenario gets worse by the second. It's like being part of a tri-amese. I just can't seem to shake these two guys no matter how I try.

63

Gary

Gary was still stunned about the conversation he'd just had. What the hell was that about? He hadn't heard from that woman for over two whole weeks. One week because she was out of the country, like that was an excuse, and the other because ... He didn't even know why. Then she calls him to break up? He was knocked for six. He'd been expecting her to say she'd been busy at work or something like that. It was unusual for them not to speak for so long but, in all truth, it had been a good thing because he'd been kind of busy himself. Tia was pregnant and her pregnancy was not proving to be the easiest: sick every morning, afternoon, evening and night. In fact, he couldn't think of a time when she wasn't being sick.

He knew he had to tell Jessica, and when the time was right he would, but that time was definitely not now. He needed her even more now than ever. He needed to know that he had a refuge from all the morning sickness and baby talk. He already had a teenage daughter; it wasn't in the plan to have another baby quite yet. It was enough dealing with that, without dealing with Jess's doubts again. She'd had doubts a few months ago; surely she couldn't be due for more so soon? How could she ask him to let her go? Right now, she was a vital distraction and he wanted to cling to her like a lifebelt. Some would say it was wrong, but if you were sick and needed medicine then it wasn't wrong to take it, was it? Well, right now Jess was his medicine.

He had no idea what could have set her off this time

though. Could something have happened while she was away? Probably holiday blues. Whatever it was, it was nothing that a long tender back and lip massage wouldn't take care of. His all-purpose remedy hadn't failed him yet.

64

Jessica

I'm sitting with the receiver against my forehead, thinking about how easy, yet how hard, that conversation with Gary had been: easy in that there was no argument whatsoever; hard in that there wasn't any closure whatsoever either. Gary. Well, I don't even know what to do about that now, and Bobby is just messing up my head for real. In the space of ten minutes, I've managed to break up with them both, but have somehow managed to remain attached to them both. Why is everything in my world so difficult when it comes to this? It's becoming a real chore to keep positive. Even looking in the mirror first thing in the morning and chanting 'I believe I can fly,' seems to remind me of everything that's clipping my wings. The one piece of good news is that Martell has been chosen to represent his school in the high jump. Oh, and Tyrone is still a sweetheart, even though I'm still not sure if he's my sweetheart.

I think it's time to get back to work. I'll be firing me at this rate. It wasn't the best idea to try to fit in telling Gary what's what with my lunchtime cheese bagel. My appetite is so gone now. That's a major feat, because my stomach was grumbling like Ebenezer Scrooge only a half hour ago. And now here comes David. As harmlessly charming as he is, I don't know if I can stomach him right now, especially if I can't even stomach my lunch. Actually, I've just had the craziest idea. Maybe if I tell him my dilemma in a hypothetical type way, he might be able to suggest the best way around it. Lord only knows much how I need a suggestion or two right now. No doubt, he's been in many a similar situation in the past with the amount of different women buzzing around him all the time.

'And how's my favourite female?' he grins through my office door.

'I'm sure your mother's fine,' I wryly reply.

'Touché! You know me so well, Jess. When are you going to give me the pleasure of having you for lunch? Apologies, I meant taking you for lunch?' He smiles that cheeky smile of his and it is clear for the world to see why the women just melt. If only my immunity to it could be bottled and sold, I'd earn enough money to buy my very own island in the sun.

'I don't need lunch, thank you,' I say waving my still cellophane-wrapped bagel at him, 'but what you could offer me is a male perspective on a little situation a friend of mine is going through.'

He immediately slides into my office and pulls up a chair, all in one fluid movement. He then throws one ankle over his other thigh and rubs both hands together as if getting ready to tuck into a good meal.

'I'm all ears,' he says.

I proceed to tell him a relatively watered-down version of my predicament with Gary and Tyrone. Except in my version its Gilbert and Tony and the 'friend' is Janet. I had to give everyone concerned a name; you can only suppose in the first and second person so many times before even you start getting confused about who is who.

'Well it's clear that the Gilbert guy just wants to control your friend. He doesn't really love her; he just loves knowing that he has some kind of power over her.'

Hmm … Same kind of thing that Tyrone (alias Tony) said in Barbados. Is it only men that can see this? It seems so transparent to them whereas I still feel like I'm wading through a fog.

'On the other hand, the Tony fella sounds like a nice enough guy. Normally I'd think he was using some kind of reverse psychology, just playing the good guy to make the girl fall all over him, get the goods, then split. I don't know, though. The way you describe him, he sounds genuine. What's stumping me is, normally those are the type of guys that, once they get the green light, are willing to go full steam ahead for some kind of relationship. The fact that Tony is stalling, but is still around, makes me think he's not sure. When a guy's not sure and the girl is, well that's a whole other ball game,' he finishes, looking thoughtful and rubbing a chin that has at least two days' growth breaking through the surface.

'Can you break this ball game down for me a little more?' I ask in a way that hopefully doesn't betray how avidly interested I am in his response.

'Actually I can't,' he says.

Just like that! He can't be for real! He's not really just going to leave me hanging with his unfinished thought of the day, is he?

'All I can say is that as great as this Tony guy may seem, he may be harder work than your friend might think. It just seems a bit strange that he's so into your friend, but still not … what's that phrase you use?' Rising from his seat, he smiles at me.

'Stepping up to the plate?' I offer.

'Yeah, that's it – stepping up to the plate. Although on the surface he seems sure of what he wants, clearly he's holding back. That's what doesn't feel right. Either he's got a secret or, deep down, maybe he just doesn't want it to go any further. That way he'd have the best of both worlds. And what guy wouldn't want that if he had half the chance? I've got a friend in a similar situation. He and his girl have broken up and he doesn't know how to get her back.'

I raise my eyebrow, wondering where this story is coming from. 'Exactly where does the similarity between your little tale and mine begin? They're totally different.' I'm starting to think that I was a little too quick to give any kind of credibility to David's theory.

'Well, my friend is at least making his intentions obvious to the girl because he really wants her back, unlike your Tony who seems happy to just "be".'

The point he's making dawns on me.

'Yes, it's all about who is – as you say – willing to step up to the plate.'

He blows me a kiss as he glides out of my office, convinced, I'm sure, that he has put the world of my imaginary friend to rights. Stepping up to the plate indeed. I know Tyrone's been a little slow in getting there, but come on now. David is nuts, and so am I for thinking he could have insight on a scenario like this. I don't even know why I asked him of all people for clarity in the first place. I should have just asked Tyrone. In fact, I'm going to tell this crazy story to Tyrone this evening. He'll bust a lung laughing when I tell him this one, again using the characters of Tony and Janet. I mean, it's not that I think there's a shred of sense in what David said, but it can't hurt to hear another man confirm it, can it? In fact, why wait until later? I could do with a good laugh right now. I don't usually call Tyrone at work so it'll probably be a nice surprise for him. I pick up my phone and dial his number from memory.

65

Tyrone

Tyrone was hoping this ninth take was going to be the final one for the scene he was shooting. His phone started vibrating in his pocket. Saved by the vibrator, he thought. He was due for a break anyway. He'd been trying to shoot the scene for nearly an hour now and it didn't look like it was going to happen until at least a few more had passed.

Taking out his phone, he looked at the number flashing. It was Jess's. What could she want? She rarely called him in the middle of the day like this, especially if he was at work. Something must have happened. He hoped she was okay. But what if she wasn't? What if she'd contracted something from the holiday, was just coming back from the doc and was calling to tell him that he may have caught it too; something that could be passed on in saliva? He might need to get checked out. He hadn't taken any jabs either; he'd booked the holiday last minute and hadn't had time. They didn't have malaria mosquitoes out there, did they? The last thing he needed was malaria. Maybe Jess was calling to tell him she was having second thoughts about them. No, that'd be crazy because there wasn't really a them, not officially. He should just answer the phone and ask what was up, shouldn't he? Of course he should.

'Hello Jess … Hello?'

Too late! She'd hung up. What if she didn't leave a message? Then he'd never know what was so important. What if she couldn't leave a message? What if someone had just grabbed her mobile phone from her? There'd been a lot of grab-and-run cases with mobile phones recently. He wouldn't even be able to phone her back.

This was going to bug him for the rest of the day. He wouldn't be able to eat lunch and definitely wouldn't be able to complete the shot for the scene. Why the hell would Jess suddenly phone him out of the blue like that? Was that what it was going to be like? Unexpected calls for who knows what reason. Maybe she was checking up on him; seeing if he was really at work. That was all he needed. It hadn't crossed his mind that Jess would be like that. But then he hadn't thought his last ex-girlfriend could be like that either.

★ ★ ★

First week – On a Tuesday – First phone call.

'Hey Tyrone, just thought I'd call to see how your day was going?' Wendy smiled into the phone.

'That's nice of you. I'm having a really good day. Even better now I've spoken to you,' Tyrone responded happily.

Third week – On a Thursday – Fourth phone call.

'Hey Tyrone, just thought I'd call to see how your day was going.'

'Wendy? Oh, hi again. It's going pretty much the same as when you last asked an hour ago,' Tyrone responded bemusedly.

Seventh week – On a Friday – Eighth phone call.

'Hey Tyrone. Just thought I'd call to see how your ...'

Wendy didn't get a chance to finish before Tyrone cut in curtly, 'Wendy, I've told you several times; I can't have conversations when I'm in the middle of shooting. If it's not an emergency please don't call again.' He ended the call abruptly.

* * *

Wendy had been really cool in the beginning too. Really laid back and just fun to be around before the increasingly frequent calls, the supposedly innocent queries about what he was doing or where he was going. Within months, they turned into interrogations, and then full-blown unfounded accusations.

* * *

'Tyrone, where were you? You were with someone else, weren't you? Weren't you?' The forceful accusation rolled off Wendy's tongue.

'No, I wasn't with anyone, Wendy. I was working late to finish a shoot,' Tyrone answered wearily.

'But I called you at the studio. I called and they said everyone had left for the night.'

'You called the main desk, so they told you everyone on the set had left for the night. I wasn't on the set, but in the cutting room at the back. Unless I informed the main desk of this they wouldn't know to tell anyone.'

'Then why didn't you tell them? You knew I'd want to know, that I'd be worried.'

'I left a message on your voicemail at work because you told me you'd be working late too.' Tyrone sighed to himself. He didn't know how much longer he could take these constant accusations.

'Oh, I ended up leaving early. I didn't get a chance to check my voicemail. I'm sorry, Tyrone! I don't know why I over-react sometimes. I'm so sorry.'

Tyrone could hear the tears in her voice, and knew her apology was genuine. He also knew that he'd be going through this again, most likely at the same time tomorrow.

★ ★ ★

He shuddered, thinking about how ugly it had all turned out. He was in no hurry to go there again. No matter how much commitment he'd shown Wendy, nothing he did could stop the cycle of angry outbursts and tearful apologies.

Thinking back, it had started just like this, with an unexpected call in the middle of the day. He liked Jess, but maybe this was a sign that things were moving too fast. He liked her a lot, but did he really *know* her? He'd thought he'd known Wendy. They'd got on like a house on fire, relatively quickly too. He knew he was probably being irrational. That call could have been to tell him something innocently simple; perhaps she wasn't going to be in later.

Whatever it was about, it was making him take stock of how far his relationship with Jess had come in a really short space of time. It also made him realise that he wasn't ready for the next phase, which was clearly some kind of commitment. There. He'd said it. Commitment. Flashbacks of Wendy enveloped him. He shuddered again. Yes, he definitely needed to slow down. He should call Jess back. No, she would expect him to call her back straight away, like he usually did. So maybe he wouldn't call her back until later tonight. Or even tomorrow.

66

Jessica

David was right. I didn't want to believe it, but he was right. He said that Tony, alias Tyrone, was stalling. I naturally thought that was nonsense, but I have to admit I was wrong and I say it again, he was right.

The one guy that I thought was no problem at all is suddenly turning out to be the strangest. It started right after that hypothetical non-hypothetical conversation I had with David a few weeks ago. I called Tyrone around lunchtime, and three days later he called me back. *Three days later!* When the first day passed I thought maybe he was just busy, but after the second day passed, and then the third, well, I didn't know what thought to have. You're probably wondering why I didn't just call him again, and I was going to. It was such an anomaly that he didn't call back straight away that I decided to wait and see exactly how long it would take for him to get back to me. And no, I didn't think anything major had happened to him, like an accident. If it had then it wouldn't have taken three days for somebody to go through his phone and notify everyone in it. I'm pretty sure my number is in his phone somewhere.

Anyway, when he eventually called after the third day (yes, I do have to keep making the point that it was *three* whole twenty-four hour filled days!), naturally, it was the first topic I wanted to broach.

★ ★ ★

'Tyrone, did you misplace your phone for a few days?' Jess jokingly asked.

'Yeah, something like that,' Tyrone answered, and then changed the subject.

Jess was a little taken aback by the nonchalant response but waited to see if any further explanation was to be forthcoming ... and waited ... and waited.

★ ★ ★

It was like the three-day phone back delay had never happened. I could even sense an I'm-calling-you-back-now-aren't-I tone in his voice. It took all of my effort to end our shortest ever conversation politely. Since then it seems that every time I ask him a question he's all vague about the answer.

★ ★ ★

'So Tyrone, are you free later?' Jess smiled into the phone waiting for his usual reply of 'Always free for you'.

'Hmm ... I'm not sure what I'm doing later.'

'Are you still planning that major production meeting, Tyrone?'

'Hmm ... Possibly.'

'Tyrone, did you call the gas people about your leak?'

'Hmm ... Maybe.'

★ ★ ★

Compared to his usual responses these mystery-filled answers are enough to make me want to scream, but I don't.

If it was just the odd isolated time, I'd put it down to him having a trying day. But when it's happening more and more often, then something is definitely up. I'm confused about where this change in attitude has come from. One minute we are getting on like a house where the roof is on fire, and now it's like the fire service has arrived and is slowly dousing the blaze. I really thought we had possibilities, but if I've been wrong, then I'm not letting ten years go by before making my true feelings known; I've been down that road already. I'm going to sort these three guys out once and for all, officially and over food. I know I've said this before, okay, a few times before, but I mean it this time; not that I didn't mean it the last time, because I did. Oh, you know what I mean.

I really am going to do it. Bobby, Gary and Tyrone: all three and all today. I'm going to clarify, simplify, edify (and any other 'fy' words I can think of) their position with me and mine with them. And I'm going to do it at that Galleon something de something or another restaurant. Why can't I ever remember the name? And I only booked it a few days ago. Three reservations more or less within ninety minutes of each other. An hour and ten minutes each to eat and explain, then twenty minutes getaway gap, which is my time to pretend to leave but really to hide out in the toilets, then make my way back for the next course, of man and meal.

5:30pm – First reservation, with Gary straight after work.

7:00pm – I'll deal with Bobby next. I'll give him an extra half hour because I'll need it.

9:00pm – Time for Tyrone and time to find out why he's suddenly turned into this mood-swinging male. Bobby, who is always going to be around in some form, will be more than enough to deal with mood-wise, I think.

I'm going to find out just what is going on between me and T once and for all. This jar of a relationship needs a label on it and if it doesn't get one then I'll have no choice but to step back. It's like a chess game. If he wants to go further with this thing, then he's got to make the next move. All this he will be told tonight. He's the last reservation because he'll likely be working until late on one of his productions.

This plan has to go like clockwork – literally. I think I've covered all possible eventualities. The restaurant, as always, is the perfect place and should prevent any unpleasantness as a result of the adverse news that's going to be on the menu. My outfit took a lot of thought. Smart casual and black is the way to go, I think; it's just about suitable for everything. Right. It's a little before five-thirty and I've got a good parking spot outside the restaurant. So far so good. Let me just gather these bits from the passenger seat that have fallen out of my bag. Hello? That's the message icon for my voicemail on my mobile. I didn't hear the phone ring. Must have been when that Amy Winehouse song came on and I turned up my radio. I do love that Valerie remix. As I listen to the message my face drops a little.

'Jess, its Tyrone. The shoot is going really well, so I should be finished earlier than scheduled. I'll probably meet you at the restaurant a little earlier.'

Damn! I can't afford for him to be too early, but it doesn't make sense to call him back because he rarely answers his phone when he's shooting, and I'll just get mad again if he sees my missed call and decides not to return it for three days. Tyrone and Bobby can *not* meet, not today. That is not a part of the plan. The plan has meant me starving myself all day just so that I can spread a three-course meal over three reservations. It had to be like that because I can hardly sit in front of each of them in such a fancy restaurant with a plate that just has the white on it; I've still got to eat. I'll order a salad with Gary, more of a main meal with Bobby (okay, also why extra time needed here) and I'll just tell Tyrone that I fancy ice cream and a coffee.

It's still early so no need to panic about time just yet. Can't believe I'm finally in this Galleon restaurant though. I'm just going to settle back and enjoy my surroundings while I wait for Gary.

Restaurant Galleon Mornay de Retro. Just reading it off this menu is a mouthful. If you had to swallow a name like that there'd be no room for food! Is it any wonder I keep forgetting the name of it? Still, it does have a high-class reputation, which is why, when you call one one eight, one one eight and can't remember the full name, they can. Does seem to be a lot of tables vacant at the moment though, but I guess it is early to be eating. I suppose this time of the early evening is in between lunchtime and dinnertime. Could be called linnertime. I smile to myself at my little punch line. Bad jokes are a sign of nervousness.

I try to concentrate on something else to take my mind away from my forthcoming meetings. This is a nice tablecloth. It's embroidered and everything, proper quality. Something my grandma would have loved. Okay, admiring tablecloths is a sign of increasing nervousness. I need to distract myself. I start tapping the table in time to a rhythm in my head – another Amy song to which, for the life of me, I can't seem to remember the words – a bit like her at her last concert actually. So I start to hum. It's only when I get a strange look from a passing waiter that I realise the volume of my humming has increased to a more than slightly perceptible level.

I give an embarrassed smile and put a finger to my lips and then continue tapping the table without the humming. In fact, if I tap this table any more, I wouldn't be surprised if I broke a nail. Can you imagine, breaking a nail from tapping? Oh, shit! I think I just have! Well, it's more chipped than broken, but damage is damage. Shit, I can't believe it! I have to worry about that later though. What's worrying me more is where the hell is Gary? It's quarter to six and he's still not here. Today is really not the best day for punctuality to go out the window. I hope my meticulously planned day is not going to be a non-starter.

Just as I'm beginning to go into panic mode, my eye catches a waiter heading, it seems, directly towards me.

'Excuse me, madam, I have a message for you.'

I look at him suspiciously with my left eyebrow up. 'A message for me?' Like that's not what the man just told me. Tch.

'You are Miss Montrose?' This time it's his turn to raise an eyebrow. I play it safe and just nod a response this time.

'The message is from a Gary Martin. He says to advise you of his apologies. He is running a little late due to a delivery mix-up. He'll endeavour to be with you as soon as possible.' The waiter bows his head slightly, turns on his heel and walks off. I too bow my head and put my hand across my forehead. Instead of savouring a three-course meal over three sittings, looks like I'm going to get indigestion because my timetable is going to be out of sync. Why didn't Gary just call me on my phone anyway? Why is he calling the restaurant to leave messages? I rummage around in my bag for my phone. For some reason it always seems to work its way all the way to the bottom. I finally find it and take it out to see absolutely no signal bars whatsoever on it. No reception. Damn. I can't even call him to see just how late he's going to be. I'm about to hyperventilate, when I see the same waiter escorting Gary to the table. He's all out of breath. No, not the waiter, Gary.

'I'm so sorry I'm late, Jess! I've had a nightma…,' Gary starts.

I'm so relieved that he's actually arrived so I can still salvage my original plan that I don't even listen to his explanation. 'It's okay. We should order.' I quickly brush off his apologies.

'Let me at least catch my breath, Jess. I've practically been sprinting to get here!'

Just like the waiter had better sprint with our orders. I'm working to a time blueprint, Honey. Without even looking up I respond, 'You can catch your breath while you're eating salad. I read somewhere it's the best way.' I can feel him looking at me strangely.

'Salad?' That's the sound of a man not accustomed to chewing lettuce leaves. That's about to change.

'Gary, this is for your benefit. I mean, face it. If you'd been eating a little healthier then you wouldn't be that out of breath from a little jog down the road.' I notice the waiter turning to leave. Before Gary can figure out what eating has to do with being out of breath, I tug on the waiter's jacket to get his attention again and quickly order two chicken salads. I can see that strange look on Gary's face again, and I know there's a question to follow. I pre-empt it with all the grace of someone working to a deadline.

'I really wanted to talk to you over a leisurely meal, but since you're *late*, there's not really that much leisure time left, is there?' I can't help but emphasise the late part to get him back for all the times he's made a point of pointing out my lateness.

'Geez, Jess, what's the rush? I just got here. At least …'

I close my eyes and put up my hand like a stop sign. This obviously surprises him into an abrupt silence, of which I take full advantage. 'Gary, please, I have something important to say, so can you just give me a minute without interruption for once?' I smile to take the edge off my words, but I can still see he's slightly taken aback.

'This is not easy for me to say, but needs must, so I'm just going to say it.'

The salad arrives, which causes a slight delay in my speech while the table is re-arranged to cater for the bowls. Naturally, I have to sample a bit. After all, eating is part of this evening. Gary's just looking at his, then at me, then at his salad again.

'Well, you know that what we've been doing is wrong; we both know that. And you know that all things, good and bad, must come to an end at some time.' This salad is so good that it's taking a little longer to say my little speech in between mouthfuls. Gary's started to play around with his, poking the lettuce and prodding the chicken. I go into a mini recap of when we met and places we've been to, you know to provide a cushion by letting him know that it wasn't all bad. Then I start to fill up with some of the stuff that was bad, and more of the salad, only this time I'm working from Gary's bowl. Waste not, want not, and I want, because I haven't eaten all day. I'm sure they put more in his bowl than mine. Gary is still unusually silent. I haven't met his eyes since the salad came. This is another part of my plan because Gary can do this puppy dog eyes thing and I am making sure he doesn't catch me with that either. As I reach over for another piece of chicken from Gary's salad, my sleeve rises slightly and I notice that the big hand on my watch is moving dangerously close to the twelve and the little hand is beginning to graze the number seven. Who knew reminiscing with salad could take this long? Time to wrap this up.

'What I'm saying is that it's time to let go. Really. And even if you still can't, I can, and that's just how it has to be.' Wow, pressure really can improve the flow of my vocabulary. Gary's face is showing a mixture of emotions; there's possibly a bit of sadness and surprise going on there amongst others that I don't have time to figure out. He attempts to say something, but I do that hand in the air stop sign thing again and cut him off.

'I totally understand if you can't finish your salad …' That makes him raise an eyebrow at me, seeing as I ate more of his salad than he did. I don't let this deter me. '… I'm a little choked up about it too.'

He tries to say something again, but I'm still not about to let him get a word in edgewise, sidewise or any other wise. 'I tell you what I'm going to do. I want us to part with at least a modicum of dignity. So, I'm going to go to the ladies' room and allow you to leave privately.' I stand up from the table and put my bag over my shoulder. He makes a last ditch attempt to speak, but I put my finger to my lips, slowly bend and give him a soft kiss on the lips, and then I walk away from the table.

I should take a bow because that was an Oscar-winning performance even if I do say so myself! I sneak a look over my shoulder just before I turn into the ladies' room and see a seriously baffled look on Gary's face. He gets up in what looks like a daze, pulls some notes out of his pocket, leaves them on the table and walks slowly out of the restaurant. I dart behind a large plant and see him stop for a few seconds to stare at the table he just left, shake his head and then continue walking into the street.

I wait a few more seconds just to make sure he hasn't forgotten something in his dazed state, and then walk back towards the waiter who's now standing at the reservation desk.

'Hi, I believe I've got a reservation for seven o clock in the name of Montrose?'

The waiter looks at me a little strangely but opens up his little reservation book. I glance up at the big clock in the restaurant and notice that it's actually a few minutes after seven. It's funny that Bobby hasn't called to say he was going to be late. Or maybe he tried but couldn't get through? Please don't tell me I'm going to have to order another salad? There's only so much rabbit food that you can use to line your stomach. I'm trying to recall what other salad choice was on the menu when Bobby appears beside the desk.

'Hey, Bobby! Is this good timing or what?' I smile hurriedly.

He's giving me such an intense, odd look that I'm just about to ask him if there's something up when the waiter closes his reservation book with a slap and tells us to follow him.

As we get to our table, which actually isn't that far from the one I was sitting at only moments earlier, I'm thinking that as we more or less still have the full quota of time I've allotted to us, I can take a little more time over this meal. I'm trying my best for Martell's sake to keep on civil terms with his father, and it surprisingly hasn't been too bad. However, that's probably due to the fact that I look at our little get-togethers as Martell catch-up time. Bobby, I'm convinced now, looks at them not like get-togethers but as get-*back*-togethers. I've tried to keep our conversations as 'in the moment' as possible, but Bobby always manages to get us on this reminiscing trip and it's hard not to just go with the flow. We do have a lot of happy memories and it's nice to mull them over with the person you originally shared them with. This evening, I'm going to be the one bringing up the past, in the hope that it will cushion the news that I've got to tell him about the present.

Even though I'm not exactly sure what direction Tyrone and me are heading in these days. We've been out and about and been seen by some of our mutual friends. It's obvious that some people will draw their own conclusion about us, be it correct or not, and maybe mention us to Bobby. If Bobby's going to smell the smoke of a rumour, I'd rather be the one to start the fire. The last time I tried to set the record straight, he hung up on me. He does that sometimes when he doesn't want to hear what I've got to say. He called back and apologised, but he needs to hear that I'm dating. Even if I don't go into the full details, he needs to hear those details, however sparse, from me. With any luck, I should be able to pace our conversation so that

I don't actually broach the main topic until after we've eaten. There is nothing like a heated discussion (no arguments in public restaurants, remember?) to affect one's appetite.

'Jess, is it okay if we go straight for the main meal instead of having a starter?'

Wow, is that amazing or what? He took the words right out of my mouth. I shrug my shoulders nonchalantly.

'If that's what you want, that's fine with me,' I smile. If only he knew just how fine that idea is with me. Finally, something in the plan is going to plan.

The food comes pretty quickly, which I'm grateful for. I seem to be doing most of the talking. Even though that's ideal, considering the purpose of this evening, it's also really weird because Bobby is not saying very much at all. Apart from nodding in a few apt places, he seems preoccupied, like he's got something on his mind. A couple of times I've looked up from my plate and he's been giving me that intense stare again.

'Are you okay, Bobby?'

He just smiles and says, 'Sure. How's your day been? Everything okay at work?'

After telling him about a couple of humorous incidents that happened at Jarrods today, I think I'm ready to ease into something a little more personal. I start just like I did with Gary. It's like a set model that I'm just modifying for each guy.

'Bobby, you know I have the utmost respect for you and you know that you'll always be Martell's father ...'

I follow that with a little bit of reminiscing and confirmation that our time together wasn't all bad. I'm really starting to warm to making my main point in a way that lays the foundation for letting him know that I'd be okay with him seeing other people, that it's only natural that he should.

I've nearly finished my lamb, an indicator that I've laid enough groundwork. I'm about to launch into the main subject of the night when Bobby suddenly scrapes back his chair mid-forkful.

'Jess, I've just thought of something that I have to do urgently. I've got to go. I'm really sorry,' he says hurriedly. I don't even get an opportunity to ask if everything's okay because he kisses me on the cheek, looks real hard at me for about the fifth time tonight, drops some cash on the table, and then he's gone.

It's now me who's baffled, mainly about two things. Firstly, obviously, what was that all about? And secondly, why is it that I'm the one who's invited these guys out for a meal, but they seem to be taking paying for it right out of my hands? My independent woman persona must be wearing off. But back to Bobby leaving like that. I'm wondering if it was really an emergency. I mean, it could hardly have been anything I said, because I only got to say all good things. I didn't even get to a remotely upsetting part. Maybe he guessed where I was heading, but just didn't want to hear me actually say it. Hmm, that sounds like a plausible explanation. I mean, from the conversation that we had the other night, it stands to reason logically speaking that if we're not going to be seeing each other then, eventually, we're likely to see other people. So, did I really need to spell that out? Maybe not, now that I think about it.

I call the waiter over and order a glass of wine to help me mull over this new thought. I can hardly believe my eyes when who do I see trailing behind the returning waiter but Tyrone! I'd nearly forgotten that he'd said he was going to finish early. Damn, how lucky am I? If he'd gotten here a minute or two earlier … I don't even give the waiter a chance to lay the glass of wine on the table. I literally snatch it out of his hand and nearly down it all in one go as it dawns on me just how close I came to being busted. The waiter gives me a strange look, again, similar to the one he gave me at the reservation desk with Bobby. On my last gulp I dab the sides of my mouth with a napkin and say one word to him, 'Thirsty!'

He raises an eyebrow and, with no further expression, turns on his heel and walks off. I breathe the hugest sigh of relief ever and promise myself, silently crossing my heart and hoping to die, that I will visit a house of the Lord on Sunday with my child. So help me God. Tyrone is busy surveying what's left on my plate. I'm struggling to think of a way to explain why I already have a plate of half-finished food in front of me. I put the wine glass to my head in the hope that the remnants in the glass will fill me, not only with a grape-flavoured liquid, but also an inspiring excuse.

'See you couldn't wait then! That's okay; I know that you're not used to eating so late and that you were thinking of me when you made the booking at this time.' He pauses to give me a thank-you-for-considering-me kiss on the cheek. 'I tried to make it even earlier, but this was the best I could do. I don't really feel that hungry. I'm still filled with the thrill of finishing my very first series. Seeing as you've already eaten …' He looks down at my plate and smiles again '… do you mind going to a bar for a drink instead? I fancy downing a cold beer to some loud music!'

At this point, knowing that my prayers have been answered so many times in so few minutes, I am ready to agree to anything that'll take me away from this restaurant. Yes, a slice of triple layer chocolate gateau with full dairy cream would have been the perfect ending to the racked lamb on the bone, of which only the bone remains on my plate. But my stomach is so tense with all these close calls that somehow I think my enjoyment of it would be a little tainted. I decide to finish the night without it. Still, if it's a really trendy bar with loud music, they might even serve cappuccino. Not quite gateau, but still a nice way to end dinner.

'Sure,' I say, and off we go. As we walk out of the door, I look over at the waiter who raises an eyebrow at me again and with as serious an expression as can be, gives me a little wink. I don't wink back lest I enhance his already, no doubt, imaginative opinion of me.

67

Gary

Gary was still super confused by what had happened at the restaurant. He was beginning to wonder if Jess had picked up some kind of tropical ailment when she was last away, because since then she'd been acting really strangely. Tonight at the restaurant was just another example of her odd behaviour. Really odd. Inviting him out, talking without taking breath, ordering his salad, eating his salad. Normally he would not have left it at that, but better to sort it out tomorrow when he was in a better frame of mind. He had felt his phone vibrate in his pocket alerting him to an incoming text. The only person who texted him, apart from Jess, was Tia.

★ ★ ★

'Tia, I'm going to be in a crucial meeting where I can't be disturbed. Text me only if it's urgent. I can discreetly look at the message then. If you call and leave a voicemail I won't be able to call you back until there's a break. You understand, right baby?'

'Sure, Gary. I know that ring vibrator on your phone is not as silent as it should be. And I'd hate to be responsible for interrupting your important meeting.'

★ ★ ★

His phone had vibrated only once, which meant a text, which meant an emergency. It had to be about the baby. He'd tried a few times to tell Jess that he had to leave, but she wasn't having any of it, just kept putting her hand up in his face like a typical American female. Some habits just never died. He'd managed to read the text under the table:

```
Come home immediately. Don't panic. Stomach
upset all day. Want to go hospital to check it
out.
```

As he left the restaurant, he did think of turning back to tell Jess, but decided against it. He'd deal with Tia now and Jess tomorrow, when his concentration wouldn't be diverted. She'd be no match for him then. But right now, first things first. If he really hurried, he could be on the tube before the second homeward rush. He pulled out his phone and pressed speed dial number three.

'Tia baby and baby-to-be. I'm on my way home.'

68

Bobby

Bobby knew his departure was abrupt, but he needed to check something out urgently. Everything happened for a reason. He'd been really happy that Jess wanted to meet up. Really thought that after the other day when he'd put the phone down on her, he'd blown it. The apology must have softened her up a little; showed her once again that he had changed. He planned to get to the restaurant early to pre-order the restaurant's special house wine so that it'd be waiting for her when she turned up. He'd imagined exactly how it would go in his mind.

'Hi Jess. Just thought I'd try out this 1985 Vin de Rouge Special while I was waiting, and thought you wouldn't mind a taste either. Here's a glass I poured for you earlier.' He spoke in a deep voice and leaned back in his chair, shirt open, chest hairs glistening.

He couldn't have been more surprised to see Jess already sitting at a table with some guy who she then kissed on the lips. And not just any guy – Gary Martin. He knew him more by reputation than friendship. Gary Martin was not the kind of guy he'd expect Jess to be kissing on the mouth.

When Gary started to walk towards the entrance where he was standing, the shock made Bobby turn aside, taking himself out of view. Gary was making a call as he got to the entrance, but Bobby couldn't catch the whole conversation. It was only a quick one, but he definitely caught 'baby' and 'home'. He didn't need to hear much more than that to figure what that conversation was about. Which led him to think: Gary had a girl, so why was he at the restaurant kissing his girl on the lips? What sort of greeting could a kiss on the cheek not cater for?

He needed to get past this kiss thing, because the more he thought about it, the more it wound him up. He had to look at things logically. They could have just bumped into each other. The two salad bowls were a mystery, but they looked like they were both in front of Jess so maybe she'd gotten very hungry and couldn't quite wait any longer. Part of him agreed this was a plausible explanation in a far-fetched kind of way, but the other part of him thought there was an even more plausible explanation that was far from coincidental. Not wanting to dwell for a second on the thought that Jess could possibly be playing him, he put the whole thing out of his mind and joined her with the intention of enjoying dinner. Throughout the meal, he couldn't get the image out of his mind. Eventually he got to the point where he couldn't pay attention to what she was talking about. What he thought he'd put out of his mind, had only been pushed to the back and with every second that passed it kept creeping closer and closer to the front again.

If he'd stayed a minute longer he'd have blurted out something accusatory and, if his suspicions turned out to be wrong, he'd have burnt his bridges for good. He couldn't concentrate on anything else unless he was sure. He needed to make some enquiries that just wouldn't wait. He had to be sure it was just an innocent meeting between them. Once he'd made some investigations, he'd feel more comfortable in casually asking Jess about Gary. And he knew just who to ask: Melinda. She knew Gary really well; he'd been at her party.

As the cool air hit Bobby outside the restaurant, something else hit him too. Maybe he was being a bit ridiculous about the whole thing. This was Jess. He'd never had cause to be suspicious of her before, so why now? As he turned around to head back into the main restaurant, a guy brushed past him, apologised for nearly knocking him down, and walked up to the reception desk. Bobby stopped in his tracks when he heard him ask for a table in the name of Jessica Montrose. The waiter pointed him in the direction of the table that he, Bobby, had just left. The guy walked over to Jess, and kissed her! For few minutes at least, he couldn't move. All sorts of thoughts were racing through his mind. Should he storm back to Jess and demand to know what the hell was going on? Smash a few plates? Punch out a few lights? He was breathing so heavily anyone would think he'd just run a race.

As he surveyed the scene in front of him, his mind cleared a little. First things first. Make some enquiries *then* find out from Jess what the hell was going on, smash a few plates and then possibly punch out a few lights.

69

Jessica

Ugh! I hope that ringing is just in my head. Who the hell can be ringing me at … where's my watch … five-thirty in the morning? Dad, this should only be you ringing from overseas. And if it isn't an emergency that is curtailing my dream about sale shopping in Shoe Heaven, two minutes before Shoe Heaven's gates officially open … Ooh, it had just better be an emergency, that's all I'm saying.

'Hello?' I must sound groggy as hell. Good. Maybe that'll let this person know that phone calls at this time of the morning are not conducive to conversation.

'So it's true. All this time. You *bitch*!'

I'm really going to have to get my number ex-directory. I can't be having these crazies dialling my digits by mistake and cursing me out like this. Especially not at the crucial point of a Shoe Heaven dream.

'Wrong bitch, buddy.' I calmly replace the receiver. Maybe if I can relax again I can retrieve part of my dream … Yeah … yeah …that's it … Oh my goodness, not again! How many times do you need to dial the wrong number before you realise that it's wrong? I'm getting pissed now. Shoe Heaven has this season's Gucci slippers. And they've gone down to half price. And they only have one pair left. And it's in my size. And I'm first in the queue! If waking up out of this dream again gives someone else the opportunity to pick up those shoes … I yank the phone out of the cradle.

'I said…' Before I can even finish, some crazy guy is yelling down the line.

'Jessica! Don't you *dare* put that phone down on me again! I want to talk to you *now*!'

'Bobby?' This nutter on the phone is Bobby? 'Bobby? What the hell is the matter with you? What's wrong?' My dream is now totally abandoned with no hope of recovery.

'All these weeks, and all the time behind my back. Leading me to believe one thing when all the time you were doing something else. Why? Why would you do this to me?' He is so livid that I swear I can see the steam coming out of his ears. What the hell is going on here?

'Bobby, calm down! Please. What am I supposed to have done?' I have to remain calm; one of us has to and it's sure not going to be Bobby.

'Oh please. Like you don't know what I'm talking about. Is that the best you can come up with? Ignorance?'

It must be the sarcastic tone he's taking with me that makes me forget for just a second that I'm supposed to be the voice of reason.

'I guess it must be because I don't work for The Psychic Hotline.'

'Oh, so now you've got jokes as well! Well …'

Okay, from that reaction, flippancy was not the way to go. Need to backtrack a little if I'm going to find out what this is all about. 'Bobby. I'm sorry!' I quickly add. 'I apologise. I didn't mean to be glib. But all this cursing isn't getting us anywhere. You need to either tell me what the problem is here or there's no point continuing this.' I think it's the way he's gone really silent on the other end of the line that makes me realise my role as peacemaker has gone to pot. I try to resurrect it.

'Bobby, can you please just tell me what this is all about?' His silence is beginning to make me feel more than a little nervous. Bobby is basically a calm kind of guy. Calming and charming, as he likes to tell me he was known back in the day. It takes a lot to work him up. Whatever he's heard, it must be a dandy.

'When were you going to tell me that you were seeing someone else, Jessica?'

Panic stations are officially go. My worse dread is now here to haunt me. I didn't tell him the other night when we went to dinner and this is my punishment. Lord only knows what he's heard, especially as some of the people we know can make a soap opera out of a sentence. What do I say? He's clearly already so mad that no matter what I say, it's not going to help this situation.

'No answer is an answer, I see,' he continues at my silence. Let me rephrase that: no matter what I don't say I'm still incriminating myself.

'Bobby, I was going to tell you, but I wanted to wait for the right time ...'

'The right time? I see. And what time would that be? Just before you moved in together? Or maybe just before you said I do? Or how about just before you give birth to my son's brother or sister maybe?'

He's actually got a blueprint of my life drawn up better than me! 'Come on now, Bobby, don't you think you're jumping the gun just a little bit? It's not even like that ...'

'Shut up, just shut the *hell up*! You've been parading this guy up and down in front of my son, no doubt, bringing him to the house where we lived, probably fucking him in the bed where we slept and now you want to tell me crap about you were going to tell me at the right time?'

Ouch. That was harsh. I'm not sure my hope that we'd still remain friends is going to be so achievable after this.

'The right time for me to know was before the rest of the world,' he splutters.

Okay, he has a valid point but, in my silent defence, I didn't tell the rest of the world either!

'You know something, Jess? You're selfish. You are a selfish bitch who doesn't give a shit about grinding the heels of her hundreds of shoes into someone's heart.'

Like I have grind-able heels on all of my shoes! Talk about exaggeration – you can't grind with flats – which I know is beside the point.

'You take, take, take all the love someone has to give and then, when you're ready or feel you want a change, then you just up and disappear, not giving a shit about how others have to deal with it.'

Exaggeration *and* unfairness. And in his current agitated state, I can't get a word in to point that out in my defence.

'I've given you everything inside of me, Jess, and you've taken it. You don't care how you've made me feel these past months, because as long as Jess is okay, that's all that matters.'

He's really not pulling any punches.

'Well, you've taken more than even you should have. You've taken the piss.'

Just because I didn't get around to telling him I went out on a date … or two? Jess to Drama King, hello?

'I've had enough of your taking, it's my turn now. To take back every damn thing I ever gave you.'

Oh, not that 'Give him Martell' one again, I hope. I'm going to have to turn him down on that again, even if it causes the apocalypse.

'I know that's not going to be possible with everything, but the Cartier watch will do for a start. You have no respect for our time, so you don't deserve to keep something that tells it. I want it back and I want it now. In fact I'm coming to get it!'

With that he slams down the phone. He cannot be serious. I have wanted that watch for two whole years. I didn't buy it myself as it would have been an extravagance, even for me, but Bobby ups and buys it for me as a surprise. And now he wants it back? There's a tug of love going on in my heart. Love for my most treasured time-piece versus love for my life. Bobby is *real* mad. I've never heard him that angry before so I've no way of knowing just how much control he has over this side of his temper, and I'm not sure I want to take the chance to find out.

It's a good thing that Martell is sleeping over at Tania's tonight. Let this be a lesson: this is what procrastination leads to. Sure, I attempted to tell him there was someone else, but I should have made sure the attempt amounted to me actually telling him. I was fooling myself with the technicalities that Tyrone and me weren't official. And I'm still not even sure about that because Tyrone's been acting strangely. I did manage to have the 'where are we going?' conversation with him, but all I found out was that he's even better at skirting around the issues than me.

★ ★ ★

'Tyrone, what are we doing?'

'We're sitting down, having a coffee,' he laughs.

'No. I mean what are we DOING? Are we dating? Seeing one another? A bona fide couple?'

'What's wrong with what we are now?'

'I'd have to know what we are to be able to answer that.'

'Does everything have to have a label?'

'Yes. So that you know what it is.' Jess barely restrained herself from adding 'Duh!'

'We like each other, we respect each other, and we spend quality time together. What more is there to know, Jess? That's what is important and that you already know.'

Jess took a deep breath. It's a wonder she wasn't dizzy from the circles he always kept spinning in this conversation.

★ ★ ★

So, even though having a new guy is still not yet officially true, it doesn't help me now that I'm officially in shit. I should have said something. Like I've said about a hundred times.

From his reaction, you'd think that somebody had caught Tyrone and me snogging in the middle of the high street or something. Ooh, could they have? I'm losing the plot now. Of course not! Tyrone and me have only been out in public on a handful of times, and even then, it's only been to check out a few shops, or have dinner with a movie thrown in. That can hardly be described as 'parading' and Martell has never even blessed eyes on him. I would always be particular about who and when I bring new people into my son's life. Frankly, I think Bobby has the cheek of an elephant's bottom to even suggest otherwise.

No doubt, Bobby's sources have added their own embellishments here and there, making this seem like a sordid scandal, which it isn't because we're over. Shit. This, I did not want to happen. What the hell am I going to do now with Bobby racing down here with his volcano head on to take my Cartier? I can't believe him. My god-damned watch? That is so petty I could spit. What does he think he's going to achieve by demanding it back? Make me cry? Okay. Maybe it might, but only a little! It is one of my favourite things in the whole world, so sue me. But I'd never let him see that. It's the fact that he's prepared to stoop to this level, to avenge the wrong he believes I've done him that gets me. Because we were/are over! I've got a good mind to just ignore him when he starts knocking on the door.

The only reason I'm thinking twice about that is because Martell might suffer indirectly if I did. I'm not going to risk an aftermath that may affect him, over a watch. There's no point in making an already sorry situation even sorrier. I'll leave the watch in an envelope outside the door. I'll do it now. I don't know where he's coming from, but I don't imagine he can be that far away. Too long a distance would give him a chance to cool down a little, and he doesn't sound like he wants to do that. He wants to be mad at me. He's wanted to be mad at me ever since I first broke it off and now I've handed him the perfect opportunity on a plate.

I get an envelope. Shaking my head slowly, and very sadly, I look at the watch one last time, slip it in, seal it up and take it outside to lay on the doormat. I look up the street to see if there's any sign of him yet, then go back in and put the double bolt lock on. When I go back inside, I pick up my nail file from the side table and set to work filing my nails. One might think, 'Huh?' and 'What kind of time is this to be filing nails?' but I totally disagree. In fact, I can't think of a more perfect time to do my nails. For one, my nerves are on edge and I find filing my nails strangely calming. Secondly, there's no harm in making sure my nails are tip-top and razor sharp. I may need to use them as a weapon of self-defence if Bobby thinks he can bully me. Just the thought makes me start to file aggressively.

The fifteen minutes it's taken for Bobby's arrival feels like an hour. And how do I know that he's arrived without him knocking the door? Because the crazed dude is banging on it with his fist!

'Jess, you better open up this door before I break it down! I'm serious, I want that watch!' Yell louder, why don't you? Meddling Mary must be having a field day next door right now. I run upstairs to open the bedroom window that is directly above the front door. Before looking down to tell Bobby to calm down, I look over to next door to see if Mary really is watching what's going on. Just as I thought, there she is curtains drawn, peering down with eyes open wide and chewing on a carrot. Carrots are her thing. She eats them all the time, cooked or raw, it really doesn't matter. I'm convinced that's why her eyes miss nothing.

Bobby is now slamming down the doorknocker continuously. His fists must be feeling a little tender after all that banging. That's a solid oak door I've got down there, imported all the way from Ikea.

I quickly pull up the window. My first thought is to throw a bucket of cold water over him. I mean, how dare he create this hullabaloo outside my front door just because I'm getting on with my life? My second thought is more along logical lines. Cold water, despite being cold, will very likely have the opposite effect on this situation.

'Bobby, will you just calm down?! Have you lost your mind?! I can't believe you're acting like this!'

'You're a fine one to talk about acting. Acting like everything is on track between us and all the time seeing someone else!'

He seems to feel the need to emphasise every other word he utters with a bang or kick on the door. Really, really hard. I hope he sprains his big toe. Damn, he is really angry! I open my mouth to shout down again then realise, no matter what I say, he isn't in the mood to listen. Best to save clarifications for another day. What day precisely I don't know. From how he's frothing at the mouth down there it's not likely to be any day soon. Suddenly I'm fed up with this whole thing and just want it to stop.

'Bobby, the watch is on the floor in front of you in an envelope. Take it and go. Just take the watch and leave.' I'm thinking that he's just going to snatch it up and storm off with the intention of never speaking to me again. Instead, and I'm not imagining this, his face, if possible, actually looks even angrier. If I could prick him, he'd likely burst with rage.

'Who the *hell* do you think you are?' he explodes. 'Do you think you can treat me like a punk?' He even adds a few other profanities I'd prefer not to repeat lest I soil my tongue.

I am truly shocked. Even though I knew he'd be upset, I would never have imagined the upset would be of this magnitude. I'm seriously considering calling the police, more for his sake than mine. I feel perfectly safe up here, but because he can't get to me, there's no telling what he's likely to do next. Okay, it's gone a little quiet now. He's not attacking the door any more. He's picked up the envelope and is just standing there, looking at it. Maybe he's remembering something. Hopefully he's realising that taking my watch is over-reacting just a bit. Looks like he's going now, thank God. What a mess.

I just can't stop giving thanks that Martell isn't here to

witness this loco display from his father. If this hasn't taught me the folly of delay then nothing ever will. There goes the phone. It always seems to ring at the most inopportune moments. Wearily I walk over to the bedside table to answer it. That little Bobby episode has really taken it out of me even though it only lasted all of ten minutes. I'm not in the mood to talk so I really should just let the answer machine take that call. Still, the temporary distraction from all of this might not be a bad thing.

'Hello?'

'Hello, erm Jessica. It's Mary. Erm, Mary from next door.' Tell me this isn't so. Tell me this woman really does not have the audacity to call my house to get the low-down on what she just saw. 'I was actually thinking about calling the police, but I thought I'd call you first. You know, save you a public scandal and all. You'd better look outside, dear.'

Meddling Mary never calls over here unless she has some very special gossip to share or wants to borrow a cup of sugar. She already borrowed a cup of sugar a few days ago so she's had plenty of time to stock back up on that. Guess that leaves only one thing. As I walk back over to the window and look outside, it's immediately clear to me how bad my situation has become.

70

Bobby

Bobby felt angry, hurt, disappointed, and like a fool. All sorts of emotions were hitting him at the same time. He just felt so stupid, which was made worse by the fact that Jess wouldn't even come to the door, but was just yelling at him from a window like some pesky door-to-door salesman. All the stuff he'd done, and said, all for nothing. He felt as easily replaceable as the watch in the envelope and saw red. He had to take it out on something and unfortunately, the oak door got it. He'd probably done more damage to himself than the door.

Unable to inflict satisfactory damage to the door, unable to get his hands on Jess, he searched wildly for another outlet on which to vent his frustrations. And there it was. Sitting there, gleaming from a recent car wash no doubt. He wanted to ruin something of Jess's so that she could see how his life was ruined. The feeling overpowered him. He didn't even feel the pain in his fists as he punched through the side windows, nor did he feel the shards of glass on his skin when he picked up a loose brick and put it through the windscreen. Slamming the metal dustbin lid against the car, with each dent he caused, it felt like a little bit of release from some of the anger inside.

The whole thing was hazy, like it all happened in a dream. His toes would hurt tomorrow after kicking dents all over that car. He couldn't think of a time in his life when he'd been that angry. When the red cloud had moved away from his eyes and he saw what he'd done, he knew he never wanted to be that angry again.

He stared at his handiwork, and then looked up at Jess who was staring at him dumbstruck. He felt nothing. He looked up at Meddling Mary who unsurprisingly had a phone to her ear, but surprisingly didn't seem to be talking into it. He turned around and did a sweeping survey of the whole street. A small crowd had gathered across the road. Neighbours were standing in their doorways and all eyes were on him. Yet still, he felt nothing. What was really weird, though, was that everyone was so silent; no whispering or pointing or anything. The whole street was just staring silently.

Holding his head straight, Bobby walked towards the cab station at the end of the road. Z Cars was once again going to help him get away from a nightmare. Melinda was once again going to help him pick up the pieces of his life. Melinda. In the dark void that was suddenly surrounding him, she was like a shard of light. If ever he needed that, it was now.

71

Jessica

I think I'm in shock. I don't know what to do or say. Bobby has totally wrecked my car. I didn't fully comprehend until now, just how much this situation has affected Bobby. I couldn't have imagined this. Never in my craziest of dreams, and believe me I have been known to have some seriously crazy dreams. Am I being selfish for wanting to leave a relationship that I'm not happy in? For believing too many times that things would change and, when they didn't, finally making a change myself? Even if I am, and I strangely don't think that, I still believe with my whole being that my decision is the right one, for both of us. Strangely, this has confirmed that for me. Bobby had somehow made me responsible for the outcome of his life and that was not a healthy thing for anyone to do. My grandma always had a saying for that. It never made more sense than now.

* * *

'Child, don't ever put your happiness in somebody else's hands. You'll be giving them the power to crush it by closing their fist. When it's in your hands, you got the choice to share it. That way, even if that other person closes their fist, you still got some in the open palm of your hand, and then you can keep on smiling. Your happiness is in your own hands, Sweetheart, right where it should be.' Grandma Pearl stroked her granddaughter's hair as she spoke. A seven-year-old Jess, just kept opening and closing her fist, hoping to get a glimpse of this happiness thing her Grandma was talking about.

Once again, I'm saved from my thoughts by the telephone bell. I pick it up automatically, thinking it must be Mary from next door, calling again to enquire whether she should still call the police. It would really be too far-fetched to think that it was Bobby calling to apologise.

'Hello?'

'Jess, we need to talk.'

It's Gary. What timing. After our last little dinner date, he's been calling me and calling me to discuss matters further, and I've been ignoring his calls. What's to discuss? But you know what? He could not have chosen a better moment to catch me than right now.

'Gary. There is nothing more to talk about. I've made my decision. I don't want to hear any of your sweet talk; it's sour to me now. Save it for your fiancée. Oh, and your baby to be.' I listen for five seconds to give him the chance to think of a response; a response I already know he can't think of.

★ ★ ★

'Jessica Rhodendra Montrose. How could you not tell me?' Maddy barked down the phone.

'Tell you what, Maddy?' Jess responded calmly. If you so much as saw a new movie, drama queen Maddy expected to be informed.

'About Gary!'

'What about Gary?' Jess's interest was now piqued.

Maddy was quiet for a few seconds. 'You really don't know?' Maddy sounded puzzled.

'Know what, Maddy?' Jess laughed in surprise. She heard her friend take a deep breath at the other end of the line.

Jess could now sense that whatever it was she hadn't heard wasn't going to be traditional feel-good gossip. 'Maddy. Know what?'

Maddy took another deep breath before answering. 'He had a girl.'

'Had a girl ... Okay ...' Jess shook her head in confusion and waited for Maddy to elaborate.

'He had a baby girl. Two weeks ago,' Maddy ended.

Jess stared at the receiver for a few seconds before slowly replacing it in its cradle.

★ ★ ★

The silence is deafening. I hang up the phone without saying another word. I bet he never expected me to find that out, and that was always going to be one of the catalysts for my wake-up call. God bless Maddy. She's like the Oracle. Nothing gets past her. Her information network surpasses CNN. Nothing Gary could have said would have worked on me after that news. He is so over and it wasn't even that hard to do in the end.

I should really be pulling my hair out over the car since I'm supposed to be picking Martell up in it later. Guess that's a no-no. I can feel hot tears building up at the back of my eyes, but they won't spill out. They're not tears of anger or frustration or even upset. They're just there because it's an appropriate occasion for tears. I go downstairs to make myself a cup of coffee. I put a little brandy in it to give it some kick. I'm not really a drinker and it really wouldn't do for my son to find me in an inebriated state so I think a teaspoonful ought to do it.

As I sit and sip, the last twenty minutes of my day are replaying in my mind, from Bobby giving me a piece of his mind to me giving Gary a piece of mine. It's a long way from how I pictured ending my relationships with these guys. I guess my romanticised notion that we could all just get along went out with Martin Luther King. And where is Tyrone in all of this? Every time we get close he draws away, and when I back off he's on my case almost like a stalker. Maybe I need to remove Tyrone from the equation too and move ahead with a completely clean slate. From three guys to none. How's that for a first?

Oh my gosh! I don't believe this. My phone again! Why is it that when I'm all alone and could do with a good phone conversation it's like my line has a fault, but the minute I want a quiet moment to reflect, it's a hotline! I sip my coffee again and contemplate letting the answerphone pick it up, but then I'd need to return the call anyway so the object of not talking is defeated.

I pick up and, speak of the devil, it's Tyrone. I can't muster up any enthusiasm for this conversation, which is not the norm for conversations between Tyrone and me. In a monotone that's new even to my ears, I speak.

'Tyrone. Hi.'

72

Tyrone

That didn't sound too welcoming. Tyrone wasn't surprised though.

'Hi Jess, everything okay?' He knew he'd been blowing hot and cold for a while so it was only a matter of time before his behaviour would have an effect. The committed relationship thing was something he hadn't done in a while. Last time he did it, it wasn't that great. As much as he liked Jess, he felt vulnerable around her. He didn't think he was ready to be at someone's mercy with his emotions just yet. At the same time, he didn't want to let her go. No wonder she was confused; he was a ball of confusion himself. He just needed time to sort out his feelings. Women were sorting out their feelings all the time, so really, she should understand.

'Well, if you take into consideration that I've just had Bobby nearly kick down my front door, then failing that, trash my car, accompanied by continuous verbal abuse for all the street to hear ... Hmm, I'd say I'm holding up pretty well, thanks.'

Did he just hear right? Did she just say her ex-boyfriend had vandalised her car?

'What? What ...! What happened? Are you okay?' He couldn't believe what he'd just heard. Jess's ex-boyfriend threatening her? Vandalising her car? He felt a surge of protective anger go through him. He wanted to go and knock the guy's teeth out and then hold Jess. In that order.

'I just told you, I'm fine. Look, Tyrone, as you just heard, I'm not having the greatest day and your temporary concern isn't going to improve it. So can we just do this another day, please?'

'What's that supposed to mean?' Tyrone responded indignantly and instantly regretted it.

'What's that supposed to mean? What's that supposed to mean? Let me *tell* you what that's supposed to mean!' Jess exploded. She had clearly been bottling up a whole lot of stuff about them and now the cork had popped.

'Suddenly you don't want to say where you're going, like it's a top secret mission ... leaving it three days to return a simple call, *three* days! ... fear of committing, like I don't have concerns too ...'

Jess was on a roll. Tyrone was astounded. He'd had no idea she was feeling like this. She was always so perceptible, he'd just assumed she would understand that was his way of saying that he needed time. How wrong could he have been? Hearing Jess lay all his issues in a list like that made it clear that he hadn't been at all clear about needing time. The extent of her feelings about the two of them threw him. She'd always seemed to accept whatever he told her with silence. That silence was now well and truly broken.

'... so, if you don't mind, I'd rather you just did your thing and I did mine ...' Tyrone could feel the emotion of everything she'd been through today, coupled with what he'd been putting her through. Right at that moment, he realised just how much he felt for Jess: everything that he'd seen in her from the very beginning. He'd made his fear of commitment, as she rightly said, temporarily blind him. Tyrone cut into her speech.

'Jess. I'm sorry.'

She continued, completely bypassing his apology as if he'd never spoken. '... and that way we can both just ...'

'*Jess!*' Tyrone shouted this time. The other end of the line went silent. 'I said I'm sorry and I mean it.'

Still silence from Jess's end. At least he'd got her attention now.

'I didn't realise. I just needed some time to deal with my feelings the only way I knew how.' Still nothing. The woman was going to make him work for this, but he was ready because he knew he deserved it.

'… and I know now how wrong I was for not considering your feelings.' Tyrone waited for a reaction. Receiving nothing, he knew he had to give more. '… and I promise I'll try my hardest to deal with us and make it up to you. If you'll let me. Please let me?' Still silence. It was too late. He didn't know what else to say. It looked like all that was left was to say goodbye, but he couldn't. Even though he couldn't think what to say, he couldn't say that.

'How are you going to make it up to me?' Jess finally asked, very quietly.

'However you want.'

'When are you going to make it up to me?'

'Whenever you want.' Silence again. This one stretched for so long that he nearly asked if she was still there.

'I'll speak to you tomorrow.' With that Jess hung up.

73

Jessica

I can't think about Tyrone and his declarations right now.
Talk is cheap; pretty, but cheap. All I want to do now is
finish my coffee in peace, which, I'm sure, must be lukewarm by now. It felt good getting all that crap off my chest.
After all I've had to deal with today, I saw no reason to
start holding back with him.

I go and sit on my sofa, lukewarm coffee in hand,
contemplating what to do next. When I next look up at the
clock, fifteen minutes have passed with me just sitting here
staring into space. The door knocker goes. Maybe Tania's
brought Martell home early so I wouldn't have to pick him
up. I hope so. Right now, I need a hug. I go to the door and
swing it open to see Tyrone standing there.

'I couldn't wait until tomorrow for your call, Jess.' He
stares deeply into my eyes and silently mouths, 'I'm truly
sorry.'

The talk is still cheap but the action of him being here
is worth a million. As I allow myself to pretend reluctance
at being pulled into his arms, two things pop into my head.
One: I don't know if this'll work out, but this guy is the
right one of the three to take the risk with. Two: I've just
remembered where that missing shoe I was looking for all
those weeks ago is!

THE END

IncorPlus

Writing That IncorPorates Words Plus Imagination

You can order further copies of this book direct from the publisher IncorPlus Ltd.

To order further copies of One Girl and Three Guys, please send a copy of the order form below to:
IncorPlus
91 Montague Road (No 4)
London
E11 3EW

Alternatively you can download an order form or order further copies via the publisher's website: www.incorplus.co.uk

---

ORDER FORM

Please complete in CAPITAL letters

NAME:

ADDRESS:

CITY:
POSTCODE:

Please provide email address if you wish to be notified when order despatched
EMAIL ADDRESS:

Book Title	Price	Quantity
One Girl and Three Guys	**£10.24** (£7.99 + £2.25 p&p)	

	TOTAL	£

Cheques/postal orders should be made payable to:
IncorPlus Ltd

Please allow 10 days for delivery. Please do not send cash or post-dated cheques. Order(s) will be sent <u>after</u> cheque has cleared. We do not share or sell our customers' details. Please tick box if you do not wish to receive further information from IncorPlus ☐